The Brickweavers

by
J.F. Williams

Copyright © 2012 by Joseph F. Williams
All rights reserved.

Cover art designed by the author.

ISBN:1478392584
ISBN-13:9781478392583

In memory of my dad

Chapter 1

As night approached, the cool breezes retreated and pleasing warmth invaded every tower in the desert city of Thujwa. A few wispy clouds of smoke, from the acacia resin burned at the evening rituals, wafted up the spiral of steps to the highest floor of the city's highest tower. Amagh paused to inhale the familiar scent. It was a short respite. The hierophant had never before sent a messenger bidding him with such urgency and so little explanation.

Unshaken by the swift journey so far – easily the measure of one hundred stories – Amagh stoutly climbed the last flight of stairs. The old priest was grateful for the ease that the forces in the steps had granted even that brief ascent. It was as though a ghost were pushing him from behind and another pulling him forward and up. Yet still he reached out to run his hand along the curving inner wall as though his balance required it. It felt burnished, almost slippery. Here, as everywhere in the city center, the bricks were tightly joined, with no mortar to break the wall's smooth surface.

From the last step, Amagh managed the short jump to the floating brickwork disk that served as the floor of the hierophant's quarters. It was a short distance to the holy man's door and Amagh hurried but his ancient legs could not carry him much faster, or without shaking. A servant greeted him.

"What is the problem, that I should be called at this hour?" Amagh blew out the words in a hiss as he tried to catch his breath.

"The waters are black, sir."

"The pool?"

"Aye."

"How do you mean 'black'?"

"Black as kiln smoke, sir." The servant boy was Thujwani, an apprentice to the priesthood and blessed by station of birth to the service of the singular hierophant of Thujwa. He gave the priest a worried look.

Amagh thought for a moment and smiled.

"That is not a problem. He is seeing the night sky under a new moon. He should see the stars."

"Nay, sir," said the worried boy. "His Holiness bent over the water and viewed as near to its surface as he could. He does not see even the stars. That is why he sent for you."

The smile disappeared. Amagh's faith told him that the images came from Thujwun himself but the god was obscure in his portents and random in their expression. Even this close to the sky, where the deity was said to reside, and separated from the earth by the forces of the all-binding, the pool produced images that were not always clear in their import and only the hierophant among all men could be trusted to understand their meaning. But Amagh knew the pool had never before darkened completely. There was either a problem with the function of the pool, he thought, or... *no*.

He watched as a door opened a short distance beyond the servant's shoulder. A figure in indigo robes appeared and seemed to gather air with his hand, beckoning the priest.

"Come along, Amagh. I wish to show you something." His voice was almost a whisper. He didn't look worried to Amagh.

"Aye, Your Holiness," said the priest. He turned to glare at the boy, then hobbled to the doorway.

"I need you to see this before it goes." The hierophant was insistent, excited. "I need you to tell me who this is."

The two stood at the edge of a shallow pool of water contained by a circular brick wall only a few hand-widths high. The surface was so still, like a sheet of glass, that an observer might feel compelled to touch it and watch the water ripple away in ever-widening circles. Amagh had tried that, years ago, and the rippling had subsided so unnaturally soon that he had felt an odd flutter in his belly at the sight of it. The water had felt noticeably thicker than what any ordinary fountain held, and it was more than naturally cool.

"There," said the hierophant, pointing to the image that floated on the pool's surface. "He is wearing a brickweaver's robe."

Amagh recognized the purple robe. There was no gold trim. Hands were grasping at it, some gently pulling on the fabric, and the hem was worn and frayed in places. Flowers the same color as the hierophant's raiment clung to the bottom of the robe by prickly stems. The man's face was unclear but his dark hair was wild and streaked with gray.

"I can tell he is a brickweaver, as you say," said Amagh. "A master. But he is not of high office. And he is not wealthy on any wise. I will inquire with my brother priests. One will know him."

The hierophant continued to stare at the pool as the image faded. There was no darkness now, just a flurry of luminous motes scattered haphazardly across the water's still surface. The sight made him grimace. "Whoever this man may be," he said. "I have a task for him. And I must meet with him on the morrow."

"Aye, Your Holiness," said the old priest. "But I have a question."

The hierophant turned away from the pool. "Of course."

"The servant told me the pool was black, Your Holiness. I told him you would see stars but he said that you did not. Is this true?"

"Aye. Until I sent for you, it was black." The hierophant spoke as if he were issuing a command. "But do not let that concern you."

Amagh would have asked another question had a second been appropriate. What vision appeared before the darkness, he wondered. That would probably have led to a third question, though, and from that, a fourth. Best to leave these matters to his holiness. He hobbled back down the staircase, the brick steps emanating all-binding forces that cushioned his descent, forbidding even the worry of a fall. He felt buoyant and safe, as though his invisible god held him in an embrace.

Chapter 2

The bricks appeared to Jeppo as they had on many nights before and while he analyzed the pattern, a small, distant voice shouted, "Remember it!" while another countered, "He need not remember it. He need only understand." It was like that every time. The bricks appeared and he would stare at the unfamiliar pattern. How do they play with the forces? He would feel frustrated and delighted at the same time, as when he was a child and struggled with puzzle toys of wood or chain. If only he could remember the pattern well enough after awaking to capture it in charcoal. But the memory always escaped him.

On this night, though, the bricks appeared for only a moment and then the wall shuddered three times. How odd, he thought, the way the bricks separated and reformed. Then he awoke.

He grabbed the jug of water near his bed and drank greedily. Matanya slept next to him, lying on her side with arms bent and her hands leisurely crossed over the top of her head. He could see her back rising and falling slowly but her face was turned away from him. As he watched her slumber, he heard three sharp raps on the door.

He moved out of bed quickly and wrapped himself in a robe. It would not be proper to see anyone in his nightclothes but he could still hear the nearly imperceptible cracking and sighing of the stressed crystals so it was earlier than he might expect to greet a visitor. Pulling himself onto the ledge of the high window, he saw that the sky was still dark but not its darkest. The window looked out onto a large but quiet plaza and the crystal lamps that illuminated the place at night were slowly dimming. He could not see the horizon for the many wide towers in the way, as well as the great wall beyond them, but he calculated that it was probably dawn. Adjusting his eyes to the dim light, he found his way to the front door and opened it.

"Greetings, Brickweaver Jeppo, on this fine morning in sacred Thujwa," said the elderly man at the door. The man smiled and tried his best to straighten up his spine though his will was no match for the devastation the years had wrought upon his joints. Jeppo thought him a beggar at first sight but in the gathering light of dawn and with the cool water draughts clearing his thoughts, he recognized the indigo, gold and white robes of a priest. And the old man had used the epithet "sacred" as well, confirming his station. He did not know this fellow and felt he should be careful dealing with him. He would need to be formal.

"My greetings are to you, priest...?"

" 'Amagh', sir. My name is 'Amagh'," replied the priest.

"They are indeed to you, Priest Amagh, on this very fine morning in sturdy Thujwa. If you need to, come in from the morning cold and rest or...."

"Please, sir," the priest said, raising both hands as though pleading. "You are most gracious but I am here only to deliver a message."

"A message?"

"A message of invitation, sir," the priest continued. "The singular hierophant of sacred Thujwa requests that you visit his high tower... before the sun is at its highest... on this fine day in sacred Thujwa."

The old man grimaced because he had not varied his epithets, as would have been proper. He had twice used "sacred" to describe the city, as though the words "holy" and "faithful" had never existed. Jeppo noticed this and smiled, as if he were dealing with a callow but earnest youth. The necessity of such formal greetings, with their rules and proprieties, had always irritated Jeppo and so he had studied them carefully.

"And does the singular hierophant of... *sturdy* Thujwa wish that I know the reason for this meeting?"

Jeppo tried to look as beneficent as possible while deliberately repeating the same epithet. The old man could easily have taken his words as mockery rather than compassion and Jeppo was not entirely sure at first whether the ploy had worked but the old man did appear grateful for the subtle gesture.

"You are a *wise* and careful brickweaver," replied the priest, now less formal in his address and more competent with his epithets. "That is all I have to tell you." He suddenly grasped Jeppo's wrist with his soft, bony fingers, then quickly let go and hobbled back to the sledge that had carried him to the brickweaver's doorstep. Jeppo watched as it lifted a few hand-widths off the ground, turned, and smoothly, gracefully escaped along a road between long rows of towers.

Jeppo closed the door, pulled his robe tighter around his shoulders and walked, pensively, into the kitchen. There was a chill in the air as the city's cooling system roused to life, triggered by the increasing heat that followed on the heels of sunrise. Jeppo took comfort in the kitchen where brick stove and water boiler would hold the cooling city breezes at bay. He turned an iron rod that pierced the side of the brick basin of water and its contents began to bubble immediately. He carefully scooped up some of the steaming water into a jug and poured it slowly over a few handfuls of dried, yellow flower petals he had dumped into a bowl. After a few moments he slowly poured the fluid into a smaller bowl, from which he began to drink. The tea was strongly flavored and deep yellow, and drinking it had the effect of further sharpening his thoughts, which turned to his schedule for the day.

He had recently been assigned a new assistant, a young man whom he had met only briefly and who was long out of his scholastics. The fellow would be arriving at the workshop this morning and there would be no one to greet him. What would the fellow do, he wondered. It would be perfectly proper for him to wait until his water was half-gone and then leave. Did this young man know what was proper? He could perish in the desert heat, waiting for the door to the workshop to open, if he were a fool. He could walk farther out to the farm town. There is water there, and shady taverns. Jeppo thought he might get a message to the young man if he could remember his name. He recalled it being mentioned that his assignee was one of Mincon's nephews, or grandsons? Perhaps a message to Mincon or one of his assistants would be sufficient. Jeppo breathed deeply through his nose, held the breath and sighed with frustration. Why was he being called to see the hierophant?

"Pardon me, lord," said the young man, pushing himself forward in the great chamber as though fighting a steady wind. "It is time for the council." He lowered his head in respect and, with hands at his sides, grasped the loose folds of his brown robe and held them tightly. In an unconscious action, he shuffled his feet back a few steps.

Mincon turned away from the scroll he had been studying and rubbed his eyes before letting his sight rest on the bowed apprentice. "Aye," he said and exhaled a sigh. "Do you know, Galel," he continued. "Do you know what I am reading?" He gently patted the scroll as it slowly curled up.

"Nay sir," came Galel's reply. "But I can guess from its color that it is very old."

"Aye. It is very old indeed. It is a secret history. It is a brickweavers history, lad, but there is not one mention of 'cooling bins' or 'tonic beds'." Mincon punctuated the statement by wiping a drop of spittle from his lips with the tip of his tongue.

Galel raised his eyebrows. Should he ask? "I would guess it speaks of towers then, or sledges."

"Nay, nay," said Mincon, nearly smiling. "But you are close to it. There are sledges, but unlike any in your ken."

"May I know, sir?"

"It is not for your eyes... not just yet. But perhaps anon. I will tell you that the scroll speaks of power." He rolled it up with care and returned it to a velvet bag. Then he stopped and decided instead to secrete it in a pocket beneath his purple robe. "You will have to aid me in crossing the bridge."

"I have the key, sire," and Galel raised his hand, which held a large iron rod of a shape so irregular it appeared to have been damaged.

"Good, good," Mincon said as he rose from the chair. He reached down to adjust a smaller iron rod near his knee. "With my debility, you will have to abate the beckoning on that bridge. It worries my device, though the streets themselves do not do the same."

He patted his robe at the spot where he had hidden the scroll, and Galel heard, and would remember hearing, the slightest crinkling of paper.

Chapter 3

Matanya pulled a blanket closer. It was cool in the sleeping room and she felt a chill. Now more bundled than she had been in slumber, she started to perspire. Her nightclothes were already voluminous and warm and so she threw the blanket down. Again the chill came and she grasped for the blanket. Her shoulders and elbows ached. The stiffened joints of her hands ached as well and then grew numb. She was in no way alarmed by these sensations. She had felt like this every morning.

"Lavena!" she shouted hoarsely, her mouth still dry from sleep.

"She is not here yet," came the unexpected response from another room, in her husband's voice. "It is too early."

The brickweaver's wife assumed that she had slept too long. Usually her husband was out of bed before she woke up. And usually he was off to his workshop soon after. Lavena, her housekeep, usually arrived well before midmorning. She took a draught of water from a jug, and slowly pulled herself out of bed, moving with such difficulty as would concern an onlooker.

"Please, stay in bed, dear," said Jeppo. He stood at the entrance to the bedroom, holding a second small bowl of morning-flower tea in his cupped hands. "I have some unexpected business ahead of me. An old priest visited us at dawn. He told me I must meet with the hierophant today."

Matanya had slowly crept back into bed and lay with one hand resting on her forehead.

"The hierophant?" she said, groggy. "Why?"

"I do not know," Jeppo took another sip of tea, slurping it

noisily as if to emphasize the finality of his declaration.

"I have never known anyone to be so invited," Matanya said with some concern.

"I have known other brickweavers," he replied nonchalantly, as though this would not be a startling piece of news at the guild. Jeppo had actually known of only a few such invitations among his colleagues. It was his understanding that only priests and councilors ever met with the hierophant. And sometimes captured miscreants, too, but this could not be the case, he thought. They were always escorted there by guards, and in chains. The old priest did not seem by his manner to be delivering such an invitation as that.

"The problem is my assistant. He will be arriving at the workshop today when I am meeting with His Holiness."

"Then tell Lavena," she offered. "She can deliver a message."

"I do not know... perhaps she can inform his uncle... *Mincon*. Yes. Mincon." Jeppo was pleased he had remembered some scrap of knowledge to work with. Lavena wasn't the best choice but it would cost him less than a messenger if she took the errand. Why couldn't he remember the young man's name? He sipped more of the tea.

"Kulkulla!" he said at last. "He is a... a grandson of Kulla. Not Mincon. His mother is Kulla's daughter, I think." He smiled and was pleased with himself. He had remembered. That problem was solved, finally.

"I will go to the Kulla tower myself. I have enough time," he decided.

"Mincon here, sire."
"Mazrash, sire."

"Tazil, sire."

"Orten of the guards, sire."

With that, each of the four most powerful councilors declared his presence. They represented the four governing industries that ruled Thujwa: the brickweavers, the merchants, the surgeons and the city guards. The minor industries, including the brickmakers and the bricklayers, textile millers and paper rollers, had seats at the council but not in these supreme sessions. The judge Kulla presided. After taking the roll, he asked Mazrash to speak, having already been informed of the mercantile lord's business before the council.

"Greetings to all of you, on this fine day in this wealthy city of Thujwa," he began. "I feel the need to alert my brother councilors to an issue of some urgency." He made a show of looking around the room at each of his brother lords in turn. "Food receipts have fallen again," Mazrash continued. "As have the receipts for the lesser goods -- pottery, basketry, and the rest. Woolens have improved, and a few other textiles, but there is such a deficit in the former that licenses will be reduced accordingly.

"I see, brothers, no improvement in any market and I fear that textiles will begin to fall eventually as well. The problem is this: we have reached the limits of our commerce. Our trade with other cities is miniscule and precious. Our industries provider all the staples of city life -- and it has been a blessing to be free of any foreign bonds -- but we have avoided the strong commercial attachments that would have increased receipts. There is no end to this that is in our favor, brothers, lest we take some actions soon."

"And what would those actions be?" asked Tazil, the four-cornered hat of the surgeon fixed neatly to his ancient brow.

"I propose that we offer treaties to the other cities of the desert. First Delgazh, then far Andli," Mazrash replied. "Such treaties might be cleverly designed to gain us advantage. We would import token amounts of the other cities' goods while assuring that our exports would exceed theirs in price. Once my managers see an increase in receipts, all licensing would increase as well, as the law requires."

"I am not sure of the wisdom of your proposal," offered Orten. "Would we not need a show of strength to ensure such an unbalanced agreement? My guards are busy enough with the towners."

"Well no, brother," responded Mazrash. "I was contemplating the use of guile and clever arithmetic to fool our trade partners."

"In that you assume," sneered Orten, "that we are more clever than any of them. We have little knowledge of the people of the other cities and most of our people have none at all. Their arithmetic may surpass ours, by now, brother."

"And how much do we know of their armories, for that matter?" countered Mazrash. "An inadequate show of force would invite destruction or enslavement. We can keep a keen eye on the words in a treaty well enough to know if it is to our benefit. We embark on war," his voice rasped. "We embark on a warring, and we cannot know what is to follow."

There was a pause as the councilors looked around the otherwise bare room. In it stood a circle of thirteen brickwork chairs nearly in the center, only five containing august bodies this day. The chairs were supposed to be healthful and invigorating owing to some poorly understood effect of the all-binding force generated from their special brick patterns. For this effect, the council itself paid a not inconsiderable license to the brickweavers guild.

Mincon spoke up. "There may be another way," he said slowly in a manner meant to induce a sense of mystery. "An ordinary show of force would be a terrific gamble but, as brother Mazrash has revealed, our current balance of receipts is sure to injure the city just as badly after some time. I know of a technic, handed down from Atos himself, which would create an overwhelming show of the most profound and intractable forces. I could not imagine any other city having discovered this."

"And the great Thujwun has entrusted the brickweaving only to His people," said Kulla with a somewhat reproachful smile, as though Mincon should have had the piety to have voiced this argument as well, as it was the overriding argument anyway. "Let us not forget the truth of Thujwun's kindness that stares us in the face every day," he added.

"Yea, of course, sire," replied Mincon. "With this gift of Thujwun, which has gone *underused* for many centuries, we will always have the advantage that His kindness has ensured. And now may be the time to uncover what has been held close to the brickweavers for so long. I will tell you only this, my brothers, so as not to break my vow until the law can release me from it, that these technics envision the design of great brickwork war engines. The texts describe how these were used against the M'butu and the nomads. The descriptions of the 'rescue' are not as mild as our common history tells us. The words in these texts convey a witness to violence that is beyond the imaginations of most Thujwani, having lived in peace with the lesser, unfaithful peoples bound to them since those distant times."

"War engines?" asked Kulla. "Do you propose a warring?"

"A warring would not be necessary, sire." He patted his hand in the air, as if to calm everyone's thoughts. "But a claim to warring and a showing of inhuman force would subdue our unfaithful sister cities without bloodshed. Our advantage is such that we need not crush a people if we can simply make them bow. And if they bow to us, judge, they will surely bow to Thujwun anon."

Kulla squinted his eyes and looked to Tazil for a reading of the master surgeon's face.

"What say you, Tazil?" Kulla asked.

The surgeon leapt to the moment, seeing an opportunity to display his piety. "I can answer only from belief, sire. The belief in our protection by Thujwun and the belief in the superiority of our most secret technics. As an example from my own experience, I know ways of staunching the remaining flesh after an amputation that the less advanced peoples would never even consider. It is surely a gift of Thujwun." Kulla raised his eyebrows at this, for it was a unique argument. Of that he was certain.

"Lord Orten?" Kulla turned to the guards master.

"Sire, I would need to know the character of these warring machines to adjudge the decision. I propose we vote on releasing Mincon from his pledge but limit any discourse to those gathered today." Orten was already warming to the idea. As guards master he would wield these new powers, whatever they may be, and in that circumstance, his personal stature, and his wealth, could increase mightily.

Kulla sat back and thought for a moment. "Lord Mazrash, sir, would terrible warring machines such as Mincon has proposed reverse our situation, or inflame it?" he asked the master of merchants.

"I am not sure," he replied. "There are many vital details in this. I would not care for bloodshed, as we have always been a peaceful people. Even the common history tells us this about the rescue of the outer tribes. Our own secret history of commerce tells me even more. Our city's wealth grew ten-fold from that act. And surely Thujwun will be pleased for his people to bind others to his worship."

"For that assurance, we would need to consult the hierophant, milord," Kulla responded.

"Perhaps not. If we can agree without controversy, it is probably the godhead's will," said Mazrash. His enthusiasm was growing now. The secret history had actually estimated the growth in wealth from the rescue at nearly one hundred times the previous state. It was the time of much technics advance in commerce, and that was the common history explanation, but he knew that the old merchants had recognized the value of the rescue and fiercely campaigned for it, even unto a murder or two, or so it was written in the books that cannot be revealed. "Depending on their character and costs, such machines may be worthwhile or not," Mazrash continued. "I agree with the guards lord and request that we release Mincon."

Kulla nodded his head and spoke to Orten. "Lord, you have made the call. Raise your fist."

At that, the guards chief raised his left fist up and at a slight angle, as though he were trying to stab a fellow much taller than himself in the chest. Both Tazil and Mazrash reached to grasp Orten's wrist. It was more difficult for the merchant because of his short arms and wide carriage, but elderly Tazil was still a tall, robust man and grasped the war chief's wrist firmly. Mincon himself did not vote in order that he might preserve the pretense that all guildsmen guard their secret histories and technics with pride and jealousy. Had it not been for this charade of decorum, his grasp would surely have crushed Orten's wrist.

"It is ruled," said Kulla. "Lord Mincon has been released from his vow. It will be noted that Mincon did not relent in his protection of the secrets but that the immovable will of the council in service to the law had overridden him."

"Thank you, Judge," Mincon said bowing to Kulla, which had the additional benefit of concealing his grin.

"I will first call out for a service of morning flower tea," said Kulla. "And you, milord, will prepare your testimony. I am assured that you will be careful not to reveal more secrets than are necessary." Kulla's eyes locked unblinking on the brickweaver's own.

"Aye, Judge," replied Mincon, more subdued than before.

By midmorning, Matanya had begun directing Lavena, a woman from the farm town, in the household chores. All the servants were from the farmlands, just beyond the brickweaver workshops, the clay pits and the kilns. Like others of her tribe, Lavena had long ago become accustomed to the strenuous morning walk, first past the workshops, where she rarely saw anyone outside, then the clay pits, where numerous men and beasts labored digging out the various clays and hauling them to the assayers, who worked in large, ivory colored tents. She would drink half her water by the time she had walked past the kilns, great squat buildings of stone and mortar, constructed the old way, like the brickweaver workshops distantly visible at the beginning of her daily journey.

The heat was greatest there and though the desert was hostile in all places save the oasis of the farm town and Lavena's usual destination, the cool thicket of graceful towers encircling the center of Thujwa, the radiance of the great kilns as they baked thousands of bricks of various standardized sizes, shapes and compositions only worsened it.

The housekeeper earned her meager wages by washing the floors and walls, replacing and cleaning all the linens in the household and cooking the afternoon meal, for which she would also shop in the marketplace. Matanya had become more and more of a recluse because of her condition, and had eschewed the late morning trip to the market, declaring that it was best to send Lavena on any account, because she could "commune better with her own people" than she, a Thujwani. The inference being that Lavena could get the best produce and cuts of meat, and at the best price.

Jeppo left the tower soon after Lavena arrived, as he did not want to leave Matanya alone. He was ever worried about her, the aching in her joints and the sadness and listlessness that seemed to consume her. He didn't know what could be done, as all the surgeons she had seen offered no treatment.

He pulled the dark purple robe of the brickweaver over his tunic and loose-fitting trousers, and wrapped his feet in nothing but bleached woolen cloth, as was the fashion. He wouldn't need much protection for them on the sledge that would carry him through the streets of the city. It was old but well made, designed by Jeppo himself. A small, oddly shaped rod of iron that hung from a lanyard round his neck was necessary to activate the forces in the device. Shaped on its sides like the silhouette of a swan, the sledge was otherwise obviously an artifact of man rather than nature. It was constructed of twice-fired bricks that were glossier than the common types found in towers, and thinner as well. So strong was its brick-binding that water splashed on its riding platform would slosh out the back instead of dripping between the bricks. Different patterns of all-binding held the rider to the platform, pushed away the ground beneath, and propelled the vehicle forward, all by control of the small iron rod twisted and turned by the rider in a discreet hole on the top of the sledge's forward hull.

On his journey to Kulla tower, Jeppo had left his neighborhood of short brick buildings tightly packed together, and rode deeper into the center of the city. Here the towers were taller and more splendid in appearance. Many had deep, colorful and fragrant gardens surrounding them, the most obvious sign of durable wealth. He passed other sledges, and people walking, mostly servants and farmers. They were darker skinned and more heavily robed in their brown raiment, unused as they were to the cool breezes of the city.

Finally, he arrived at the Kulla tower. It was tall and old and almost square at its base. It must be thirty stories high, he thought. Already his mind was analyzing the brick pattern on the front of the edifice. Decades of sunlight had reduced the vibrancy of the small motes of color identifying the different types of bricks but a trained eye like Jeppo's could still read their ancient language. This tower had much brick-binding, he deduced, more than was needed for its height. And some 'slowing' force as well, no doubt to further cool the air. These were antique patterns, not unlike his own, but as noticeably different as the sound of his own name when spoken by a foreigner.

He parked the sledge along the side of a wide brick path that led from the street to the great brick door of the tower. Every step he took toward the portico became easier and somehow more urgent as a long and subtle all-binding pulled his feet forward. This was the 'beckoning path' that was common in the old times and is more of a quaint annoyance these days. The household already alerted, the great door opened and a tall servant woman appeared.

"May I help you, sir?" the woman said.

"I am calling for Kulkulla, a young man of this house. He was assigned to my workshop but I will not be there till after midday. He should wait here until I arrive on my sledge. My appointment is not far from here but I am not sure how late I will be," Jeppo spoke slowly, unsure as he was of this towner woman's command of his language.

The woman nodded frequently as Jeppo told her the message. When repeating it later, she would nod at the same points, as was the tradition of her tribe, a nomadic people long ago tied to the lands of Thujwa.

"And please offer my respect to the judicious Kulla of this house," Jeppo said as an afterthought. When visiting the tower of one so prominent as Kulla the judge, it is expected to leave a message of flattery or praise.

"Judicious?" said the woman with knitted brow, "I do not know this word."

Jeppo turned around, realizing the word was a bad choice, and one that might appear to be mocking.

"I am sorry, housekeep," he continued. "Please tell your master that Jeppo the brickweaver stopped by only to leave a message." Great Thujwun, that sounded cheap, he thought. "And for the opportunity to relate his long-held respect and gratitude for the just Kulla's service to our well-standing city of Thujwa."

The woman stopped nodding her head and smiled. She had understood every word, and had detected no hint of mockery this time. She closed the large brick door effortlessly and picked up a basket of linens she had put to her side. Kulkulla's chamber was three stories up but even with the heavy basket, the climb would be easy. Patterns in the brick steps eased the effort of it, pulling her body up the staircase and she ascended as though she were unburdened. A few shafts of light had found their way past the dense array of towers in the neighborhood and through the generous windows along the walls above the steps. It was late in the morning now, and time for young folks to wake up, she thought. In the better families, adolescents were left to sleep till this time, as the practice was believed to make them less recalcitrant to their elders.

She arrived on the third floor platform that surrounded the spiral staircase. There was no need for a railing here as the forces manipulated by the brick floor prevented falling to the bottom of the tower-high atrium. The drapes in front of the entrance to Kulkulla's room were already open. She ventured in farther and saw that his bed was empty, and the drapes on the window had been pulled open as well. He had left early, she thought, which was probably a bad idea.

Chapter 4

The heart of Thujwa, the shimmering city of the desert, was among its duskiest places. So thick with towers of various heights that little direct sunlight reaches the winding, antique streets. The addition of catwalks between towers further deepened the shadows. Wealthier tower masters stretched brick platforms across walking bridges at high stories, ensuring a permanent night on all the architecture beneath it. Except that crystal lights as had once been only used during the nighttime were now embedded in the undersides of these platforms, an accommodation of little cost save for the constant but barely audible hissing and cracking and sighing of the quartz lamps as enormous pressure was applied to them by brickwork casements. It was through one of these blue-lit areas that Jeppo rode his sledge as midday approached. The yellow glow of natural light ahead betrayed the only open land in wide vicinity. It was a white brick plaza, clean and glowing in the midday sun, that encircled another ring of gardens, itself surrounding a great, vastly tall tower.

The building's top was the highest point in the entire city and even the most ambitious of the other towers did not reach within forty stories of it. What a marvel of the craft, Jeppo thought, his eyes happily discerning the patterns on its face. He followed them up the sides of the great octagonal structure where they disappeared beyond the strength of his vision. These were rich, complicated patterns, harnessing much brick-binding, as was appropriate for the tower's exceptional height. But there were also all-binding forces of complicated play here, and far more sword-binding than one would expect. This was an ancient building, a thousand years old, and no matter how elegant the weaving of the great Atos, the building's architect and the first brickweaver of any consequence, it was bound to appear odd to the modern 'weaver's eye. Jeppo approached the great brick door of the hierophant's tower and was greeted by a guard wearing the official yellow robe.

"Are you expected here, sir?" The guard asked. He was a severe, middle-aged man, with shortly cropped hair and hostile, squinted eyes.

"Yea, I am," Jeppo responded. "I have been called to a meeting with the singular hierophant of this beautifully designed city of Thujwa. I am Jeppo, a brickweaver."

A demon plagued Jeppo, though not one from the old tales. It was a demon of the mind, in which every pronouncement he brought forth, more with the formal than the informal, was followed by unholy regret upon recognition of its now obvious irony or mockery. How ironic, he thought, to call that tangle of brickweaving exuberance he just sailed through "beautifully designed", and yet did not the utility of those bridges and platforms and quartz lamps speak of a certain beauty by some measure?

The interior of the hierophant's tower was designed in the old manner. A staircase clung to the exterior wall and spiraled up, punching through a rectangular opening in the floor of each story. There was no high-rise atrium here as might be found in the old residential towers so that from inside there was no clue to the great height of the edifice or the lengthy walk required to reach the higher floors. Just a few foot-lengths from the edge of the staircase was the base of a tower within, which rose, he presumed, in parallel to the walls surrounding it and probably had doors at every story. The door at the base was brick and closed shut. Jeppo surmised that priests lived beyond those doors and engaged in preparations and rituals that would be forever unknown to him or anyone else outside the priesthood, just as he knew the many secrets to which only brickweavers were privy.

His progress up the staircase was not wearying. Strong forces played by the patterns in the brick pulled his legs forward and up. Even without the cool city air that encircled him and gently blew against his skin at times, he would not have broken a sweat in this climb. All the work of it was performed by manipulation of the all-binding force through the genius of the ancients' 'weaving skills.

At what he had reckoned to be the tenth floor, Jeppo

encountered only the second person he would meet at this place, a guard less hostile in manner than the first but just as stern in aspect. He motioned the brickweaver to leave the staircase and enter a door in the center tower.

"It is late," said the guard, as though that were a reason for redirecting Jeppo, who opened the door easily and entered a dark chamber. No sooner had he done this then the darkness was broken again by the door reopening. Now Jeppo could see the sunlit sky through what he first thought were great windows. They were instead open spaces periodically broken by narrow brick columns. He walked to the edge and looked down. Below him, he could see all of Thujwa, its mighty walls and the great expanse of lifeless desert beyond. Had he walked to the other side, he would also see the farmlands stretching to the south and the industrial areas that supplied his craft with well-assayed bricks. He would even have made out his own workshop far off to the southeast and, had he not continued climbing upward on the staircase, he might have seen a lone figure slowly advancing to the locked wooden door of that distant building.

Jeppo realized now that he stood more than one hundred stories above the street. How he had risen so high so quickly and without effort or jostle was a mystery to which he now applied his mind. If only the chamber had not been so perfectly dark, if only he had taken a quick glance at the walls to examine the brick patterns when the sunlight flowed in the opening doorway. But he had not left the chamber so quickly under his own direction. An unseen force had gently pushed him out.

This next story must have been nearly at the top of the tower, Jeppo thought. Here the staircase ended. The floor was nothing more than a ledge jutting out a few foot lengths from the exterior wall. It encircled a great brick disk that floated another few foot lengths from its edge and slightly above it. Jeppo could see a crack of light beneath it, and assured himself that it was, indeed, unconnected by any tangible means to the tower itself. At the center of the disk was a circular brick wall and beyond it, he reckoned, the living chamber of He Who Never Touches Earth.

A double brick door opened at one side of the chamber and out of it stepped a figure in indigo robes, the color of a rare flower that only grows in the most hostile desert lands where piles of stone provide shelter from the sun and winds, and deep aquifers are the only source of water, and only for the longest, most ambitious and most hopeful roots.

"Greetings, brickweaver," said the figure in a sonorous voice, no doubt aided by the clever acoustics of the carefully designed structure. "What is your question, first?"

It was a tradition well known to Jeppo that he had learned as a child, along with the many stories and fables that account for the mysteries of the world in a manner digestible to young minds, that the hierophant knew all things, and should one meet him, the eminent personage would be bound to answer one question and one only.

"Please, sire," Jeppo bowed to ask his question, "My wife, Matanya, is feeling poorly and has had no comfort for as long as I remember. Will this illness pass while there remains many years to her life?"

The indigo figure waited a moment before answering.

"This burden will pass," he said at last, "but your woman will take up many others."

Jeppo bowed again in response and a grin grew broadly on his face. He struggled to contain it lest he be chastised for being less grave in manner than the situation demanded.

"There is not much time left for your task," the hierophant continued with pausing. "Before the new moon rises, you must begin a journey far to the south, beyond the walls. There you will find the flower from which my robes acquire their singular hue. It guards the first place of your craft. Among the sands of that place is a chamber as old as Thujwa itself where lies," and here he paused as though collecting his thoughts. "Where lies *the duty to which we are bound.*"

The hierophant finished his statement with, "May Thujwun guide you." He abruptly turned his back to Jeppo and disappeared behind the door from which he had first emerged.

Kulkulla had been walking for a long while before the entrance to Jeppo's workshop was in sight. Two stories tall and many arm-lengths wide, it was located on the most remote land still within the great wall, well past the other workshops. Here the wall itself was larger and higher and more crudely fashioned of plain stone. There were no bricks to be seen. Beyond it to the south was the farm town, whose inhabitants still lived in tents or crude adobe huts and suffered the desert heat.

A great wooden door was the only entrance to Jeppo's workplace. It was painted a deep purple to signify that this was brickweaver property, and was firmly attached by thick, tightly woven fabric to the walls. Kulkulla knocked on the door and waited. There was no answer. He knocked again and waited. There was still no answer. The sun was well high above the horizon and Jeppo was not at his labors. Why? Kulkulla wondered. His gangly, spider-like body seemed to crumple and collapse onto the sand as he tried to figure out what to do next. If he entered the tent without Jeppo's permission, he could be punished for trying to steal brickweaver secrets. But Jeppo was not likely to prosecute his own assistant and Kulkulla thought it a reasonable argument that the old master might be ill or on some other wise adversely restrained from answering his call.

"Master Jeppo," he shouted to the door, his hands cupped like a horn around his mouth. Would that I had a ram's horn, he thought. He quickly pressed his ear against the painted wood but heard nothing save the beating of his own heart, the rush of hot, dry wind across the sand and the distant cacophony of the farm town marketplace. The intermittent "whoosh" of the wind made this solitary place seem still emptier, and lifeless, but that was only a trick of the mind. In Kulkulla's reasoning, it was also a portent of a bad result, but which one? If he tried to enter the workshop, and Jeppo were not there, he would surely be found out and his fate would be sealed. If instead he were to leave and make the lengthy trip back to the city, he would be adjudged a malingerer, or worse, a fool, by his new master. And what if the new master were unconscious from some grave accident, perhaps more severe because of the powerful forces with which the 'weavers struggled daily in their ancient craft? How would his actions be accounted should he abandon him there to languish, and possibly expire?

He stepped back a few paces and looked up at the second floor. There were a few large windows there, open to the air but grated. Probably affixed to let in the sunlight and fortified to prevent burglary, a likely occurrence considering the shop's proximity to the farm town. He had been taught that many of the farmers and servants and laborers who lived there were not of the faithful and so their morality was as suspect as their propriety.

His eye caught sight of a small stone, which he hefted in his palm and then threw with alacrity at one of the window grates. It hit the iron and made a deep clanging sound. He rushed to the door again and pressed his ear to the wood. Again, no sound was heard coming from within. He looked around the dunes. No other person was to be seen. Even the farm town was too far away for anyone to catch sight of him. Far to the north, rose the towers of the city, which seemed at this distance to form a bristle of long, rusty needles within which rose, nearly twice higher, the single rusty needle of the hierophant's tower.

Kulkulla resolved to find a way in. That appeared to be his only choice.

The judge called the council to order, as all had had a refreshment of yellow morning-flower tea and were ready to listen to Mincon's testimony. All seemed anxious save Mazrash, who was beginning to think through some doubts. How harmful must the display of force be, he wondered, and how costly the licensing? These were the two issues on which he would need to find assurance during the negotiations. But if there is warring, to what assurances would the guards be adhered in the chaos of the battlefield?

"My brothers, the technics I will speak of are far beyond the homely devices used in our daily lives or in the industries," Mincon began. "Two employ unique principles of binding and playing with the forces to achieve a level of mechanical violence that is awe-inspiring to even the distant observer.

"The machines are of three types, brothers. First, the 'concussor'. This one is particularly forceful and spectacular in its effect," Mincon looked around to each of the lords as he spoke. "It is a long pipe of circular, glazed brick. Within it are placed charged missiles, which are special glazed spheres made with the same earths and displaying the same properties as woven brick. When activated, the concussor pushes the missile out at tremendous speed. It will glide in a great arc until it collides with an obstacle, or the earth's all-binding returns it to the sand. In either case, the missile explodes in a blinding display of destruction, shaking the earth far past the horizon. Or so the secret history recounts.

"The second machine was called the 'compressor' by its maker. It is for all appearance a large wall, a square plate of twice-fired bricks affixed to the front of a large sledge. This plate will concentrate the all-binding into a point in the air some distance before it. All things on the other side of the point will be drawn to it, without exception for size and weight." Mincon held up his left hand, fingers together, and slightly curved, the thumb facing his mouth. With his right, he pointed to a space a few hand-widths from the palm of his left. "All things in this direction will eventually move toward the point, it only being a matter of how long the force is left active."

"Excuse me, sir," said Mazrash. "All things? What becomes of humans in the machine's range of action?"

"Human bodies are just as drawn to it as stone or wood, or goat. All things will be crushed into a small but very heavy ball, the same weight as all it consumed but of a size beneath measurement. It will sink into the desert because of its unbearable density."

Mazrash appeared stunned. He wanted to raise an objection to the potential for bloodshed but feared that Kulla would counter him, and tacitly chastise him for such unfaithfulness. It was a common belief among the Thujwani that the unfaithful live desperate, tragic existences and death my actually come as a gift to them, relieving their daily suffering and poverty of spirit, and hastening their future rebirth, if they had advanced sufficiently, into the blessed bosom of Thujwani parents. He would need to "skirt that dune" as climbing it could prove tiresome.

"Milord," Mazrash spoke at last, "while such bloodshed might be a boon to the lesser ones, as our faith tells us," he shot an earnest glance to Kulla, "it might also have the effect of reducing our accounts. How am I to sell a fine piece of Morso pottery to -- we shall say perhaps an *Andlian* -- whose brother we have just compressed into a heavy ball that is even at the time of our negotiation not yet completely submerged beneath the sands?"

"We are not likely to truly use this on people," Mincon replied. "I expect all here agree that what we are contemplating is a show of force, a powerful display, a beating of the chest. It would be like the roar of a well-fed lion, frightening but without peril."

"Indeed," interjected Tazil. "This is what I expect as well. As a surgeon I do not recoil from the sight of meaty violence, or its vivid description. But I am as pragmatic as you are, brother, and wish commerce to flow free, like the blood of an unstaunched wound."

"Let us allow the brickweaving master to finish his revelation and we shall happily argue the breadth of our plans," said Kulla. "Continue, please, milord."

Mincon resumed, "The third, brothers, is called the 'cabinet of forgetting'. It has a simple action and is not intended for show as the others are because its effects are not dramatic. We have secret histories that describe the use of the cabinet and its victims. Mostly rebel leaders, warring enemy generals, spies. Those were times of much warring and this device provided a quiet but effective advantage when a single man needed to be eliminated."

"But how is that so much more effective than a secret execution and burial, or burning?" questioned Orten.

"Aha, but that's the thing. The victim who enters the cabinet will disappear at the closing of the cabinet door. He will disappear completely, including the memory any friend or kin had ever had of him. All his works and influence will disappear as well. His children will have new fathers; his woman, a new husband; and it will be as though these new bonds had always existed."

Mazrash laughed. "I am doubting the existence of such a device itself. Think of this logically, brothers. What proof would there be of its efficacy after the victim has disappeared? Could I not say that I have already acquired such a device and have used it to send a hundred enemies to oblivion, and you will not recall their names because this cabinetry will have erased our knowledge of them, even unto the memories of them, as well? It seems an improvable matter, milord."

Mincon waited patiently throughout the merchant master's arguments. "That small logical issue," he said anon, "can be explained. But first I will begin with a question for you, Mazrash. What is the reason, brother, for which we keep the secret histories?"

Mazrash thought for a few moments, trying at first to discern the direction into which Mincon was leading him and, failing that, composing an appropriate response for which his brother masters could not readily find objection.

"As any apprentice that had mastered his scholastics would know, there are three reasons for the secret histories: to preserve the knowledge between generations of skilled men, that each should improve on his father's technics; to celebrate and praise the accomplishments of our skilled guildsmen; and to circumscribe those technics that Thujwun has given our respective guilds so that no guildsmen would know the vital technics of his brother guilds."

All eyes turned to Mincon again, confirming that Mazrash had said it right, at least according to the common history.

"Aye," responded the brickweaver, "That's well enough, but why might you think that the chronicles *begin* at the time of the 'rescue' of the southern tribes? Is it perhaps no coincidence that this strange machine, this cabinet, made all this record keeping *necessary*?"

There were knitted brows all around, and Tazil shot a glance to Kulla, to see what opinions might be registering on the aged countenance. Mazrash seemed to be staring at a point on his nose, indicating he was deep in thought.

"Brothers, the last revelation I will tell you today is this," Mincon continued. "The cabinet's maker, Atos, knew that while all the expanse of life connected to the box's victim would disappear, the inscription of a victim's name on cured hide, *would not*."

"So clarify this for me, milord," said Orten. "A victim's woman would have another husband all at once with his disappearance, but a written history of their marriage would remain unchanged?"

"The symbols that form our alphabet are unaffected by the power of the all-binding. As they can create a false history, such as the kind that is sometimes performed in dramas before the unfaithful in farm town, they can preserve as well any forgotten truth. This 'writing' was a young skill to the Thujwani at the time of the rescue and they did not need to take it on in earnest until the appearance of this machine and the understanding that its powers were absurdly useless without it. Scribes became a guild at that now misty time and their own secret histories might have more writing on this, but as proof of the machine's efficacy, I offer this argument of logic. We all know that a false thing can be written, a fiction. So it is on hide or parchment or paper that a truth could be written and still survive its transformation into a falsehood by Atos' cabinet. That was the most urgent purpose of the writing for the brickweavers, to prove that the machine was actually working."

Mincon took a deep breath and returned to his chair.

"I must say that should Hecult have been here, he might have made a stalwart defense of the veracity of our scribes," offered Kulla. "In my eyes, they take great care to ensure the accuracy of their chronicles."

"And that is proof again of how elusive the truth is," replied Mincon. "That men must struggle to record it."

The brickweaver glanced at each of the councilors, trying to read their reaction.

"I am convinced of Mincon's words, brothers," said Orten. "I have found this revelation to be a most exciting one. That the first of the secret histories began due to the power of this machine is a strong argument for its efficacy."

"And convincing of the efficacy of all three, I warrant," added Kulla.

"This is too much to digest," said Tazil. "Can we distill from this a vote, so that the for and against can debate?"

"It is my issue at hand," said Mazrash, "And I can work out of this news a proposal that we might prudently embrace. Desirous as I am of the purest utility, I can see only one of these machines as advancing our diplomacy, which being the horrific *'concussor'* machine. It could be used to teach quite a lesson to the other cities of the power of our armaments and without harm to anything but a dune on the high desert. What say you, brothers?"

"Aye!" said they all. Because this was not the more solemn vote of law, they merely voiced their approval for the action to go forward.

"Then we shall plan a demonstration for all the council, judge?" he spoke to Kulla.

"Aye, milord," said Kulla, turning to Mincon. "When can the device be made ready, milord?"

"Three days should be adequate time, judge," he replied.

"Then we shall see this concussor in three days' time. May Thujwun guide us on that day."

Chapter 5

Jeppo returned to the sledge dazed by the thoughts that roiled in his mind. He was relieved to know that Matanya would survive her suffering, though would the burdens that followed be more vexing? He had already dismissed her unease as a minor complaint, acute but self-limiting, now that a voice of prophecy had given him leave to dismiss it. What concerned him now was this task. It would be five days before the new moon would rise. In that time, he needed to prepare for a journey into the desert, something he had not done since his youth, when he had schemed to escape the cruel life of an orphaned child in Thujwa. He had run away from his master and sought the world outside, only to discover, almost at the price of his life, that there was no such world awaiting him. The other desert cities were, like Thujwa, great walled places, their inhabitants suspicious of strangers, their secrets of craft held closely, jealously.

He knew where to find the indigo flower. It grew in the old city of Koosh, first home of the Thujwani who, before that time, had been a nomadic tribe. Dye gatherers still ventured there to pick the blossoms though there were fewer and fewer each year.

Koosh was an oasis in the old time, before the great city was built some many days north. It was taught that Koosh lost its water when Thujwun's people abandoned it to build the great city in His name, because Thujwun "would bend the earth itself" to please His children, especially in response to such flattery, which was considered the highest form of devotion. The king Azrom had been thought a madman to move his people there, though he was later revered for it. But the brickweavers' secret history teaches that the exodus was the idea of Atos, the Receiver of the Gift, the founder of the brickweaver's art.

"The sands have a rhythm," Atos had written, "and the wind has an agenda, and where they meet is a pattern that tells of all things." The legend says that Atos could read the patterns of clouds in the sky and know all about the sky, while the patterns in the sand told him all about the earth, and all patterns instructed him in the secrets of the wind. It is said that this knowledge was to brickweaving as the orator's speech is to a baby's babbling, yet brickweaving, perhaps the crudest of his arts, was all that remained of his fabled wisdom.

Jeppo had never been to Koosh but had heard stories from the dye-gatherers, who, like the other merchants in Thujwa's marketplace, were crude, unfaithful, farm town people who felt the need to relate the entire history of a pomegranate before selling you one. He had bought red dye from an elderly nomad once and the toothless fellow proceeded to regale him with a poorly articulated memoir of his last trip to Koosh, to explain why the red dye was so much cheaper -- because it was made from beetles that swarm around garbage dumps, which men can always produce with little effort -- while the indigo dye comes only from a rare flower in that abandoned city.

Great rocks burst from the desert long ago to build the city, the dye-seller had told him, and near the greatest outcropping was an edifice built on fertile earth where the sweet waters of the oasis still provided for thirsty flowers. The rest of the city was a ruin of old brick-and-mortar, crumbling back to the desert centuries after it was abandoned, he had told him.

It was not long past midday that Jeppo arrived at the Kulla tower. The dark-skinned servant woman he had seen that morning opened the door before he could raise his fist to knock.

"Please, sir, know that I tried to deliver your message but the young man Kulkulla was already gone from this tower," the woman said in one long breath, making sure that both the failure and the excuse were heard in the same moment. "I did not know that he had already left. I am just a housekeep."

"Then tell me, woman, where did he go?" Jeppo demanded.

"I know not where he was off to, sir," she said in the awkward dialect of the M'butu, her head nodding.

Kulkulla had identified several large stones in the vicinity and was busy collecting them and carrying one at a time to the workshop. It was strenuous work but he managed to build something of a crude tower along the western wall of the building. Working at this for some time, he felt thirsty and exhausted. Most of his water was gone and how much more of it could he lose in the strain of lifting and carrying those stones?

He began his ascent of the crooked tower. The stones allotted random spots of purchase, which he navigated awkwardly in the soft bags of stitched leather that covered his feet. Standing on the top stone, which wobbled slightly, his hands could just reach the iron bars of the window grate. His searching fingers fell not far through the spaces between and touched, to his horror, a smoothly polished surface. A sheet of quartz thick as a bricklayer's battered thumb was affixed behind and against the grill. It would allow light in but reveal nothing but shadows when seen from without. The same quartz was used for its own luminescent properties in the night lamps of the city but on this crude structure it was only an inaccurate but generous vehicle for the sun's own light. Its primary purpose, though, was to keep out insects and burglars, both of which were thought to heavily populate the farm town.

A little desperately, Kulkulla imagined that both the grate and the pane might have been loosened by neglect or harsh conditions. No sword-binding could be practiced here so only the inferior old technics held the iron-grate to the stone frame. He briefly thought of lifting himself onto the narrow ledge but he was not sure how he could get down. The fall would not be great but when one is alone and in the desert, any mishap would sizably increase the likelihood of a tragedy. First he would give the possibly loosened pane a gentle push with his fingers. At once with this effort, his toes pushed out away from the wall and the top stone flung outward. A cacophony of dull thuds accompanied the toppling of the other stones once solidly beneath it, while Kulkulla's gangly arms and legs beat the air until he landed on his back. Everything was dark now with just a few stars in the sky but they glowed brightly, and in different colors. Somewhere, from far off in the distance or from down a deep well, came his own voice, saying only "Unh." And then there was nothing.

Chapter 6

"Lord Thujwun, preserve me!" Jeppo shouted, grateful that no one could hear his profanity but worried that the figure lying in the sand before him made no reaction. He jumped from the sledge and ran to Kulkulla's side, squatting down to get a closer look at the fellow's face. To his knowledge, he had never met his assignee before. The grand council chooses apprenticeships based on the number of vacant duties and the qualities of the applicants. A good scholastics record is often a guide to the professions of oratory or academic. A reputation for rough play in athletics would guide the council toward the surgery or merchant managing. Artistic youths are directed toward the priestly or craftsman managing professions. The solitary students who develop grand schemes of imagination to comfort themselves in their loneliness are the type invariably sent to apprentice in brickweaving.

  Kulkulla's sudden appearance in a post left vacant for years was the result of none of these reckonings. He had failed at other assignments and his family's prominence was somewhat endangered by the prospect of his ultimate failure as a respected and faithful citizen, one who would earn his wealth through the power of his intellect. His grandfather no-doubt had wielded a heavy hand in finagling this apprenticeship. And the youth's desperate fear of yet another failure had urged him to overplay his earnestness and arrive at the workshop early on his first day of assignment.

  Jeppo wet a rag from his water bladder and patted the youth's forehead. His cheek was hot to the touch, and flushed. He lifted Kulkulla's seemingly lifeless body onto the sledge and brought him into the cool, dusky interior of the workshop. He placed the limp body on a table and tried to revive his new apprentice with splashes of water, and slaps on the cheek and pinches on the arm. I know nothing of surgery, Jeppo thought to himself, I swear he is breathing still but that is the limit of my knowledge, a thing that any farm town goat would know just as well.

He resolved to ride the sledge to the farm town marketplace where he might find a surgeon, if even a farm town one. He feared that the time it would take him to ride to the city would render moot any advantage in acquiring the services of a respectable surgeon.

It was only several leagues to the edge of farm town and the marketplace was not far beyond. As Jeppo approached, a variety of farm people -- who did not all work at farms but nonetheless worked at labors of similar cleverness and remuneration -- were drawn to the sledge. Such vehicles were not often seen this far from the city and usually they carried members of the city guard, who never visited without tragic consequences. Farm town wagons were pulled by men and women, or goats and asses closer to the crop lands. In the farm town itself, buildings were constructed of adobe or buried in the earth, though there is much shade here from various palms and fruit trees like pomegranate and blood lemon. Fewer animals were found here than on the farms, which raised goats and cattle along with grains like wheat and millet. A variety of bush berries and vegetables were also grown there.

The town itself was nothing more than a tight accretion of adobe huts and nomad tents around the central great fountain that pulled water from deep within and across the earth to turn the desert lands into a cornucopia. Underground brick conduits spread out from its buried heart to feed the irrigation pipes of the thirsty southern farm lands. The farm town folk were of all types, tribes of the rainforest or nomads of the desert, all colors of garment and postures of body and each had their own language. They all learn a broken Thujwani though so that they could bargain in the marketplace of the great city.

Among the crowd of faces, more of a medley of humanity's many forms than Jeppo had seen in a long while, he spied a man with a black robe and crimson sash.

"Please, fellow, are you a surgeon? I am in need of one," Jeppo pleaded.

"I am no surgeon... now... but I may be of help. What ails

you?"

"It is not me but my new assistant who had just started today. I found him prostrate in the desert and not responding to water splashes."

"Where is he now?" the man replied with concern.

"My workshop," said Jeppo. "Please board my sledge and we can be there in a few moments."

At first hesitant, the black-robed man jumped onto the sledge, which was rigidly still and hovered a few hand-widths above the stony street way. Though he wore the robes and sash, the traditional costume of a surgeon, he was not wearing the black four-cornered hat on his head or the opal pendant round his neck. Jeppo began to distrust him but was sure that even this inadequately attired farm towner could do a better job of treating his felled assistant than he, who only knew to splash water on the unconscious.

The journey was only several leagues, a distance the swan-shaped sledge could cover in just a few hundred heartbeats. It would take many more palpitations though for the black-robed man. He spent the short time standing nervously behind Jeppo and trying to reach out to the brickweaver's waist for support. But he was unable to do so. Some invisible force kept him separated from the pilot and held him still, as though his feet were bolted to the base of the sledge.

Jeppo realized as the fog of the crisis lifted from his thoughts that his passenger might likely be a burglar. And here he intended to grant him admission to his workshop, the most secret of places, to which few had ever ventured and every one of them a brickweaver himself. There were great drapes of rough cloth, hung from dowels, covering the deep shelves and alcoves, and a tarp of the same fabric draped over the models and calculating table, so there was not much this fellow would see. But what was in the towner's black bag? A surgeon's bag would be holding many gleaming sharp knives and saws, and glass bottles with wooden stoppers containing plant extracts, oils and mineral solutions, all of them poisonous to one degree or another. What if the bag were itself a stolen property of one of the city's respectable practitioners. In the hands of an ordinary man, and especially those of one of these desperate types who idled in southern places, it was a veritable armory, a toolkit for murderous burglary.

"What is your name, towner?" Jeppo shouted brusquely to his passenger as the sledge slowed and the workshop appeared like a small brick on the horizon.

"Sir, I would be Vomcot, formerly an assistant to Surgeon Axil," said the man nervously, owing to his inexperience with sledge rides rather than any reluctance to identify himself. "I am no surgeon but employ myself in treating the people of the Surrel by use of the old healing arts."

The stranger's proper speech was a relief to Jeppo. Already much uncertainty and potential tragedy had been visited upon him this day -- even the prophesy about Matanya was not entirely without foreboding -- but now he was marginally assured that the stranger would not slit his throat and make off with his precious tools or invite a swarthy gang of towners from "the Surrel" to ransack his lonely desert roost.

As they arrived at the workshop, a small panic arose in Jeppo and he pulled Vomcot by the arm as both men ran to the freely opening purple door. The worry at hand now loomed largest to him so whatever residual fear he had of the towner was put aside. Jeppo secured the door soon after they were inside and Vomcot approached his patient, whose long, thin limbs were stretched out on the large, waist-high wooden table near the center of the building's cavernous single room. Though the youth's brown robe and purple sash were sandy and rumpled, there were no marks, no scratches or bruises or bumps on his head or arms. There was some bruising to his palms and some sand around his neck though Jeppo had washed the youth's face in his limited attempt at reviving him.

Vomcot unlaced his black bag and produced from it a glass bottle filled with clear fluid.

"This is an extract made from a common flower that grows in the mountains to the west. The flower itself is poisonous in handfuls but this extract has been prepared to reverse that inclination of the flower's spirit." Vomcot held the bottle out for Jeppo to see, then set it down on the table near Kulkulla's left ankle. He proceeded to examine the patient. A steady palm close to Kulkulla's nose and mouth and then two fingers alongside his neck assured Vomcot that the youth was still breathing and still had blood pumping through his veins. But Kulkulla's skin was hot to the touch while his forehead was cool.

      Vomcot's eyebrows rose. He had taken the wrong remedy out but gratefully the correct one, an extract from the bark of a deep-forest tree, was secreted in his black bag. He exchanged the bottles, removing a slim white cloth from the bag as well. He opened the new bottle and poured a small amount on the cloth, compressing it in his hand to ensure that every square measure of it was soaked through. Then, with delicate care, he spread out the wet cloth on Kulkulla's face. The youth awoke and tried to rise at once but Vomcot easily pushed him down.

      "What...?" Kulkulla tried to speak but only made a tortured rasping.

      "Stay quiet, boy," Vomcot spoke sharply having just attired himself in the invisible cloak of authority that dresses the singular healer in the company of folk of any other station when a medical crisis is at hand.

      "Get me some water, sir," he said to Jeppo and the brickweaver quickly filled a goat head-sized jug with cool water from the shop's stone cistern.

      Vomcot held up the skinny youth with one hand behind Kulkulla's back and, with the other, brought the jug to Kulkulla's mouth. The youth drank and coughed, and breathed deep breaths, and drank some more.

Chapter 7

Lavena took a thin, tightly woven woolen cloth and washed it in the nearly scalding water of the great basin, wrung it out in her leathery hands and gently stretched it on a carefully designed block of brickwork nearby. It was immediately dried and rendered exquisitely soft to the touch and so white that it glowed in the afternoon sunlight that streamed through the kitchen window. Lavena enjoyed the first touch of the revived cleaning cloth, when it became softer than even the piled cloth of the silk merchant, and the many other small benefits of housework as well. But she tired of the drudgery and worse, the constant, invisible horror that seemed to hold her fast in its grip at all times. She resented that she was bound to servitude simply because of an accident of her birth. I have a nomad's blood, she would ponder, and this life to us is not unlike to be enchained. Lavena knew that should she ever harm her mistress or master in even the slightest way that she could suffer death. It was the cruelest law, she thought, and had been executed against people she had known, or were known in her tribe. The Thujwani had well established the conceit they were protecting the tribal peoples from their own innate urges rather than binding them to near slavery as a source of inexpensive labor. The M'butu and the Tawani, the Gelgak and the Morso, and all the other southern tribes, had once roamed free in the rainforest or the sparsely planted desert. Those lands were deep desert now, ruined by the scouring wrought by great engines, the terrible armaments that destroyed their camps and villages and terrified their ancestors into submission. There was knowledge of this in the secret history of the tribes, a history told in song and oratory, or drama, or dance. Because it was not a history written in books, the

Thujwani knew none of it. They only trusted the common history, inscribed in large, bound scrolls and promulgated through the teachings of the scholastics. Should one be a guildsman, however, he would ascribe more veracity to his own guild's secret writings.

She wiped the cloth along all the walls and furnishings, as it transformed from snowy white to gray and then black. All the loot abandoned by the air and breath and footfall, the touch of hand to wall or door, all was collected by the attracting cloth. Lavena had not the slightest understanding of how the process worked, only the correct sequence of events for washing and drying the cloth. She failed to comprehend, as well, the means by which the water font could produce scalding water that had only moments before been cool as that of the great fountain in the Surrel. All that with the turn of an iron key, she mused.

Despite her resentment of the Thujwani people, she bore no ill-will to her mistress, a sad woman, she thought. Perhaps as bound a servant as I, Lavena would think as she was bringing her mistress the morning tea and would catch the brickweaver's wife grimacing in pain. Matanya would strain to smile and appear comfortable as soon as she caught sight of anyone, even the lowly housekeep. She never abused nor was unfair to Lavena. Of that, the Morso woman was cognizant and grateful. She had kin who worked as house-servants to other Thujwani and they engaged in the "whisper war". They would gather in small groups at taverns in the Surrel, when they were sure no Thujwani were around, and mock and insult their masters, and tell long stories of the undiscovered practical jokes they had played on them.

"Lavena," came Matanya's voice from the sleeping room. "I wish to take a bath."

"*Adoo*, madam," Lavena replied. "I will prepare it for you."

As Lavena went about her water carrying to fill the oblong bath basin with just the right combination of hot and cold draughts as would be comfortable to her lady's touch, Matanya lifted herself out of bed, marking with some regret the late position of the sun as it shone through the sleeping room window. She raised herself up before a large looking glass and scrutinized the old face she saw there. Her skin was still soft but small folds had already begun and what had once been the glowing homogeny of young flesh was now an ill-concealed network of tiny veins and pallid fat and blotchy freckles. Her eyes were the worst of it. Having been the paired gems of her beauty in youth, they were now pinched to squints, like the eyes of a boar, and cloudy like those of a goat of long years. She cleared her throat and assured herself that a bath would be her palliative. There is healing in water, she thought, "mild to the body and strong to the throat," her mother would say. She gulped a draught of cold water from the sleeping room jug and made her way to the bath chamber.

"I will want some hot tea after my bath," sad Matanya to her maid.

"It will be ready for madam," Lavena spoke while helping to lower her mistress awkwardly into the lukewarm water. She recalled some stories from the whisper war of what servants had done to their masters' bath. It was not Matanya's fair treatment of her that restrained such petty rebellion, she thought, but rather her lineage and breeding, that as a member of her clan she was above all such hooliganism, though she knew that other members of her clan were not.

The brickwork bath basin was sealed from leakage with the power of the brick-binding. The bricks from which it was constructed were patterned like those used in the great towers but not so thick as them. Their smooth, glossy surface was the result of painting them with a slop of watery clay before a hotter, longer stay in the kiln than construction bricks would need. But they still played with the same forces, sword-binding, all-binding, cooling-and-slowing, heating-and-rising. These bath basin bricks had simple patterns only to bind the bricks together and hold the water within. But it was rumored that all-binding in excess of this task would caress the body and wake aged flesh to vigor. Matanya was not convinced of the rumor, for she had taken more baths in recent times than in her youth and had not found it to slow the advance of the years, which seemed to chase her nowadays on swifter feet. But the warm water was a comfort and a tonic. The folds in her face and dullness in her eyes, she felt, were merely hallmarks for the pain in her joints, which only the water soothed.

The bruise on the back of Kulkulla's head was now swelling slightly and aching in pulses. The youth reflexively raised his hand to it and winced as his impatient fingers touched the scalp, inflaming the dull ache into a stinging pain. More draughts of water and he was able to speak, though he coughed and strained at the task.

Vomcot narrowed his eyes. "Did you fall, boy? Is that a blow to your head?"

"Aye, sir." Kulkulla answered. "I may have fallen and injured my head." He was just collecting his wits now and made a cursory glance around the room. He was no longer outside in that perilous sun but found himself, instead, in a great, dimly lit, cavernous place. The iron grating on the high windows was a sufficient clue to his location and a small note of victory came to him, having accomplished his earlier goal but not, apparently, according to his original plan. The room was square and high, with a line of windows all around the top. Below that where great stone shelves and raised alcoves. Each was covered by a heavy cloth that hung from dowels affixed to the wall above it. In the center of the room was a large open space save for what looked like a low, wide tent with points at random heights. The thick wooden table on which Kulkulla reclined was near the room's entrance and away from the low tent. Near to him stood two figures looking down at the youth with concern. He recognized at least their stations and could deduce more from that. Clearly the purple-robed man of his mother's age would be Jeppo himself, his new master. But he could not guess the identity of the surgeon and was not entirely sure of the man's station because he lacked the traditional four-cornered hat and opal pendant.

"Sit up, boy" said Vomcot, who had prepared another wet cloth and pressed it firmly against the bruise. The pain was quick and deep now, and Kulkulla rose up with the sting of it as Vomcot gently grasped his shoulder and held him from rising farther. And then the pain was gone. Had I a dull ache as might worry someone for seven days, thought Kulkulla, but delivered to my nerves in only moments all at once, it might approach the ferocity of the suffering I have just endured.

The swelling went down as well and there would be no trace of injury remaining on his scalp by sunset. But he still felt a little tired. "Drink more water," Vomcot adjured, "But slowly, boy."

"Are you well now?" said Jeppo to the youth.

"Aye," he took another sip and wiped his mouth. "Aye, master Jeppo. Please forgive this introduction... on this fine day in the healthful... no, the well-made city of Thujwa," he added.

"You are Kulla's son, no?"

"Aye. Or rather his grandson, sir."

"How many years are you then, Kulkulla?"

"I am born seventeen years past, sir. I am old for the first year of apprenticeship and I know that."

"And why would that be?" Jeppo continued his interview.

"I had apprenticed, sir, in other trades."

"And did you find the other trades wanting, or they found you so?"

Kulkulla thought carefully about his answer. He had apprenticed to the lawyer Gigmal, and in the surgery of Tovis, and in the reckoning chambers of Mazrash, all with poor results. He had surely earned a black mark in those guilds and surely Jeppo would find that out. But the work had not interested him either and perhaps that was the root of his failure. He had not known a calling as his peers had. They were already on their third years and could order about their lessers and earned good stipends, a few even keeping their own servants. But he was surely the worst of dullards, having found no attraction to any of the professions.

"The wishes of Thujwun have brought me here by a twisty path, sir, and I can only guess that His will has planned it so," he said with the earnestness of a priest or a lawyer.

Jeppo suppressed a chuckle. This canny response was just as he should have expected from the grandson of that orator. If there were proof that this was not indeed the boy named Kulkulla, he would be sure it was judge Kulla himself.

He turned to Vomcot, "Will he be well from this, healer?"

"He grows stronger by the moment. There will be no legacy to this mishap, I can warrant, but he must take care, drink heartily of the jug and sleep well this evening to finish the cure."

"And what is your license, for this?" Jeppo asked in the brusque manner of the merchant class.

"Four small pieces, sir," replied the healer.

"I will pay the license," Kulkulla interjected. "It was my folly that brought me down and I have a small stipend. I can give you two pieces today and the rest on the morrow."

With a wave of Jeppo's hand, the youth cut short his declaration.

"You are in my care now, assistant, and I will pay the healer's fee." The relaxed formality of his discourse comforted Kulkulla, as it made him realize he was not yet routed out of brickweaving by the mishap, though he reckoned that would come on another day. He shuddered as he wondered what tragedy would cause the break - a flying brick, a plunging bridge between high towers, a bath basin poaching some wealthy matron.

"Once you are strong enough," continued Jeppo, "your first task will be the removal of that pile of stones near the south wall. It will invite burglars if left there."

Vomcot turned at the sound of the word "burglar", knowing that the peoples of the Surrel were often slandered that way, despite their intimacy to the Thujwani's households and the frequency with which they minded their betters' children.

"Healer," said Jeppo, grasping the man's left wrist, "I will pay you now and return you to the town. I give you praise, sir, for your skills." The wrist grasp was an honor Vomcot had not expected. Jeppo produced a small leather bag attached to a leather thong that disappeared under the many layers of his clothing. He handed out four small pieces of gold which Vomcot secured in a pouch under his sash.

As he walked Vomcot out, Jeppo turned to Kulkulla, still reclining on the table but up on his elbows. "You, son, are to stay here till my return. I bid you rest on that great table, and keep your hands away from anything in this shop."

Once outside and aboard the sledge, which Vomcot now approached with less hesitancy, Jeppo sought an interview with him before the rush of wind during the ride could drown out his words.

"Before you depart, healer, I would have you entertain some questions. What is the nature of your practice? I saw you treat the lad with great gentility and swift result. And yet you did no bloodletting, and did not force any poisons down his throat?"

"My skills," replied Vomcot, "Are not of the surgeon guild's tradition. I am using the old healing ways of the Tawani and the Morso. They are fond of water and weak plant extracts for their dispensary, and have not advanced enough to let blood or give poison. But I had never had the stomach for such practices on any wise, and left my apprenticeship after encountering a healer from the Surrel, who had done as much as I did for her patient and had brought him back to health and vigor in as short a time."

"Know that there are rumors such practices as yours are said to erode our faith and they are not encouraged. You look Thujwani, man, and I wonder if you have lost your faith."

"I am Thujwani, of the house of Axil, surgeons for as many generations as the common history can tell, but I have not lost my faith in Thujwun and believe it is He who has brought me down this path."

"That is good, sir," replied Jeppo. "It is good you have not abandoned your faith. So tell this old brickweaver, what nostrums might you have in your dispensary to ease the suffering of a Thujwani woman, whom all our fine surgeons have waved away because she has not borne issue?"

"Tell me the nature of her distress and I will reckon on it. There is so little that plagues the Thujwani because of their good food and water, their restful homes and their faithful manners, that I may already have a suspicion. But tell me her complaints, in plainest language now, sir."

"Aye," said Jeppo. "She is suffering from her joints and in general is forlorn and sad. She is weak at all times and late to rise from bed. Only warm baths seem to comfort her."

"Enough, perhaps," replied the healer. "And does she go to the marketplace many times a fortnight?"

"She does not today, nor in recent days," Jeppo was trying to think of the last time Matanya had gone to the market. "But she would go each day in times past. We have a cooling bin but it was never full as in other households. My Matanya resolved that all our evening meals would be made from the freshest victuals. It was a special concern of hers though something of less urgency to the other Thujwani wives, who busy themselves with other matters."

"Does she feel as though she has aged more years than the calendar would reckon?" said Vomcot.

"Well I have heard some talk like that," Jeppo answered. "But all the women of Thujwa talk that way. It is their custom, as I have always believed."

Vomcot's brow knitted in thought for a few moments.

"Let us go to the Surrel now. I will direct you to my shop, where I may have a therapy for this woman," he said at last.

"Aye, sir," said Jeppo, and he plunged the metal rod into its obscure hole on the front hull of the sledge. With that, the vehicle rose a few hand-widths above the desert sand. He seemed to play with the metal rod, as though it were a crazily bent wire that was stuck in the hole, and he was trying to release it. But his maneuvers had a purpose as the sledge slowly accelerated and reached the Surrel while the sun continued its descent well away from its midday height. What was normally a sixth-of-a-day's journey on foot took the two riders only a few hundred heartbeats in time. As they rode through the streets of the farm town, they passed people of every variety of color and build and costume. Once occasional enemies in intertribal wars, these peoples now lived and worked together in peace and mutual fear of their masters. Whether the passerby was a Howoo cattle farmer, tall and dark-skinned almost to a blue that reflects the sky, or a pale and freckled Dazhragg goatherd, or the M'Butu, tall, slender and of haughty posture as one might recognize in a king, or the Morso, clever, moralistic, and prideful of their pragmatic philosophies. They passed Tawani tribesman wearing traditional tunics and leather breeches, and Gelgak, the primitive mud people, who cover themselves in different colored clay slurries to express their spiritual state. Regardless of the tribe or clan, all the onlookers stared at the sledge as it sped by. Some reacted with alarm as the last appearance of such a vehicle heralded a punishment from the city guard.

"Look there," Jeppo said pointing to three Gelgak walking along the side of the road. One was covered in crusty yellow clay, the second, in deep red, and the third, who was strolling more casually, wore a thick blue mudskin. "They are rarely seen in the city and to see three at once, in different colors, is surely a sign from Thujwun of a good result."

"They are very quiet, even in the Surrel, at least during the day," added Vomcot. "The sight of this machine has attracted much attention."

Vomcot directed Jeppo to his dispensary, a single-floor adobe building reinforced with great wooden beams. Inside was a good water basin, connected by the underground aqueducts to the great fountain, and a few specimens of the brickweavers' art, but not many. Mostly, the walls were lined with thick wooden shelves, covered by thick cloths. It was in some ways a smaller version of Jeppo's own workplace. Vomcot put out his bag on a waist-high wooden table and walked over to one of the shelves. He went behind the curtain and emerged with a bottle in his hand. Around its neck was a short leather thong attached to a thin wooden tag. Jeppo looked at the tag and said "Is this not the godhead of one of the tribes?"

He pointed to a picture burned in the tag that looked to him like an old king with two eyes, no nose or mouth but a beard of tentacles.

"No," said Vomcot, "No god at all. That is a sea creature. Far to the west, probably many months' journey even in your sledge, there are great seas of water with many creatures that would seem strange to us. This is one such creature, a tiny monster that defends itself with the squirting of a dark fluid. The western tribes use the same fluid as an ink for their brushes. This bottle contains the essence of that dusky liquid, and it may be a cure for your woman."

Jeppo's eyes were wide as he tried to absorb all that the healer said.

"But what does this monster have to do with my wife's condition?"

"It is the principle," Vomcot returned to a speech he had often given to Thujwani patients, "That Thujwun in his infinite kindness has provided the earth with all the remedies to disease. Given such a truth, it would follow that a disease that might be obscure, as this one that has confounded other surgeons, is probably only suffered too far from its companion remedy."

The logic made sense to Jeppo, at least theologically. The healer was already decanting a small portion of the contents of the tagged bottle into a smaller ceramic bottle. He poured another clear liquid from a jug to fill up the small bottle, stopped it with a cloth and a piece of wood and handed it to Jeppo.

"You recall how I treated the young man, at first?" asked Vomcot.

"Aye, sir. You did moisten a towel and gently lay it on his face," replied Jeppo.

"You are to do the same to your woman, before she retires this evening. You must later report back on how she appears in the morning," said Vomcot.

"Aye, healer. And what is the fee for this?"

"No fee can be determined unless there is a cure."

Jeppo smiled and bid his leave. He secured the small bottle in a pocket within one of his robes and rode the sledge past the rows of the many desert trees and palms that lined the streets of the farm town. Farther west, the orchards are thick with fig, coconut, pomegranate and other thirsty trees, and could likely not be navigable in a sledge this size. The sunlight was waning now but he expected that he could be home before dusk. In a few moments the workshop ahead was visible and there was still plenty of light to make out the pile of stones collected against the south wall.

Chapter 8

Lavena had found a seller at the marketplace with a special selection of small game. There were cotishes, and wild dramagan, and, unusual for this season, a good selection of gaumji, the tiny wild birds that flock in swarms in the outer desert when a storm approaches. They rarely cross the wall and enter the land of the Thujwani. Lavena guessed that someone had left the perimeter but she would not ask who or how. The wild poultry would be a special treat for her masters and that was enough to know.

"One small piece of gold for a handful, madam," the seller quoted. "These are not often seen in the market, and their tiny hearts are said to be tonic for the ill."

"Need the measure of the handful be mine own or could I find a large man to do my shopping. Wait as I search for my cousin Olmak," she said with a smile. Olmak was many hands tall but of normal count should his own hands be the measure.

The seller laughed. "You know how to bargain, madam," he said. "I know of Olmak and would not make him such an offer, or I would leave here in poverty."

"But note how small my woman's hands are," she returned. "Surely neither of us need to leave this place a pauper. I will give you one piece for two handfuls, and promise to make my first stop here in days forward."

"A deal then," said the seller.

"A deal... as long as the hands that measure are yours," she added with a coy smile.

While the guamji are tasty and satisfying, their preparation is not difficult and takes very little time. A metal bowl is inserted in the hot bin and filled with the oil of crushed olives. The heat is activated by the turn of an iron rod and the oil speedily rises to boiling. The birds are plucked but not dressed because even their tiny bones are no hazard to the throat after cooking. A batter is made on them with goat milk and millet flour and then the quamji are dropped in the boiling oil. Their battered skin cooks up crisp and slightly burnt, but their meat and organs are steaming and give away easily to the tooth.

Lavena prepared the meal simply, placing the browned bird carcasses, each about the size of Jeppo's second finger, onto a bed of vinegar-soaked tamran leaves, where they would keep company with slices of lemon. Alongside she placed some bowls of seasoned cracked wheat and a sauce made from pomegranates. The repast was set on a large tray in the feasting room, a generous, well-decorated chamber near the modest kitchen. She covered the dish with a heavy bronze dome that would keep it warm until her masters were ready to consume it.

Her tasks were completed and she was ready to return to the Surrel for the night but she needed to look in on her mistress and bid her a good evening.

"Madam, I have served the dinner. Shall I wait with you till master Jeppo returns?" she spoke from the opening to the sleeping chamber, with the thickly piled cloth cover pushed slightly open, and hoped that Matanya would not take her polite offer as anything more than good manners. The walk to the Surrel would last well past dusk and there were dangers along the way. But she would be traveling in the company of the other house servants and the industry laborers for the evening's trip home though the desert twilight. They would chat of many things along the way, but mostly about the small, remarkable occurrences of everyday life, such as her bargain at the market, or the incidental follies of their masters, and some in small groups would engage in the whisper war. They would be stealthy at first but once catching sight of the amber glow of oil lamps emanating from the farm town ahead, their voices would rise and laughter could be heard at intervals.

"You have done well today, Lavena," said Matanya, her voice lightened by the expectation of a fine dinner. "Perhaps it is good I no longer visit the market. I could not have won such a bargain." She was busy with her evening clothes. These were lighter than the robes of daytime that were woven for the rough service of ambulation about the brickwork streets of high Thujwa. They were less modest as well, and the silhouette of Matanya's unhappily stooped form was readily discernable through the layers of silk and thin cotton.

"It is a pleasure to me, madam, that you should enjoy these rare victuals." Lavena backed out into the hall as her mistress emerged, re-appareled, her face nearly beaming as in the old days.

"Please go, child," Matanya said, as she quickly grasped Lavena's wrist, then let it go. "You will not want to travel alone in the night." She closed the great brick door behind her housekeep and daintily made her way toward the feasting room to get a glimpse of the dishes Lavena had cooked that afternoon.

The farm towners at end of day gathered at the edge of the high city where the tightly packed brickwork streets played out to irregular avenues of smooth but bumpy stone, which themselves ran down, anon, to paths of gravel and pounded dirt. The travelers formed a great swath of diverse heritage and occupation. Most were house servants or merchants or their assistants. Many were farmers selling their produce in the markets, delivering it directly to the larger and wealthier households, some of which populated nearly entire towers with just their extended families and the weight of their possessions.

By the time the road was nearly dirt, they merged with the last laborers from the industry sites. There were brickmaking and bricklaying laborers, and the workers who drove the massive looms of the textile houses or sweated the vast furnaces of the iron and bronze foundries, or unloaded the great basin sledges of their cargo: ore plied from the southern mountain mines, grain from the thirsty farmlands just beyond the Surrel, or long-traveled planks of hard timber from the deep forest.

As they gathered and mingled, all steadily marching as if commanded by a general, they would remark on the brightness of the stars in the sky, or the character of the moon, or the swiftly moving specks of light as could barely be seen far off to the east, on another road that brought the brickweavers on their sledges back to the city from their safely shuttered workshops.

One such light that loped across the darkening sands was mounted on Jeppo's sledge. That he was not alone on this trip made little difference to the experience. Behind him stood a thinner, more slackly postured passenger but neither bothered speaking as the rush of wind allowed no voice to be heard clearly without the tiresome effort of shouting.

They passed smaller, residential towers near the edge of the city, the architecture of which rose in height, story by story as they reached the neighborhood of wide streets and thick surrounding gardens that housed the wealthiest families near the edge of the old city's tightly packed quiver of tall old towers with their bridges and platforms.

Here the sledge halted, near the deep garden affront a great tower and Kulkulla stepped down, awaiting leave from his new master.

"On the morn, boy," said Jeppo with a deliberate note of sternness, "You will wait for me here. I will arrive on this sledge and deliver us both to the shop thereafter. We shall not have another calamity as today's"

"Aye, sir" said Kulkulla, and the sledge was off to the west. Kulkulla turned to enter the tower just as the door opened and the tall housekeep woman, T'Mota motioned him inside.

"You are late for the evening meal, young master," she chided him.

"There was much to do today," he replied. "There is always much to do and late hours on the first day." He realized upon saying it that such knowledge was bought through failed apprenticeships, of which he now had quite a string. But there was still a day, at least, left on this current venture. Jeppo had curtly instructed him to wait for his arrival on the sledge. That he hadn't chastised him too much nor had talked of refusing the arrangement was considered a good sign in Kulkulla's considerable but regretful schooling in these matters. He brought his right hand up to the back of his head and pressed as hard as he could. There was a slight ache, but nothing much, and only when his fingers were pressed their hardest.

Jeppo's journey through the streets of Thujwa was unusually swift as most of the guildsmen, priests and other masters had already ridden their sledges home and only the odd, lonely citizen walked them now. An occasional city guard was passed and here and there a messenger, but mostly the streets to Jeppo's neighborhood were as deserted as they would be in the middle of the night. It was the time when most enjoyed their evening meal and Jeppo's stomach told him such and he was happy to park the sledge near his garden and pull the iron key from it.

Matanya greeted him at the doorway, having seen him arrive with his lamp, having watched for him for many heartbeats.

"Why are you so late, husband?" she spoke with concern and not offense.

"Aye, Sparrow," he said with a tired smile, "It has been a day of much circumstance and I have much news."

She frantically motioned him inside and closed the door.

"Please, Monkey, the news can wait," she said. "Your stomach must be empty and our dinner awaits."

He pulled off his outer robe and hung it on a carved wooden hook in the foyer. Matanya took his hand and led him to the feasting room. With some effort, emphasized by her dainty grunts, she lifted the bronze cover of the platter, revealing the repast Lavena had laid out for them. Steam still wafted from the bowls of cracked wheat and the splendid tray of deep-fried wild birds. Jeppo's eyes widened, as did his grin. The two settled down on either side of the low table, arranging large and highly decorated pillows of fine red, purple and gold cloth to buttress their half-reclining bodies. Jeppo took one of the small birds and bit off its tiny head, its endearing features, thankfully, obscured by golden batter.

"Is this... ?" he asked.

"It's guamji," said Matanya, her mouth full of some cracked wheat.

"Guamji?" Jeppo replied, as his tongue freed a strip of meat from between his teeth. "We've not had guamji for some years. This is wondrous, Sparrow."

Matanya laughed as she chewed on one of the cooked birds. "Tonight, sir, the sparrow is a predatory bird!"

Jeppo laughed.

Kulla himself had called Kulkulla up to his chambers and they met in the room where the old judge did his writing, recording his opinions and their rationales. Kulla sat in a large wooden chair that was sturdy enough to sport an entire writing desk on a swiveling hinge off to the right of it. The desk was made from thin tiles the color of dried dates. Their surfaces had lost most of their glossy finish from years of use. When the desk swung away from the chair, one could see the seated figure and at the same time his leaves of paper, half-filled with his careful script.

"I am impatient to hear how your day went, grandson" said Kulla smiling. He sat in the great chair as though he were a prince or king, and folded his hands on his lap.

Kulkulla would need to choose his words carefully. He did not want to convey his own doubts about the day's events, his foolishness and injury, and certainly not the odd treatments from the healer, for there was surely something foreign about Vomcot's ministrations and they were likely to enjoin the old judge's criticism, possibly unto his wrath. He had not much experience with the guild surgeons, save for that one disastrous day of a surgery apprenticeship, and having still all his limbs and no chronic pains in his belly, he reckoned enough on his own that their offices were different and possibly in conflict with those of the farm towner.

But lying would be worse, as Kulla's fabled discernment would catch him in his ploy as the jurist had done with common miscreants.

"It was a momentous day," replied the youth with a smile, his eyes wide with wonderment, his words spoken in short, gulped breaths as though he were expressing his excitement over his new position, when it was actually the fear of discovery that rattled his demeanor. "I met the master Jeppo, and he was gracious too me. He brought me into his workshop.... There are many mysterious things in that place and I have not fully taken account of them all as yet."

"Say no more, grandson," said Kulla cheerily, "I will not have you revealing any of that guild's secrets to me."

"Of course not, grandfather," he responded with solemnity, "I will follow my vows and keep my knowledge close to me."

"Now off to your rest, apprentice," Kulla was now roused with pride over what he had convinced himself had been a promising first meeting with the brickweaver. Such pride was all the more intoxicating after such a long abstinence. He had pulled the levers of his power and notoriety to enroll his grandson in one failed apprenticeship after another. The brickweavers were the last of the major guilds he could try before remanding him to the likes of the brickmakers or the paper rollers, or some other of the lesser guilds. I owe Jeppo a personal debt of gratitude, he thought, and as the night wore on he contemplated an appropriate favor for the master, being careful not to consider any gesture that could be confused as a bribe.

Chapter 9

Jeppo's arrival that morning at the Kulla tower was congenial and awkward at the same time. He hadn't quite decided on Kulkulla's prospects but he would not judge a man on just one impression, he thought, regardless of how much his pessimistic nature might demand it. Of course, one might do so if the first impression were that of a crazed miscreant. Should Kulkulla have tried to murder him while grimacing with a bloodthirsty aspect, Jeppo would readily have rendered a bad judgment on him, and hopefully in enough time. But Kulkulla's poor showing yesterday was nothing like that. The youth had nearly perished, though. Perhaps he only needed a watchful eye and a clearly defined office to survive at least the apprenticeship, if not a long and healthy life. It did not hurt Kulkulla's prospects either that unbeknownst to the youth, the occasional abrupt smile and suppressed laughter that he saw registered on the brickweaver's face belied a curiosity of Jeppo's mind that it would briefly replay the imagined images of Kulkulla carefully stacking stones, climbing them and foolishly falling on his head. The acts of the fool and the miscreant are sometimes indistinguishable, he thought, in the type of philosophical declaration that to Jeppo was itself indistinguishable from a joke.

"How are you feeling today, boy?" said Jeppo, still standing in his hovering sledge.

"Fine, master," said the youth, who was carrying a heavy cloth bag. He held it aloft and said, "Some fruit and dried sausage for the workshop."

"That is appreciated, boy," said Jeppo. "I often get hungry after midday, when the work has finally taken its toll on me. But all I demand of you today, boy, is to pay attention and watch what you are up to."

Kulkulla jumped aboard the sledge and they were off, back through the winding streets heading out of the high city, encountering fewer and smaller buildings as they neared the industry lands. Once in those lands, they saw the march of laborers arriving for work at various foundries and factories and mills. Most of them arrived via the southern road while the brickweavers' route was along the eastern way. Brickmakers and some layers walked this road along with the 'weavers, though the latter like Jeppo commuted by sledge, especially considering their journey was the farthest east and then south to the barren, unbrickwoven land of their distantly scattered workshops.

When they arrived at the great stone building, the sun was still far enough to the east that they saw the building in silhouette, it's high windows only discernable as they grew closer but its large purple door apparent well before that. As they were near enough to halt and leave the sledge, a small flock of birds of indeterminable color took flight, in silhouette as well, against the eastern sky.

As they entered the workshop, Kulkulla was directed to put his bag aside on an empty table. He then aided the master brickweaver unrolling the canvas drapes that covered all the shelves. One shelf contained nothing but scrolls and it was thick with them, in various sizes, all of them seemed to be randomly packed together. Another had various glass bottles and iron tools and several bolts of colored woolen yarn. The other shelves contained bricks of various sizes. One large set of shelves made of the thickest planks contained only the standard construction bricks in carefully labeled slots, numbering to a few hundred or so. Another of only slightly less hefty wood contained hundreds of shiny, ceramic bricks, each less than half the thickness of a construction brick. The remaining shelves contained thousands of bricks shaped and colored like those but at only one-fortieth scale. In the center of the great room was a low table covered by a canvas blanket which Jeppo and Kulkulla removed together due to its awkward size. Their action revealed a series of colored dowels of various sizes affixed to what seemed random positions on a large, flat sheet of dark wood the thickness of a construction brick. The dowels had holes cut through them at random heights and through these holes pulled taught were a variety of colored yarns, some of them ending in notches cut into the edges of the board, others ending in knots atop the dowels. The yarns zigzagged in all directions. At certain points some sturdy bronze bars were slid into angled holes in the board. They were affixed in pairs, each of which ended in grooved spheres of wood that channeled some of the lengths of yarn so that not all their turns were abrupt angles, as with the junctures at the dowels, but rather curves of various sizes and degree of turn.

Jeppo took a cursory glance around the contraption and then spoke to his assistant standing on the other side. "This, boy, is my reckoning machine. It is not like those of the merchants for I have widely modified it to my own uses. If you succeed at last in this apprenticeship, you will have learned how this device works.

"It is unlikely that anyone might figure its use just from its appearance, so abstract are its principles," he continued, "But whatever you come to understand about it is a secret business between the two of us. I am not yet ready to reveal this machine to the guild. Is that understood?"

"Aye, sir," said Kulkulla, with the same confidence as a blind man declaring he will not leer at a naked woman's body.

"Very well, then," he continued. "I will have to record the formulae that this machine displays." Kulkulla's eyes quickly darted to the device again but he could see neither formulae nor anything recognizable on display save for the odd amalgam of yarn and wood and bronze. The master continued making careful notes on ink and paper, appearing to his assistant as though he suffered visions that others could not see. At length he looked up at the wide-eyed, slack-mouthed youth standing across the table and spoke to him, "While I am busy at this task, boy, you may recite what you know about the brickweaving art, what you learned from your studies or the common knowledge. That might give me a fix on what is still left to teach you."

"Aye, sir," Kulkulla said. "The bricks, sir, are most sacred and most magical. The priests bless them many times and implore the blessing of Thujwun as well. Once properly blessed, the bricks cleave unto each other in strong fidelity and rise to great towers, seeking commune with the maker of all things and raising the faithful to that height as well."

Jeppo stopped what he was doing, sighed deeply through his nose while his mouth clenched tightly and he looked at Kulkulla as though he hated every particle from which the boy was comprised.

"Is that all you know, boy?" he spoke with a pronounced note of derision that made Kulkulla's stomach clench. "Is that what they are teaching in scholastics these days?" Jeppo put down his leaves of writing and stood erect with has arms akimbo. "Brickweaving," he bellowed now, "Is an art, boy, and a science! There is nothing magical about it! The bricks are not prayed over, good Thujwun, they are not! The priests are not involved in these efforts at all! They have their own offices and cannot interfere." He was shaking, as was Kulkulla but Jeppo shook from anger while his assistant was clearly struggling to keep himself from sobbing.

Jeppo had long been without an assistant as no prospective candidates had been assigned a position in his workshop in many years. His reputation as a skilled brickweaver was without challenge but his social connections were the least of anyone's. Most of his contemporaries had grown sons by now, or marriageable daughters at least. And they could trade assistants or make more complicated arrangements through marriages. For example, Xexeen had only a daughter of the apprentice age but Mincon had a son who fancied her and soon married her. When Mincon's son apprenticed with Lalbor, this made the latter beholding to either one or the other. His young son in a few years would apprentice with Xexeen, thus ensuring that the debt was paid to both Mincon and Xexeen, the two of them sharing in a chance for an assistant because of the marriage. But Jeppo's assistants had been few, as his marriage had brought no issue. After seven years without an heir, it was legal to abandon one's woman in favor of a more fecund mate. When asked by colleagues in private why he had never done so, Jeppo's answer was always to attack the question philosophically, as it was considered to be foolish and immature to express romantic feelings about one's woman. "It would also be legal for me to beat my housekeep if she should spill hot tea on me or commit some other insult to my person. I would fail to engage in such beating because it would not give me pleasure, it would not improve my lot nor that of the housekeep, so why bother to do it?" The answer told his colleagues that the question was a thorn to him and they wondered why. Some thought him lust-mad with his woman, or bewitched by her, and a few thought him so bound to her as justly humans can be that he would be lost without her company, and they were the ones who quietly admired and envied this in him. The brickweaver Jeppo for his part entertained all three of those same opinions of himself at various times.

Jeppo's anger cooled as he was reminded of the sorry state in which he found the boy the day before. It was no small matter that the boy could have perished under those circumstances. Perhaps the knock on his head had rendered him a fool, at least temporarily. No, that would not explain his foolish attempt at entry to the workshop in the first place. Perhaps it was the satisfying meal he had last evening that had urged his compassion but he was willing to give the boy a chance at all of this and hoped he might grow to be less annoying in his ingenuousness.

"Let me tell you the basics, first, boy," he said at last. "Listen carefully for I am loathe to repeat these lessons...."

And so Jeppo taught Kulkulla the fundamentals of the brickweaving art. The bricks, he explained, are made with special clays carefully mixed from the well-studied clay pits of the industry lands. There were twenty-seven special types of brick, each type being distinguished by the mixtures of the various clays, and perhaps other impurities as well. Only the brickmakers themselves knew how the bricks were made and how they were assayed, a process by which the brick is determined to be adequately representative of its desired type. The bricks are called by the names of their types and the brickweavers knew which types form the numerous patterns of three. A simple pattern describes the positioning of three bricks together in a standard design, for example, two bricks adjoined at the bottom while the third rests equally upon both is the form of a pattern, while the specific types of bricks and where there are placed in this form is the completion of that pattern. There are many forms of placement and combinations of brick types but mostly a standard set of completed patterns is used. Each such pattern has a known effect and these effects are variations on the two prime forces: the sword-binding and the all-binding. The first has only two states: attraction and repulsion and aside from other brick patterns these forces seem to act primarily on iron, hence the name from the Thujwani's warring past.

The all-binding force, however, acts on all things. It can hold objects in place, such as the riders on a sledge, and lift the same sledge off the sandy ground. It blows the gentle breezes of Thujwa and pulls the water from deep below the desert earth. It is one force with one inherent nature, to attract and repel, but it can be manipulated by the brick patterns into manifesting as daughter forces, these being the brick-binding force that holds bricks together and enabled the construction of high towers without the need for mortar. The same force holds ceramic brick so tight that even water cannot find a place where the bricks meet from which it can escape. This same force produces light without a noticeable heat by careful calibration of the pressure from brickwork sconces containing cut and polished blocks of quartz. These gems release much luminescence when they are squeezed to the point of audible cracking and hissing by the power of the brick-binding.

Another daughter force of the all-binding is the cooling force, which chills the air in cooling bins and prevents decay of perishables in the citizens' kitchens. This is a strange force that can be played to do far stranger things than cooling. Its opposite is the heating force, and where the cooling slows the subtle actions of nature, so does the heating speed them up. It is used to warm the homes on cold desert nights and boil the water and cook the foods of those who live there. It too has more extreme uses.

As the day wore on and Jeppo completed his transcriptions of the reckoning machine's deductions, he took time to lecture Kulkulla on the forces and how the bricks produce them.

"It seems as though the sword-binding is not so valuable a force as the all-binding," offered Kulkulla, an observation he had made and thought worthwhile to enunciate.

"That is truly not the case," said Jeppo with some satisfaction as though he had wanted to hear such an argument as a pretext for beginning the next lesson. "The sword-binding may not seem so useful as the all-binding yet it is necessary for our control of that force, and so it is equally as necessary as the force itself. The sledge, for example, is operated by an iron key. This key manipulates the sword-binding force, its direction and intensity. Now listen closely, boy, for this is important. There is no power in the all-binding force save that which is derived from the sword-binding. Sword-binding patterns create the sword-binding force -- there are few of these -- and all-binding patterns drink in this power to use in all-binding ways. We cannot as men manipulate the all-binding directly, only Thujwun can do so. But we can manipulate the sword-binding and it drives and empowers the all-binding. Do you see this?"

"Aye, I am thinking this through, sir. When I am trying to learn something new, I fear I try to grasp it by drawing from my own experience and seeing it in light of everyday things, including my previous apprenticeships. The surgeon master taught me that a strong body is useless when bound to a weak heart or a weak mind. So when you were talking about these forces I began to think that the all-binding is like a strong body, capable as it is of many powerful and remarkable things but the sword-binding is like its heart when it drives it and its mind when we cajole it to our bidding."

"Aye," said Jeppo. "That may be a good comparison though such comparisons are never perfect and neither shall be our knowledge if we embrace them without restraint. But it is a good model. The reckoning machine itself is a model, too. But it models the play of forces and in no way appears to be anything like a wall of bricks. All models fail at some point but we tolerate these occasional failures because of their ongoing usefulness."

"In that respect, are they not like an assistant, sir?" said Kulkulla, first loud and steady but ending with rapid mumbles to the point where "sir" was nearly unintelligible. He had crawled out on a tree branch by making this wry comment and quickly retreated to the trunk once he feared that the branch might crack beneath him. But Jeppo caught the joke and responded with guile.

"Yes. And it is the models that fail so badly at times that must be the most useful," he replied, hoping he could subtly get much more work from the lad with this comment, and loyalty as well, for that was more important in an assistant than most of the work they performed, labor itself having been so gravely devalued through the technics of the brickweavers.

"We speak of models," he continued, "and I have yet to build one today. The sun is high now and our talk has made me peckish. Talk always does that with me. We mock the belly, Kulkulla, when the mouth is kept open so long and no food arrives. We shall enjoy the victuals you carried here and then we shall build a model, a very good and useful model."

Kulkulla's bag contained nearly five pomegranates, various berries, a few large dried sausages, made from the meat of pig and goat, and two large rounds of crusty sesame seed-covered bread. It would have been considered a feast in the farm town but it was standard midday fair for the Thujwani, many of whom had grown fat from the day-to-day conveniences that brickweaving had afforded them, as well as the ample supply of good food enabled by the brickwoven extraction and distribution of water, a rare commodity outside Thujwa's impermeable wall. This recipe for corpulence was no better exemplified than in the means of cooking the cornucopia of victuals they enjoyed. No longer was much work needed to prepare and cook the foods, or clean the utensils and bowls afterwards and such ease left only the eating of it to human effort.

"I will consider you useful today," he said to Kulkulla after noticing the pomegranates, "If you take a bowl from that shelf and wander to an alcove were you can clean a fruit of its jelly seeds and bring just those back to me. I admit to you that I cannot abide the look of the inside of a pomegranate though I find the fruit itself especially tasty."

Matanya climbed the steps to the second floor of tower Jeppo. Unlike the great towers that housed large extended families, theirs was a solitary place, only a few stories high but built with all the brickweaving gadgets a modern home would need. Her ascent was not difficult despite the pain in her joints and the leaden way she felt these recent mornings when she was always sleeping in, as the much younger Thujwani were by custom allowed to do. The staircase was brick and powered to ease the pull of the earth on feet so that whether one is ascending or descending, the use of these steps was never tiring. It had no railing either for the all-binding was manipulated to prevent a body from moving past the edge. She simply walked as though on a flat surfaces, using far less effort than that of the peoples who have not known brickweaving. Even the streets and floors were designed to subtly reduce the pull of earth for pedestrians, so that walking around Thujwa was unlike walking in any other city.

The second floor had a few chambers with brickwork doors arranged around the central platform through which the spiral steps emerged. There were storage rooms here and she opened one, entered, and shut the brickwork door behind her. There was a high window in this room and plenty of light. The brick patterns captured what sun rays shown through this window and diffused it throughout the room. There were quartz lights here as well that could be activated after the sun had abandoned his duties each evening. But for now the sunlight was adequate.

The room contained a series of tall glistening shelves made of ceramic brick. On them were folded a collection of differently colored fabrics. Unfolded, they would reveal themselves to be robes or gowns, skirts or tunics, and various shawls and headscarves. The lower shelves contained a variety of footwear, placed below the shelves of the raiment for which they were appropriate. Many of these items were no longer wearable by the mistress. They included the clothing of her youth when she was a slim, fresh sapling of a girl, her aspect more hopeful than today. Some of the robes were ceremonial. They were to be worn at great annual feasts and elaborate rites in praise of the one god Thujwun. But as soon as it was clear that Matanya was barren, she and Jeppo were no longer welcome at these festivities. The tradition developed as a way to encourage the husbands of barren women to abandon their wives for younger mates more likely to produce offspring. Thujwun is a lonely god, it seemed to them, and the greatest gift to Him would be to increase the company of His people. In this way, they argued that such tactics merely strode the path that morality follows beyond the point were justice does not continue walking.

Matanya's wardrobe was also her secret history. Here on these dustless shelves lay the loci for all her memories, from childhood frocks to the elaborate silken robes of the winter festivals. She was in a mordant mood today as she often was in recent times, and sought to slake her thirst for melancholy by running her hands along the luxuriant vestments from a life now gone. Her wedding robe is here, all gold and shimmering, even in this indoor light. It was made from golden silk and muslin, and a front of the thickest wool from rare mountain goats whose coats are softer than an infant's tousles. She grabbed it in both hands and pressed it to her bosom.

At once she heard Lavena's voice, "Milady!"

She re-folded the robe and placed it carefully on the shelf. The bricks assured it wouldn't fall off.

"Yes, Lavena," she shouted as she closed the wardrobe chamber's door behind her. "I am on the second floor, seeing to my wardrobe."

The housekeep climbed the steps quickly. "Madam," she said, "A messenger just came to the door. You have been invited to a wedding. You and the master." Lavena was excited, having known that her madam was a pariah of her own class.

"This is a surprise," replied Matanya, her eyes wide and her mouth agape. "When is this wedding? What did the messenger say?"

"It is the wedding of Mincon's grandson Modeen, who is at twenty years, with a granddaughter of Tazil. It will be the day after the new moon, at the old Temple, milady. You are invited to the feast at Mincon's tower."

"It is such a surprise," she said again. "I have not been to a such an event in years."

"Shall we select a gown then, madam?" said Lavena as she waved her hand at the door that Matanya had just secured.

Chapter 10

Kulkulla was instructed to gather a few trays from the far shelves. Then over to the shelves of miniature bricks he went and filled some of the pockets in the wooden tray with the tiny bricks. These were of the ceramic kind and their glazed surfaces sparkled like crudely made jewelry. He had to be careful to place each of the small bricks in the right slots so that Jeppo could identify their types without thought. The youth then carried the now heavier tray with much effort and brought it to one of the long tables where he set it down. At the center of this table was what looked at first like a step stool but was actually a pedestal for constructing the model. The table itself was waist high and suitable for the pieces and tools but the pedestal came to Jeppo's chin and allowed more careful observation of the model building. Today he was making a bath basin but it had to be of a wider girth than the standard designs such as the one in his own bathing chamber. The client was a wealthy bread merchant who had consumed too much of his own inventory. He and his wife had twelve children only eleven months apart for most of them and though he had a fine tower with plenty of room for these blessings, they had sought to refrain from producing anymore and had avoided the conscious decision by indulging themselves in the obsessions of the gourmand. They spent well on exotic foods and commanded their house servants to procure and learn to properly cook the rarest delicacies. As a result, the tailors were well employed in expanding the couples' robes and now Jeppo would find gainfulness in providing them with adequate space for bathing.

"It is a delicate balance, this design," said Jeppo, his eyes fixed on the written notes he had derived from the reckoning machine. He abruptly switched back to the model half-constructed on the pedestal. "Watch carefully boy and note the order in which I am placing the bricks. As patterns of three they come together and note which patterns are mixed with which others."

"Aye, sir," said Kulkulla examining with some interest the slowly constructed miniature bath basin before him. Watching a brickweaver work was like watching no other craftsman.

"It is a delicate task because there are rules," the master continued. "One cannot create a basin so deep that it is likely to drown the bather as the bottom must hold the bather there as the sledge holds its rider. With such a condition, a basin too deep might hold the bather underwater like the hand of some invisible demon. There are many facilities we use to ensure that cannot happen. Control of the height of water poured in, for example. On most of the standard basins, a jug will cease pouring when that waterline is reached.

"A heating bath basin -- and they are all heating basins now -- cannot get too hot either or it might poach the bather like a bird poached in a cooking basin. Its controls must be well calibrated or tragedy is assured. It is not well known, but a brickweaver once built a tub with a faulty control mechanism. The patterns that play with the sword-binding force are, cajoled, as you said, by the movement of an iron key. Using this faulty mechanism, the bather tried to increase the temperature of the water and became instantly frozen in a block of ice. He was revived anon only to die some time later when recovering in the care of the surgeons."

Kulkulla suppressed a laugh, knowing that it was improper to make jest of a fellow citizen's death, but he had found imagining how surprised he would have been had he been the bather provoked in him a desire to do so.

"There are other rules," Jeppo continued. "They can be found in the neatly gathered scrolls on those shelves. One knows them well after a time. The issue we must face involves the extra girth of the tub. The rules say that it should not be so wide as could be shared by two persons. That would be perceived as an occasion for consort, and consort under water has been prohibited by the opinions of the surgeons, the priests, the merchants and the judges. Each has his own unique argument in disfavor of the practice. So the tub we are building must be wide enough for a corpulent merchant but not so wide that his woman might join him there."

Kulkulla was stunned by this revelation. He had not imagined that sex had any bearing on the industries or their technics.

"Do you have a measurement of this client?" asked the apprentice.

"Aye, boy," said Jeppo. "That I do. It is this figure here," pointed to a chart carefully drawn on paper. "And this is the tub's girth."

"That would seem a good fit," said Kulkulla. "But what if the client should lose weight?"

"Aye, that is what I am trying to calculate and account for."

Jeppo continued working on the model and explained his actions as he went along. By the time the light in the workshop started to dim, the brickweaver had finished building his miniature tub. Its appearance was similar to the one in his own bathing chamber but more squat and wide, though not so much that it could be called a pool. He believed these dimensions were adequate. He need not take too many pains in expectation of the client's future diminution of physique, considering that it was, at best, an unlikely prospect.

"Let us go, soon, boy," said Jeppo once he had completed the model. "Gather what you need, and we will be off to the bricklayers so that they can construct the true bath basin. All we build as brickweavers are models."

"Let me ask, then, master," said Kulkulla. "You have said that models fail and yet are useful. How is it with the wide bath basin model?"

Jeppo appreciated that some of his words had stuck with the lad. "That is an easy question Kulkulla. Their model fails in that it is so much smaller than the object it portrays and we don't always know the true character of the brickwork till it's manifest at full size. So that is the failure."

"And why is it so useful, then?"

"That is easy as well. It allows me to work in separation from the bricklayers themselves, who can be a difficult sort and wont to complaining about the designs."

They gathered their robes and bags, and Jeppo noticed as he pulled on his outer robe that something heavy was secreted in his pocket. The healer Vomcot's remedy for Matanya's illness, he now remembered, which he had forgotten to give to her. With the workshop secured, they walked to the sledge. Kulkulla carried the model in a large wooden box and handled it gingerly, even though the force that held the miniature together would not abate if it had fallen even from the very top of the hierophant's tower. Jeppo stood in the front while the heavy box rested securely on the floor between them. A few awkward manipulations of the iron key and the sledge rose and headed toward the west, to the industry lands and the workshops of the bricklayers. On this journey they would be following the setting sun and were blinded most of the way. Kulkulla took the chance to watch the desert landscape rush by. They rose in crossing the great swath of house servants walking south to farm town at the end of a day's work and continued on to the noisy, well-lit bricklayers' compound.

That place was secured against wandering visitors by a great brick wall, and a guard held station there to protect the secrets of the 'layers from rivals and miscreants. Jeppo stopped the sledge at just before the gate and the guard, recognizing him, motioned him forward. "Master Henrix is in his studio, sir," said the guard. "Who is this with you, sir?"

Jeppo swung his arm out in Kulkulla's direction. "My new assistant," he said. "His name is Kulkulla, from the tower of Kulla."

The guard bade them go into the direction of Henrix' workshop. When they arrived, they found the place well lit by quartz lamps, noisy from the ministration of the 'layers as they fabricated a tub in one corner, a heating basin in another and a tonic bed in still another.

"Have you got the wide tub?" said Henrix eying the wooden box that Kulkulla carried. Catching sight of Kulkulla's face, he looked mildly shocked, and Kulkulla appeared embarrassed, and looked down at the box.

"Aye, 'layer," said Jeppo with his usual congeniality when talking to the bricklayers. "I finished just moments ago. And I was helped by my new assistant here." He pulled Kulkulla over to him by the far shoulder, rattling the youth who had gone a little limp, like a robe on a hook.

"Aye, Jeppo," the bricklayer went on in measured voice, his

eyes moving up and down Kulkulla's form, as though the youth were some strange creature of improbable origin and little utility. "We've met." Then directly to Kulkulla, "I thought you were apprenticing the surgery, boy?"

"That...," he mumbled. "That did not work out so well."

Henrix looked around as some of the clatter in the room had died. His assistants quickly returned to their work as soon as he caught their eyes and the workshop noise returned as well.

"So let us take a look at the model," said Henrix, returning his attention to Jeppo. "Come to my chamber in the back there and we'll open her up."

Jeppo and Kulkulla moved forward in unison but Henrix held his arm out to halt their advance. "I think you will not be needed in our discussions, boy. Give the box to your master." Henrix pressed his index finger alongside his generous nose to signal to Jeppo that he wanted to talk to him privately.

With knitted brow and a forced air of nonchalance, Jeppo held out his hands and Kulkulla handed him the box. "Stay here, boy," said Jeppo, then whispering. "And stand up straight. You are representing the brickweavers here."

Jeppo followed the workshop's master into another chamber and Henrix closed the large wooden door behind them, leaving Kulkulla to stand by himself in the busy workshop. The other assistants looked up from their work at intervals and smiled at him, though without making eye contact. An apprentice working on the tonic bed spoke in whisper to another working with him. From halfway across the room Kulkulla could not make out what they were saying, but the word "camel urine" somehow found his ear. It made him blush and sent a tiny shudder through him. The workers were snickering now.

In Henrix's chamber, Jeppo carefully opened the box and with even more care produced the model of the tub and set it down on a large, cleared table. The bricklayer examined it, squinting at times and raising his eyebrows at others. "This should not be difficult to lay, Jeppo," Henrix said at last. "Is this tested and true?"

"Aye, it is master Henrix," replied the brickweaver. "I have reviewed the patterns many times and found no fault in them. Note how close the arrangement of bricks would be here. And that it is so shallow but sufficient for the client's girth."

"And your assistant...," said the layer. "What hand had he in its design?"

Jeppo thought for a moment and decided he should feel offended. His word was as good as in the past and there was no need for such questioning. True, this was a new model, unlike the hundreds of tubs Henrix had made before, but the bricklayer had no business asking such a question.

"I am forced to ask you another question first, bricklayer," said Jeppo, his choice of words indicative of his rising anger. "What business have you with my assistant that you have asked such a question? Is not my word as good as always?"

Henrix was becoming angrier as well but knew the point was well made and an honest one. He suddenly switched postures to that of a frustrated man pleading with the benighted. "I am worried, sir, that this fellow may have ruined the design. And I will give you a clue to this. Some time many days ago I dropped a glazed brick and it shattered on the stone floor. A shard flew with great speed to my right calf and cut a gash in it as easily as my housekeep chops a leg of lamb. My assistants helped me onto a sledge and took me to the shop of Tovis. They rushed me into his surgery and lay me down on his examination bark. My robes were cut away at the leg and Tovis went to cleaning away the blood and preparing the stitching. It was a horrible gash and blood was everywhere. My pain was so great at that time that a leather bit was placed in my mouth as the surgeon sewed the wound with gut and needle. When he was finished, he called in his assistant to bring a cloth soaked in goat urine, that it might promote the healing of the wound. The fool brought such a cloth, wet and yellowed, that Tovis laid and pressed on the sutures."

The bricklayer took a deep breath, and continued, his face getting redder with each word. "I swear the liquid bubbled when the cloth was applied and I felt such a sting as would kill a man with a weaker heart. It was as though the very meat beneath my skin was caught fire! I nearly hit poor Tovis with my bad leg but he jumped away in time, being a surgeon of much experience."

"And what does this mean to my office?" said Jeppo sternly.

"That foolish assistant of Tovis," said Henrix. "That fool was none other than your Kookulla."

"*Kulkulla*," said Jeppo.

"Whatever his name," said Henrix. "He had been told to bring a soak of goat urine, which would have soothed my suffering mightily. Instead the fool had soaked the cloth in the piss of a camel!"

The gravity of the mistake was not lost on the brickweaver. He knew that camel urine was a sharply burning fluid, even on healthy, unbroken skin. It must have caused Henrix great deal of pain in a short period. Still, he made an effort to hold back his laughter at the picture of the incident that his mind had created.

"And so he brought the wrong jar. At least it was not camel spittle that he brought," offered Jeppo in the weakest possible defense.

"Spittle!" bellowed Henrix, his bombast sounding like a blow from outside the chamber. Kulkulla heard it as a thump from where he was standing and he feared the two masters might be fighting. Oh, this is not going well, he thought. Had his imagination been brave enough to even consider grandfather Kulla's reaction to all of this, he probably would have found a shard of brick on the floor and sliced his own neck with it. But for now he was more worried how his master might react.

After a few more moments, no noise was heard from the chamber. The large door opened at last, and Jeppo emerged with Henrix behind him.

"So when do you think you will have it ready for the client?" said Jeppo, his manner focused and professional.

"Not long master, perhaps a few days. I will be sure to apprise you of the results," Henrix spoke with his head turned up slightly and his eyes a little lidded, as though to make a play of his professional demeanor before his own assistants.

"Come apprentice," Jeppo said to Kulkulla, not halting a step in his advance across the workshop floor. "It is late and we must get back to the city."

Outside, as they walked the way from the workshop to where they had left the sledge, Jeppo stayed ahead, handing the empty box to Kulkulla who walked behind, not wishing to let his shame-filled eyes meet those of his master.

"So you were an apprentice to Tovis, I hear," Jeppo began.

"Aye, master. I was not a good apprentice to him," he

volunteered. "He dismissed me after I had brought the wrong soak for master Henrix' wound. It caused him great pain. I wished to beg his forgiveness but he would not see me though I would understand that."

"Well surely Thujwun did not want you as a surgeon, it takes no priest to know that," replied Jeppo, trying to keep his lips tight as he imagined again the surgery incident and the blowhard Henrix' discomfort.

"This is true master," replied Kulkulla, still speaking with shame in his voice, and holding his head down.

"Know, boy, that your actions in the surgery had put me in a difficult circumstance with the bricklayer." He did not look at the apprentice when saying this but climbed atop the sledge and motioned him to do the same.

"I am so sorry, sir," the young man was starting to shiver as though the evening air were colder than at truly was.

"Aye," said Jeppo as the sledge rose from the desert sands. "I was nearly close to laughing when Henrix told me about the incident. And that would have been an embarrassment." He turned around briefly to Kulkulla and smiled when he said this, and the youth looked up to the master, his eyes now wide with relief.

The sledge made its way through the gathering night with the quartz light affixed to the hull now glowing a bluish light. The sound of wind rushing past forbade any further conversation as they traveled back to the south road and followed it, now almost empty of travelers, back to the city proper and through the outer districts to the wide streets and tall towers of Kulkulla's neighborhood.

The apprentice disembarked near the garden of the Tower Kulla and placed the empty wooden box behind Jeppo on the sledge.

"I will meet you here tomorrow, boy," said the brickweaver. "We will not be going to the workshop at first, but will make the rounds of our accounts in the city."

With that the brickweaver stood alone on his sledge and disappeared into the darkness.

Matanya waited for her husband to arrive home for the evening meal. She did not often have a meal of lamb like this served on an ordinary day. It was the special braised lamb of her mother's recipe, garnished with pine nuts and tamarind seeds, infused with the flavor of stop-witch leaves that covered it, leaves that remained a bright green throughout the cooking. She had used the great oven for this, a brickwork device not often needed. The rough-cut chunks of lamb were served on heaps of that rare grain, rice, mixed in with tiny, cooked wheat-flour dumplings. A sauce was made from the drippings of the roast flavored strongly with the stop-witch leaves, combined with a golden honey produced by bees kept to pollinate the crops far away from the edge of the city proper in the southern farmland. She had already sent her housekeep home and expected to begin eating soon, but raised herself off the lushly adorned pillows that circled the low dining table to keep vigil at the door, away from the temptation of the generous repast.

The sun had already set and the entranceway, the kitchen and the dining chamber were all well lit by candles and oil lamps. The facility for quartz lamps existed, in brick sconces recessed into shallow spaces of the brick walls. But they gave forth a light with hints of blue and green, and Matanya had decided that it made the food look strange. So Lavena had brought out more oil lamps from the storage chambers on the second floor, as well as the great platter. And together with her mistress and the convenient devices of the brickweavers' art, with their shiny surfaces of ceramic brick, ubiquitous in the home and hearth as the rougher surfaced construction bricks were to the streets, she had prepared the feast.

Now Matanya stood awaiting at the door, her ears tuned to the sound of the whoosh of wind in the wake of her husband's arrival on the sledge and his first footfalls when disembarking the vehicle.

At last he arrived and was in good spirits. The day had gone well, meaning he had gotten the chance to spend most of his time building the model for a vexing custom device, which he could do any day at all, but also because he could spend the time talking about brickweaving, a subject that after many long years still excited his mind with its powers and mysteries. This Kulkulla, he thought, may be a good student. He is honest to me. This I can tell. And he is also somehow broken, as a sledge is broken when it ceases to hover at points. He certainly is not the smartest apprentice I have ever had, who would be Azelfof, I would guess.

As he disembarked and grasped the empty wooden box from the sledge platform, he thought of his confrontation with Henrix only moments earlier. The bricklayer had questioned the stability of the model if Kulkulla had had a hand in its building. When Jeppo lied and told him that the apprentice did indeed have a hand in it, Henrix had blustered a speechy overture to a refusal, as a straightforward rejection of the model would have been a serious insult to the brickweaver. Jeppo was expected to take the model back and return the next day with a new one, after having banished the youth from his workshop. He would not stand for it and told Hendrix outright that if he wanted further business from him, he must display the necessary confidence in all the work he supervised. Now it was sounding to Henrix that Kulkulla had built the model with his own hands, and so he was doubly suspicious of its reliable function. But he had no choice given the demands of his business and agreed, with some prejudice, to accept the model.

As Jeppo approached the front door of his small tower, it opened seemingly on its own accord but behind it was the night-garbed figure of his wife Matanya, smiling and seeming ready to burst from holding something inside her.

"Husband, welcome," she said, embracing him.

"You must have news of some sort," he replied. "Or you would be resting as you should."

"Aye, we have news today," she said, pulling him into the dining room.

"Let me first put this box away, woman," he said with a jolly air. He lay it on a small table in the entranceway and made his way behind his wife. Despite her good spirits, her pain in moving was noticeable and he recalled the words of the hierophant.

Once again in as many days a feast awaited Jeppo on the low

table in the dining room. He and Matanya ate heartily but she paused at least to tell him her news.

"I wonder," she said, "if there will be lamb roasted this well at the wedding banquet."

"Wedding banquet?" Jeppo replied. He sucked air in between his lips to dislodge some strips of lamb meat.

"Aye," Matanya smiled broadly. "We have been invited to attend a wedding. A wedding! Guildsmen families, too."

Jeppo looked puzzled. Why had this happened so abruptly after all these years, when their lack of issue, it seemed, had meant the closing of so many doors? There was some stratagem afoot, he reckoned.

"Who sent the invitation, Sparrow?" he asked.

"It was from Mincon himself, for the wedding of his son Modeen," she said.

"I know of Modeen. He was apprenticed to Bashul. He must be in his fifth year," said Jeppo. "That is about right for him to take a woman now."

"And we are invited," said Matanya again, as she enjoyed saying it.

"Who does he marry, then?" said Jeppo, hoping to gain another clue.

"The granddaughter of Tazil. I believe it is Rapusah, the one with the large monkey eyes," she said.

"Oh I am sure she has outgrown those," said Jeppo. "We all have something too large or too small or the wrong shape as children, but we grow into them or out of them. We begin life like crumpled leaves of paper that He slowly unfolds."

"I saw Rapusah only ten days ago at the temple," said Matanya. "She is completely unfolded and her eyes are still too large and the lids seem to have grown thick all around them." Now ashamed of such criticism, and ingratitude, she offered, "But she will be a handsome bride on that day as all brides are."

"And so when is this wedding?" said Jeppo, who was busy cutting up a particularly tender chunk of the lamb.

"It is four days from today," she replied. "I will need to visit the tailor. You only need your best guild robe."

"Aye," said Jeppo, his voice muffled by chewing. "I must tell you that I have business the day after tomorrow at the far end of the wall. I may not return that night for the journey is long."

"Then I will not eat so much that evening," she replied, her mouth filled with rice. "And perhaps that is good for I have gotten larger these days with so little walking."

"I have not complained, Sparrow," he replied and followed with mock sternness. "So it is your duty not to worry. I will be taking accounts tomorrow and will set aside a good sum for your gown. And I have no care how many lengths of cloth are needed." He gave her a broad smile and she struggled to get herself up with the pain in her joints and make her way to her husband, to whom she gave a playful punch in the chest, then cradled his face in her hands and kissed him forcefully on the lips.

Chapter 11

The brickweavers temple was built wide and tall to further enhance the reputation of the guild's members. It was more elaborately decorated than the temples of the other guilds and the bricks were arranged in colors and patterns engaging to the eye, obscuring the more discreet patterns that exploit the brick-binding force to hold the massive edifice together. The bricks were colored in shades of yellow, orange, red, brown and purple. Black bricks formed a trim that traced lines across the walls horizontally and encircled the great windows made of the smoothest quartz. Its builders' intentions to showcase the art of brickweaving in an eye-catching manner were well served. At dawn the play of colored brick and golden sunlight distracted even the two figures that approached it this morning. One was a tall man in a robe that fell to only one ankle, the other having been lost to the surgeon's saw. Like other patients so bereft of limbs, a ceramic brickwork block replaced part of the length of his leg, his thigh resting on a fleece-lined indentation at its top while all-binding forces induced it to hover at just the right height to keep his pelvis level. Even this device was awkward at times, so much so that the surgeons often recommended more stability would be attained if only their patients would agree to have the other leg removed so they could rest their thighs on a single, doubly wider hovering block.

Along with this one-legged man, who was Mincon the brickweaver, chief of his guild council and senior councilor on the grand council that answered to no one, along with him walked his apprentice Galel, a sixth-year student, nearly a brickweaving master himself and already with a wife but not yet his own tower.

"We must be quiet about this work," Mincon reminded him.

"No telling the wives as some of your generation are wont to do."

"Aye," said Galel. "I am to say nothing about this."

"It will all be told in a few days time on any wise," Mincon said. "But for now, as we prepare the engine, we are not to speak of it to others."

They entered the building by the use of Mincon's key and shut the great ceramic brick door, which was enameled in a deep purple hue, behind them. The two made their way to the center staircase and walked up two flights with no effort at all, as though they were being pulled by some invisible rope to the third floor. Here was another great ceramic brick door, enameled in black but shiny in the blue-tinged light of the quartz lamps as though the bricks were perfectly smooth stones with a thin wash of water flowing over them. Beyond it, the room was revealed to be vast and cavernous as the light of the rising sun filtered through the frosty quartz windows and illuminated row after row of great wooden shelf-cases that were lined up carefully across the floor and along the high brick walls. On these shelves were placed items of various size and shape, each covered with a cloth so that only the crude dimensions of the object could be known. The two men made their way past this inventory and continued on to the far side of the room, a distance of many steps, until they arrived at the back wall. He was another great case but deeper than the others, made of a different wood, older and burled, and fashioned with a great door secured by an iron lock about the size of a man's fist.

"What we have come for at this early hour is behind this door," said Mincon to his assistant. "Or so it is written." At that the master brickweaver produced a large key from within his robes, a rod of iron with smaller rods protruding from it in every direction. It was colored orange from rust and he held it by a large oval handle at its end. Squinting one eye, he pushed the key onto a star-shaped hole in the lock, turned it one way and then another until he heard a click. The key was now held fast in its purchase and the effort to pull it back unbalanced Mincon so that his assistant rushed to catch him from falling.

"I am fortunate to have you with me, Galel," he said as he let go of the key fob and righted himself. "The key must be pulled with effort to open this old door. I cannot do that so easily with my debility."

"Aye, master," answered Galel, and the young man grasped the fob with both hands and pulled at the door. Three tries were made as the hinge creaked and the swollen wood scraped and whined before Galel, red-faced and grunting, had gotten the door to swing open. With this sudden break in his effort, the young man fell backwards and Mincon stepped out of his way to avoid a fall himself.

There were five shelves in the cabinet and they were twice as high and nearly three times as deep as the others in the room. There were no cloths protecting the objects that lay there so all were visible in the growing morning light. On the top shelves were objects made of tiny ceramic brick that glistened in that light. One looked like a bathtub, another like a small cabinet but with the door slanted at an angle instead of upright. There appeared to be models of sledges and cookers and cooling bins and tonic beds, and other devices that were not so readily identified. Unlike their familiar counterparts, these models seemed cruder, oddly shaped, or unfinished in one way or another.

On the lower shelves the models did not glisten. They were made of tiny construction bricks and dully reflected the captured sunlight. These were not recognizable at all, at least to Galel. Though they were not substantially larger than the ceramic brick models, he assumed their scale was different and that they were designed for the ultimate fabrication of larger structures.

Mincon stooped to get a better look at them. He held his hand to his mouth at first as his eyes darted from one object to another, then stretched it out to point at one in particular. It looked to be the model for a large brick bark with a freestanding wall of the glossier ceramic bricks affixed to one end. In the center of the bark was a chair that faced the wall, the size of which gave Galel a clue as to how large the final product would be, assuming that the chair would need to fit a sitting human. Between the chair and the wall was a block of brickwork with tiny crooked wires emerging only hairbreadths from its surface.

"No," Mincon said, pulling back his hand, "I am mistaken." And his survey of the lower shelf's contents continued. Finally, his glance fell upon another large model off to the side. It was larger even as a model than the bark with the wall and was a bark itself, much longer than it was wide. It too had a chair but far to one end and before it another block of bricks with crooked wires. A taller block of bricks rested near the center of the bark, atop which was a bowl containing a pile of tiny ceramic balls. But none of these appointments had at first captured the notice of Galel. Instead it was the large conical arm that thrust out at an angle from the center block that aroused his curiosity. Galel had seen brickwork cones before, especially among the towers of the old city, some of which reached toward the heavens with a gradually diminishing girth. But they had ever smaller rows of bricks placed in ring after ring just as the cylindrical towers of much more recent construction. The cone of this model, though, was fashioned by an ever turning single spiral of bricks, reminiscent more of the common spiral staircases such as the one in this temple or the edges of a scroll that has been rolled up on only one side.

"Do you have cloth and twine in your bag?" said Mincon to Galel.

"Aye, master," he responded, clearing his throat.

"Then take a piece of cloth and cover that bowl," he said, pointing to the model with the spiral cone. "Secure it well with a length of twine."

Galel produced a bag from his robes and found a small cloth that seemed the right size, as well as a roll of twine from which he bit off a suitable length with his teeth. He covered the bowl, pulling the excess cloth down around its rim and wrapping the twine around its base several times before tying it off.

"Well done," said Mincon. "Now you must fetch boxes for these models. I will wait guard here as you find them. We will need a large one such as might hold the model of a small tower and then another, but not so generous in size."

"Aye, master," said Galel and he went off to the tool room to find the boxes.

It was mid morning when the messenger arrived at Jeppo's tower. He was a youth still in his scholastics and he was out of breath having run a good distance to the doorstep.

"What business have you?" said Jeppo greeting the fellow at the door, a bowl of tea still in his hand.

"I bring news from master Mincon," said the youth. "He has called a meeting of the masters at the courtyard... of temple."

"A meeting on accounts day?" said Jeppo, perturbed. "What is the reason for this meeting?"

"I am not wise on that, sir," said the messenger, still breathing deeply.

"Come and get some water, boy," said Jeppo, his annoyance sounding through despite the hospitable offer.

"No, sir, I would not...."

"Lavena," Jeppo shouted, turning his head away. "Get this runner a bowl of water. He is thirsty."

"Adoo, master," said a woman's voice from inside.

The bowl was brought and handed to the boy, who gulped hearty draughts from it, spilling some on his robe at times.

"And you were given no reason then?" asked Jeppo. "Perhaps you forgot it?"

"Nay," replied the boy. "I am sorry, sir."

"That is not your worry," said Jeppo, his eyes stared out into the street at nothing in particular. The boy bid his leave but the master called him back.

"Are you finished with your deliveries, son?" asked Jeppo.

"Aye," the boy replied. "I must return to the dispatch."

"I will give you a penny if you can deliver a message for me," Jeppo said. "Do you know where to find Kulla's tower."

"Aye," said the boy unhappily.

"Yea, it is far and I will pay three pennies for the effort," replied Jeppo, sighing. "Tell the housekeep there that I will be late to arrive this day. The fellow Kulkulla will be waiting for me."

"Kookulla?" said the boy, repeating the name he had heard.

"Nay, it is *Kul*-kulla," said Jeppo, emphasizing the first syllable. He gave the boy his fee and sent him off.

Jeppo closed the door and returned to the kitchen with both bowls.

"Lavena," he said to the housekeep as she rubbed the cleaning towel across the walls, "I will give you your wages now as I will not be able to collect the accounts till later. I am called to a special meeting of the guild." Then he produced a coin bag from his robe and counted out the woman's wages. "This will be a long day, I fear."

Jeppo returned to the sleeping chamber where Matanya still reposed and gingerly took his guild robe from the shelf on which it lay, unfolded it and donned it quietly.

"What?" Matanya said, her eyes barely open. "Monkey, what are you...?"

"Sleep, Sparrow," said Jeppo. "I am off to an urgently called meeting. I will take accounts later and give you your robe fee. Do not worry." And he reached down to kiss her on the cheek. And then she fell back asleep.

The guildsmen had gathered in the courtyard, all wearing their guild robes and engaging in whispers. All were standing save the older masters who were given places on the few brick benches. Jeppo arrived late and sought a place near Zamchin, his old friend.

"Do you know the reason for this meeting?" he asked the stout master.

"Nay, I do not," replied Zamchin. "A messenger came to my door just moments ago. I was so surprised and worried, for I did not know it was a meeting of all the masters."

"My messenger told that much," replied Jeppo. "But I am still unsettled by it."

"Aye, as am I," said Zamchin. "There must be something of

import. Perhaps it regards the wedding."

"I would doubt that," said Jeppo, bristling at his friend's speculation. He did not want Matanya to be disappointed.

Now Zamchin was again surprised, expecting that the affair scheduled some days hence might be news to his friend, and he could make time by discussing it at length.

"Are you and your woman attending?" said Zamchin, his eyebrows raised.

"Aye," said Jeppo, his face turned up and eyes squinted but with eyebrows high as well.

"Well that is great news," Zamchin replied. "My daughters will be with us but you must join us at the banquet. We do not often see you at these affairs."

"Aye," said Jeppo. At the mention of his friend's many daughters, which ensured the master's social standing and an adequate supply of apprentices, he was subtly reminded of how vacant his own society had been all these years without the accomplishment of offspring.

"Have you heard, Jeppo," Zamchin continued. "That my daughter Wisira has been betrothed to a grandson of Kulla, the son of Amzin?"

"No I had not," replied Jeppo preparing for a bombast.

"Aye, she has," he went on. "They met at youth banquet. He is quite a fighter I hear, and a sportsman, too. He and his fellows have gone to the far wall, the forest, to hunt boar. And he took one, after much chasing, with a spear. He is quite the fighter, too, as I may have said, and has bested many opponents. He is wont to draw blood in his contests, or so I hear from the other families, so he is well set for a surgical apprenticeship. Of course his father is a great jurist and he could easily follow his path, and that of his grandfather. Did I say that his grandfather is Kulla himself?"

"Aye, friend, you did say that at least once," responded Jeppo with a forced smile. Jeppo thought Zamchin a social-climbing braggart but he was a good friend nonetheless who always spoke to him. That Zamchin had never invited him to one of his daughter's weddings was something Jeppo could forgive though he often sensed some resentment when he ever brought the man's name up to Matanya. "As long as the topic is on Kulla, I have news you might not know."

"Aye?" Zamchin was stunned. What could Jeppo know about such people?

"I have a new assistant, who is a grandson of Kulla also," said Jeppo.

Zamchin paused to think. "Would it be that one who was the son of Mincon's... of one of Mincon's lesser sons?" he asked.

"Aye. I believe there would be some of Lord Mincon in his heritage," Jeppo was surprised by the question. He believed that was the case but realized he knew little about the youth.

"That poor boy," said Zamchin, his head shaking. "His father was said to have been one-sixteenth Morso, on his mother's side of course, as you probably already know...," Zamchin paused to see if he had opened a fresh line of conversation with which he could impress his friend by his exclusive wealth of knowledge.

"I know little of his father," replied Jeppo. "His father is not my assistant."

"Nor could he be, I warrant," said Zamchin, "having already passed many years ago, as he did. The cruelty of wine on those people is legendary. It was his end to be sure. He was not a respectable man, even in the farm town, I have heard."

"Let us pray that Thujwun guided him at last," said Jeppo in the type of theological argument that is supposed to "skirt the dune" of such discussions concerning people and their worth. Jeppo found such discourse tiresome. "Perhaps he will be reborn to one of your daughters," he told Zamchin, with a note of frustration.

"Aye," said Zamchin, now weakly, as he paused to calculate whether the souls of any of his infant grandchildren might have had such a provenance.

Jeppo had not needed to bludgeon his old friend with such a bothersome suggestion, for the chatter around them had already dissipated as all eyes turned to the great double doors that opened near the back of the courtyard. From the shadows behind the doors emerged a figure with the awkward stance and dignified air of Lord Mincon, walking with his well-recognized halting gate and followed by four assistants carrying a large wooden panel. Atop the panel was some object covered with a large linen cloth that rose oddly at two distant points. As Mincon approach the crowd of masters they fanned back and away from him, allowing him access to the center of the courtyard where the assistants carefully lowered the panel to the ground.

"Masters," Mincon spoke soon after the burden was set down. "I have a commission for the city that is of great value and will require many hands. We must build a structure, a great engine, based on the model beneath this cloth. It is a matter of great secrecy and all who hear this are bound to keep this close.

"Brothers, we have only two days to complete this work. It is for a demonstration of this engine for the full council. You are requested to speculate on its purpose or use, though not on the greater scheme for which it is designed. That is the council's business alone at this time. Know only that it is of interest to you as a fine example of the brickweaver's art and its construction will bring a good and lucrative license.

"We will need one of you to supervise the making of this and you shall have a choice of one or two 'layer shops to assist. My own apprentices will be at your disposal during this time."

At that, Mincon instructed those assistants to remove the cloth, a task which they performed in unison as they delicately lifted it by all four corners and walked to the side to fold it, like the charnel sheet of a corpse just after it is consigned to a deep trench in the earth.

What was revealed to the gathered brickweavers was one of the models that Mincon and Galel had retrieved from storage earlier that day. It was the length of a grown man's arm and should its scale be common for construction brick, the structure it described would rival in size Jeppo's own home tower.

"Shall this odd brickwork be the size I imagine?" said one of the gathered, Folgis, with his arms spread wide to indicate the enormity of what he was imagining.

"Yea," replied Mincon. "It will be the size of a two-story tower at least."

The answer was met with murmurs and whispers that rippled through the crowd. Mincon stood with his hands folded before him and looked not at the model itself, which was being scrutinized by his brother brickweavers, but around to each of them at a time, awaiting more questions.

"I say, milord," queried Zamchin. "What is the license on this task? What are the terms?"

"I can only say that there is a generous fee for completing it in the required time," replied Mincon. "One hundred twenty gold pieces for the effort above supplies and resources. That's one hundred twenty profit."

"And ongoing, sir?"

"Ongoing will yet to be decided. But for its value to the city, there will be an annual license on it, I am sure, should its use be sanctioned by the council," replied Mincon.

"Its use, sir?" said Bashul, a puzzled look on his face. "What would that be, milord?"

"Aye, that is the point of this meeting," replied the old master. "Who has an eye good enough to discover this engine's use? I would be prejudiced to give such a clever master the commission."

The brickweavers spent many moments examining the model. Some pointed at the small chair on one end of it and the block with wiry protuberances and guessed that it was some station-like structure as would be seen in a foundry where a human operator sitting in such an arrangement controls the great smelting engines. Another compared it to the similar structures for the great sawing engines built to harvest lumber from the forests, and the earth-clearing engines that mined ores from the mountains, as well. Most if not all had deduced that end of the model, but the front of it was another matter entirely. There were conical structures aplenty in the city but all pointed straight up. A structure like this one, which points at such an acute angle, is generally a sign of structural failure and poor design. And that it was tilting was less remarkable than the very structure of the cone itself. Many remarked on how the spiral comprised only a single row of bricks, spiraling closer together to a point, rather than the succession of separate rings of bricks as were found in the conical towers. One master, inspecting it closely, determined that there were clearly two rows of bricks in the spiral as though that were significant and a sign of his singular cleverness.

For his part Jeppo was intrigued by the design, as he was of few others. Brickweaving had become so accomplished and standardized, and therefore lucrative as well, that some of the more passionate 'weavers, especially the elder ones, bemoaned the lack of innovation and the loss of any spirit of daring among their brothers.

So it was a treat for his mind to examine this strange spiraling engine and the bowl atop its center with its tiny, pearl-like balls.

"I know it," said Tormandun, who had been an assistant to Jeppo many years before. "This bowl has a small hole that if widened would fit the girth of the ball. Brothers, I think this may be an engine for producing these balls. Imagine the size of them at scale."

"And why would one need to create such balls?" asked Ezrob.

"Aye," replied Tormandun. "That is the question we next need to answer. This appears to my eyes to be an engine for creating such balls. The whole at the end of the cone is clearly a channel that leads to some chamber in the center block of bricks. This chamber, I theorize, must fabricate the balls when fed materials that are deposited here," and he pointed to the tip of the conical structure. "Once fabricated, the balls are forced out into the bowl here," as he pointed to the bowl atop the "engine" chamber.

Jeppo listened to this and knitted his brow. It seemed to him that Tormandun had gotten it backwards somehow. Jeppo suspected the balls were created elsewhere and fed into the engine through the hole in the bottom of the bowl. From there they would be projected up through the channel in the cone and out. Such principals are used in staircases to aid in the ascent of them. But this was much thinner and much longer than any staircase he'd seen. He calculated roughly that the ball's ascent up the channel would become much swifter than any stair-climbing human could abide without perishing, especially on impacting a wall at that speed. This was a warring device, and the realization changed his expression from studious to awestricken once he had began to envision the limited uses for such an engine. It could shatter walls and towers and reign shards of those balls on a populace. It might even shatter a brickwoven wall, he thought.

"Hail, Jeppo," said Mincon, having noticed the brickweaver's abrupt change in posture and aspect. "Have you a theory, brother?"

"From its looks and the patterns of the bricks," said Jeppo. "I would see it being used as a warring machine."

"How so?" said his lordship.

"I would surmise from these shapes and the patterns of bricks that the spheres are dropped in that hole at the base of the bowl-shaped structure," Jeppo continued, trying to be precise and objective in his description. "The sphere is then by some means propelled upwards through the long cone's channel. Note, brothers, that the hole at the tip of it is just the right berth for the spheres, which are of identical size and shape yet useless in construction. They are missiles, as the pebbles in a sling, only these are far less crudely propelled."

"I see," said Azelfof, to whom the machine's function was now so obvious he convinced himself that he had known it all along but that his conscience, no doubt, had raised a moral wall against the thought. "It would surely deliver the missile at very rapid speed. My rough estimate is that it could break a city wall. Other peoples may have such missile devices but we had never sought the need to develop one, until today of course."

"Are you an expert then on warring machines?" Mincon asked Azelfof.

"I am as good an expert as any here," he replied.

"Jeppo," he said, turning back to the other brickweaver. "What do you say about this?"

Jeppo did not want this commission, though surely he had uses for the fee. Accounts had been poor lately but he expected some improvement today, if he yet had a chance to collect them. But he had business of the hierophant's on the morrow and could not well manage the job in two days and be out of sight for one of them.

"I agree with Azelfof's surmises," Jeppo offered. "Even when he was my apprentice long ago he was a clever student of the weaving."

"Then Azelfof," Mincon said, "Can you take this commission?"

"Aye, milord," said Azelfof. "I wish Tormandun to aid me in this task and I will hire Henrix to lay the bricks. We will use his building ground."

"Then we shall see this in two days, young master," said Mincon sternly, as though there might be some punishment otherwise. "I will be visiting your site each day as well for my own scholarly interest and to protect the ancient writings that describe this machine's fabrication. These are scrolls rarely seen by less than guild lords, or the occasional scribe."

Mincon bid the other masters leave and get on with their days. "But be advised, brothers, that you are to afford Azelfof every means of assistance he may request."

The sun was not high yet and Jeppo hurried back to his sledge, turning it north toward Kulla's tower. On the sledge with him sat a large wooden box filled with scrolls.

Kulkulla was relieved that he had a position now and for a third day no less and, as things had gone so far, there were no problems as in his last few apprenticeships. There was of course his disastrous first day at the workshop and his poor scholarship yesterday. And the difficult time with Henrix that evening. But these had not swayed his master against retaining him. Perhaps, he thought, that calumny had been so often visited upon his short life that he was now immune to its effects. The possibility comforted him and his posture improved at the thought of it as he stood behind Jeppo on the sledge, which made its way, sometimes swiftly, haltingly at other times, on crowded streets.

It would be Kulkulla's task during the accounts taking to hold the great box and be ready to hand his master the proper scroll. Account negotiations had increased in frequency and had become more tiresome of late, and Jeppo thought he might get an advantage if his hands were unburdened at those moments.

Their first stop was in the old city, at the marketplace, where merchant managers met with him in small offices in an arcade off the main market-grounds. Sissel was a master of textile industries and owed license fees to the brickweavers who designed his looms and those who had designed his barks for carrying the bolts of cloth into the city. Jeppo had done both types of design work many years ago and his license fees were withering, as they do over time, but they were nonetheless substantial and Sissel protested them down as often as he could. "I do not sell as much cloth as I once did, sir," he would tell Jeppo. "Please see my accounts and you will know." And Jeppo would review the accounts and they would bargain a change in scale.

The same was true with the baking industries, and the tea-sellers, the cooker and cooler sellers, the rope-makers and salt-evaporators, the foundries and warehousers and transporters. All had devices or vehicles or engines that Jeppo had designed. He had devoted more of his time to such work as the trade in construction transitioned from lucrative tower and wall building to bridge and platform construction on existing structures. Fully half of the street area in the old city was in shadow for most of the day due to the interconnecting tracery of bridges and platforms that form a sunlight-blocking canopy several tens of stories high there. The thought of it was unpleasant to Jeppo. Why not extend the boundary of the high city to the south, he would say, but the only area for growth would be into the farm town and the city council did not want to introduce too many of the conveniences of brickweaving to those living there, especially as it might cause an increase in the price of the food they grow. So he had shifted his interest to the variety of dynamic objects that could be fashioned of plain or ceramic brick and even that market now grew leaner. The shortage of gold was some of the cause but the complex arrangements of licenses and fees, while spurring more innovation, in brickweaving most extensively, but other industries as well, had only brought wealth as demand rose. As soon as growth of the city slowed and the Thujwani had reduced their birthrate ever so slowly over the years, in some reaction perhaps to the higher cost of limited resources, such as land, distributed among ever more people.

So by the end of the day of accounts taking, with Jeppo and Kulkulla having visited as many as thirty different concerns and residences, the brickweaver was still a man of some respectable means, and Kulkulla would be paid a stipend, and Matanya could buy her gown.

It was sunset nearly when Kulkulla was brought back to the gate at the entrance to Kulla's tower and Jeppo gave him his instructions for the morrow.

"I will be embarking on a two day journey early tomorrow before dawn, boy," he told him. "I will not need your services tomorrow. It will be a day free of work for you."

"What business would you have that you would not need your assistant, sir," said Kulkulla, ever doubting that he would keep his position. "Have I not done well for you today?"

"Aye, boy," said Jeppo smiling. "You were a great help in keeping that box so that I could use my hands to point and confuse my clients."

"Then why wouldn't you need my help on the morrow?" asked Kulkulla.

Jeppo thought for a moment. He could use another hand in this task but he was bound to the privilege of his audience with the hierophant. Yet surely he should make every effort to accomplish that which the hierophant had actually tasked for him.

"To say the truth, boy," he spoke in a measured tone, carefully choosing his words. "My business takes me outside the wall but I must pass through the farm town and the farming lands and these routes can be dangerous. It would aid me to have another rider, if only to intimidate potential miscreants and bandits and their like."

"Outside the wall, sir?" Kulkulla was puzzled.

"Aye. I need to fetch some... artifacts from the old city," he replied. "Now this amounts to a trade secret, boy, so you are bound by your vows on this."

"I swear I could be a help... and I would not betray your trust in me... and I could learn much, could I not?" said Kulkulla.

"Very well, boy. It's settled then," said Jeppo. "Be prepared to leave before dawn tomorrow. We may take less than a full day but a long journey is never predictable and tell your housekeep that you may not return till the day after."

"Aye, sir," and Kulkulla bid his leave. He was not looking forward to waking so early but there was a note of adventure to their plans and he might be sure to regret it if he were left behind.

Chapter 12

In the moments before dawn, Thujwa appeared to Jeppo to be an abandoned city. As he sailed through the market district on his sledge, fitted in front with a quartz lamp and carrying in back a large woolen bag partially filled with dried sausage and fruit and a few loaves of bread, he saw hardly another person. Absent were the street vendors and the open produce markets and sellers of meat and delicacies. He was wise to have depended on his cooling bin for his victuals as no food was available for trade at this early time. He had stocked the provisions bag well but also expected to trade for more just before leaving the wall, which they would likely encounter by midmorning. As well as the victuals, he had packed a large woolen tent and the string of ceramic blocks that would hold it full open and erect even in the strongest wind. He brought tools as well, and a map that traced the route down past the farm town into the southern farmlands. They would follow the road in its turn southeast and out through the great southeastern gate. From there, the way passed through a forest that abuts the foothills and plays itself out to desert wasteland a few leagues farther west. They would continue southeast over more wasteland after leaving the forest until reaching the now sparse oasis and ruined city that was Koosh.

Once past the marketplaces, Jeppo sailed deeper into the old city but turned quickly east to the wide streets of the great families. He arrived shortly in the neighborhood of Kulla's tower and spied a lone figure holding a great bag slung over his shoulder and yawning and pulling his robe tighter together for warmth.

"Quickly now, boy," he said brusquely, without taking time for the usual greetings, and Kulkulla hefted his bag and placed it in the rear of the sledge near Jeppo's larger burden.

"Greetings, sir," said Kulkulla, yawning, as he jumped aboard the hovering vehicle. With his passenger secure, Jeppo fiddled with the iron rod on the sledge's front pedestal and the vehicle advanced to the southwest to meet up with the eastern highway. This route confused Kulkulla but with the wind whooshing by he could not ask questions as his words would be flung backwards before they had a chance to reach Jeppo's ears.

It was still the dark sky of early morning that framed the façade of Jeppo's workshop as they approached it. Jeppo at last slowed and then halted the vehicle, foot lengths away from the building's main door, which glowed a deep purple in the light of the now stationary quartz lamp.

"Come with me," said Jeppo once the craft settled onto the sand. "I need to get a large box here. I need this box for the samples. I had nearly forgotten that necessity." He had actually only just that morning realized he might need such a means to conceal and protect the "duty", whatever that may be, of which the hierophant had spoken.

"The duty to which we are bound" was a phrase he had thought of many times in the past few days. The Thujwani are taught to have two duties: the duty of family, which many considered Jeppo to have neglected, and the duty of rescue, as the Thujwani had long ago rescued the southern tribes from their primitive and unfaithful existence, so is every Thujwani child taught the imperative of the rescue of one human by another. It struck him as he pondered this mystery that he might be obliged at length to marry a fecund young woman should he find one in the abandoned city, thus finally obeying the first duty. He hoped that was not the case.

Jeppo lit an oil lamp just inside the big purple door and he motioned Kulkulla to follow him to the far wall where rested a great cube, nearly the length of Jeppo's arm on each side. Kulkulla looked with disbelief that they could carry such a thing but Jeppo gave the lamp to Kulkulla and soon produced an iron rod, which he manipulated in a discreet hole on one of the ceramic bricks near the top of the object. At once, the cube rose and Jeppo easily pushed it back toward the entrance doorway while his assistant held the lamp well enough aloft for them to find their way in the darkness.

Just outside the building, Jeppo let the box hover in place as he secured the great door and then he pushed the box toward the sledge with Kulkulla following behind. Upon reaching the sledge, Jeppo pushed the box onto the far end of the platform, driving his and Kulkulla's luggage forward. More manipulation of the iron rod and the box lowered to the platform, making a slight hissing noise as it became fixed to the surface and any air between it and the sledge floor was squeezed out.

"We are running late on this journey," he said to Kulkulla, "because of my detour to the workshop. Let's be as quick as we are able. I wish to pass through farm town by dawn as that is the safest time for travel, miscreants generally not being early risers."

"Aye, sir," said Kulkulla climbing onto the now rising vehicle.

Any passerby on the stretch of the southern road where it first emerges from the established boundary of the farm town would be surprised to see two travelers appearing from the eastern horizon, with the first fingertips of the sun's hand scraping the sky behind them. It was a sledge first of all, seeming like just a hovering wall from the front and shaped like a swan's neck in a side view but with the neck ending in a long, broad platform floor of ceramic brick, near the end of which appeared a large box made of the same, two swollen traveling bags, and two standing men ahead of them. This might be a remarkable sight in itself to the servant maid heading for the residences of the city or a foundry or bakery laborer just beginning his early working hours, but the appearance of the same silhouette with a bright, bluish light emanating from it would raise concern beyond its sheer novelty. The appearance of such machines in the past had always meant an urgent visit from the city guards searching for miscreants or bandits or anarchists, or even spies.

A few of the early laborers on the road took cover to the side where there were trees or rocks, and the braver of them would simply move aside to give the machine a wide berth.

As they followed the road down into farm town proper they passed tent after tent, followed by adobe buildings and finally a few stone-and-mortar structures new the town center, a large, open marketplace of colorful tents and great standing tables heaped with produce and meats, pelts and textiles. This small market seemed opulent to Jeppo after having just passed through the deserted cityscape of pre-dawn central Thujwa. And it was still early enough that the full bounty of the farm town's market was only slowly being revealed.

The eastern faces of the mud brick buildings glowed golden in the long morning light and soon their roofs would glow as well. Jeppo and Kulkulla continued on till the adobe reverted once again to a mix of mud brick next to tent and finally mostly tents. As the sun began to rise, they encountered more farm towners -- they saw Howoo, Tawani, many Morso and even some Dalgleesh.

As they passed the extent of the town where even the tents became sparse, they saw three small figures up ahead and Jeppo reckoned that some cultures did not keep their children in at such times. As they drew closer it appeared they were not children at all but the short race of people known as the Gelgak. They were covered in thick coats of colored mud that adhered to them like too many coats of paint. It was elastic enough that few cracks appeared as they moved but roughly formed enough to conceal their figures. Oh, if I could only converse with these creatures, he thought, I would be tempted to delay this mission for the chance.

Jeppo's fascination with the Gelgak harked back to his scholastics in his childhood where he was taught the romantic stories of Atos, the first brickweaver, who alone among figures in Thujwani history was a friend to the Gelgak and counted one of them among his senior apprentices. It was generally understood that Atos' genius in so many fields had so exhausted his analytical ability that he was in error about the Gelgak, who most thought of as a more primitive subspecies, incapable of faithfulness or civilization. Many Thujwani considered it as a mark of their own generous nature that they tolerated the Gelgak at all.

The three pedestrians turned to watch the sledge as it went past them, staring, it seemed, at the passengers aboard and particularly at Kulkulla but the mud skin betrayed no expression on their faces. As the sledge continued on to the vast farmland ahead of them and the Gelgak receded progressively into the distance behind them, Jeppo thought he may have heard a burst of clicking noises emanating from their direction, sounds that were indecipherable to begin with but quickly became fainter and were ultimately lost in the rushing wind of sledge travel.

Here the roadway changed from the stone pavement of farm town to the gravel of its tent-strewn borders and finally the packed dirt of the farmlands, dark, rich and fertile, lands through which it pushed unbroken toward the distant wall. They passed through citrus orchards and stands of pomegranate trees that seemed to stretch out forever to the west as Jeppo's sledge came up a rise from which they could see the tops of those rugged trees laden with crimson balls of fruit, sacred to the Punic traders that had first brought the seeds to these lands centuries before.

The road descended abruptly and the travelers sailed through this shady path, surrounded by pomegranate trees and the crude fencing fashioned from their own timber that held the trees from advancing to the road and prevented only the hungriest of passersby from poaching their succulent bounty. It was only from this sudden filtration of mid-morning sunlight that they realized how oppressively hot the day had become and they were thirsty. Kulkulla turned to the baggage behind him and widened his stance for balance on the vehicle, which traveled faster than the swiftest Howoo runners, though the all-binding manipulations of its design would prevent any inadvertent fall from the platform.

He opened his bag and produced from it a goat bladder stretched tight with cool water. He lifted it to his mouth to squirt the cool liquid down his grateful throat, then tapped the shoulder of his master before him, who turned and smiled and hefted the bladder to his own mouth for a few generous draughts.

As the sun climbed higher in the morning sky, the sledge continued its way through the orchard lands, the road piebald from the bits of sunlight and shadow that painted the leaf sheltered way. Here and there they saw a smashed pomegranate along the side, perhaps the refuse of some nocturnal animal or large bird, and Jeppo turned his sight from them. Even at this speed he feared to see a specimen of that fruit's many-pocketed flesh exposed.

The way ahead would be long and hot and sunny as they approached the grain fields and they kept their robes hooded as had been a protection from the early morning chill and would now be a shield from the heat of the high sun. They passed many Morso along the way, grain growers as they were and goat keepers. To the east where the Howoo grazing lands and to the west, the rocky domain of goatherds and the olive orchards, and row after row of grape arbor. But their way was through the shimmering brownish-yellow waves of wheat and millet and barley.

By midday they could look behind them and see nothing but grain fields in their wake. But forward the land changed, rising, with a cluster of large trees in sight. As the sledge climbed up in parallel with the road an arms-length beneath it, they caught sight of the vast cultivated lower lands that spread around them, scored by a long narrow ribbons of rushing water that twinkled in the sunlight, and they could make out for the first time the seemingly endless breadth of the great southern wall, fully ten times the height of a man but at this prospect merely a ruddy brown band that edged the horizon.

Jeppo halted the sledge and the two enjoyed more draughts of water.

"Drink all you want, boy," said Jeppo to Kulkulla. "We can replenish our bladders at the gate, which lay behind the grove of trees ahead. There is a fountain sheltered by those trees, if my history is sound. The great fountain of the farm town feeds it through the underground aqueducts."

"Aye, sir," said Kulkulla, now beleaguered by the heat. "How much longer, master, till we reach our destination?"

"Aye, it's another half day I think," said Jeppo, unrolling his map, "The charts are not as precise beyond the wall but I reckon we have at least as much distance to travel yet today as we have already borne. There would not be a road in the desert but there will be markers as the dye collectors must make this journey twice a year themselves. And now we must think of a story to tell the guards."

"A story, sir?" said Kulkulla putting aside his now shriveled goat bladder. "Why should we need to tell a story?"

"The orders of the guards demand it," replied Jeppo. "They will not prevent our exodus from the city's walls but will need to record what manner of business we are on and the time of our expected return. They are fearful of spies and agitators and are always on the lookout for them."

"And so we are just on our way to gather samples, then?" said Kulkulla repeating the fiction Jeppo had told him.

"They may ask too many questions, about that, boy," replied Jeppo, half-regretting his subterfuge, "And I have no letter from

Mincon approving it."

"Aye, sir," said Kulkulla with a concerned expression. "Yet how would they know that, sir? Are they familiar with his seal?"

"They may not be," replied Jeppo, pensive now and slightly ashamed. He was entertaining the notion now of forging such a missive from his lord. He might have requested one instead yesterday, but surely he would have needed to tell Mincon a false story and his lord would be a less gullible audience for his lies than some remotely stationed guards. Now he was faced with the prospect of committing what would be a grave crime and he would be counted a miscreant should he be discovered in it. Yet the words of the hierophant could not be ignored, nor could they be exposed, and he was bound to find a way to complete the task.

"Fetch me the writing tools and some paper from the bag," he said to Kulkulla. "And a taper."

Kulkulla pulled open Jeppo's great bag and found a smaller bag of stationary items. There were a few sheets of blank scroll rolled up together, a glass bottle of ink, a pen carved from bone or possibly ivory, and a small, square red wax taper. Jeppo took these things and rested squatting on the platform of the sledge. Using Kulkulla's back as a writing table, he wrote in carefully obscured and elaborate script the words, *"Be It Known That This Man Jeppo Is Given Passage On My Business. Question Him Not That No Secret Be Betrayed To Thee. Signed On This Fine Day In Sturdy Thujwa. Lord Mincon."* And Jeppo had the fleeting thought that this action of his may be in no ways different in effect than a suicide drafting his last words. He completed the ruse by breaking off a small chunk of the taper and kneading the blood-red wax till it was warm and malleable. Then he carefully blew on the paper to dry the ink and creased it twice so that the words were concealed behind its folds. Where the edges of the paper met, he applied the soft and flattened wax to them and pressed it down against the floor of the sledge as hard as he could press. The letter now seemed crudely official yet the wax seal had no identifying marks. What was the seal of Mincon like? He knew he had seen it.

Kulkulla had already guessed his masters' quandary and reached into tunic to produce a pendant that he wore around his neck. It was made of gold alloy and did not shine so bright but had the unmistakable image of a tamran tree in relief on its face.

"This was a gift from my mother as it was my father's possession and I received it after his death. I did not know him well for I was so young when he passed," said Kulkulla handing it to him. Jeppo examined the pendant and a smile grew on his face.

"This is the shield of the house of Mincon as sure as I am a brickweaver," said the master.

"Aye, my father was of that house though that is rarely spoken of."

"It has the wrong attitude, I fear," Jeppo continued. "A seal would carry a depressed image, leaving a raised one such as this on the wax. This will invert that familiar aspect of the seal but it may just do."

He pressed the face of the pendant hard onto the wax and left there an inverted impression of a tamran tree. In doing so, the narrow chain that held it came free as a link was forced open. Jeppo was pleased with the appearance of the seal and held the letter up at different angles to test the look of it.

"I am afraid the chain was broken, son," he said to Kulkulla, returning the pendant and chain to him. "Worry not for I will have it remade for you. It has done a good service for me."

Kulkulla thought any damage to this pendant would sadden him but the prospect that he had been of good service to a master, at least this once, though possibly never again, alloyed his sadness with a token amount of unexpected joy.

Jeppo fiddled with the iron key and the sledge was off again, climbing a gentle slope out of the fertile valley and up into the frontier terrain of scrub bushes and a few gnarly olive and horse-chestnut and tamran trees. Kulkulla turned around to see the great swath of golden grain fields that lay behind him, criss-crossed with dirt roads and shimmering ribbons of irrigation channel. Beyond that he could see the random clump of adobe buildings in the farm town and farther on, the many towers of Thujwa, which, at this distance, appeared to be the bristles of a boar-hair brush.

Before them, in all directions, they could see nothing on the horizon save the great wall, but directly ahead, where they expected to reach the south gate anon, the base of the wall was obscured by a thicker clump of trees than had been seen this far. The passage through this grove was short and almost as soon as they had entered it, the gate and the buildings of the station appeared. More striking though to travelers through so sunny lands was the appearance of a fountain. It was nearly the size of the station barracks which could sleep six guards at a time were it ever necessary.

Jeppo sailed the sledge over to the fountain and set it down so they could replenish their bladders. Kulkulla busied himself with that task as Jeppo walked the short distance to the guard station.

"I have business beyond the wall," said Jeppo to the guard, who stood with a spear and a bludgeon resting at his side.

"By whose order would that be," said the guard.

"By master Mincon, the lord of all brickweavers," said Jeppo.

"You are a brickweaver, sir?" said the guard. "What business would a brickweaver have outside the gate?"

"It is all in that letter," said Kulkulla, done with his provisioning. "Master Jeppo has a letter explaining it all, in detail."

The guard stepped back. "You have a letter, you say?"

"Aye, said Jeppo," taking it from his robe and waving it about. "There is Mincon's seal upon it."

"So it is, so it is. And this Mincon, he is your lord?"

"Aye, sir," said Jeppo. "He is the High Lord of Brickweaving."

"Of course, he is," said the guard. "I do not need to break the seal on that letter. Does it give you passage to take a sledge out to the desert? Does it say that in your letter, sir?"

"Aye," said Jeppo, fearing no verification. "It is all clearly laid out there."

"Then let me not detain you, sir," said the guard. "Please be on your way and have a safe journey. There has been banditry out in the high desert."

"We shall take care, then, sir," said Kulkulla as he and Jeppo returned to the sledge.

"This was far easier than I had expected," said Jeppo out of the corner of his mouth once they were safely out of earshot. The guard was obviously illiterate, a deficiency too often seen in the guards services, who were mainly comprised of washouts from the other guilds.

The guard opened one door of the great gate to let the sledge pass through. Jeppo made sure to have part of the letter sticking out of his robes, conspicuous to the guard's eyes.

As they passed through the gate, Jeppo noticed a large quartz lamp high above its arch. It appeared to be the type that was triggered by darkness. He would expect to see it as a beacon should they return in the night.

"Be on the lookout for bandits, boy," he told Kulkulla. As they sailed across the landscape, the trees were smaller and farther apart and they eventually gave way to grasslands and finally the scrub land that borders the edge of the high desert.

Jeppo turned back to Kulkulla again and shouted to him. It was pointless for the apprentice to talk back because of the rush of wind. "We are approaching the high desert. We can follow this road but it is not well-traveled and you shall keep your eyes peeled for cairns that serve as markers should a dust storm obscure the road itself."

By this time the desert heat was at its worse and they were thankful that they had brought plenty of water. They depended on finding water at Koosh though and Jeppo had not heard any reports from there in a while so he did not know what condition the wells might be in. If it were any indication, the textile makers continue to produce fabrics dyed with that hue, which is only obtainable from the flowers that grow there.

"And there's a sledge, you say?" Bakau's eyebrows were raised, noticeable even through the narrow slit in the heavy black cloth that encircled his head.

"Aye, sir. No horse or camel. They travel by sledge," came the answer from Dugel.

"And there are two of them. Hmmmm...," Bakau mused.

"But no escort. Not like the dye collectors," said Dugel hopefully.

"Aye, but the sledges can travel fast. And we don't know what witchcraft the Thujwani may be concealing." Bakau was warming to the idea but wanted to knock down his own reservations before committing to the action.

"They are carrying a great box and some large bags. But I saw no weaponry," said Dugel.

"Aye, you wouldn't. The Thujwani are a crafty bunch, to be sure. They enslaved our kin many generations past with their witchcraft." Bakau rose up from his chair and looked around at his lieutenants, "What say you, men?"

"A sledge!" said Kormu, his arms raised as though the object were just before him and he could grasp it with both hands. "We have not often seen such a device with so little protection."

"Yea," replied Balaku. "But why would the lords of Thujwa allow such exposure without the needed security?" he turned to Kormu, then back to his grandfather. "I think this would be unwise, sir."

"Well it is a risk, Balaku, but if we should capture this device we could rule the sands," Bakau replied.

"Aye," said Zasu, grinning, "The price of ruling the sands is our bravery. The Thujwani have known no such challenge in a thousand years. They have become weak and vulnerable."

"And you say they are heading to Koosh, the old city?" Bakau asked his spy.

"Aye, sir," Dugal replied. "They follow the road. They were at the fourth cairn when I caught sight of them. They will be at the twentieth, near the red rocks, by dusk, if I reckon their speed well."

"If we make a move, it will have to be there," said Kormu. "We can surround them. And cast our nets on them."

"We will indeed have to make our stand there," said Bakau. "A few cairns past and they are in Koosh. We cannot attack them in Koosh, ruin though it is. The place is thick with their dark magic."

Bakau needn't remind his comrades of the attack at Koosh nearly five years before, when his son and ten others were caught in the sandstorm. They had sought to plunder the old building that was surrounded by blue flowers. Kabak had led the charge, ignoring his father's warnings.

"I am not so happy to take their device," said Balaku. "Their machines are cursed. And how will we operate the device?"

"If there are two travelers," answered Kormu. "One must surely have knowledge of the device. The other we will hold in peril to break the first man's will."

"And if they have taken any vows?" said Balaku?

"Then we will use pain to take his knowledge," said Zasu, gleefully, too gleeful for Bakau to stomach it.

"We will not torture a man no matter the prize," the chieftain bellowed. "We cannot embrace the evil of the Thujwani, even in defeating them, for it will make us Thujwani as well. Know your history, man!"

"Aye," said Zasu, crumpling to the carpet, and shaking. "It would be such a great prize and the prospect of it banished my clear thinking. Forgive me."

"See what dark magic has already been brought here, grandfather?" said Balaku.

"Aye, son," said Bakau. "I respect your concerns. But we have a path to follow and the gods have handed us this opportunity." He spoke to all gathered now. "I will need twenty men riding. We must make haste to the red rocks and conceal ourselves there. There is plenty of cover where the road rises."

Chapter 13

Kulkulla felt the cooling rush of wind against his face and was grateful for it. This would be the worst of the trip, he thought, as the sun seemed to keep itself high in the cloudless sky. The road ahead was not clear, the heat of the afternoon playing tricks with his eyes. At some times it looked like a river, at others like a fog. The rare piece of brush, the scattered rocks and the undulating field of dunes they passed all shimmered and diffused from the relentless heat.

"It is not much farther to the red rocks," shouted Jeppo, turning his head slightly back, his voice raspy from the dry air. "We have passed the sixteenth cairn already. We will stop to rest our eyes a bit, in the shade of the great rocks. A few leagues after we leave that place, we will have sight of Koosh on the horizon."

Jeppo had never been to Koosh but had tried as a youth to find his way there. City guards escorting a dye gathering bark had found him just past the red rocks. What a fool he had been as a youngster. He knew the city was just a ruin now and not the place of his childhood fables. And yet the thought that plagued him was that this journey was itself like the fables, obscure, full of promise, and prompting actions that were perilous and inadvisable, just as the adventure of his youth had been.

They continued on in the sun and heat, the sledge running swift past one cairn, then another. The road began to rise, and here and there the landscape of dunes that stretched to the horizon, which appeared to writhe and sparkle with the play of light and heat, displayed a sparse but noticeable line of rocks, some the size of a boulder. The road grew dense and dark, and a rim of red rock slowly appeared to the right in the way ahead of them. Kulkulla welcomed the chance for a rest. Even though no effort of his own was needed to hold his body on the sledge, he did not enjoy being whisked through this oven of a desert regardless of how swift the conveyance. He wished the sledge had a cover, but Jeppo had probably thought it wasn't needed owing to its speed.

They had passed the nineteenth cairn, and the great red rocks and their generous shadows were visible now, obscuring the horizon. As the sledge slowed on the last stretch of road approaching another cairn, the twentieth, they entered a passage through tall dunes that nearly encircled them. Behind them was the sun and the land ahead had just begun to grow less bright. Each had pulled a thin muslin cloth over his eyes, adjusting it when wishing to see. As both Jeppo and Kulkulla removed these cloths they saw small black spots bobbing on the tops of the dunes around them. There where twenty-one of these dots in all if they had had the time to count them. But they grew with their approach and soon the two were surrounded by bandit riders, each dressed in black robes from head to foot, with only the eye line of their faces showing. Most brandished swords while others held out the ends of what appeared to be wide trapping nets.

Bakau, the bandit chieftain, led the charge giving a cry of "Halloo! Halloo!" at which the riders spurred their horses to a gallop. The ground shook as those hooves beat the sand all around the sledge, until they were nearly upon them and two of the net carriers cast the veils of rope out and onto the travelers.

Jeppo stopped abruptly but the machine still hovered. He manipulated the iron rod on the top of the sledges forward hull, and the machine began to rise, the ends of the nets that covered the two hanging from the sledge's sides, the sand beneath it began to churn and raise some dust, confusing the bandits. They halted their advance as Jeppo struggled to gain more altitude while Kulkulla tried removing the heavy rope nets that blanketed them.

No sooner had Bakau halted then a tiny bird fluttered past his eyes. He saw another, and then another. He turned around and saw a great swarm of the tiny birds, called guamji, coming toward him. With a look of horror on his face he shouted "Ootah! Ootah!" and his horse turned round as did the rides of the other bandits, all of who repeated Bakau's cry. Jeppo and Kulkulla watched in disbelief as they disappeared into the south. They had discarded the nets by this time and soon Jeppo lowered the sledge. Kulkulla was laughing.

"Master, that was very funny, don't you think?" said Kulkulla. "Those men on horseback. They were frightened by that flock of little birds."

"Aye, was not the birds that frightened them," said Jeppo smiling. "It was that," and he pointed to the northeast where now the entire sky had darkened though it was not that late in the day. What they saw was a wall of sand approaching them at a terrible speed. Jeppo manipulated the rod again and raced the sledge to the shadow of one of the larger rocks, a great swath of stone that seemed to thrust up from the sands. It was a refreshing change from the heat and desert glare.

"Do not worry, boy," said Jeppo to Kulkulla, who had stopped laughing once he caught sight of the approaching sandstorm. "The sledge will protect us but the way will be obscured till it passes. We will wait out the storm here."

They landed in a deep shade made darker still by the looming wall of sand. Jeppo fiddled with the iron rod again and as the storm was upon him the air felt suddenly still.

"This is a lesson for you, Kulkulla," said Jeppo, in the several moments it took for the storm to pass. "The all-binding can be bent and shaped. That is known well and widely. But there had never been much progress in making it bend *predictably*. My reckoning machine has solved that problem. I have the force in this sledge bent to surround us and protect us from the storm. We can not remain this way for long, though, or we will run out of fresh air."

They both refreshed themselves with draughts from their bladders, which were now at the halfway mark. As the sands dissipated and the sun began the last leg of its slow descent to the west, Jeppo removed the invisible, protective shields of force and turn the sledge back toward the road.

The desert was starting to cool now and the change in temperature was bracing for them. Jeppo activated the forward hull's quartz lamp as the sun became less generous, and the lantern was bright enough that they would not need to reduce their speed from that of the daytime travel.

They made good time along the still distinguishable road despite the frequent sand storms that are raised in this high desert.

The effort of these winds and the rarity of rains had made this land as barren a place as whither a traveler had ever gone. Everywhere all around and stretching to the horizon were wave after wave of sand rippling so slowly that it appeared on first observation as though it were a frozen, ivory-colored sea. That conclusion is soon discarded as a traveler crossing that expanse comes to know that it is an ever-moving thing, as living a thing as any river.

Mincon stepped into Henrix' workshop with two assistants following behind. At once the gaze of all three was fixed on the large structure that occupied the center of the shop floor. He caught sight of Azelfof standing on the bark, with unrolled scrolls propped up on the brick chair next to him and held open with a few pieces of loose wood. On his other side, a large, empty brickwork bowl rose nearly to his head from a great brickwork cube.

"Azelfof," he shouted as he approached the tall, thin brickweaver, whose long mane of black hair had been pulled together behind his neck and tied with a strip of purple fabric. The brickweaver turned at the sound of Mincon's voice.

"Greetings, milord," said Azelfof. "We are nearly ready as you can see."

"Aye," said Mincon, making a great show of looking around at the structure. "I see you have the bark constructed, and you have the chair, the controls and the great bowl," he held on to the block beneath the bowl to swing himself down, closer to the large circular hole at its center. "But where is the cone? I was sure on my visit yesterday that you had almost completed it."

Henrix stepped forward to answer. "Sir, the door of my shop

is not high enough so we have taken the cone outside. We will attach it there."

"Yes, milord," said Azelfof, "we encountered that issue, as Henrix said. We had attached it in this room and could not see a way to move the entire structure outside without tearing down a wall. We will attach it to the block, what is called in the old scrolls an 'arming chamber'."

"So we will be ready on the morrow?" said Mincon.

"Aye, milord," answered Azelfof.

"And the missiles. I have not seen them at full size."

"We have had some trouble with the missiles, sir. These old plans required some adjustment as they employed obsolete practices but I have managed to work them out. The missiles are a different matter altogether. We have tested the model three times and each time saw the missile projected at great speed toward a target wall of brick. Such ballistics would noticeably damage any wall on impact but the testing produced results beyond our calculation. I need only say sir that we were required to build a new test wall each time. These walls were only five bricks wide and ten rows high but on the scale of the model, they would be as tall as the great wall of this sturdy city."

"I have read the plans from the secret histories," said Mincon. "And that does not surprise me. They tell of a great noise and a blinding flash of light when the ball meets its target."

"Aye, milord, the plans are true on this," Azelfof continued. "I have reckoned that the balls manipulate the heating/quickening force at high tolerances, but if there is pattern to these balls," he held up one of the model's, a shiny pearl-like sphere, green and opaque, to show Mincon. "I have not found it. The instructions are not detailed on their manufacturer though we have fabricated full size versions that look the same." Azelfof directed Mincon to a wooden crate containing some six or seven large, shiny green balls.

"And they were not easy to fabricate, master," said Henrix. "We have not much use for balls in our work, at least in my experience. But Ashon the brickmaker found a way to glaze and kiln them nonetheless."

"And you could give Ashon no wisdom on their proper manufacture?" asked Mincon of Azelfof.

"Nay, sir. The instruction I gave him was no more than I

could find myself in these scrolls." He held out one of the ancient documents, which Mincon took from him, held up close to his own face, his head moving back and forth and his lips opening and closing.

"Yea, I see the problem," said Mincon. "We must include another brickweaver on this project. Have you a choice?"

"That has been studied, milord," replied Azelfof. "Both Henrix and I agree that Master Jeppo may be able to help us with this problem. I apprenticed with him and learned how he solved many others. He is a good scholar of the craft."

"Then it is done," said Mincon, and he turned to his assistant Galel. "Take a sledge to Jeppo's tower and bring him here. He should be home by this hour."

"Aye, milord," replied Galel, who bid his leave at once.

Lavena opened the door with one hand and helped her mistress climb the step with another. The crumpled expression on Matanya's face was punctuated by grunts at times as she made her way into the tower.

"I will get you some tea, madam, once you are settled," said the housekeep.

"Aye, Lavena, that may help," said Matanya. "You have been helpful to me today and you should be on your way to the farm town, but may I seek one more task of you?"

"Aye, madam," she responded.

"If you could draw a bath, a soothing hot bath for me," she winced at the next step.

"Aye madam," she replied. "Let me get you to your sleeping chamber first, so that you may know some comfort."

"Aye, dear Lavena," Matanya replied, still taking careful,

awkward steps as the pains in her joints seemed to burn regardless of movement now. The aching and weakness were not so much her concern this evening as whether she could rest well enough on the morrow to have the strength for the next day's activities. Many years without a call to such a grand occasion and now that such a moment was nigh, she feared she would not enjoy it so much, or worse, that her debility might prevent her attendance.

"Are you sure you have time, dear," said Matanya, as she settled haltingly into her bed.

"Aye, madam," said the servant woman. "There are groups of late travelers, nannies and house servants and a few laborers. I will travel with them, some of whom I know well. My cousin labors in the house of Ramjin at this hour. He is a tall man who can protect me on the southern road."

"Well that gives me peace, dear," replied Matanya, forcing a small smile. "I would not want my problems to bring you to tragedy."

What a fine thing to say, thought Lavena. She would have a troubling walk home, she thought, hearing the complaints of her fellows and their harsh treatment by their masters, hearing the whisper war. Yet none was more beleaguered than her cousin Olmak and he would keep quiet. The poor man was not as clever as the others and failed to voice his complaints save when asked outright. Nor could he engage in the practical jokes that formed the little aggressions of that war: a garden ruined by some strange wild animal, a tiny drop of itch oil in the bathwater of an officious matron, a bowl of soup viscous with the spittle, or worse, of some kitchen servant.

"I am at least content with my purchase," said Matanya as Levana ushered her to the bath chamber. "Fetch it for me while I bath so that I may see its beauty and draw strength from that," she continued in a self-mocking tone.

"Aye, madame," Lavena smiled, happy that her mistress's spirit was not diminished by her pains.

As she removed herself to the entranceway to grab the parcel she had carried back from their outing that afternoon, she heard three knocks on the front door and put the parcel aside to answer the call.

On the porch stood a young man in the robes of an apprentice. Behind him was a sledge, its quartz lamp still glowing in the darkness.

"Woman, I am here to fetch the brickweaver Jeppo," said Galel. "He has urgent business with my master Mincon."

Lavena bowed slightly, "He is not here as yet, sir," she spoke with some concern. "He had business south of here, past the farm town, but I do not know the nature of it. He was not sure of his return before the morrow."

Galel fumed. "This is urgent business, woman. How am I to find him?"

"Please, sir," she responded. "Neither I nor my mistress would know. The brickweavers keep their secrets close."

"Then I must need to travel there. Would he be returning by the south road?"

"Aye," she said. "That would be his route."

"Then I am off to the south. A messenger is sure to come here after some time asking for 'Galel'. Please remember to tell him where I have gone."

"Aye, sir," she said as the young man returned to his sledge and directed it toward the south road. He sailed off in that direction before she had gotten the door fully closed. I hope the walkers that man passes keep their stories to themselves, she thought, not knowing how difficult it is to hear when riding a sledge, as she had never had that experience.

The light from Jeppo's quartz lamp illuminated the path before them as it was now dark night and the moon had waned for many days before. What was left of the moon and what little the stars could offer was all that revealed the desert around them. Kulkulla frequently turned around to check whether bandits or Thujwun-knows-what-else might be advancing on them. But he saw nothing.

"Koosh," said Jeppo after a while. "Koosh is directly ahead."

Kulkulla turned to look and saw a cluster of rocks on the horizon. They were barely visible to him because the lamp's beam did not reach that far. As they continued, the rocks loomed larger and obscured most of the horizon directly behind. They were almost on top of the great gate of the city of Koosh when the lamp's beam first revealed them in its brighter light. Jeppo halted the sledge and the two took in the sight illuminated before them.

There were two august pillars that formed the gates. These were made of brick, and Jeppo guessed by their lack of mortar that they were brickwoven. He could even make out some of the patterns but they were slightly different than he would expect, as when one converses with a speaker of the same language whose word choices are odd or formal but nonetheless intelligible. There was little left of the stone wall to which the pillars had once been attached but that the pillars themselves remained a millennium past their construction was an homage to the art of brickweaving.

Jeppo started the sledge forward again but now at a slow speed. They passed between the gate pillars, and the terrain became less smooth. There were no great rambling dunes and swells and curves here. It was a flat plaza in which they were standing, most likely brick beneath the sand. But the surface itself was punctuated by numerous small depressions, like the steps of animals or human feet. These were probably not fresh as the terrain appeared not to have been bothered by windstorms in a long time. They may be, Jeppo thought, the impressions of dye gatherers who were likely here a few new moons ago, or that of the unbound nomads. They might even be the recent impressions of bandits, he feared.

"We need to look for the blue flowers," said Jeppo. "They should still be in bloom if I can tell by the state of the flowers in Thujwa."

They traveled slowly past the ruins of what appeared to be a circle of great buildings with smaller ones scattered around them. They traveled toward the great rocks that thrust some sixty stories from the desert surface and had replaced whatever wall once surrounded the city at the end farthest from the gate. The rocks appeared to rise higher as they approached them until they had risen so far above the quartz lamp's beam that they disappeared into the darkness, discernable only at a distance as a rough silhouette against the stars. They came across a large stone building, well intact but without a door where a deep drift of sand had flowed into it. Jeppo pointed the hovering sledge's lamp inside and caught the sight of something glowing. In the lamp's bluish light, blue objects glowed as though they emanated the light themselves. These were clearly the blue flowers prized by the dye gatherers. He turned the sledge into the great building.

"I can hear water flowing in here," Jeppo said. "Just a trickle but enough to slake the thirst of these plants. The rock itself appears to form the back wall of this building and likely provides a small spring."

"Aye, sir," said Kulkulla, himself looking about the cavernous room.

"There is adequate water for these plants and adequate shelter from the sun and heat," said Jeppo, relating all he had figured out about the place. But I see nothing here that appears to satisfy my mission, he thought. "I have two oil lamps in my bag, Kulkulla," he said to the youth. "Take them out and we shall explore this place more closely."

Kulkulla rummaged through the bag and produced the lamps. They were heavy to heft with glass light chambers and ceramic brick bases. Jeppo manipulated a looped metal rod on each of the bases and the wick of each produced a strong, steady flame of amber light.

"These lamps are ignited by the quickening force," he lectured to Kulkulla. "But they burn oil."

"Why not have them illuminate with the force alone?" he asked.

"That would be too dangerous," Jeppo replied. "The force is too hot at the temperature needed to produce a flame and the heat would eventually become unbearable to the lamp carrier."

"Aye, sir," Kulkulla replied. "I have much to learn."

Jeppo directed Kulkulla to search to the left while he would investigate the area to the right. There was little that remained here from before the time of the migration. Most of what Jeppo found were scrub bushes and flowers enjoying the hospitable environment.

"I've found something!" shouted Kulkulla, prompting his master to turn and run in his direction

"What have you found, boy?" said Jeppo, gulping air.

"I felt something sharp as I walked through the sand here. So I dug a bit and found this," Kulkulla held up a shard of green clay that had been buried just under the sand. Jeppo examined it. It did not look like any piece of pottery he had ever seen. It was an odd color, as well, but that may easily be due to its age.

"Could these shards be the specimens you have come here for?" asked Kulkulla, hopeful that he had done well. The youth was not aware that his master was equally as unable to answer that question as Kulkulla himself.

"These may be," said Jeppo, entirely unsure but hopeful as well. "Let us continued digging."

As they dug with their hands down the few hand-widths to the bare brick floor, they carefully brushed away the sand surrounding the pieces they found so as not to disturb their original order. There were many large pieces scattered near the entrance and smaller ones farther away. They seemed to form a crude line pointing toward a section of the side wall they had yet to explore. Jeppo held up his lamp and carried it in that direction, discovering a great ceramic brick cabinet, with an angled top, that seemed to rise out of the sand.

Jeppo approached the cabinet and examined it carefully. It was unlike any he had ever seen. Why the door would be at such an acute angle was what intrigued him the most. He would need to open it but there was no catch or handle, just the obvious break in brick patterns that aligned with the rectangular shape of the door. His fingers could not insinuate themselves for any depth between the edge of the suspected door and its jam. He returned to the trail of pottery shards to aid Kulkulla in retrieving the pieces as the assistant gathered them in an empty cloth bag. Among the smaller pieces, oddly shaped and not readily revealing the whole of which they might be part, he found a rusted iron rod. It resembled enough the cabinet keys with which he was familiar and he thought a try with the slant cabinet door was in order.

"This may be just what we need," Jeppo exclaimed. "Come with me, boy, and we might see what is in this cabinet."

Kulkulla put down his bag for the moment and followed Jeppo to the object near the wall.

Jeppo rubbed as much rust off the rod as he could and dragged the end of it down both sides of the seam. Halfway down and inside the seam, the rod found purchase. Jeppo pushed it in, turning it either way until it had an effect. A double clockwise turn was followed by an audible whoosh of air and Jeppo pulled on the rod's small crossbar, at once lifting the door open.

Jeppo had imagined finding any number of things in this cabinet: ancient scrolls, bricks of various types, a model perhaps, a cache of gold pieces. But he had not imagined finding a man there, nor if he had, one so covered in fresh blood. As the light from his oil lamp fell upon one of the man's eyelids, they opened and the man was struggling to move though with obvious difficulty. He was breathing well, at least, and he opened his mouth, his eyes already wide now, "Ockuckuck!" he said or something near to that. "Ockuckuck!" he said again and then he fell unconscious.

"This man has been beaten, and recently," said Jeppo, as he and Kulkulla carefully pulled him out of the cabinet. He was not a large man thankfully, about normal height like himself, Jeppo reckoned, but terribly thin. He was wearing only a single layer of robes and much of that had been ripped open at the chest, no doubt when his persecutors attacked him, and Jeppo could clearly see the man's ribs and the morbid thinness of his arms.

"Kulkulla, take our bladders and replenish them," Jeppo ordered, once they had laid the man out on the sand. There is sure to be a spring at the back wall, which is part of the earthborn rock itself.

"Aye, sir," said Kulkulla, who ran to the sledge, grabbed both bladders and quickly returned with them.

"First, sir, I think he will probably need to drink," he said handing a nearly empty bladder to Jeppo.

"Aye." Jeppo lifted the spout to the man's mouth.

At the feel of water against his lips, the man awakened again and sputtered but drank thirstily as Jeppo squeezed the bladder carefully so as not to give him too much at once.

"Here, boy," he said to Kulkulla, handing the goat bladder back to him, "Do as I said now. Refill the bladders and be prepared to leave this place anon."

Jeppo sat watch over the man and noticed him shivering. He must be chilled, the master thought, and he removed one of his many layers of robes to cover him with it. At that the shivering ceased, and Jeppo thought about what the provenance of this discovery must be.

Surely, he reckoned, the man was beset by bandits, who beat him, perhaps to the point where he appeared to be dead. They hid the body in the slanted cabinet, which must have been opened before the crime was committed for surely they did not have the skill to open it themselves. How fortunate the key was found among the shards, he thought. Looking at it, the iron rod did not appear to be much unlike the keys he used. Perhaps it was not. He had made unpurposed keys before himself and was planning to try the sledge key in the cabinet had this one not been found, as that would sometimes work with cabinets.

Now as the man seemed to be sleeping and with hardly any fits or shakes most of the time, Jeppo began to think of his mission. "*Among the sands of that place is a chamber as old as Thujwa itself where lies the duty to which we are bound*," is what the hierophant had told him, and the common history says that the two great duties are the duty to family and the duty to rescue. He and Kulkulla, he thought, may have just performed the latter. This would explain why the seer had set a time. Had he already known the man was injured? Or did he know that a man would in time be so injured and our journey would be scheduled in adequate time to both save his life and yet avoid the identical fate ourselves? He was tiring himself with these thoughts and even amidst his gratitude that he had probably fulfilled his mission, the awe with which he recognized the depth of the seer's power shamed him a little, for he should have had less spare room for his faith to grow this much.

When Kulkulla finally returned, he found his master sitting near the sleeping stranger and dozing off himself.

"Master," said Kulkulla, grabbing his shoulder to rouse him, "We have plenty of water now. The spring was near the rock as you had guessed."

"Aye, son," he said groggily, and took a draught from one of the bladders. "We will have to ride through the night as soon as we are ready."

"Are we not endangered by the bandits, then?" asked Kulkulla.

"If this man is any testimony, boy, I would say we are in as much danger here as on the high desert. Have some faith boy. We are bound by the duty of rescue, is this not so?"

"Aye, sir," said Kulkulla. "But I had thought that duty only one of the olden time, when there was so much strife and hardship, and many required rescuing."

"Nay," said Jeppo. "We are always wont to think that the gravest demands of our faith were made on those of times past. This is not always so. Just as the good fortune required to complete these duties has not diminished in our time either. We escaped the bandits once through Thujwun's hand and we may do so again."

"Aye, sir," he replied. "I will finish collecting the samples in only a few moments and then we can be off."

"Hurry," said Jeppo.

Kulkulla picked up the remaining pottery shards and gathered them in the bag. He secured the bag and the other luggage in the great box to leave more room for the stranger to recline. They carried him from the sand and placed his feet against the inside of the forward hull of the sledge, laying him down as straight as they could with his head nearly touching the tip of the box. Jeppo and Kulkulla would have to straddle his body, with their legs in a wide stance, during the entire trip but the effort would be reduced considerably by the sledge's facility for holding fast its occupants.

Once they were ready, Jeppo took his place at the front of the sledge with Kulkulla behind him; the two of them standing over the prone body of the stranger as though he were their prisoner. Jeppo turned the iron rod in the control slot of the sledge and navigated the vehicle back toward the entrance. They sailed through the now familiar cityscape of Koosh past the gate pillars and onward down the road through the high desert on their way back to the great city of Thujwa.

Chapter 14

"More tea, sir?" said Affel.

Mincon heaved a sigh and took the bowl of steaming beverage from the bricklayer's assistant. He sipped it slowly and the bitterness contorted his face to a grimace his current attitude found agreeable.

"Azelfof," he said. "Have you a spare apprentice to go to Jeppo's tower?"

"Aye, sir," replied the brickweaver. "Young Qestril here can drive a sledge there in no time." He stretched his hand out in the direction of a brown-robed youth who was cleaning tools to pass the time.

Mincon turned to Qestril and said, "Boy, do you know where Jeppo's tower is?"

"Aye, milord," he replied. "He is not far from where the edge of the city meets the south road."

"Then off with you, and ride as fast as you can."

"Aye, sir," and Qestril, who put aside his cleaning cloth, bid his leave to all three masters and ventured out into the night.

"I do not know what has become of Galel," Mincon said, turning to Henrix, who was sitting on a bench drinking tea nervously. "But he may have been told that Jeppo was elsewhere. He is a tenacious fellow and would have sought him out on his own. He would also expect me to send another messenger by this time." Then he turned to Azelfof. "Please, brickweaver, bend your mind to this problem some more as we await Jeppo's arrival."

"Aye, milord," he replied, despondent.

"Layer Henrix and I have some other business to discuss in the meantime so we will leave you to your problem." At that Azelfof unrolled a scroll that he had read numberless times before but he now perused it closely, as though it were written in a cipher. Mincon motioned Henrix to follow him into the bricklayer's master chambers and closed the door behind them.

"I am beginning to think that all of this night's sledge travel is for naught. Even if we can find Jeppo, there is no assurance that he can solve our problem with the missiles. And it is far too late to rouse another brickweaver out of his sleeping chamber and expect any good council from him." Mincon did not want to say it but he had felt Azaelfof's suggestion to be the only reasonable one. He had known Jeppo for the man's entire career and knew him to be among the most skillful men in the guild. An orphan, he recalled, who had so readily grasped the principles of brickweaving during his scholastics that he was given a special admission to an apprenticeship.

"Aye, milord," he responded.

"So what is the status of the compressor. Have you had any trouble with that design?"

"Nay, milord," Henrix replied happily. "I borrowed a crew from Fignon's shop and they were working on it as late as this day. They may be finished as the design was quite simple, not like this machine. It is in the back workshop."

"Take me there," said Mincon. "This machine may be our resort. I do not want Kulla or Mazrash to think we cannot meet our promised time for the demonstration."

The two left Henrix' chamber and returned to Azelfof who was deep in study.

"Have you any wisdom on this problem yet, Azelfof?" asked Mincon.

"Nay, sir," said the younger brickweaver nervously. "But I am still pursuing some logical approaches to it."

Mincon restrained himself from a cynical response. "Keep at it, then. Henrix and I will be in another workshop for a bit but we will return anon."

Mincon and Henrix left through a small side door and walked around to the back of the building. They entered another structure there, of smaller size but with great double doors just the same. Through the high windows they had seen the blue quartz light still emanating from the building. Inside were two laborers cleaning the surfaces on a large brickwork machine. It was another bark but smaller than the concussor. Like the machine that so vexed Azelfof, this one had a chair and a small block with protruding wires in front of it. Forward of that arrangement was a large brick wall. It was a perfect square and about the length of a man's height on each side, but it was gently curved as though it were a smaller piece of some great sphere.

"Greetings, master Henrix," said one of the laborers, as they both bowed to the two visitors.

"Greetings, men," he replied. "Is the machine complete as yet?"

"Aye, master Henrix," said the first laborer. "All that is needed is the adjustment of the controls. For that we need a master brickweaver." He looked over to Mincon, whom he did not know, but recognized the purple robes of the master's guild.

"I will perform the adjustments," said Mincon, walking toward the machine's control block. "Bring me the model."

"Chief Bakau, I have seen the sledge again," said the scout. "It had a bright lamp on the front of it, the blue kind I have seen in the city."

"And where?" replied Bakau, rubbing his beard. "Were they on the road?"

"Aye, sir," he replied. "They had just passed the red rocks. They are on the way to Thujwa. We can meet them at the edge of the forest if we are swift. Their machine was traveling very fast, swifter than we saw earlier this day."

"And why would they travel at night?" Baukau thought out loud, then turning again to the scout. "Get to the forest, if you can, and lie in wait. You are to do nothing and they are not to see you or hear of you. But report back to me all that you may see and hear. There is something afoot these days and I cannot guess what it would be."

"Then we are not to take that prize?" asked the scout.

"Nay," said the chief. "Their magic is too strong. They may raise another storm as they did today."

The scout bid his leave and left the great tent, returning to his horse and mounting the steed with one jump. Hunkered down against the animal's neck, he dug in his heels three times and shouted the command "Choo-cha!" The horse took to a gallop with eyes wild and much neighing.

Galel stayed on the sledge but kept it hovering for fear of miscreants or bandits. There were two guards posted here as there were at all times and they had known about a sledge leaving the city with two men riding it but little else. At least Galel knew he had not overshot them, that Jeppo's mysterious business had not been among the rows of wheat or the craggy groves of olive trees he had just passed. He decided he would question the guards again.

"From whom came this report of the men passing the gate?" said Galel to one of the guards.

"Was that Torkul or Mayda who told us that?" the first guard asked the second.

"It was Torkul, brother," he replied, smiling. "He was stuttering as he does when he is excited. He said he could count on his fingers the number of sledges he had seen leaving the gate in his memory."

"Where is this Torkul now?" asked Galel.

"Oh, he would be asleep now in the barracks," said the first guard.

"Dreaming of his wife back in the city, no doubt," said the second.

"Take me to his bunk, then," said Galel. "I must need to speak with him."

The smile left the second guard's face as he motioned Galel to follow him. He walked the short distance to a two-story stone building that leaned against the great wall itself. "You can not ride the sledge in there, sir," said the second guard. "Wait here, and I will fetch him."

Galel waited and listened closely. He heard Torkul's name being called and soon saw streaks of golden light appear around the edges of the door. It opened suddenly and the second guard appeared with a portly man dressed only in nightclothes. The guard was holding him by one arm and led him toward the sledge as the man turned his head away from the beam of the vehicle's quartz lamp.

"Are you Torkul?" asked Galel.

"Aye," the man answered groggily, his eyes squinting, "What b-business have you that I am... that I am woken up at this hour?" he said stammering.

"Your brothers have said you let two men on a sledge pass through the gate earlier today?" said Galel. "I am looking for these men on an urgent matter. Did they tell you their business?"

"Nay, just that they were on a mission for one of the great masters," Torkul replied. "They had a letter... with a seal."

"And what did this letter say?" Galel continued.

"I did not read it, sir," said Torkul, as the second guard suppressed a guffaw.

"Then whose seal was it?" asked Galel.

"I am not sure I remember the name," Torkul replied. "It was a red seal, though, and it had the image of a tree pressed into it."

Galel could not believe what he was thinking. By the color and image described, it sounded like the seal of Mincon himself. Why would his lord not tell him of this?

"Do you know when they were to return?" he asked, now more perplexed than frustrated.

"Nay, sir," said the sleepy guard. "I would have expected them on the morrow, though. No one leaves the city for more than a day, sir. And no one travels at night on the high desert, because of the bandits. They will surely attack any nightrider. Even in the sunlight, the way is not safe."

Galel felt as though all his dinner had vanished from his belly. There is no likely destination for a traveler out the south road save for the old city of Koosh, or one of the bandit camps.

"You may return to your dreams, guard," said Galel, unhappily. "At least I know that I have waited here in vain." To the second guard, he said "Should by chance these travelers appear, I will be waiting for them in farm town, at the great fountain. Is that understood?"

"Aye, sir," said the guard as Galel turned his sledge around and doubled back on the south road.

The rapping noise woke Matanya easily as she was suffering a fitful sleep. She reached across the bed, expecting her arm to stop anon against the nightclothes of her husband. But her arm extended farther than that, finding no obstruction, and she realized that Jeppo was not beside her. The room was dark save for the few rays of bluish light that trickled through the high windows from the illuminated plaza on the other side. She heard the rapping again and rose from her bed. On a shelf near Jeppo's side, she found the rod and turned it in its discreet hole. At once the house was lit by many quartz lamps scattered among the different chambers. She could hear the subtle cracking and hissing of the quartz as it complained about the robbery of its light.

Matanya shivered and pulled another robe over her nightclothes, grasping it closed at her chest with one hand and pulling up her walking stick, which she now used at all times. She leaned on the stick as she moved her painful limbs toward the entrance way.

"Who calls at this hour?" she shouted down the hallway. More rapping on the door followed.

Once she had made her way to the entrance and the great door, she pulled a smaller one found in the wall near to it, at eye level, allowing a look outside. She saw a young man in apprentice robes. She did not think they were the color of a brickweaver's assistant but could not be sure because of the dull, blue-tinged light outside and her sleepy eyes.

She cautiously opened the door just enough to converse with the stranger.

"I say," Matanya spoke. "Who in the name of all-seeing Thujwun disturbs my sleep?"

"Madam," said the young man. "I am Qestril, an apprentice to the bricklayer Henrix. I have been sent by Lord Mincon to find his own apprentice, whose name is 'Galel'."

"There is no one here by that name," she said, and began to shut the door, fearing the man might be a miscreant. And then she remembered the messenger too whom Lavena had spoken earlier. "Wait," she said, opening the door just a sliver again. "There was a man here earlier. His name may have been 'Galel', sir. My servant... one of my servants had spoken to him. He left a message that he would be past the farm town, if anyone asked."

"Is this the tower of Jeppo, then, madam?" Qestril asked.

"Aye, sir," she replied.

"And is Jeppo here now?" as he spoke he tried to look over Matanya's head to see whether the master was standing behind her.

"Nay, sir, he is on a long journey far to the south," she said, and shut the door as tightly as she could. Through the small spying door, she could see the man step onto his sledge and turn it to the east and disappear from view.

Galel took a quick draught from his water bladder and leaned back as he stood on his still-hovering sledge, waiting for Jeppo in the large plaza that surrounded the great fountain. The power of the all-binding generated from the sledge's brickwork would keep him from falling and it felt to him like something close to an embrace. The vehicle's errant forces agitated a dusting of sand on the ordinary brick ground, and even the plain bricks beneath slowly scraped and bobbed a little in reaction to them.

Now dark as any time at night, the area around the sledge was dimly lit by torches that encircled the fountain, their amber glow enfeebled by the bright bluish-white light that emanated from the sledge's quartz headlamp. Galel extinguished the lamp with a few small turns of the sledge key as he realized that the glow made him more conspicuous in this strange place. The entire plaza was otherwise deserted, save for the occasional towner filling his water bladder. At the far end of the plaza, after a while, Galel could make out more lights and a gathering crowd of towners. He stood erect at the sight but the distant torchbearers made no advance toward him, nor did many of the crowd even bother to look his way. They seemed to be focused on something at the crowd's center. He heard their distant talking and laughter, but he could not understand the words that floated to him on the evening breeze.

Most of the crowd dropped to sitting on the plaza floor at once. They surrounded a group of ten or so who still stood and began dancing in circles, wearing robes that were slashed to ribbons of intertwining colors: black, white, red and tan. Though Galel could well enough discern the traditional garb of various tribes: the Morso with their long robes, the Tawani leather tunics and britches, the dark blue, magenta and green togas of the Howoo, he could not remember seeing these strange costumes before. The spinning of the dancers gave these ribbons a disturbing aspect. They throbbed and roiled like sandstorms streaked with blood and skin. And the dancers shouted mournful cries and indecipherable words that they repeated, again and again, as they spun.

Galel knew that the towners engaged in dramatic recreations of events from their distance past, and that most recalled events at the time of their rescue, or the warring period that preceded it. Yet at this distance, and without any understanding of the strange Tawani language, he could not discern what sort of event the dancers could be portraying. He was comforted by the thought that at least his faithfulness could not be endangered by such witness, yet the sight of it still worried his mind and perturbed his belly. It would be better, he thought, that Jeppo return anon and he could go about his business.

Jeppo's sledge and its three riders arrived at the gates near the darkest moments of the night. They were thankful that the gate had affixed atop its arch a quartz lamp that served for them as a beacon through the last stretch of the south road, where it cuts through the ragged edge of the forest. Jeppo knocked loudly on the small, inner door of the great gate.

"I have a man in need of surgical attention here. He was attacked by bandits," Jeppo told the guard.

"There are no surgeons closer than Thujwa, but in farm town there is an infirmary," he replied. "But first, sir. Are you the man who came through earlier today on a sledge?"

"Aye," replied Jeppo. "We have rescued this man now but there is not much time," he spoke with the force in which he would have ordered a recalcitrant servant or laborer had he ever had experienced that occasion. "This man is a Thujwani who was attacked, sir... by bandits!"

"Aye, Aye, of course," replied the guard, now startled from his walking slumber. "Follow the south road to the healer's house. He is sure to be there at this hour."

They pulled in through the gate and Kulkulla stepped off to replenish the goat bladders at the fountain.

"If you are the same as came here earlier, a man was desperate looking for you. He said he would be at the great fountain," said the guard. "The great fountain in the farm town."

"That is very odd," replied Jeppo. "Pray I hope it is not concerning my woman Matanya. Did he give any reason for his search?"

"Nay, sir. But I will tell you he was taller than you or me, and he wore a brown robe with a purple belt."

Then he was on brickweaver business, thought Jeppo. He could think of no reason to avoid meeting this fellow once the stranger was in good hands. It must surely be an urgent matter for it to be addressed at so late an hour.

Once Kulkulla had finished filling the bladders, the two stood astride the sleeping stranger again and continued on through the orchards and fields well south of Thujwa. At another time of day the speed that Jeppo drove the sledge would have been a hazard and a terror to the laborers walking this road, but at this hour the road was nearly empty. They passed a few figures along the way that appeared to be the strange mud people. Who knows what hours they keep? thought Jeppo, who would have stopped to try conversing with one of them, had he not been in such a desperate hurry.

Jeppo was hopeful to see the mud brick buildings at the edge of the city and he soon slowed the sledge so that he might not miss the turn to Vomcot's infirmary. He knew that if he saw the great fountain he had passed it and did not wish to delay much longer. Finally, his memory served him well, even though he had been to this building only once and during the day. The seemingly random pattern of buildings in farm town was not at all daunting to a man with an eye trained to discern the discreet patterns in brickwork. As they pulled up to the entrance, Jeppo was grateful to see a sliver of amber light spill out between the loose fitting door and its jam. He knocked and called out at the same time.

"Please open, sir, I am Jeppo the brickweaver, who is known by you," Jeppo shouted. "I have an injured man, a Thujwani, who is in need of your care."

The door opened and Vomcot appeared from behind it, his eyes wide and mouth agape. He looked first at Jeppo and then at the man lying on the sledge.

"Swiftly, Swiftly," he said to Jeppo and Kulkulla. "Carry this man into my infirmary." The two rescuers picked up the stranger by shoulders and knees and gingerly carried his withered body into the building. Vomcot had them lay him down on a waist high table covered with layers of clothes. He went to a basin and gathered a jug of hot water and from a shelf took several towels and brought them to the table.

"You," he ordered Kulkulla. "Wash this man's wounds while I prepare some bandages." Kulkulla went to work and carefully cleaned the man's face and then proceeded to wash the many slashes on his arms and chest.

"Had this man been tortured?" he said to Jeppo after he returned with the bandages and began to examine the wounds. "Over there," he pointed to another basin with a shelf of bowls and bottles above. "Fetch me a bowl of water," he had the man's head cupped in his hands and it appeared that the stranger was becoming conscious.

"We are guessing he was beaten by bandits," replied Jeppo.

"Not bandits," said Vomcot, taking the bowl from Jeppo's hands. "I have seen their work and they do not torture. It is a rule with them. They murder, of course, but they have no stomach for torture."

As he lifted the bowl to the stranger's lips and poured just a little, the stranger began to sputter, then drink greedily, then sputter some more. Vomcot started taking the bowl away and the stranger lifted himself up, with difficulty, to a sitting position and took the bowl with his own, shaky hands. He took a long draught of the water, nearly tipping the bowl sideways, coughed a few times, and tried to drink some more from the bowl. Jeppo had already fetched another and handed it to the stranger.

"Master Vomcot," he said, with a deference that surprised the healer. "We must bid our leave. The guards at the south gate have told me that I have urgent business with someone waiting at the great fountain. I am assured that this stranger is in good hands now."

"But what is his name?" asked Vomcot. "What can you tell me about him?"

"We found him in the old city," replied Jeppo. "We must leave as I have said."

Vomcot turned to the stranger who now appeared weak but fully conscious. "Sir," he asked the stranger. "What is your name?"

The stranger looked around the room, at Jeppo and Kulkulla and Vomcot and at the shelves of bottles and tools around him. He then turned directly to Vomcot, and said "Brumajin... my name is Brumajin."

"The man can probably tell you more now, master," said Jeppo. "I will pay for his treatment. Jeppo pulled out his bag of coins.

"For this service, I ask twenty gold pieces," answered the healer. "I will keep him in this infirmary until he is fit to be on his way. As long as we are reckoning, sir," he continued, turning to Kulkulla. "Are you well boy?"

"Aye, sir," said Kulkulla. "I am thirsty though, and hungry too, and very tired." Jeppo shot him a glaring look for his complaining.

"Then that would be another twenty pieces, sir," said Vomcot, matter-of-factly. Jeppo opened his purse again, producing five of the larger coins.

"Aye, that was the deal sir," replied Jeppo. "And thanks are to you for these services."

"And one more item, master," added Vomcot, securing the coins in his purse. "What of your woman and the remedy I gave you for her treatment?"

"The remedy?" at once Jeppo was ashamed. He had left the bottle at his home, in the pocket of another robe and as it had left his person so it left his mind as well. "I had forgotten, sir."

"Is your woman no longer in discomfort, then?" he replied.

"Yea, she still suffers. And it is a shame upon me that I had not pursued this action," he said with his head hung to emphasize his regret.

"Well as long as she is still living, sir," he replied. "You can apply the remedy as I told you. At the first opportunity, I would suggest."

"Aye, master Vomcot," said Jeppo. "Aye, I will."

Vomcot returned to his patient who was drinking water, and still shaky, and cringing at times from pain or hunger or dread, it was not easy to discern which. But as they bid their leave, the stranger turned to them, and said, "I am most grateful to you, gentlemen. I am forever in your debt."

At that Jeppo bid his leave again, and he and Kulkulla returned to the sledge.

Vomcot closed the door behind them and fetched a tamran fruit from the cooling bin. These had a tender flesh and a bland effect on the stomach but were nourishing nonetheless. He cut off a few chunks of the fruit and handed them in a bowl to his patient.

"Do not eat too much, sir," said Vomcot. "Your body does not appear to be used to it."

But the man named Brumajin was ravenous and finished the bowl in a few moments. While he was still chewing the last few remnants of the fruit, he made another careful look into the empty bowl. Vomcot had taken a bottle from the shelf, the same remedy as he had used on Kulkulla a few days before. He poured a little of it into a small square white cloth, then he crumpled and wadded the cloth until it was soaked.

"Now you lay back, Brumajin," he said to the stranger. And he placed the thin, gauzy cloth soaked with remedy on the stranger's face.

Brumajin laid with other cloths soaked with other remedies as well, one on the stranger's chest and two separate ones on his arms. He lay like this for the time it took Vomcot to finish a cup of tea. After Vomcot removed the cloths, the stranger sat up and pulled his robes back around, for it was cold here at night.

"You are a great surgeon, master," said Brumajin, smiling. "I feel almost revived from your treatment. Now please tell me where we are?"

"First you must tell me something, sir," Vomcot said. "You must tell me your true name and explain to me why you wish to conceal it." He pointed to a large bottle on a shelf near Brumajin's table. It was a remedy bottle, and the label on it read, in large letters, "Brumajin root".

Chapter 15

It was only a few turns and a few long stretches of farm town street before the two arrived at the great fountain. Galel was alone in the plaza by this time.

"Hail to you, Jeppo, sir," said a smiling Galel. "You are requested by Mincon himself, my master, to aid in solving a problem with a particular machine that must be ready for display on the morrow."

"What sort of machine?" asked Jeppo.

"It will all be known to you shortly, master," he replied. "Please follow me and stay close."

Jeppo and Kulkulla followed Galel up through a wide northwestern road that cut through farm town. They were on their way to the industry lands, and followed the trail of scattered mud brick buildings till structures of any kind disappeared in the high desert. They had passed only a few large dunes before catching the walls of Henrix' compound in the glare of their sledge lamps. The guard waved them in and they brought their sledges onto the grounds, stopping before the entrance of the workshop, its high windows still glowing blue in the deepest part of the night. Kulkulla remained behind to guard the luggage, and avoid another encounter with the bricklayer, while Galel and Jeppo continued into the workshop.

Once inside, Jeppo encountered his former student.

"Is it you that brings me here, Azelfof?" said Jeppo. They grasped each other's wrist in a greeting of fidelity. Because surgeons often perform the same gesture with their patients but for the purpose of checking a pulse, it is often joked that their profession has many false friends.

"Aye, Jeppo, master," Azelfof replied. "I have a problem. This machine that you see here is from an ancient design and it is to be demonstrated to the council on the morrow after midday." Jeppo stood listening but his eyes were following the contours of the large brickwork before him. It was a larger version of the model he had seen at the guild temple but he was not entirely sure of its purpose.

"We have a model as our guide and the ancient texts describing its design and function."

"And its history, if that is any help," said Mincon who had just entered the building with Henrix in hand. "Greetings, master Jeppo," he said breaking the brickweaver's gaze at the machine.

"Greetings, milord Mincon," said Jeppo. "What is the function of the machine in plain words, then master?"

"Do you see that cone?" asked Mincon, pointing to the large obtuse conical structure made of spiraling bricks lying to the side on the workshop floor. "That is to be placed on the front portal of this great block...." And Mincon continued on trying to describe the problem as best he could despite the exotic nature of the device. Jeppo listened intently and looked at the machine and asked questions of Azelfof and Mincon, and sometimes of Henrix.

"Can you demonstrate the model for me," Jeppo said at last.

"Aye," said Azelfof, who took the model from his work table and set it on a large bare section of floor. Two assistants helped to align a large, freestanding wall of brick as a test target. "We are ready to demonstrate the model, master."

"Azelfof," said Jeppo. "You have models of the glazed balls that the brickmakers kilned?"

"Aye," he said. "That is the requirement. But these are plain like the full-size missiles we had made. In our tests, those missiles did not perform as described in the ancient texts. That is why we need your help to determine the proper manufacture of the balls." Jeppo hefted one of Azelfof's missiles. He could not think of how they could be specially manufactured as his thoughts were always with the nature of bricks and not spheres.

The assistants set up the demonstration, which was designed to launch a model ball through the model cone and have it hit the target wall. Jeppo substituted one of the newly crafted model balls for the same-sized originals found in the bowl. An assistant fiddled with the small wires and at once they heard a high pitched whoosh and something glowing emerged so quickly from the nose of the model's cone that it was only seen in a flash of light and just before a greater flash, and a concussion that shook the building occurred as the swift glowing ball obliterated itself and fully half of the test wall.

"The problem is not in the missiles, then," said Jeppo. "Their design is not the source of the violence. There is something wrong with the controls or the firing chamber."

"Fetch me the ancient texts and a large bowl of strong tea," said Jeppo. "And I will try to solve this."

The stranger looked at Vomcot and thought for a moment, then he surveyed the room. This was unlike any surgery he had seen. The items on the shelves were stacks of cloths and towels and labeled bottles containing various liquids and creams, as any surgery would contain, but there was no collection of saws or mallets as would be expected in a surgery, and no tell-tale spots of old blood on the floor that could not be washed away.

"How am I to trust thee?" said the stranger. "I may have enemies who are in pursuit of me."

"You are safe here from the bandits, sir," said Vomcot. "Are they not the ones who had beaten you?"

"Nay, sir," said the stranger. "It was the guards of the city who beat me. It was the guards of the city known as Thujwa."

"Are you a miscreant then, stranger?" said Vomcot, his eyebrows raised.

"In their way of thinking, I am," said the stranger, hanging his head for a moment. "Where are we now, sir?"

Vomcot stared at the stranger and wondered what manner of

trouble had been brought to his infirmary. The man was weak so no danger to him, he thought. He was well spoken though there was a slight accent to his speech. He sounded Thujwani but it was a different form of the dialect, as though he were born and raised in Thujwa but had left as a youth to live among foreigners.

"You are in the farm town sir," replied Vomcot. "You are not in the city proper but you are within the great wall of Thujwa and the jurisdiction of the city guard. I will not remand you to them, for fear or respect or bounty even, as I cannot imagine any crimes that would justify the torture you had received."

"Then I will tell you that my name is 'Atos' and I am a master brickweaver," said the stranger. "My crime was to threaten a general strike of the guild in protest of the use of warring machines, machines we had designed, and many of which I myself had designed."

"Why did you design these machines, then," said Vomcot, "if you did not want them to be used?"

"Aye, we were told they would only be used as a show of force," said Atos. "We were assured this by the lords of the council, who may have even been honest about their motives at the time, but they are Thujwani and often I wonder if the brickweaving has weakened them. A strong man will choose his weapons carefully but a weak man will take the most violent one he can find, it is said. Once given these weapons, it was not long before they saw the strong advantage in using them. They are using them still, I would reckon, unless my fellow guildsamen have shown that they possess some backbones at last."

Vomcot stared at Atos. He did not know what his next question should be for there was so much this man said that made no sense.

"Against whom were these machines used?" he asked at last. "I have heard nothing of warring machines."

"Do you not know, man?" said Atos, now in greater disbelief than the healer. "We have already enslaved the Howoo and the Tawani. The Morso will be a tougher opponent but they cannot resist against these machines."

"Great god Thujwun, I have no idea what you are talking about, sir," said Vomcot. "The Morso cannot be an opponent at all. They have been bound to this city for centuries."

Atos looked at him in horror. "Centuries?" he said.

"Aye, sir," Vomcot replied. "You may be suffering an affliction of the thinking organs. It is not unusual in cases of great trauma, as you have suffered. There are beds in the next room and I insist that you take rest there. You are not healed though you may feel well enough at the nonce. Only sleep will make your therapy complete."

He walked the shaken man to the nearby wardroom and helped him into a bed.

Jeppo felt as though he were going to vomit. He had spent some length of time by now reading several stanzas of the secret histories and he could not believe the words he had seen. He felt shaky, whether by the impact of his reading or his profound exhaustion, or possibly the several bowls of morning-flower tea he had consumed. Or perhaps it was not the story that the histories had told so much as the necessary conclusion that such practices would be countenanced by the lords that rule Thujwa this very day.

In his reading through that night he learned of the 'rescue', and how enslaving the southern tribes would please Thujwun because it would give the unfaithful the opportunity to know of his worship and ensure the wealth of the faithful by providing a ready source of labor. The Thujwani themselves had become so used to the comforts of the brickweaving technic, and the wealth generated by a complex system of interconnected licenses, that they were no longer attracted to the meaner tasks on the farm, in the mine or foundry or factory, or in the gardens, markets or households of the city. For that they needed to conquer less advanced cultures, the M'butu and Howoo at first, then the Tawani. At the time of the history's writing, the Morso had not yet succumbed. These rescues as they were called, were induced by the action of warring machines designed by the brickweavers, many of them by Atos himself, who was the great old master of brickweaving in that time.

Of the warring machines, the most frequently used were these three: the concussor, the compressor, and a third that was called the "cabinet of forgetting". The concussor, which Jeppo had determined was the machine on the floor of the main workshop, was well-described in both design and usage. The writings told of its use against Howoo villages, even beyond attacks against the warriors to those that were aimed at the common people. It was used against the M'butu and the Tawani in the same way. As was the compressor. While the concussor produced a powerful explosion and a blinding light when its projectile met its target, the compressor was even more violent in its employment. Whole bands of people and animals and buildings, and anything else that it encountered, were compressed, as horrifically described in the old account, into writhing, hovering spheres that became so heavy in weight they would pierce through the earth's crust and tunnel downward through the dark, unimaginable kingdoms below. But even that fate may have been less than the one that greeted those tribal chieftains and other great eminences of the captured peoples. Those souls, Jeppo read, were remanded to the cabinet of forgetting, a device in which the victim is placed and at the closing of its door becomes both nonexistent and unremembered. The scrolls said that the men forced into this cabinet not only disappeared, there works were gone, their wives had different husbands and their children had different fathers.

The texts went on to tell the story of Atos and his treasonous attempt to end the rescue by an uprising of his guildsmen brothers. His reputation among the guildsmen was high, at least among the three brickworking guilds, and so was he seen as a threat to the lords' activities, which were only in the interest of the city after all. Atos was the last victim of the cabinet, it said, but only because with his disappearance, it failed to work properly again. Without access to the cabinet itself, until placed inside it without tools to alter its construction, Atos had nonetheless effected its debility. Somehow, the cabinet door that closed behind him remained sealed forever after, the key to it as useless as any other rod of iron.

The account of Atos' treason continued with the murder of his Gelgak assistant, who was named Oku-kuk. He had escaped but would surely have died of his injuries. As a child, Jeppo had read the common history about Atos and his Gelgak assistant, but the man's name was not mentioned and he was characterized as nothing better than a trained monkey, an animal to which he was alike in size, being described as of child's stature like the rare Gelgak Jeppo had seen in his lifetime, and covered head to foot with a thick coat of green mud. The tribe always fascinated him and he was doubly horrified that these ancestors had murdered even one of these harmless people, his only crime that he had befriended the Thujwani who threatened their continued warring.

Jeppo saw the first few rays of amber light from the high windows piercing through the diffuse bluish glow of the quartz lamp. It was dawn and he decided that there was no time to digest all that he had read and come to an acceptance of what it would mean. He knew how to adjust the machine to correct what was changed in Azelfof's design. The correction would only take a few adjustments of the brick patterns on the firebox, and a few related adjustments to the controls. He had known that soon after he had started reading the secret histories, but he had kept reading till nearly dawn despite that he was detaining Henrix and Azelfof, and their assistants, but most of all Mincon, because he had wanted to read more than was needed. And every strange account he had read had urged him to read further.

Jeppo rose from his chair, put away the scrolls save for one roll that charted the precise design elements of the firebox.

In the great room Jeppo emerged from the chamber and called Azelfof over too him. Mincon and Henrix rose from their benches at the sight of him. They had not thought to check whether the brickweaver had fallen asleep in the chamber as they had fallen asleep themselves.

"Master Azelfof," said Jeppo angrily. "Why did you change the patterns of the brickwork on the fire box?" and he held out the design scroll himself as proof.

"Master Jeppo," said Azelfof, startled by his former mentor's obvious displeasure. "I was merely following the advances we have made in this sort of design. I replaced a few patterns in the ancient design with our more modern variants."

"Then you have misread the design," he said, shaking the scroll in his grasp. "These 'modern variants' are not aligned as you think with the ancient ones. There are more bricks in these patterns than those to which you are familiar."

"More bricks?" said Azelfof, with a look of genuine surprise.

"Aye," said Jeppo. "This is how the fire box works: it focuses a powerful thread of the sword-binding generated here," he pointed to a section of the scroll, "and transformed to all-binding here. This third pattern is not for brick-binding, as you had apparently surmised. It actually converts the all-binding into the most intense quickening force embodiment I have ever imagined. That is what makes the balls glow and explode upon impact. The balls themselves could be fashioned of wood or goose feathers and twine, the effect would be the same."

"Say master, Jeppo," said Mincon as he approached the brickweaver from across the room. "Have you solved the problem of the missiles?"

"Aye, milord," he said, "I have read these few stanzas over many and many times, even to the point at which I must confess I fell deeply into sleep, and slept for a long time."

"That is not a concern, master," replied Mincon cheerfully, "If you have truly solved the problem."

"I have solved it milord, but we must get ourselves onto correcting the error," said Jeppo, turning to his former student. "The error was assured by the poor descriptions in these stanzas. I fear the scribe who compiled this account had not worked with many brickweavers before. I am fortunate to have made a study of ancient descriptions that were available to me."

Chapter 16

Kulkulla woke up. From the angle of sunlight that entered the room through the high windows, he calculated that it was mid-morning on the same day on which he had slipped so readily into sleep after dawn. He was still groggy and his mouth was dry; his belly was empty. But exhaustion still plagued his spirit and hunger had to wait in line behind it. Thirst was another matter, as there was a jug of water kept in his sleeping chamber. He drank a few draughts and felt renewed at once.

There would be no working today as Jeppo had told him to rest from their long night of adventure, advising that he would do the same himself. But Kulkulla's mind was racing. Where he had found himself sleepless in the past because of the specter of failure that would greet him on most days, he found that at this time his mental disturbance was at least free of regret. It was borne today of questions, a thousand questions for which his mind could not readily calculate the answers. The last being Jeppo's sternness and anger when he last spoke, as Kulkulla was left at the garden gate of his grandfather's tower not long ago that same morning. That he was angry about something was easy to discern, and Kulkulla was confident that at least for now the anger was not directed at him, for which he was grateful.

As his thoughts returned to the events of the day and night just past, he tried to recall them in order and see if he could cobble together some meaning to the mysteries he had witnessed. He recalled the bandit attack and its fortunate preemption by the sandstorm, the stranger, the work at Henrix' shop, the sample he had found. He had almost forgotten about those shards of green pottery he had collected.

They were secured in a cloth bag on a shelf in this very room. He leapt to where it rested and took it back to his bed to examine the contents.

Sifting through the fragments, he caught something sharp on his fingers and pulled the thing out. Unlike the rest of the pieces, this small scrap of metal was not green but a rusty brown. He held it up to the morning light and turned it this way and that before his eyes. Here was something he had not often seen except in sport. It was an arrowhead, but it was larger than those he remembered from the archery competitions of his scholastics. This would be an angry blade in a creature's flesh as it was probably at one time as sharp as any knife and had extending from its tip three wing-like blades that would have done too much damage to an archery target to be suitable for practice. What animal had this brought to the ground, he wondered, although no proof was evident that the missile had ever found purchase in flesh.

Putting the rusty piece of iron aside, he reached into the bag again and pulled out a few of the larger pieces of oddly shaped green pottery. They were roughly made and unglazed. One piece in particular was puzzling. It was not as rounded as the others he had laid out on his bed and it contained a strange depression on one side about the size of his thumbnail. It was not a deep depression but it was clearly delineated and at its center was a much smaller cavity that was only several hairbreadths deeper. Some instrument that was the size and depth of a small coin with a millet seed attached to its center could make this dimple. He held it up to the light, turning it to watch the play of shadows as they leapt about the impression. The shape seemed somehow familiar to him and yet it still escaped identification. Then a realization entered his thoughts at once and he let go of the piece, which fell to his bedclothes. With knitted brow, he pulled aside his robe revealing his breast and looked quizzically at his left nipple.

The proving ground was in the desolate barren lands far south and west of the city, far north and west of the farm town and well beyond the scattered workshops of the bricklayers. A flotilla of sledges converged on the place, twelve of them each carried a lord of the council and that lord's most trusted assistant as well. There were other sledges numbering as many as those twelve that carried a force of city guards, and a few more occupied by various brickwork guildsmen and their assistants. They gathered in a half-circle on one narrow side of a large, oblong bark that had been covered with several large cloths, revealing little of the shape of the objects beneath. As the arrivals completed, Mincon stepped off his sledge at the front of those gathered and began to speak, shouting to be heard in the hot and windy desert venue.

"Greetings, masters," he said. "I will ask you all at this time to park your sledges and quiet them as this demonstration demands your full attention. As has been explained by lord Mazrash, our commerce is withering and may soon reach a state of dissolution. There is not adequate trade in our city to support the continued assessments of license that we have enjoyed these many years. This situation demands that we should open our gates to greater trade with the other cities of the desert, with Delgazh, and distant Andli, and the cities beyond those with whom we have had little contact at all. We have always taken comfort in the great wall that surrounds us but now we must set out beyond this wall without the fear of conflict or submission by these other peoples.

"What we will demonstrate this day will be our prod to the other cities to grant us favorable terms for trading and our shield as well against their possible aggressions. This demonstration will be of a warring machine that was used in times past to convince the southern tribes of our power and prevent the bloodshed that would otherwise have attended their reluctant acceptance of the benefits that only Thujwani culture and technics can afford."

Jeppo stood alone on his own sledge, exhausted still but having known some sleep and groggy for having known it just recently. He had been roused at midday to join the gathering so that should a problem arise, his skills could be put to correcting it. The brick pattern changes on the firebox and the controls adjustment of the machine's console had been completed soon after sunrise and he was assured himself of their reliability but Mincon had insisted he be at hand just the same. Now he rankled at Mincon's depiction of the machine's history, which he knew was not as benign as the lord stated.

"Be advised," said Mincon. "That this machine will display a horrific violence against the earth some leagues from where we stand. Watch carefully and know the horror and wonder of its action for it is that same sense that will goad our future trading partners to reasonable fear and submission without the need for the device's actual use against their property or people."

At that he directed his assistants to remove the cloths that covered the machine. They revealed a large bark with a great conical prominence rising at an angle and pointing away from the throng. In the forward side was a center block of brickwork atop which rested a large, bowl-like structure, concealing a few large ceramic balls inside it. On the other end was affixed a chair that faced the brick block and cannon. Between the two was another, smaller block with iron rods protruding from it.

Azelfof walked onto the bark and settled into the chair. He began to adjust the iron rods and a door opened at the bottom of the bowl permitting one of the balls to fall into the firebox. The door then shut and Azelfof made more adjustments to the rods. From the center of the bark came a great rushing noise and a high-pitched whine. He manipulated the rods again and the audience of councilors could hear a sound like muffled thunder as the ball rolled rapidly up through the channel in the cannon. There was a great blast when it exited the muzzle only a heartbeat later and witnesses saw a glowing ball of bluish green light exit from the bore at a speed that caught their breath. The glowing mass continued up at the same angle as the cannon's placement, describing an arc that at its highest point was higher than even that of the great wall. Though lightning fast already, it gained velocity as it approached the barren expanse of sand to the west. Upon impact some many leagues away from the gathering, it exploded. Even at that distance and in the oppressive sunlight of the desert afternoon it produced a blinding light from which the observers instinctively turned away. Coincident with the eye-piercing flash was a great, ground-shaking report that moved the observers to cover their ears and shook the land around them like an earthquake. This display was followed anon by a great, irresistible wall of hot wind that swept past the councilors and their retinues. Because their sledges were quieted, the attendees where not bound to them, and every rider was thrown from his mount without exception.

The blast was felt and heard across the lands of Thujwa. In the spire-thick city, pottery and glassware rattled in the great homes, the armaments of the city guards shook in their cases, pomegranates in the great marketplace fell from the stalls and ran rolling through the street, water splashed out of brimming jugs and ponds and fountains, children froze in their boisterous play, but the towers themselves stood firm.

In the farm lands, the blast spooked goats and cattle and horses, who ran amok; guinea hens made frantic but failed attempts at flying off in every direction; orchard trees dropped oranges and olives; the great fields of wheat and millet that waved lazily in the sun were shaken and flustered by the tremor. From deep within the sparse forest that ran toward the southern wall, a great cacophony of clicking was heard, as though a thousand crickets or locusts were roused. But the noise continued well past the tremor and in moments became a rhythmic sound, a living thing that ebbed and flowed and seemed at last almost like a melody before it ended just as abruptly as the quake had called it forth.

Vomcot rushed to the infirmary soon after the farm town shook from the concussor's blast. He had been worried that the stone and mortar building might have suffered damage during what he had thought was an earthquake. He also needed to check on his lone, billeted patient.

He opened the front door to the infirmary with an ordinary brass key in an ordinary lock cut into the thick wood of it. As he entered, his eyes scanned the room. There were some bottles turned on their sides, some disheveled bowls, one broken, but nothing else was out of place. He set the fallen bottles aright, and straightened the bowls, and then saw the figure hiding beneath one of the beds close to where he stood.

"Are you alone?" the stranger whispered to Vomcot.

"Aye, sir," he replied. "I have brought no one with me if that is your concern."

"The windows?" he said, and Vomcot caught his meaning at once. He walked over to the front of the ward room and lowered the rolled up canvas shades on the three front windows.

"Thank you," said the stranger, who pulled himself out from under the bed and lifted himself to a standing, using the side of the bed as a crutch. He patted his night robe, and then his hands, of whatever dust or sand had been on the floor.

"You felt the quake, I would guess," said Vomcot standing in front of the shade-drawn windows and folding his hands.

"Aye, healer, I did," replied the stranger. "But it was not an earthquake."

"Really?" Vomcot had known many deluded people in his practice and knew well how to humor such patients so that they might not become violent. "I was sure it was an earthquake. There were goats near the home from which I have just returned and they behaved as though it were an earthquake. What was it then?"

"I have told you, sir, that I am a brickweaver. Have you not heard of me? Atos?" he said.

"I know few brickweavers by name," Vomcot replied. "I left the city many years ago. I only really know of Jeppo, the man who rescued you."

"Jeppo?" Atos stared deeply into Vomcot's eyes. He had not known so much frustration of thought as even when exploring the very limits of the all-binding force. This man appeared as honest in his aspect as any Atos could judge yet he was speaking nothing but falsehoods.

"I have been, until just recently, the lord of the brickweavers," he spoke as though Vomcot were the one with illness of the thought organs. "There are only five masters and their names are Pecel, Romdah, Teliak, Ashor, and Klymteh. There is no master named 'Jeppo' nor any apprentice with that name."

"I may not know the brickweavers well," replied Vomcot. "But I am sure that there are many more than six in that guild."

The healer took a wooden chair and pulled it closer to the bed on which Atos leaned one arm. He adjured the madman in the night robe to sit on the bed, and Vomcot returned to the chair and sat down himself.

"Please, sir, as I said last night," he spoke to Atos in the gentle tone of one dealing with frightened children or the deluded. "You may not have all your mental faculties as yet. You have suffered badly at the hands of the bandits."

"There is no convincing you, then, of the jeopardy in which I find myself?" said Atos, now catching his breath with fright. "Please do not betray me to the guards and I will leave this place at once, never to return," he pleaded.

Vomcot tried to give a reassuring smile. "Atos," he said, "The words you are saying do not make any sense to me. And I would wager a moon cycle's accounts that any towner I might find walking past my front door would agree with me. Listen to me very carefully, putting aside, if you can, what you might deem the truth as your mind grasps it now, there are, first of all, many brickweavers, I would guess at least forty, and among them is master Jeppo. I have been to his workshop and it is a great structure full of multifarious brickweaving items both large and small."

"Healer, you have been kind to me," said Atos. "So I am bound to trust you and your words. There are few conditions of the world that could accommodate both of our assertions, but one of them may be that I have encountered another people like my own in many ways, but with a different history. Pray tell me where I am."

"You are in the farm town, man," said Vomcot, as though it were obvious. "Some call it 'the Surrel' but most just say 'farm town'. We are many leagues from Thujwa proper. You will note if you look around," and Vomcot spread out his arms and turned his head to look from one side of the room to the other. "That there are very few examples of the brickweaver's craft here."

Atos sat back against the wall and thought for a few moments.

He then bent forward and held up his chin with his hand, resting his elbow on his knee. He had the look of worry on his face that accompanies those who recklessly contemplate the possibility of a tragedy that is not only unbearable to the heart but far beyond the ken of ordinary life.

"Perhaps you are correct, healer," he said at last. "Perhaps I have forgotten the events that preceded my rescue. I am a Thujwani but I may have been gone longer than I had thought. I am many years past your age, sir, and my knowledge of the guild may be from a time that is earlier than your memory."

"That would make some sense," replied Vomcot, pleased that his patient was beginning to exhibit rational thought. "If it has been many years as you say it is likely the guards are no longer looking for you."

"Aye," said Atos, still puzzled. "But it is surely to revive their memories if I were to appear in the city again. There may still be some there who would remember me. This farm town... is it safe here for me?"

"The guards do not come here often but they do come at times," said Vomcot. "And guildsmen as well. Apprentices often visit the taverns here as strong drink is not allowed in the city save for weddings and other events."

"Then I must find a way to leave here before I am found out," said Atos, regretfully. "It would only be a matter of time, I assure you. I am desperate, though, to learn of my loved ones. My wife and sons and my assistants."

"I could ask this of Jeppo. He is as honest a man as I have known among the Thujwani. I sense that he is of the earnest faithful, those whose faith restrains their hand rather than excusing it."

Atos laughed, "I know of such people. They are a dangerous type. I had an assistant named Morgel who was always talking of his faith and his god. When he caught his own father preparing to beat his garden servant, Morgel staid his hand, even to the point of pushing the man to the ground, his righteous passion was so enflamed. Now this is a crime, of course, but his father did not call the guards on him. Morgel argued a parable his father himself had taught him when he was a child, in which the man who stayed the hand of angry servant master was held in higher regard by Thujwun than the master himself.

I wonder what may have become of him, for I have guessed he would have found more trouble by now."

"I can make inquiries, if you like, sir," said Vomcot. "We need a better understanding of your current status with the guild as well. I will learn these things only from those I can trust. There is no fondness for the guard in farm town, or most of Thujwa for that matter."

"Please, sir, I would especially want to know the status of my wife," said Atos. "Her name is Kallila. I have just now realized I have been gone from her for many years." His eyes where glistening with tears now. "And my assistant, Oku-kuk. I want to know what has become of him as well. He is a Gelgak and he covers himself in a green mud skin. Have you seen him?"

"A Gelgak?" said Vomcot. "You know the Gelgak?"

"Aye, healer," said Atos, anxious to speak of familiar things. "They are a very shy people but I have known some. Oku-kuk was a rare one in that he found us Thujwani curious and eschewed the isolation of his people. He taught me many things for the Gelgak are the wisest of peoples."

"Yea, they are a wise people," exclaimed Vomcot. "I have made a study of them myself. Wait here. I have something to show you." Vomcot left the room but returned presently carrying a clutch of large scrolls in his arms.

"As you can see," he said rolling out one the scrolls on the bed. "I have sought to record their speech." In the Thujwani alphabet there was no figure to represent the odd clicking sound that the diminutive tribesman enunciate when they spoke. Vomcot had substituted a simple dot to represent that sound and had transcribed the syllables that Thujwanese could accommodate with his best approximation in that language. Atos perused the writings with careful attention, saying the words aloud so that he could match their sound with what he had heard of Gelgak speech.

"These dots must indicate the clicks," said Atos. "But there is more than one type, I am afraid, and one figure is not sufficient to convey the variety of their meaning."

Vomcot was more amazed by the stranger's knowledge than resentful of his criticism. He had suspected there was more nuance to the Gelgak language but felt as though he were groping in the dark.

This first attempt at transcription he had felt might be a light on that path to understanding, albeit a dim one.

"I have wondered that myself," replied Vomcot. "Can you help me with this study?"

"Aye," Atos replied. "But find Oku-kuk and he will be a better teacher. He is fluent in our language and many others. Many of the Gelgak are talented linguists. I believe that is due to the complexity of their mother tongue. Used as they are to such complexity from infancy, they easily master other, simpler languages as our own."

"Aha!" said Vomcot. "And yet the Thujwani consider them to be simpler of mind than goats or cows. Many even in farm town have that opinion, as well."

"You seem a man of good study," said Atos. "And believing that I must again insist to you that the tremor was no earthquake."

"Then what was it, sir?" asked Vomcot, now curious of everything the man named "Atos" was saying.

"It was a warring machine," replied Atos. "I know this because I myself designed and built such a thing. I would think you would be accustomed to its use by now. At the time of my departure, the thunder of this machine was heard often."

Now Vomcot was perplexed. Again the words of Atos were not making any sense to him. How knowledgeable he appeared at one moment, how obscure the next.

"This machine," he continued. "It is a loathsome thing that causes great misery. Pray tell me which of the southern tribes is it being used against today?"

"Here, sir," said Vomcot as firmly yet congenially as he could. "Here is the cause for my concern about your mental state, sir. The southern tribes as free peoples are no more. For easily nine hundred years they have lived here in the Surrel, in peace and in servitude to the Thujwani. Now pray tell me from where do these false memories come, sir?"

"Nine hundred years?" said Atos, his squinted, skeptical eyes slowly opened wider and his jaw fell limp. He bolted away from the bed, ran to the front door, flung it wide open and ran out into street. Here he saw passersby of every shape and size and color, every sort of garb and manner. Not far away was the great fountain which was as familiar to him as his own heartbeat but it was surrounded by a random variety of one-, two- and three-story adobe buildings, many so seamlessly connected that they appeared to be a ruddy, sun-baked, amorphous creature rambling around the source of precious water. He looked to the north, down what was called the southern road and saw the scattered buildings made of white stone and mortar and farther away the brickwork structures with their tell-tale multiplicity of hues from dark brown, through deep red to dusty yellow. Beyond that, far to the north, was the silhouette of the great city shimmering in the afternoon sun. Like the bristles of a boars-hair brush, the many towers of Thujwa clustered thick around a single doubly tall needle. Atos recognized the needle and little else around it. *It is true*, he thought, and at once realized there would be no memory of him in this city.

Vomcot had followed him outside and was pleased the man had lost some of his shyness. "Do you recognize this place now," he asked Atos.

"Aye," replied Atos in a raspy voice. He turned to look Vomcot straight in the eye. "I have something important I must tell you, healer, but I am vexed at how I can convince you that it is the truth. So I will not tell you now but anon, when I have come to understand it in full myself."

"That is well enough," said Vomcot. "For now you can stay in my hospital. All that I require is you follow my instructions to get well and that you not cause any trouble." He smiled, put his hand on Atos' shoulder and led the man back inside.

Chapter 17

As Jeppo lifted himself off the ground, he looked first toward the great machine. There was Azelfof still seated firmly in the command chair, unshaken by the blast within the protective aura surrounding the bark. He looked around him and saw all the guildsmen thrown from their sledges, most were still lying on the ground. Their assistants and servants had arisen more quickly and were busied with helping their masters back to their feet. Jeppo climbed aboard his sledge and set it running. It lifted an arm's-length off the sand and he steered it toward the place where the projectile had finally come to earth. He raced the sledge in that direction and after several moments of travel, when he feared the gathered audience would disappear beyond the horizon, he saw a great wide green ellipse before him in the sand. As he came closer to it, its shape became less oblong and more like that of a circle. It was a wide, shallow bowl of green glass with steam or smoke rising from its surface. In the center was a deep dimple, a smaller deeper bowl of the same green glass. The glass surrounding it fanned out for many times the length of Jeppo's sledge. It looked like a large shimmering pool of green water that had been suddenly frozen, with endless rings of concentric waves rippling toward its rim. Even in the normally breathless heat of the high desert, the area surrounding the great glass bowl was especially searing and Jeppo maneuvered the sledge far enough away to escape the intensity of it.

Other sledges soon joined Jeppo though most of them held themselves slightly farther back from the glasswork than he. Alongside him came the sledge bearing Mincon.

"This is a great warring machine," said Mincon, he turned to

Jeppo and whispered, "You have done well, master Jeppo."

Mincon smiled broadly and turned around to face all the guildsmen gathered there. "A demonstration of power this great is sure to make our trading partners bow to our demands for the fairest and most favorable terms. I propose we send emissaries to the other cities at once to plan a suitable presentation."

"Aye," said Mazrash, farther back in the crowd. "Let use convene the full council anon to prepare."

With that the many sledges were turned around as their riders sought to escape the terrible heat of the glasswork's rim. Jeppo turned his sledge about as well and steered it toward the northeast, and home. He knew of the council's intentions well enough but he was uneasy about these warring machines. What he had read of the secret history while in Henrix' private chamber worried him. He was not in the least assured that this venture of the council's would not end in ruin but he had not their ear nor would there be any hope in speaking to Mincon, unless he could find the best opportunity to do so.

Kulkulla had neglected to spend his day sleeping as expected by his master. Instead he had acquired a tub of pottery paste from the housekeep and set about rebuilding the piece of pottery from the shards he had found at the stone building in Koosh. The pieces aligned well as long as he eschewed his expectations for the appearance of the final shape. He merely attached the edges of each piece with those of others that fit more or less precisely. Halfway through he began to see a shape emerge. It was a human form but small, like a child's. He had never seen a statue before as such graven images were frowned upon in Thujwani society. They were thought to reduce the human form to its mere animal-like components, so this piece of pottery fashioned to give the appearance of a human fascinated him with its novelty. The nipple had been the first sign that the form might be human and that he had only found two pieces so embossed convinced him that it must be human, or possibly ape. He had seen a bushman once in the menagerie and this could well have been the model for the sculpture but as the form progressed, the proportions of the limbs and torso had become ever less apelike.

The sun had long passed its zenith in the desert sky when Kulkulla had finished piecing together the pottery puzzle. It was indeed the form of a child, a boy child of ten to twelve years old. The form depicted the child's entire body save for hands, feet and head. Why, Kukulla thought, would anyone remove the limbs of a sculpture? And why were the sharper details of the torso, such as the nipples, inverted rather than appearing on the surface? He recalled what he knew from his scholastics of the forging industry. They would create well-defined shapes of flowers or beasts by a process of inverting a form then reverting it many times, using a tool called a 'mold'. Perhaps, he thought, this pottery was such a mold but for a human statue. And the molds for the head and hands and feet were separate. He had seen no sign of any head or extremity molds in the old workshop but it was dark there and ministering to the rescued man had consumed their time and attention.

Kulkulla soon embraced the possibility that the puzzle was indeed a mold, as that would explain its value to master Jeppo. He allowed himself to hope that this work he had done, both in collecting the shards and rebuilding the artifact, would please his employer. It would certainly, he thought, remove any regret for Jeppo that he had wasted precious time attending to the stranger. Their mission was not, apparently, a failure.

The housekeep appeared at the entrance to Kulkulla's room and called him to the dining chamber. "Your dinner is ready, young master," she said, her head nodding as though to emphasize the truth of her declaration. "Your family is waiting."

"Aye," Kulkulla responded. "I will just be a moment." He took a large folded bed linen from a shelf, unfolded it and carefully draped it over the incomplete statue. "I will be there anon."

The dining chamber was large and well appointed. Six oval tables, each accommodating four diners comfortably, were arranged around a large circular table that accommodated eight. Surrounding them where various large, overstuffed pillows on which the family members would recline, serving themselves from wide communal bowls containing various delicacies, and steaming plates piled high with cracked wheat, or boiled millet. Because this was one of the wealthier homes, there were also dumplings and that rarity, wild rice. Smaller plates were heaped with chunks of braised beef or chevon, rarely there could be the occasional horse or, even camel, or wild game, such as boar or antelope. Wild birds were served as well and often a guinea hen or two provided a respite from the steady fare of goat meat.

By the time Kulkulla had arrived, all of his many relatives were seated and the only space remaining was that to the right of Judge Kulla at the central table. This was a place of honor at which Kulkulla had not found himself since he was a child. In Thujwani tradition, the seating of a grandchild next to his prominent grandfather was not a sign of honor until he had at least reached the age of what little self-sufficiency the upper-class demanded of its offsrping. Kulkulla felt he was well into that category and as he walked toward the table, his mother Antilla rose from her seat and took him by the shoulder.

"Your grandfather," said the short, stern-looking woman. "Something is troubling him. Some council work. I think. Or perhaps the earthquake. I do not know. Be nice to him. Tell him your apprenticeship is going well. It will ease his mind." And she smiled at the end, pulling her son closer for a kiss on his cheek. Antilla had had a closer relationship to her son than most women of her status, who generally left their children's upbringing to nannies and house servants. That was largely because the rough treatment they had both known at the hands of Kulkulla's father, a son of Mincon who had died when Kulkulla was young, of the same trouble with the drink as had made him a horror to live with. The beatings and rows and ultimately his untimely death had forced them into an alliance that few Thujwani parents had known with their children. But it was a help to Kulkulla that his grandfather had taken special interest in him, knowing that his start in life was less favorable than that of his cousins.

"Greetings, apprentice Kulkulla," the judge said smiling. "How is your work progressing?"

"Well, sir," replied Kulkulla seating himself down on a pile of generous pillows. "I have been hard at work this day on a new project for my master."

"Aye?" replied Kulla, as though his grandson's work had been the most important activity to occur that day. "Can you tell me what this work entails?" And he brought a morsel of beef to his lips to savor while hearing Kulkulla speak.

"I can tell you only this much, sir," replied Kulkulla, not wanting to relate the events of the past two days as Jeppo had sworn him against it. "I have been examining an artifact that is of interest in our brickweaving."

"An artifact," Kulla replied, still chewing on his beef. "You have said enough, boy, to gain my interest but I will bow to the wall of secrets that any guildsman can maintain. Tell me only whether you are doing well in the work."

"Aye," said Kulkulla, smiling confidently now. "I warrant my master will be pleased with what I have learned." By this time, Kulkulla had convinced himself that the strange torso sculpture he had partially mended with potter's paste was a specimen of an ancient technic for the creation of brick clothing, or something not unlike that in any event.

"What troubles you, Monkey?" asked Matanya, using her pet name for her husband.

"Oh Sparrow," he replied, drawing a deep breath. "I have witnessed a horror this day and I pray it can be contained."

"What is that, then?" she replied, the pain in her joints having been made more severe by the cloud that seemed to follow her husband.

"Did you feel an earthquake today?" said Jeppo.

"Aye," she replied. "All the pottery shook. The jug in our sleeping chamber sloshed water the tremor was so great. It woke me up, Monkey. I had hoped to rest late and revive myself. I have been growing weaker and tomorrow is the great wedding at Mincon's tower and I don't know if I can bear it." Her face was taut with worry.

"That tremor was the report of this machine's action," said Jeppo. "This machine I witnessed in demonstration earlier this day. Or rather it was the concussion against the earth that a missile from this machine delivered."

"But why? Why dear Monkey would you create such a machine?" she looked askance at him.

"It was not my creation, dear Sparrow. It was the creation of another but I aided in its finishing. I am responsible for it as much as any man. I have been assured it will not be used in warring but will instead be used as a brace for trade with the other cities of the desert."

"A brace?" she asked.

"Aye," Jeppo replied. "The council seeks to open up trade but there were fears that Thujwa would appear weak or gullible to the other cities, who have traded among each other for many years."

"There is no need for trade, Monkey," she responded. "I know the market well enough to see that farm town and the industries supply us with all we need."

"They do not supply us wealth," he replied. "They supply us with goods and we subsist, but there is a desire for the wealth of which many have become accustomed. The gold piece is more elusive now because we have all we need. Younger guildsmen envy the great towers of their elders. Their thirst for wealth cannot be slaked unless they find others who need more and more of their goods."

"You are far wiser than I," said Matanya. "I do not understand what one needs beyond a third story."

"Aye, well perhaps you are wise to not understand these things," he said to her, smiling. But she did not return the facial expression. The lines of her face were drawn down in pain now and would not permit the passage of a smile.

"I am sorry, Sparrow," said Jeppo, reaching his arms out to her. "Are you in pain?"

"Aye," she replied, then pressed her lips together tightly and briefly closed her eyes in a wince.

"Good lord Thujwun!" shouted Jeppo, startling her. "It has been three full days at least since I had found a remedy for you. I have been an absent-minded fool!"

"Pray what, Jeppo?" she replied. "A remedy?"

"Aye," he let go of her and spoke, shaking his outstretched arms. "I had met a healer from the farm town just the other day. I mentioned your complaint to him and he gave me a remedy for you. I must apply it in an odd way but it will neither hurt you nor discomfort you much." He ran to the foyer and returned with his old guild robe that he had worn on the day in question. He spoke while rifling through its internal pockets. "His name is Vomcot. He is Thujwani."

Reflexively Matanya pulled her legs up under her robe.

"But he is not of the surgeons guild," Jeppo continued. "You need not worry that you will lose a limb from this remedy."

He held out the bottle to her and she took it in her shaking hand. She examined the thin wooden tag attached to the bottle by a leather thong.

"Is this an old king?" she remarked, examining the image on the tag.

"Nay," Jeppo laughed. "I had made the same mistake. It is a creature known to the Tawani, a creature of the sea. It is a sort of writing creature for it makes its own ink and gives it to the Tawani for their writing."

Matanya looked at Jeppo in disbelief. What a strange story, she thought. And yet, a remedy for her complaint would also be a strange thing to ponder. And don't strange things tend to follow one another just as ordinary things do?

"Must I drink this," she said, hefting the glass bottle.

"Nay," said Jeppo. "Come lay here." He arranged a row of pillows in the dining chamber so that Matanya could lie across them, straight and comfortably. She was already half reclining anyway but he helped her lie down, as she appeared to move with much effort, and took the bottle from her hand. He left the room for a moment and returned with a small white cloth from the cooking chamber. Carefully, Jeppo opened the bottle and poured some of the clear liquid onto the balled up cloth. He squeezed it in his fist a few times to saturate the fibers. He stopped the bottle and put it aside, then held out the cloth with both hands.

"I am going to put this cloth on your face, Sparrow," said Jeppo. "Please relax and give no concern to this wet cloth."

He lowered it to her and draped it over her face. She lay there for a few moments, trying to keep herself still. After a while Jeppo thought he could hear her snoring. He removed the cloth and she did not react. A slight push of her shoulder roused her.

"What?" she said, drunkenly.

"Do you feel well, Sparrow?" Jeppo said softly.

"So tired," she said. "So sleepy."

"Aye," he said and helped her up and walked her to the sleeping chamber. He clumsily helped her change to her nightclothes and guided her into their bed. No sooner was she there than she fell into a deep sleep.

Chapter 18

The servants arrived at Mincon's tower on great sledges, barks actually, but they were called sledges for those occasions when they carried human cargo. While the brickweaver lord retained twenty servants at any time, there were going to be an additional forty loaned by other masters so that guests could be attended to properly. These were all of kitchen staff and wait staff though a few were brought just to lift and carry. Ramjin had loaned the services of his garden laborer, the giant Morso named Olmak, who would be pressed into service waiting on guests. There was also a trained ape from the city's menagerie that would be waiting on guests as well. Most forms of entertainment were frowned on in Thujwani society in the belief such activities as drama or dance or song would eventually lead to as yet indeterminate blasphemies. So the remaining form of amusement at large gatherings was the conspicuous display of oddities. Olmak was a popular choice because he was so well known to both Thujwanis and farm towners as the tallest man in their experience. His protruding brow and large hands and feet only increased his value as an object of entertainment. The ape was also a prestigious addition to the staff, arriving in chains, as he did, with two city guards in his retinue.

In the great courtyard at the center of Mincon's atrium, there were fourteen large oval tables arranged around a central, larger, circular table. The chambers around it were used for preparing the food that would be enjoyed all day and into the night. One chamber held several amphoras of wine and beer, beverages infrequently consumed in the city save for special occasions. Another was established for cooling and stored the animal carcasses that provided meat for the plates of the wedding guests. There was horse and pig and cow and guinea fowl, and plenty of goat. All cleaned and dressed and carved into slabs that would cook readily or boil or fry in the cooking bins. Next to it was another chamber designed for cooling. It held the selection of fresh produce: figs, pomegranates, lettuces, goat milk, lemons, various olives and grapes. Here also were bags of cracked wheat and rices and dried beans. And then there was the cold room. Here was kept the ice that is rare anywhere else in the desert but easily manufactured in Thujwa by applying the slowing force to water. Rarer still were the confections kept in this room. There were custards of goat milk and flavored ices, including the pomegranate ice that traditionally finishes great banquets.

    A dozen cooks and cleaners manned the great kitchen rooms while twenty others awaited the time to serve and water the guests that would be arriving later. In one cooking room, workers busied themselves with soups, boiled grains and meats, and sauces, while the roasting chamber was the venue of the butchers of camel and goat, cow and game, including a fine side of boar that had been kept in Mincon's meat-cooling room since the hunting adventure in which the beast was slain. A crew of old women spent the morning in an otherwise empty back chamber plucking the feathers from innumerable guinea hens and small game birds. Though he was not an especially strong man, Olmak was tasked with lugging the heavier provisions from the barks that delivered them. He often carried slabs of beef or bags of game. At other times, some produce or cereal or flour. Once the guests began arriving, he would be an attentive waiter for one or more tables. The wait staff master had already advised him that at serving time he was to stand near the shortest persons as much as possible so as to appear more bizarrely tall himself.

    In the chamber where soups and stews were prepared, there were heaping bowls of braised goat and cattle bones and smaller platters containing piles of steer and poultry meat cut in small pieces and only recently removed from the roasting ovens.

    Here two stewers stirred great pots arranged on long heating tables. They mixed the meat and bones with a variety of herbs, oils and juices, and goat-milk cream or butter in some of the mixtures, or flours in others. The stewers were Morso and as such used much pepper in their preparations.

"This is an old recipe," said Lallikon, who carried both the exuberance and arrogance of youth though he was past his thirtieth year. "It never fails to please my own master Ramjin," he said with his smile widening as he worked. As a skillful servant, he was wont to think of himself as almost the equal in standing of his masters.

"Will you add a secret ingredient?" replied Tabshir, laughing. Lallokin looked at him darkly, though he continued smiling.

"I will not," he whispered. "You must be careful here. There are many guards at this banquet."

"Ah, yea," responded Tabshir, who now whispered as well. "But did you not remark last evening at the tavern that there would be a... surprise?"

"I had too much wine last night, brother," he whispered back to Tabshir. "I would be a fool to do what I had said. Fetch me some of the purple-leaf herb."

"Aye, you are right, Lallikon," said Tabshir. "There is no way it could be concealed, I would guess," as he walked to the herb table for more purple-leaf.

Lallokin thought about it for a few moments. It would be a great joke to play on these eminences to dose the soup with some rank excretion. It would make him an honored hero in the whisper war. Servants would mark him as the man who had been bold enough to adulterate a prestigious wedding banquet and he might even be portrayed in the dramas sometimes performed in farm town. Of course the character in the play would have a different name but all the towners would recognize this hero as Lallokin and the playwright would disguise the act as well to further protect him. He might be portrayed in a character named something like Smileman or Soupmonger, and his act would be portrayed as subduing a boar or a hippopotamus. But in the shopworn symbolism of farm town dramaturgy, all would know which real-life secret act was celebrated. The audience would applaud the play as indirect praise for Lallokin, and so the whisper war was spurred onward by the promise of such rewards.

"It is not a matter of my skill," whispered Lallokin when Tabshir returned with the purple-leaf. "I would know precisely how to adjust the other ingredients to mask the secret one."

"Still, that would be quite a risky thing," replied Tabshir.

"Fetch me a small bowl," Lallokin whispered to Tabshir. "There is an empty chamber off that doorway. Keep an eye on it while I am there."

Tabshir's eyes widened. "You are going to do this?" he whispered, excited.

"Keep an eye on the curtain to that room," Lallokin replied, smiling. "I will not be gone more than a few moments." He took the bowl that Tabshir had fetched and advanced to the curtained room, his eyes darted all around as he went but he strode with an air of circumstance nonetheless.

When Jeppo awoke, Matanya was standing over him. She had pushed him gently with her arms. "Wake up, husband," she said, smiling.

"Matanya?" said Jeppo, his manner changing from drowsy to alarmed. "What? Have I overslept?" He looked toward the high windows along the same wall as his headboard. A dim light shone through them, but Jeppo imagined by her presence that it was well past midday.

"It is dawn, Monkey," she replied, laughing. "You have not overslept, husband. Come with me. I have made the tea."

Jeppo followed Matanya into the kitchen and each filled a bowl with tea and sat in the wooden chairs near the small table used for chopping. He was perplexed at Matanya's behavior. She was vivacious now. Here color was better and her face wore a constant smile. This was not a foreign aspect for her, but a return to her manner of years before. Had he dreamed Matanya's complaints? Had he only dreamed all the years that she had suffered so?

"How do you feel, Sparrow?" he said to her, and he took

another sip of tea, all the while his eyes darted busily around her face, searching for the signs of age and despair to which he had reluctantly become accustomed. They were not there. This is a years-younger woman, he thought.

"I am fit as a young mare," Matanya exclaimed. "And I have much to do today. The wedding."

"The wedding," said Jeppo. "Aye. And it is just past dawn now."

"Aye," she replied. "And it is the most beautiful, glorious morning."

"Then I beg you, Sparrow. Do not exhaust yourself today. I know this wedding is very important to you."

"Do not worry, Monkey," she said cupping his cheek in her palm. "I have no pain and no stiffness in my joints. At least not much, and it seems to reduce as the moments pass. I feel it has lifted my spirits. And my appetite has risen to meet them. I shall prepare a board from the cooling bin, dear. What do you want?"

"Whatever fleshy fruit, there might be," Jeppo focused momentarily on breakfast. "And some of the bread. And the goat cheese, the firm kind. And grapes. Oh, and the fruit of pomegranates. Please prepare them yourself and throw...."

"Aye, Monkey," she replied, laughing. "I have not prepared breakfast for a long time but I still remember. You will not have to see the pock-marked flesh of the pomegranates."

"Do you think it was that treatment last night?" He asked his woman.

"That must be it," she replied, startled. "I had forgotten that." She held her hands over her face to mimic the treatment Vomcot had prescribed. "I had forgotten it. Aye, it was probably that treatment with the wet cloth. Was that sorcery?" Her brow was knitted with worry now.

"Nay," Jeppo said. "It was only the work of the surgeon... healer named Vomcot. He is a devout Thujwani and would not practice sorcery. But I would not tell others of this treatment. It is to be our secret."

"Why is that, husband?"

"It is frowned upon by the priests, and the surgeons, of course," he explained. "They believe it is a spur to unfaithfulness. I think they just want to discourage competition. But this is not something we can pursue. It has served us well for the nonce but we are bound by our fealty with a our brother guildsmen."

"Then if anyone asks me why I am so hearty," she replied. "I will credit the meal of guamji we had."

Jeppo smiled and started chewing on a grape. He was thinking about why Mincon had invited them to the wedding. The brickweaving lord had hosted numerous weddings before and he and Matanya had never been invited. It was not unusual, considering their lack of issue. But why the change now, he wondered. Perhaps it didn't matter. Matanya was happy to have been called to attend after all these years of isolation. And she was also healthier than she'd been in some time. He decided he must make it a point to thank the healer on the morrow, and pay his fee of course, and perhaps inquire about the man they had rescued. He recalled the man's name was "Brumajin".

Vomcot went to the infirmary soon after waking. He entered with two bowls of tea and found the stranger's bed was empty. Looking around the room, he caught sight of a figure in the shadows, the stranger, who emerged into a ray of light shining from one of the high windows.

"Healer," said Atos his arms outstretched to display his figure. "I am cured. My wounds are healed."

"That is good, master," he offered Atos one of the bowls. "I am not surprised. How are your legs?"

"Strong as a goat's," he replied smiling broadly and jumped from side to side as proof.

"That is good," said Vomcot. "That is good. I would expect to release you today but you have no place to go, do you?"

"Aye," said Atos, losing his smile, but speaking as though it was not a bothersome condition. "My absence has been prolonged, far longer than I had guessed. There is sure to be no memory of me here."

"Had you not children who might still reside here?" asked Vomcot.

"Nay. My children are long gone," Atos replied. "They would have no residence in this city now."

"That is unfortunate," said the healer. "What of your craft? Would you find employment there, and then build a residence?"

"Aye," wondered Atos. "That might be my future, though I question it. I must find the man who rescued me first. Perhaps he can employ my skills. He is a brickweaver, you said?"

"Aye," said Vomcot. "His workshop is not far from here. But he may not be there today. There is a great wedding in the city and all the guildsmen and their families would surely be attending. We can go there tomorrow."

"Aye, aye," Atos replied. "That would be a good plan."

"Until then," added Vomcot. "You can stay here another night."

"That is kind of you, healer," Atos replied. "I have no gold but I may trade some knowledge for my lodging."

"Knowledge?" Vomcot was intrigued. "Of what sort?"

"You have showed me your writings of the Gelgak speech. What more do you know of them?" said Atos.

"More than most Thujwani," he said. "More than most towners as well." And then he paused and looked down as though he should be ashamed. "Very little, sir. I know these things: the Gelgak wear a cloak of various wet clays. It is called a 'mud skin' and they are of various colors due to the types of clays used. These colors signify the spiritual state of the Gelgak but I have not deciphered which color indicates which state.

"The Gelgak worship a godhead that rules the sandstorms in the high desert. They eat no meat, only fruit, and as such reside in the great forest near the wall and the orchards. That is all common knowledge but beyond those facts I have learned that the Gelgak language is complex and sought to grasp its meaning by first recording the sounds in writing, using the letters as they would sound if it were

Thujwani words that they speak. That is why I have used only a dot to represent the clicks.

"Beyond the facts, I have a theory about something far less well known. There is at times a great buzzing noise heard in parts of the farm town. It begins like the din of the cicada or the locust but soon acquires a rhythm that slowly plays out to silence. Towners believe it is a swarm of insects that produces these sounds. But I am sure I have recognized amid the noise of these events, the sound of individual clicks such as those enunciated by the Gelgak. I believe this noise to be caused by the Gelgak, all clicking at once in various ways, and I believe the rhythmic conclusion to these events to be a moment of agreement among the arguing tribesmen."

Atos appeared stunned. "That is truly remarkable," he said at last. "Let me tell you this to begin with. Save for their diet of fruit and their forest habitat, the 'facts' that you relate about the Gelgak are incorrect. Your 'theory' however, is so near the truth that I am astounded by your analytical powers. Had only you not been burdened by legend, you might have found the truth on your own.

"First, I should make it clear to you that the Gelgak have no god," Atos folded his hands as if to emphasize the point. "Let me explain. The human being is born with two strong traits: curiosity and reverence. The latter trait is found in both Thujwani and Gelgak in equal measure yet the Thujwani have invested only one being with their reverence while the Gelgak have cast it around to all creatures. For them, harming another being is as great a sin as disobeying the will of Thujwun for our people. This has made them a very gentle race. And without the shackles a single god can place on the mind, their curiosity is without bounds. It is enhanced by their complex language, which enables them to share their knowledge and powers of thought to understand truths that would evade the learning capacity of a single mind."

"The great noise?" asked Vomcot.

"Aye, the great noise," replied Atos. "That is their reckoning time, with every Gelgak voice taking part. It begins much like the bustle of the marketplace, many voices speaking in different keys and tones. They argue much and with vigor, but that is their only violence, for while our language and the languages of most men can boil the blood with rhetoric and spur men to fighting, the baser urges are exhausted by the Gelgak's strange speech, if it can be called a 'speech' at all.

"As that swell of anger dissipates, and agreement arise among them, the great noise becomes a rhythm anon. This rhythm becomes the solution to a problem, the recognition of a truth or a well-agreed call to action. I have not deciphered the specific meaning of any such event myself but I have learned this much from my Gelgak assistant."

"And what of him, sir?" asked Vomcot, trying to grasp all that the stranger had said. "Would there be memory of him among the Gelgak?"

"There could be," said Atos. "The Gelgak have no writing as you rightly know. But they maintain their history through recitation. That is another use of the 'great noise'. It assures that the important details of their history are remembered through the generations. As long as even one Gelgak lives, a good part of their history will be known.

"But I do not know what details they would record in their history," Atos continued with a sigh. "It is possible that Oku-Kuk was not of as much importance to them, though in my Thujwani perspective, he would have been of great importance."

"Why is that?" responded Vomcot.

"Before I reply, sir," said Atos with some formality. "May I ask how much I have told you do you now accept as the truth?"

"I have no quarrel with anything you have said," replied Vomcot readily. "Your description of the Gelgak is in far more agreement with my limited experience than the beliefs I had held up to a few moments ago."

"And then one more question, sir," said Atos. "Can you be trusted to keep what I am to say to you a secret? What I am to tell you may be of interest to the city guards."

"Abandon that worry," said Vomcot laughing. "I am no friend to the guards. I am Thujwani but I do not hold much respect for the city guard knowing that they have caused hardship in the past for my neighbors. Let us go to my chambers nearby and you can speak freely. I reckon you are fit enough for a bowl of some Tawani ale."

Chapter 19

As Modeen and Rapusah retired to their wedding chamber following the ceremony in the temple of Thujwun, their relatives and friends and invited guests began to file into the great room of Mincon's tower where they would dine and drink until a priest delivered the word that the young couple's marriage had been consummated. Wedding banquets in the past had sometimes been long, worry-filled evenings, with guests departing well before the assurance was reported. At other times, the banquets had been embarrassing in their brevity because such alacrity in the marital chamber could be charged to either the wantonness of the bride or the brutishness of the groom.

Mincon and his woman were the first to arrive with their extended family following close behind. Tazil, his woman and their children then joined them, and finally the close relations of both families arrived as well as unrelated or distantly related persons of prominence. As Jeppo and Matanya strolled slowly into the room, a servant asked Jeppo his name and then motioned him to seats a few tables away from the great round one in the center of the room, on the side assigned to Rapusah's relations. It was, in fact, Kulla's table and Jeppo nodded to both the great judge at the other end of the oval and his own assistant who sat at Kulla's right side.

Zamchin sat far across the great room with his woman and his three young daughters, unhappy that his colleague was seated so far away. Alongside them sat Emblin, a trade master who dealt with towners all day, and next to him, his wife Sallin and their young daughter Sulluh.

"I am glad there are guards here today," Emblin whispered to his wife. "There are far too many towners here for my digestion to operate efficiently."

"I would ignore them, husband," replied Sallin. "I do not think they would dare steal from us with all these eyes watching."

"One never knows, woman. I swear my own commerce has fallen because of their treachery. Mazrash said there is another cause altogether, but I have my suspicions."

"Please, husband," she replied, forcing a smile to him. "Put that aside for today. Let our daughter enjoy this banquet."

At that moment the Morso giant Olmak walked past their table carrying a large bowl of steaming cracked wheat.

"Look at that one," Emblin continued, pointing to Olmak. "That is a freak and an abomination... a monster"

Olmak did not respond to what he heard but reflexively nodded his head in Emblin's direction, as a token bow to the guildsman.

"Look how he mocks me," he whispered to Sallin, who gently pushed his arm down to the table, signaling that he should desist in his complaints for the nonce at least. But Sulluh turned and smiled at the sight of the giant. She had never seen any other human as tall and his prominent features reminded her of the toy dolls made by Howoo craftsmen that she played with throughout the loneliest times of her day. Olmak reminded her especially of one of her dearest dolls, the old baker Slit-eyes, who was formerly known as old Fat-chin and before that, old Sausage-nose.

"What is your name, sir?" she asked the giant as he passed by her.

"Olmak, milady," he replied and hurried off with his bowl of cracked wheat.

"Please father," she said turning to Emblin. "May we have master Olmak fetch our food? He is very entertaining."

His daughter's formal address of a mere servant had such a ring of sarcasm to Emblin that he laughed out loud though he did not doubt the earnestness with which the sheltered child had said it.

"You need not call them 'master', child," said Emblin. "You are their better in all ways."

"Yet I will never be nearly so tall," she argued in return. "In that way I cannot be his better."

"All important ways, then," replied her father. He waved Olmak over as the servant had just placed the large bowl a few tables away. "Over here, 'master' Olmak," he shouted. The diners within earshot of his daughter's remark laughed at the mocking tone of Emblin's address.

Olmak turned and walked toward Emblin. "What is your wish, master?" he said, bowing and looking down.

"My daughter finds you amusing and wishes that you could fetch some food for us," said Emblin. "Please fetch us a bowl of spicy goat stew and for my daughter a plate of fruit and cold beef. That is all she eats."

"Aye, master," replied Olmak who backed away and navigated the clutter of tables to make his way to the larders were meats and fruits were kept cold. At the cold fruit stall he found sliced tamran and a pomegranate that he arranged on a plate with a half blood-lemon. At the nearby meat stall, carvers had laid out thin slices of beef, goat and boar. Olmak carefully arranged the choicest slices of beef on the same plate.

He carried the cold meal in one hand as he made his way to the stew kitchen. Here the cooks helpfully fetched bowls and filled them with whatever is requested from the several great heating bins they supervised. The cook Tabshir greeted Olmak as he approached.

"Hail to you, Olmak," said Tabshir. "What is the order?"

"I need a bowl of stew for man and wife to share... a bowl of the spicy goat please, cousin," said the giant.

"Aye," said Tabshir waving him to bend down closer, to hear his whisper. "There are two pots, Olmak. The stews are the same save for one ingredient, an adulteration provided by the stalwart Lallokin," at this Tabshir started to snicker. "He... he... well I tell you that you choose which pot by who is being served." Tabshir was now nearly unable to speak from his restrained laughter.

"I want none of you folly, cousin," Olmak whispered. "This is for Emblin, the trade master. He is a very prominent guildsman."

"Emblin?" said Tabshir. "He is well-known in the town. Well-known as a donkey's ass. Never mind. I will score this myself. You will not be credited with it."

Olmak thought of Emblin mocking him and the names he called him. He certainly deserved a citing in the whisper war. Tabshir thrust a bowl of spicy goat stew into Olmak's free hand.

"Be sure to serve this to master Emblin, cousin," he said with mock solemnity.

"And how has Lallokin tainted this stew then?" whispered the worried giant. "I will not be poisoning any guests."

"Aha, Olmak," whispered a smiling Tabshir. "You know how the whisper war works. Let me just tell you that before tainting the stew, our sturdy friend Lallokin repaired himself to a discreet chamber with a small bowl," Tabshir could hardly contain his amusement. "He returned flush-faced and pleased with himself."

Olmak noted the thick steam rising from the tainted pot in the chilly kitchen and decided the taint would do no harm. He was surprised by his own unbidden grin as he reminded himself that the guildsman had called him a "monster".

With two large bowls in his hands, he navigated the bustling banquet room floor with urgency. The chilled city air was wont to cool cooked food too rapidly and Olmak was determined to complete this service as quickly as possible, and without complaint. At Emblin's table, he set down the bowl of stew before the guildsman and carefully set the dish of cold dinner down before Emblin's daughter.

"That is well enough," said Emblin to the giant without looking directly at him. "My women and I will share this," and he pushed the bowl between them. They both drew spoons and Emblin took the first taste, smacking his lips loudly.

"This is a good stew," he said to Sallin. "Please partake of it."

"Aye, husband," she replied and took a spoonful, blew on the still steaming dollop, and delicately sipped the gravy. Sulluh watched as her parents enjoyed the dish. "May I have some of the stew, father?" she said. At that, Olmak, who had been walking away from the table, turned and stopped a short distance away.

"It is too spicy for you," said her father. "But lest you protest, I can give you a small taste." He dug into the bowl with his spoon and filled it. Then he carefully moved the full spoon over his daughter's plate and let a small amount of gravy fall to a slice of the beef. As she reached to take the gravied slice, Olmak acted without thinking to prevent the child from eating the sullied fare. He tried to move her plate out of reach but he stumbled in the attempt and fell against the girl, his large and heavy frame pinning her to the table.

"My arm! My arm!" Sulluh screamed and soon her left arm began to redden and swell. Two guards were already upon the giant and two more soon joined them. They took hold of Olmak's long arms as one of the guards raised his bludgeon high and struck the giant across the head. Sallin looked horrified as she rose and leaped to her daughter's side while her husband reflexively leaned back away from the scene. Olmak was swiftly removed by the guards, still conscious but woozy from the bludgeon's blow. Soon surgical assistants arrived with a litter and carefully laid the young girl upon it. She was crying now and holding her arm, which had already started to return to its normal size and complexion.

At Kulla's table, Matanya turned to the woman who sat next to her, Migdilla, the wife of one of Kulkulla's cousins. "I think I know that servant," she said. "I think he is related to my housekeep. I hope the child will be ok."

"The child will fair better than that servant," Migdilla replied. "My husband is a judge and he has told me of such incidents. The servant will be tortured," and here she whispered. "That will be done to extract the reason for his miscreancy. He will be tried on the mere fact that he caused harm, regardless of his intentions."

"And he should be," said Tavan, an older woman with a pinched mouth and deep voice who sat across the table from Migdilla. "He was doubtless intending to attack her."

"For what?" said Matanya, sharply. "Why would the fellow attack a young girl?"

"He was doubtless lust-mad for her," Tavan growled with an air of certainty that had always ended debate. "This is the state to which these people have fallen."

"There are steps, milady," and here Matanya showed a sarcastic edge to the epithet. "The ablest servant might easily trip on them. This fellow is tall and his footfalls are awkward. I would guess he is not a house servant at all and these floors are foreign to him."

"That may be true," said Tavan, raising one graying eyebrow. "But the law must ensure the safety of our children. This is a faithless servant, after all. There can be no chance taken with his fate as long as it is possible he is lust-mad. I tell you I sleep deeply knowing my husband and yours, Migdilla, will follow the law and banish all the possible dangers."

Matanya returned to her plate as most of the other guests had already done. Inside she seethed with anger. Such talk among other women, which in recent years had only been at temple or in the marketplace, had usually saddened her and slowed her steps or made the ache in her joints flare exquisitely for a moment. But without her usual complaint, she now felt only the early stirrings of a bitter rage.

"This draught is good," said Atos as he poured more Tawani ale into his mouth. "I can feel it down in my belly and there is a warmth that radiates from there to my entire body."

"Have you not known this drink before?" asked Vomcot. "It is very common in the farm town. Less so in the city."

"Nay, I have not known much from the Tawani," he replied, feeling more relaxed with each sip. "I tell you, there is much I will say that you shall choose not to believe."

"Then try out my gullibility, sir," said Vomcot jauntily, having already imbibed a few draughts himself. "I am in the mood for a good story, true or not."

"Very well then," said Atos. "Remember that I have been away from Thujwa for many years."

"Aye," said Vomcot. "That much I agree. You are a brickweaver by trade yet your rescuer knew not of you."

Atos laughed. "I would reckon that the man knows something of me but not by the name with which I had disguised myself."

"That may be a truth," said Vomcot. "Why would you not give your true name, Atos?"

"For this simple fact, sir," he replied, his tone now shifted to the more grave. "I am not just a brickweaver, sir. I am the first of that trade."

"This is truly a good story," Vomcot chuckled, adjusting his posture to make himself more comfortable. "I have encountered fanciful boasts from guildsmen before but this is surely the best."

"This is not a joke, sir," asserted Atos. "I have told you of the Gelgak and their mastery of the clays, and of my assistant Oku-kuk. Together, the two of us contrived a way to hold the power of the clays in brick."

Vomcot stared at his guest. His thinking organs had so surely begun to analyze the man's words that he felt his intoxication from the ale drifting away. The man's assertions made some kind of sense, at least in that there was consistency between what he was claiming and his odd behavior. Vomcot had encountered many men and women in his practice who had lost their thinking but they did not speak so carefully and logically about the world their madness had created.

"Sir," he said at last. "I have some schooling in the history of Thujwa. The trade of brickweaving has been practiced for at least several centuries. It is an old trade."

"Aye it is," said Atos. "The walls of the old city Koosh, where I was found, are brickwoven, and I trust they still stand despite their age. While walls in this farm town that were likely raised within your lifetime fall now to cracks and rubble.

"I am not an elderly man, as I appear to you," he continued. "But in truth I have been gone from this earth for myriad years."

"Gone?" asked Vomcot. "Gone to where?"

"I can only guess at the proper word for it," Atos said. "But I think that it would be 'oblivion'."

"Oblivion?" said the healer. "The sacred texts speak of this. It is a place that is no place at all, a nothingness," the retreat of the ale's effects had only been for a moment and now they advanced upon his sobriety in a wave. "By what miracle of Thujwun did this occur?"

"This was no miracle," said Atos. "It occurred by the application of the all-binding power, the same power that pulls a thrown rock back to the sand beneath it. Imagine that power so focused on a single rock that all the space around it was pulled to its center. And do you know of the sword-binding as well?"

"Aye," said Vomcot. "It is a magical power entrusted by Thujwun to the brickweavers, or so the common history states. It causes the sword to bind to anything that wields such a force, and anything made from sword metal as well."

"You are good student," said Atos. "It is unfortunate that your teachers were themselves so poor at the task. This sword-binding force is no magic itself. It is found in small amounts around us and the earth itself has given up rock that wields it without a brickweaver's crafting. But in the hands of a brickweaver, this force can be applied in terrific strengths to produce all-binding in equal measure, which can itself bend the very contours of earth and time. I designed brickwork that did just that very thing and it has brought me here, across the many centuries."

"And to what purpose did this occur, if even it did?" said Vomcot, now so puzzled by the words spoken by his guest as to avoid astonishment at what he at least thought the man might be saying. "You have journeyed through time? I am not ready to believe so."

"It was not a journey, healer," said Atos, a little puzzled himself now that he was enunciating his suspicions about what had happened to him. "I had made a special box of twice-kilned brickwork that was placed beneath the city. It was a prison of sorts and the guards had beaten me and thrown me into it. This prison exerted both of the powerful binding forces in great amounts. It was to be my... execution chamber." Atos was carefully holding back some of the truth, that of which he was ashamed. "What the guards did not know proved to be my rescue. I was expecting my arrest and so had built a second box in Koosh and these two were tied together by the forces such that their interiors could be said to have been one.

"I was imprisoned in the Thujwa box many centuries ago," he continued. "And released from that very same place when your brickweaver friend opened the other box's door in Koosh only a few days past."

"If that is true, sir," said Vomcot. "How would a man pass the time for so long?"

"You do not quite understand, I am afraid," replied Atos after a few more sips of ale. "You could say that I did not so much pass time as time itself passed me."

"I think my bowl is empty, sir," responded Vomcot. "Perhaps if I refill it I can grasp your words better. I am trying to understand but you give me little proof. And I have yet to even reckon what proof would be for these strange things."

Vomcot poured himself another bowl of the ale.

"Then walk with me outside, healer, and I will try to make an argument in my favor."

The two men had had enough ale that when they stood up their legs felt a little wobbly but they both managed to gain their footing after a short while. They stepped out through Vomcot's front door and stood at the edge of the town street, though it was nothing more than pounded earth here. Atos pointed up the road past the cluster of adobe structures that surrounded the great fountain. From here one could see all the way up the south road to the city, where the distant towers at the city's heart appeared like a cluster of bristles in the waning afternoon light.

"Do you see that highest tower?" said Atos.

"Aye," replied Vomcot. "I reckon that to be the hierophant's tower."

"That it is, healer," replied Atos. "Now how many stories is that tower?"

"I know the great towers of the guilds or the prominent families are twenty to forty stories high. That one seems to be twice as high is the others. I reckon a hundred stories?"

"Aye," said Atos. "Or thereabouts. Have you ever been in that tower?"

"Nay, sir," said Vomcot. "I have never been called there."

"Well at least entertain this argument: As you may know, the hierophant lives at the highest story of that tower...."

"In a level that does not touch the level below it. So that his holiness is not bound to earth," added Vomcot, looking to the sky to avoid distraction as his ale-soaked thoughts fought to unearth the well-learned lessons from his scholastic days.

"Aye," said Atos. "And his holiness is wont at times to call a citizen for an audience. Such a visitor would have to climb one hundred flights of stairs. Even though the all-binding can be used to ease that ascent, it is still a lengthy journey. So an accommodation was made. These boxes I told you of, there are two more like them, earlier models with slightly different properties. One is placed at the tenth floor, the other just below his holiness's chambers, a hundred stories apart. Ask any you know who has been there, and he shall confirm this."

Vomcot looked out at the cityscape and pondered Atos' argument. He could confirm none of this save the very fact of the distant tower's phenomenal height and the situation in which the hierophant lives. An accommodation might be necessary for visitors, he thought. He found Atos' story to be convincing at least in regard to the man's unfailing assuredness in telling it. Atos was no liar, thought Vomcot. Either that or he was an unnaturally good liar. Or he was mad.

As the two men stood at the roadside, they could also see great barks filled with servants moving down the south road. Vomcot had seen the great rush of returning servants and laborers nearly every day in the Surrel. They were always on foot and tired but boisterous. He could hear their voices as they approached the farm town's center. There was laughter and shouting at times. But not among these servants who were quiet and sad-faced. City guards piloted the barks, manning four or five to each one. They carried swords along with their usual bludgeons and continually surveyed the passengers in their charge.

"Something is wrong," said Vomcot as he watched the barks arrive at the great fountain north of the infirmary. "The tribal people are returning under the command of the guard. I know that some left that way this morning but not this many."

Ten to twelve barks stopped at a time and the servants disembarked soon after at the fountain piazza. There they headed toward their homes, slowly at first, the younger ones running as soon as they were out of sight of the guards. The sun-baked structures around the area where the barks gathered began to shift slightly but audibly, sounding like a fine rain, owing to the interplay of the powerful forces created by so many of the vehicles together. Even the woven bricks of the great fountain could be heard to move slightly in the wake of the barks' errant forces.

As he opened his eyes and shuddered from the cold water just splashed against his face, Olmak found himself in a chamber illuminated entirely by the blue light of pressed quartz. The light was bright and eye piercing unlike the subdued quartz lamps of the city streets. Even the cracking and hissing of the lamps was louder and in a higher pitch in this place. He sat in a large chair made of twice-fired brick, glossy and glowing in the bright lights.

He had been stripped down to a simple, knee-length tunic, now smudged with blood and sand. It was heavy and cold from the drenching. He could not rise though there seemed to be nothing holding his limbs to the chair. It was the all-binding, no doubt, that held him, a force to which his people ascribed the magic of the Thujwani's dark demon god.

Another splash of water and Olmak thrashed his head one way and another, like a goat that had splashed through a puddle.

"Are you awake then, giant?" the guard Atavis stood before Olmak, grinning and hefting a large jug of water with both hands. "Are you ready to confess your miscreancy?"

Olmak felt a blow to his belly as the other guard, Donyon, wielded a bludgeon to it. The thin, excitable guard was not the strongest bludgeoner on the force but that was no comfort to Olmak, as an electric flare of pain spread from his solar plexus.

"I am sorry for hurting the child," he said at last, after the shock of the blow had diminished enough for him to speak.

"That has no meaning here, miscreant," said Atavis bitterly. "The facts are that you fell upon this child, the child of a guildsman, and we must know why."

"I fell, sir," replied the giant. "I missed a step and fell. It was a happenstance."

"A happenstance?" said Atavis. "I think it was no happenstance. You were seen by reputable Thujwani to have reached out to harm her with," and here he produced a scroll that he rolled out to read from directly. "To harm her with 'a look of madness on your face.' "

How could he explain, Olmak thought, about the tainted stew?

Why had he suddenly turned to stop her from eating it? What real harm was there in that? He did not himself understand his motives but was now expected to explain them to the guards. The pain of his bruises, the cold of the chamber and the invisible grasp of the brickwoven chair drained his mental faculties. I am a fool, he thought, for trying to stop her from eating the stew. He shuddered again as a cool draught of air brushed past his soaked raiment. He would have to fashion a fiction for this incident, the truth about the tainted stew would only bring more trouble for his cousins, and maybe all of farm town.

"I saw that she was being given the spicy food and feared it would upset her digestion," Olmak said weakly.

Donyon had been grinning with amusement at the insults to this giant man that he, a scrawny, poor student of a guard could deliver. But his expression grew sterner now as he sensed an affront from the prisoner.

"Are we to believe, sand-eater, that you have better say over this child's care than her own father?" he was angry beyond Olmak's understanding. The guard had taken offense at his prisoner's assertion despite the long history of towners as house servants and nannies. Olmak's kin had spent more time with the Thujwani's children from birth to the first year of the scholastics than their own parents.

Atavis pulled Donyon aside and whispered to him. "It is not just to call this man a 'sand-eater', brother," he admonished. "We are required by our office, and our faith, to abandon such name-calling."

"Yea," said Donyon, his rage cooled somewhat by this sanction. "That was an error I made. But I am so astounded at times by the conceit of these dusky, unfaithful people. I have been to the farm town and, you know, they treat us like miscreants there. They walk with the posture of a king among us and their children snicker and point to us when they are out of reach of the bludgeon. They are such cowardly fools."

"Aye, brother. It is hard work for us but we are above them and must always practice to be that way."

The two turned to their prisoner again. "I find no truth in your story," said Atavis officiously. "I suspect you had a foul motive for attacking the child. I am a faithful man," he continued, leaning close to Olmak's bruised face. "So I have no ken for the foul motives of the unfaithful. You will have to confess your reasons anon. All that is unknown is how much you will suffer before speaking the truth."

"But I swear, sir," pleaded Olmak. At that, Atavis walked around behind the brickwoven chair and adjusted a small iron rod that prodtruded from the back of it. The seat pulled tighter against Olmak's thighs, the arm-rests prevented even the spreading of his fingers much less the movement of his hands from its otherwise slippery, well-glazed surface and his back was held so fiercely that he felt his belly might be pulled completely inward. Pain again flared in his abdomen and as the all-binding tugged inexorably at his lungs, he became alarmed at the shortness of his breathing. He felt as though he were drowning but this alarm was trumped by a pain like a strong hand grasping his heart and clenching it unmercifully. Moments passed and the clenching did not relax and if it had been an actual hand, it surely would have been a hand of stone or iron.

Soon the cold, blue-lit chamber fell away and Olmak was sure he was in the desert again. The guards were gone and he was lying face down, feeling the warmth of the desert sun on his back, hurting from some trivial bruise. How good he felt, though. Something wet and warm was touching his hand. He turned to look and there was a small grey goatling, a kid with no horns, staring at him with bright eyes. It had been licking his hand and now with Olmak showing a sign of life, the creature made an exultant "Baaaah!"

"Ashpot," he said without emotion, if only to convince himself that this long departed companion was real and this was not a dream. The goatling, he remembered, had grown old and had died many years past. "Baaaah!" insisted Ashpot, as though to assure him that this moment was indeed real and all that he had thought he remembered was a fevered dream.

He turned and saw two small dark feet in sandals. Looking up he saw a young girl, which reminded him of the issue at hand though his mind was wont to let that slip away. Compared to the Thujwani girl, she was darker skinned and wore a more brightly colored robe. She extended a slender hand to him and spoke.

"Cousin, you are crying," she said. "There is no need for that. You are better than those boys. You are the son of a prince."

She smiled at him and extended her hand.

"Little Bird?" he said, as she grasped his hand and helped him to his feet. And then this gentler grasp released, and the desert was gone, and all was darkness, and there was nothing.

The wedding banquet had not lasted much longer past the incident with Olmak and Sulluh. An aged priest had appeared anon and had carefully made his way to the center table on a small floating cart, as he was missing both his legs. When he was at Mincon's side, he had introduced himself with much formality and because his speech had slowed so much with ill health, the greetings had taken a while and his chosen epithets were so archaic some allusions were lost even to Mincon. But he eventually managed to produce a large, crumpled white cloth and hand it over to the lord of the brickweavers. Some guests recoiled in horror when Mincon made a show of sniffing the opened cloth. He then declared in a loud voice that the marriage had been adjudged as consummated and the guests could be on their way.

Jeppo was not a little intoxicated by the rare treat of Tawani beer at the event and was a less than careful pilot of the sledge that carried him and Matanya back to their small tower. At times the conveyance accelerated abruptly or halted at random moments. This was the hour of the day when many servants were heading in the same direction, toward the south road, and he needed to take pains to avoid hitting any of them. But there were, thankfully, fewer of them today, as many had already been conveyed away by great barks on which they were accompanied by many guards, owing to concerns over the incident at the banquet.

As they entered their home, Lavena greeted them at the door. She was crying.

"Milady," she said to Matanya. "I have been told that Olmak

has been arrested. Is this true?"

"Aye, dear," Matanya replied, as she pulled her closer to embrace this woman she had never seen cry before. "There was an accident at the banquet and he was taken away by the guards."

"What happened?" she replied. "The boy who told me heard it from another. You saw what happened?"

"Aye. Our table was away on some wise from where it occurred but I heard a child scream and saw that your Olmak was atop her. I think he had fallen from a step."

"Then he is not regarded a miscreant?" she said, hopefully. "They have not arrested him for miscreancy?"

"The guards did take him away," interjected Jeppo. "But that does not mean he was arrested. It is purely a formality."

"I have never..." and here Lavena paused and eyed Jeppo. Then she looked down and spoke in a careful, measured voice, "I have never heard of one of my people, or any of the Surrel people, who had been taken by the guards and not arrested."

"Aye, you are right to worry," the beer had rendered Jeppo's manner blunt and casual, even when speaking to a servant. "The guards do not like to take action without justifying an arrest so they may have had him charged a miscreant for this accident."

"I am afraid that what my husband says is true," said Matanya, and she turned to give Jeppo a bitter look. "Even if he is so unkind in his saying of it."

"I shall make some tea, then," said Jeppo, who left them in the entranceway and made his way to the kitchen feeling wobbly due to both the beer and the reproach.

"He will be killed, I fear," said Lavena through her tears. "Olmak is very special to me. His size is an accident of birth and it came with other problems as well. When we were children the other boys would tease and bully him, so we would play together. Can anything be done?"

"I am not sure, dear," and Matanya looked wistfully towards the kitchen. "Sometimes the old monkey has more in him than one would guess. If something can be done, then we shall do it, my dear."

"Your words grant me hope, milady," she said.

Matanya hugged her tightly, then pushed her away and said with mock sharpness, "But you must be away now. It is time for your journey home and you would not want to be left by the throng, dear Lavena."

"That is true, milady," she said and took her leave.

Matanya joined Jeppo in the kitchen and asked him for a bowl of the same tea that he was sipping noisily.

"Anything for my Shparrow," he said, jauntily. "Lavena... she is very upset."

"Aye," said Matanya. "This will not go well. Is there anything you can do, Monkey? Lavena has been a good servant."

"She hash been more than that, for my dear Shparrow," he replied. "She ish your good friend, ish she not?"

Matanya recognized the effect that beer had on her husband, though she had not seen it for a long time. Such a quiet man usually, but when given beer his aspect became jovial and sentimental at the same time.

"Aye, Monkey, she is my good friend. And I hope this does not hurt her too deeply or for too long."

"Then, my Shparrow, I hoist thish bowl to declare that I will do what I can tomorrow to rectify thish," said Jeppo as some hot tea sloshed out of the raised vessel and burnt his fingertips.

Chapter 20

Dawn had not yet broken when the bark made its way down the south road. A single quartz lamp, glowing a bright blue and making an occasional cracking noise, was mounted on its front hull. Four guards stood fast near the edges while a fifth, their master, stood at the front piloting the conveyance. On the bark's bed lay a cloth bag that bulged irregularly in places along its length, which was two footlengths or more beyond the length of the average man's body. It was cinched at the top by a leather thong and remained motionless throughout the journey, held fast as it was to floor of the bark.

Long after the road had run down to pounded dirt, the guards could see the first glow of dawn to the east and by the time they had reached the great fountain, the farm town itself was bathed in the honey-colored light of early morning. Here Howoo and Tawani gathered, along with M'Butu and Morso, as the laborers and servants stopped to fill their water bladders at the large, circular brickwoven basin. The bark finally halted at the square near the fountain as marketsellers began to set up their stalls and lay out their wares. Though it was stopped, the bark continued to hover, which was the usual practice of guards in this hostile territory. The master motioned to his lieutenants to carry the bark's cargo to a nearby bench but they had miscalculated and the bench was not long enough. Instead they lay it down on the stone floor that surrounded the fountain and stood in formation around it, as if to protect its contents from thieves.

"Hear ye, people of farm town," the master shouted to the crowd, which continued to thicken yet encircled the guards and their bludgeons at a safe distance. "Who shall claim this body? It is the remains of one called 'Olmak'."

The sound of the master's words reached Lavena, who had been filling her bladder, and she dropped it into the basin. A Morso man beside her bent down to fish it out as the housekeep pushed her way through the crowd toward the guards.

"My cousin! My cousin!" she shouted, close to tears. "What has happened to him?"

"This man," replied the master. "He had attacked a child at a wedding banquet. When questioned, his guilt was so strong as to have weakened his heart. That was the report of the surgeons who examined him after death."

Lavena hastily loosened the top of the bag and pulled the cloth down to reveal the familiar face of her giant cousin. "Giraffe," she said to Olmak's bloodied, lifeless face. "It is I, your little bird." She cradled his large head in her hands and was not so much shocked by the dried blood and dirt as the stiffness of the cold flesh she now held so gently. She turned to the guards master and shouted, "Murderers! Murderers!" The crowd followed her refrain, alarming the master who directed his men to return to the bark. One of their force was standing near Lavena and reflexively sought to silence the woman by raising his bludgeon but another hand took it from him. And soon the unwary guard felt a sharp blow to his own head. He fell unconscious and his three comrades quickly returned to the bark, raising their bludgeons at the people who followed them.

"You must return that man to us or there will be consequences!" shouted the master, his eyes bulging from fear, his words choked by it. At the same time he adjusted the iron key on the bark to turn the vehicle around. The towner who hefted the bludgeon now threw it toward the bark and despite the vehicle's rising velocity, it found its way to the leg of another guard standing in the rear, who bent down to clutch his bruised limb and wince from the pain of the blow.

Amid cries of "Murderer!" and "Devils!", Lavena, still crouching near the body of her dead cousin, shouted in a clear voice to the crowd around her, ready as the people were to pounce on the fallen guard. "This guard shall come to no harm! We shall send him back to his comrades with our demand."

"What is our demand, mother?" said Effel, the young Morso standing near her.

"We demand the murderers of our good man Olmak. We will show them Morso justice. We will not harm this man further. We are not Thujwani," she said, reminding herself that her long passed father was a king of the Morso. There will come a day, I pray, he had told Lavena, that you will rise up and lead. His father had told him the same, and his father before.

She gently lowered Olmak's head back to the ground and Effel helped her up to the edge of the basin's wall.

"Hear me, people of farm town," Lavena spoke loudly to quiet the noise of the rabble. "Hear me now. You are all workers in the city. Have you ever seen more masters than workers?"

"Nay!" came shouts from the crowd.

"We Morso may not outnumber them, but with the Howoo and the M'butu and the Tawani, we are more than their strength."

"Aye!" many shouted.

"We will serve them no longer! We will not be murdered by them again," she roared. "You have all known my cousin, the giant Olmak. We have all known his kindness and charity. He was such a gentle man and ... and they have murdered him."

Shouts of "Murderers!" rose again from the crowd.

Lavena's words came strong and forcefully, but with great effort. Her chest heaved at every sentence, as though the breath were being sucked out of her lungs. "You shall not tend the fields today, my people of the Surrel," she continued. "You shall not herd the goats, nor empty the barks, nor work in the kilns or the mills or the towers. We shall walk north as we do every morning, but we shall walk in the same gait, like our armies of old. We shall bring them their abandoned guard, unharmed. And we shall demand those who murdered Olmak for his return. We shall show them our justice!"

Shouts of "Huzzah!" rose from the crowd, along with more shouts of "murderers" and "justice".

"Fill your bladders, for we have a long walk and we must leave anon!" She said finally and some of the throng scrambled to the fountain's edge. A few of those gathered withdrew slowly, in fear. Many thought of the dramas performed there in the fountain square, in the evenings, when no regular Thujwani could be seen in the vicinity. Actors would portray the great chiefs and kings and generals of the various tribes in stories held since the oldest times, well before the rescue, when their people's lives were fraught with great struggle but they governed their own destinies, for better or worse. It seemed so foreign a time and world to most of the towners that such stories became the tales told to children or rousing entertainments for a beer-besotted audience of laborers. But having retained the narratives of freedoms past, they knew the world did not have to be the same as they had known it in their own lives.

As the marchers began forming, the captured guard was crouched down and shivering from worry. A few of the towners had tied his hands behind his back and were preparing a long leather thong to use as a slip-noose and leash. Lavena stood nearby talking with the chiefs of some of the other tribes. Her posture and speech were still forceful and strident. Part of her wanted to crouch over Olmak's body and wail with abandon. This is how the women who had raised her had taught her to react to the death of a loved one. But grief only seemed to fuel her anger. She could not think of her loss just now, or the effect her actions today might have on her people, or her employers. All that was of any importance to her in this moment was the attainment of justice.

When the march began, the vanguard was formed of Lavena and the other leaders, but just ahead were two Morso brothers who tended to the captured guard, himself forced to walk ahead of them, the noose of his leash loosely wound around his neck, the other end given to a Tawani chieftain to hold. Behind the vanguard was as diverse a mix of human forms as could be seen on any normal day at the farm town market or the morning and evening journeys of servants and laborers along the south road. Indeed, this was the hour when they would normally be walking to the workplace. It was not entirely clear to those farther back in the crowd that this was not their regular morning journey.

When Jeppo arrived at Kulla's tower, his assistant Kulkulla was already waiting with his water bladder and two bags, a small one that contained some sturdy food and a much larger one that was challenging to carry due to its weight and size.

"Hail, master," said Kulkulla, smiling.

"Greetings, boy," said Jeppo unhappily. The rare beer drinking he had done the day before had produced another rare experience for him, a miasma of nausea, headache and what the surgeons grandly called a "pitiable shyness of the sensory organs". "I wonder," he said to the youth. "I wonder if you could pilot today?"

Kulkulla's expression fell quickly from smile to frown, and then he took a deep breath.

"Aye, sir," he replied. "I have a fair knowledge of the fundamentals, sir. I've been watching how you fiddle with the key and to what effect, when we have been on our rides. But sir, think not poorly of me if you could remind me of the maneuvers once again," he said, making his best effort to speak with confidence but he did so in a halting manner.

Jeppo looked askance at him. That the sunlight hurt his eyes made the prospect of Kulkulla's piloting only a little more comfortable than it would normally but he was dubious nonetheless. Given his condition, however, it was riskier perhaps to pilot himself and it would certainly be more comfortable to simply ride with his eyes closed and feel the brisk morning wind against his aching body.

"Aye, take a close look here and I will show you," said Jeppo at last. "Follow my hands as though I were touching the key," he began. The lesson did not take long and the two were up and off at near enough their usual time. Jeppo shaded his eyes from the sun and looked over Kulkulla's shoulder along the way. He said little to direct his assistant, largely because the rush of wind was too loud for any talking below a shout to be heard. The sledge's speed was sometimes variable on this journey and the direction was not always straight nor the turns always smooth but they had encountered no other travelers, not even the familiar wave of laborers advancing to the industrial lands. Jeppo glanced toward the sky and determined from the sun's position that this was the usual time for such migrations. Yet there was no sight of any figures crossing the desert in that direction. Something had happened, thought Jeppo, but as ominous as the prospect was, he was grateful that Kulkulla's first test as a sledge pilot could be completed in such abandoned landscape.

As they caught sight of the workshop off to the east, Jeppo look in the direction of the south road. Normally there would be a stream of servants and sellers making their way toward the city at this hour. But Jeppo saw no one. He wondered if Lavena would be attending to Matanya today. She was so upset last evening, he thought, about her cousin. He reminded himself to visit the guild in the afternoon and discover what he could about the cousin's fate.

With the workshop just rising over the horizon, the sledge abruptly halted and the two were thrown forward from it into the sand along with their baggage. Kulkulla apologized repeatedly to Jeppo for the error. He had maneuvered the key in such a way as to sever the influence between the sword-binding and the all-binding brick matrices. This simultaneously ended the forward advance of the vehicle as well as the hovering and the fastening of cargo. Fortunately, the large parcel was unharmed, its consignment of pottery shards glued together with potters pitch was undamaged in the throw to the sand, possibly because the midmorning heat had softened the pitch enough to make it elastic.

"You are not to stop a sledge with those turns of the key," said Jeppo sternly. "That will cause happenstances as we have just suffered. Turn the key in these ways, but slowly. That turn you did is how you must leave the sledge but stopping is more complicated." He showed Kulkulla a few more times and then the two gathered up their parcels onto the sledge.

"I am curious about something, apprentice," Jeppo said as Kulkulla prepared to restart the vehicle. "There is something amiss in the farm town, I think. I need to run an errand there so we might as well go now."

"You wish to go to the farm town?" replied Kulkulla. "Is it to a place I know?"

"Aye," said Jeppo. "I need to repay the healer Vomcot. You know his infirmary?"

"Aye, sire," replied the youth with some excitement. "We can inquire about the man from Koosh."

Jeppo's headache was worse. Both from the heat and the swirl of thoughts he was trying to process. He had forgotten about the stranger. Aye, he thought, it would be another curiosity satisfied to learn his story. Perhaps Vomcot would have much to tell about him.

After a few awkward lunges, the sledge took off toward the south. Skirting the south road they would be entering farm town from the east, closer to Vomcot's infirmary. But even at this distance they could see the crowd gathered where the south road meets the fountain square. From his perspective, Jeppo could also see, at last, some movement on the road. A few sledges were charging down from the north. They disappeared behind a dune as Kulkulla piloted the sledge closer to their destination.

The library of the brickweavers guild comprises a vast chamber with great shelves rising from floor to ceiling. There are thousands of scrolls carefully organized by era and discipline. Galel was rummaging through the history section, particularly the early guild histories. Mincon waited at a great dark table where his assistant had already piled documents. He was deep into study when the otherwise quiet room rang with the sound of footsteps. Mincon looked up and saw a guards master before him, with the brickweaver Betran at his side.

"Excuse my intrusion, lord," said the guildsman. "This guards master Ollon is here with urgent news. He insisted I bring him to you."

"What is your news master?" said Mincon. "That it should justify this intrusion into our library by another guild."

"Sire," replied Ollon. "I have no wish to steal your secrets. I am here on orders from Lord Orten. The towners have not shown at their workplaces. They are gathering on the south road but their numbers are too many. Lord Orten said that you would have a solution to this problem."

"Why have they done this?" asked the aged lord. "What has happened?"

"The giant, sire," replied Ollon. "The giant who disrupted your banquet. He was taken for questions and in the effort to find the truth, he succumbed to his own weakness."

"And what is the problem with the towners? Surely there have been deaths before. I assume you used the chair."

"Aye," replied Ollon. "The chair was too much for his heart. The surgeons who examined him have ruled that. But the towners claim we murdered him."

"And so we did," said Mincon with a cynical laugh. "They have no rights to bring that charge and they know that. Why is this death so special to them?"

"Because he was a giant, sir," replied the guards master.

"Of course he was," said Mincon, chuckling at the declaration, which to him was as obvious as it was not relevant. "He was at the banquet to entertain the guests as an oddity."

"But sir, because of his stature, all the people of the town knew him. In their strange ways he was probably a great leader, commanding loyalty from as simple a thing as his height. Their thinking in these matters is like a child's."

"Aye," Mincon grew serious. "I see what you mean."

"And they have taken a guard prisoner, sir," said Ollon. "That is the meat of it. We must act quickly to retrieve the guard or there may be no stopping their advance."

"What do they want with the guard?" said Mincon. "Do they think your men will not attack with spear and sword if there is a brother guard among them?"

"Nay," said Ollon. "They want to trade the guard for the guards they say murdered their giant."

Mincon rose awkwardly out of his chair while adjusting the small hovering platform upon which his left legless thigh rested. "Enough, master," said Mincon angrily. "We cannot stand for this." He turned in Galel's direction and called the apprentice over.

"Come with us now, Galel," said Mincon. "We three will take

our sledges to Henrix' shop. We must hurry. Galel, you will use the machine. You must take it to farm town. I will be close behind."

Galel was surprised but a little intrigued by the mission. "On what shall we be testing the machine, lord?" said the visibly pleased apprentice.

"Towners, lad," said the master brusquely. "As many as it will take to stop a riot."

Betran made his way closer to Mincon's ear and whispered, "Lord, you cannot use this machine without the approval of the council, or Kulla at least."

"There will be no Kulla or council if these servants rebel," replied the lord in whisper. "Our laws are not the final writings of a suicide. But I should be careful to follow the law, or at least make an effort to follow it. While we are on our mission you are to see the judge and convince him to sign a writ allowing this emergency endeavor."

"Aye, Lord," replied Betran. "Galel, take custody of the guards master till you leave the hall. I am off to see judge Kulla."

Galel was now more nervous. He was the only man who had ever used the machine, at least in this incarnation, owing to Mincon's infirmity. He knew its effects on a pile of bricks and stacks of lumber. But no test had been done with living creatures other than that unfortunate stray goat, and the old texts were unclear on this, at least those that Mincon had allowed him to see. Perhaps it would just not be necessary. The thought comforted him as the men rode three separate sledges southwest toward the bricklayer yards.

Chapter 21

Kulkulla halted the sledge abruptly, unused as he was to the graceful, unthinking maneuvers of the practiced pilot, but he at least did not break the influence between the patterns so that unlike the earlier incident, he and Jeppo were not thrown off into the sand but held firmly to the sledge's deck by the all-binding. I shall count it a success, thought Kulkulla, whenever I have not been the cause of a happenstance. With a sudden air of confidence, the fledgling followed his master to the infirmary door.

Jeppo knocked three times on the green painted door and a groan was heard from inside. "Who is there? I am at surgery," shouted Vomcot weakly.

"It is Jeppo, the brickweaver. I've come to pay your fees," the brickweaver shouted with his hands cupped between his mouth and the door.

"Aye!" Vomcot shouted in return, but he was now sounding stronger. The door swung open and Vomcot stood with a wet square of cloth on his face. Behind it was a jovial smile. "Please enter, sir. I have been hoping to speak with you."

"Aye," replied Jeppo. "You have waited long enough for your fee. My wife, healer, is as hearty now as in the days of our youth. You had said there could be no reckoning till a cure but surely she has been cured by my eyes. So what is thy fee for this boon?"

"I demand little for that," said Vomcot. "I charge the least for the worst diseases. These may not always be the deathly ones. Ten gold coins would be sufficient," and Vomcot thought for a moment, the remedy he had administered for his morning fever had worked well because now he was thinking with less effort. "As well as a confidence from you."

"A confidence?" said Jeppo.

"Aye," and he looked over to Kulkulla.

"You know my apprentice," said Jeppo, stretching his arm out in the youth's direction. "And you must know that by the guild rules he is bound by my confidences."

"Aye, then," said Vomcot. "There is this. I have a patient in the next chamber. He is the stranger that you rescued."

"Brumajin," said Jeppo. "I shall not forget his name."

"Aye, master Jeppo," replied Vomcot. "But that is not his name. I caught him eyeing a bottle with that same label in my dispensary. 'Brumajin' is a common remedy. But he now claims to be named 'Atos' and to be a brickweaver."

"Atos?" said Jeppo, laughing, though it hurt his aching temples to do so. "If a man were to pretend to be a brickweaver, there is no higher pretense than he."

"Eh?" Vomcot thought the master's grammar might be poor, or else he didn't understand what Jeppo said.

"Atos," he replied smiling. "He was the very first of the brickweavers and, by my accounting, still the wisest in our history. I have heard of poor fools with addled minds that they would claim to be a king or a prince, often to be the lord god Thujwun Himself. Perhaps this fellow takes his name from his surroundings. He sees a bottle of herb and takes its name and he was found in the old workshop of Atos so he takes that man's name," his voice slowed as he finished speaking. There were no writings in that workshop bearing the brickweaver's name, he thought.

"I reckon that he might be a brickweaver, though," replied Vomcot. "Because I was a guildsman of trade and never new of this Atos. Who but a weaver would know of him?"

"There would be 'layers – bricklayers – who would know. And I would expect most brickmakers would know of him," replied Jeppo, arguing the case without confidence. Had it been a dream, he thought, about Atos and his treason. Had the story about the cabinet of forgetting been a dream as well. No. He remembered that night and his exhaustion after the trip to Koosh. He remembered reading the secret histories but he had been so tired at the time that the memory wasn't always present with him, just the bitter feeling that followed him since opening the scroll. Men were monsters then, in that distant time, he thought.

"What would you have me to do with this stranger?" he said to Vomcot.

"He has told me many things that I cannot assess," said the healer. "I am sure the man is suffering a debility of the thinking organs but I wish to understand, for both his remedy selection and my own curiosity, how much of his story is the pure fantasy of a suffering mind, and how much of it might be the truth."

"Where is he now?" replied Jeppo. He had been curious as to the fate of the man he rescued but his curiosity had grown after listening to Vomcot's report.

The judge's chamber comprised an entire floor near the top of the great court tower, with a ceiling three stories high. The walls were lined with great shelves from floor to a point halfway to the ceiling. They groaned and bulged with tightly pressed books and scrolls. Here was the collected legal wisdom of the Thujwani, each directive, finding and verdict still extant after many centuries of laws accreting to the simpler codes of the past. Clever minds like that of Kulla swam effortlessly through this maelstrom of provisions and arguments while the common folk, even many guildsmen, were perplexed by it.

Kulla sat at a great wooden chair, older itself than many of the towers in Thujwa. Before him stood a great table cluttered with papers, some flat, some rounded, some crumpled. They were briefs and arguments and opinions from the vast library that surrounded him. The crumples were Kulla's own writings, words ready for discard because they suffered from either inadequate scholarship or doubtful persuasiveness. He was just finishing a writ when he was disturbed by his assistant.

"Excuse me, milord," said Jafree, who had pulled back the heavy purple curtain that secluded Kulla's chamber. "I see that thou art writing, milord, and for that I am doubly apologetic to have disturbed you but there is an urgency to this matter, I am told." At that he waved in the brickweaver Betran.

"Sire, greetings to you on this morning in the wondrously designed city of Thujwa" the brickweaver said to Kulla while making a hasty bow. "There has been a revolt of the farm town peoples. They have captured a guard and are sure to be torturing him as we speak."

"Aye?" said Kulla. "Have the guards been dispatched with swords?"

"Aye they have, sire," said Betran. "But there are too many of these town people and they are preparing a march to our city. They are laborers, sire, but they have not arrived at their workplaces this day."

"Why do they march, guildsman?" said Kulla squinting his gaze. There had been many incidents in the past between guards and town people that had not been squarely reported by the servants of the law. Kulla's mentor, Lord Boggom, now gone many years, would often instruct him to be dubious about a guard's testimony, in light of their well-nurtured desire for the powers of violence and subjugation, for whom only they and the surgeons enjoyed a license.

"It is because of the giant's death," he replied. "The giant servant died in custody of the guards."

"And this is what the guards have told you?" said Kulla, "Or do you know this by other ways?"

"This is the challenge, as the guards told me," replied Betran.

"So why are you here, then?" said Kulla. "The guards need no writ to draw their swords."

"Aye, sire," Bertran spoke more rapidly, mindful of the situation's urgency. "The Lord Mincon has offered to assist the guards in quashing the rebellion. He has a machine that can subdue the marchers before they advance to the city. He needs your writ to use this new weaponry as this matter is too urgent to wait for the council to be called."

Kulla's eyes widened at the mention of "machine". "Is this the machine that was demonstrated before the council, master?" he asked, his face hardened now as though he were questioning a miscreant.

"Nay, sire," Bertran said. "It is another machine. This has not been demonstrated. It is called the 'compressor'."

"The compressor," repeated Kulla. It was at the supreme session of the council some days earlier that he had first heard the noun variant of the verb 'compress'. He recalled the description and in his mind the image came of stones pulled into a small, turbulent cloud of sand. That was how he had pictured the device when it was described by Mincon in the council chamber. It seemed a foolish, absurd weapon, so foreign in its effect from what one commonly pictures an act of violence to be that it was almost beyond one's usual revulsion to such matters.

"Will this machine cause great loss of life?" asked Kulla.

"Aye," admitted Bertran. "It may cause the first of the marchers to perish, but those behind them will have adequate time to disperse.

"Explain to me precisely what will happen to these marchers who perish," said Kulla. "I must know this before I can sign a writ."

"The compressor, sire," began Bertran. "Will squeeze together whatever stands a few arm lengths before its screen. It will squeeze everything so tightly that a ball will form, and this ball will become so weighty despite its size that it will tunnel below the sand."

"And what happens to a human standing before this machine?" said Kulla. "To but it bluntly, is this a gory death?"

"I do not know, sire," replied Bertran. "I have seen tests with lumber and the planks did not break. They became compacted, smaller, but equally in all dimensions. I have seen tests with jugs of water, and the jugs did not break, nor did any water spill."

"Have you tested on animals, then?" asked Kulla.

"Aye, sire," Bertran hesitated. "I saw a test with a goat. It was consistent with the other tests. There were no bones breaking or... or splatter of fluids or blood." He hoped Kulla would not ask him more. There were no words for what he had seen but his demeanor in trying to describe it would surely upend his mission.

"Very well, then," the judge sighed. "Are you sure that the city is in imminent danger?"

"Aye, sire," said Betran. "There are too many rebels for the guards to hold. This machine will save the life of many guardsmen, I would expect."

"May it not be said that I do not revere the guardsman," replied Kulla. "But I have never been comfortable with the notion that a guard's life is more or less valuable than any other Thujwani's. But I must agree to the dictum of Lord Thujwun and respect that a faithful life can only begin when an unfaithful life ends. You shall have your writ but it will be very narrow. Mincon must take great care to operate the device for only the needful extent of its power and only for as long as is urgent and necessary."

"I will advise Lord Mincon of that, sire," replied Betran, who waited for Kulla to finish the writ, then bid his leave as soon as the jurist had sealed the scroll and placed it in the brickweaver's hand.

It had only taken a few moments for the three men to cross the city and travel west through the desert to Henrix' workshop. Mincon spoke brusquely and excitedly when ordering the bricklaying master to retrieve the machine and he in turn set his assistants off to removing cloths that covered it. They then attached a sledge to the front of the machine and dragged it out of the large chamber in the rear building where it had been secluded and pulled it across the sands to where Mincon, Galel and Ollon stood.

The machine sparkled and glowed in the morning light. The twice-fired bricks had a thick coat of glaze and at some points they were so glossy as to anger the eyes. Galel squinted as he carefully seated himself at the control chair and Mincon brought his sledge to a hover alongside the bark that carried the device. Ollon followed him from behind.

"Ollon and I will follow you at some easy distance, Galel," said the master. "You are to head straight toward farm town from here."

"You will see a crowd, sir," interjected Ollon. "They have massed at the edge of their town, last I heard, but they may have advanced. You should aim your weapon toward the vanguard of the crowd. They may be marching in step, like the armies of old."

"The crowd?" said Galel. "Am I to use this against a crowd of people?"

"You may have to," said Mincon forcefully. "Move the bark slowly toward the crowd after you start up the device. I am sure as you affect the first few of the marchers, the rest will scatter. These people have no will or courage. There will be deaths today but there need not be many." Then the master produced from within his robes a small, oddly twisted bar of metal and handed it to his assistant.

Galel was nervous and gulped a few deep breaths to gain some composure. He took the key and inserted it in the well-fit hole in the control block where it belonged. A few turns and the bark lifted up and hovered. After a few more turns the bark slowly accelerated forward.

"We are following behind you," shouted Mincon, in the last moment before the rush of wind past Galel's ears would prohibit conversation. Behind the two guildsmen, Ollon had called another four sledges of guards, each with two riders. They all advanced carefully, making sure they were each many sledge-lengths behind the bark carrying the device. Of the entire convoy, only Mincon and Galel had a firm idea of what the device would do. Ollon himself imagined the curved brick wall on the front would heat up, even to the point of flame. And this was the effect, he though, that would pacify the towners.

The curved brick wall that formed the front section of the device was raised only high enough for Galel to see the road ahead. He was grateful for the reduced visibility given that this mission required him to sail the bark into the morning sun. He maintained a moderate speed, not as fast as he would pilot a sledge but not as slow as the speed he planned to use after activation of the device. In the tests he had performed, the device had been stationary. They had not planned for its use against an advancing force, which would require it to advance as well. He wasn't sure whether the effect would be the same and reckoned he should keep the bark as close to stopped as possible. This restraint, he reckoned, might reduce the casualties as well. The thought of casualties plagued him and so he reminded himself of Ollon's argument, that this action may save guards' lives that would be lost otherwise.

As he came closer to the south road, he shuddered at the first sign of people ahead of him. On the horizon to his left he could make out a wave of guards sledges slowly traveling down the road. They were no doubt ordered by Lord Orten to approach at that speed. As he grew closer, he could make out little more of the distant convoy but could readily tell that they had stopped abruptly, first the vanguard then every row of sledge behind it. He could not at this distance calculate the size of the force but was sure that they had ceased moving. He realized they might have been ordered to stop at the first sighting of him and the machine.

Galel continued on until the south road was plainly in sight just below the horizon. There was no sign of the towners as yet. He hoped that they had already dispersed and his mission was unnecessary, though that would probably be disappointing to Mincon, he thought. The old man liked to show the power of the brickweavers whenever the opportunity arose, and this was quite an opportunity, he reckoned.

The bark's tangential approach to the south road halted when Galel spied the targeted marchers farther to the south. He could turn south onto the road at this point, then continue in the direction and confront the vanguard of the marchers directly. Or he could just follow the road south at some distance west of it and turn to approach the crowd from the side.

By this time Mincon and Ollon had caught up with the hovering bark.

"The marchers approach," said Mincon as his sledge stopped alongside the bark. "Just follow the road itself in their direction. I had just remembered that there are two problems here. The first, you must remain on the road because that is the only piece of land where it is guaranteed no water pipes lay below it. When the compressor creates it, the 'mass' will be so heavy as to drill itself into the earth. We cannot have that occur to the water supply. Nor can we know what effect the brickwoven water pipes would have, themselves, against the mass. The road here is ordinary stone so it will sever but that is easily repaired. How long after your tests was the land useful again?"

"It was many days, sire," said Galel. "And those places have known occasional small tremors since the test."

"That is no great matter then," said the lord, forcing a smile. "Now the second problem is this. They have a guard which you may even now see," he pointed down the road. "He walks ahead of the marchers. He is their hostage. His life is forfeit anyway but we must take pains to preserve it if we can."

"And how would that be done, master?" asked Galel.

"As you first approach the crowd, turn right and away from the guard then turn left again into the end of the first rows. This will address the vanguard and avoid the hostage as well, at least as we hope it will."

"But, master, when am I to turn on the device?"

"Just as you are clear of the hostage and you've settled on a straight course."

"But the towners will be nearly upon me then, master," said Galel, his shuddering speech punctuated with alarm.

"This will go well, Galel," said Mincon as he moved away from the bark. "I have great trust in your skill."

Chapter 22

The ward room was empty save for a single patient sleeping fitfully on one of the ordinary hospital beds. As Jeppo and Vomcot entered, followed by Kulkulla, the footfalls roused the patient to life. Atos felt the head and joint aches of the morning fever that befalls those who had consumed too much good Tawani beer the night before. The nausea had left him as it had not Jeppo because he had slept later, but he moved more stiffly now than the brickweaver and spoke with less assurance. He took a nearby water jug and gulped as much as he could. It felt as though the walls of his throat had been stitched together and this draught tore open that seam as he swallowed.

"Forgive me condition," said Atos to his visitors. "We had much of that fine beer last evening."

"Aye," said Jeppo. "I myself imbibed too much at a banquet and suffer for it this morning. Worry not about they condition, sir. The healer has said that you have much to tell us. Do you recognize me and the boy?"

"Aye," said Atos. "You are my deliverers. I am forever in your debt." And he slipped out of the bed to standing position, wobbled a little, then grasped the wrists of Jeppo and Kulkulla with his hands.

"You can pay your debt then by telling of yourself," said Jeppo, who then turned to look at Vomcot. "The healer said that you had given the name 'Atos' and that you are a brickweaver, yet I am a brickweaver, better known than some, and I know all the masters in my guild by sight." He turned back to Atos, "Yet I know not of you."

"You know of me, master," Atos said, smiling broadly. "Does the name mean nothing to you?"

"Aye, that is a storied name but not when attached to you, sir," said Jeppo with a grin. "The great Atos succumbed centuries ago. No brickweaver dare choose that name since, so revered is he in our histories."

"Then if I can prove myself a brickweaver, you have only the choice of accepting that I am the one from the past," said Atos.

"Nay, proof of one thing does not prove the impossible," rejoined Jeppo. "But perhaps you know what only a few men, including Atos, would know."

"And what would that be, master?"

"Atos is supposed to have died in a certain way...." As Jeppo began thinking about the secret histories he had read, which described the fate of Atos, other ideas crowded his mind for attention. What of the heirophant, the mission, the wild ride to Koosh and the discovery of this man in a cabinet there, he thought. And this man claims to be Atos himself.

Atos looked Jeppo squarely in the eyes. "I can tell by the look on your face, master, that you may know even more than I do about my condition. But here it is, anyway. I had tried to foment a rebellion by the brickweavers against the use of warring machines, especially as they were being used to enslave the southern tribes. This tells you how long ago the time was."

"Aye," said Jeppo. "But continue even so."

"One of the warring machines was a cabinet. It was a foul thing I had first created to dispose of refuse. It was neat and useful in that way save for one problem. Once the refuse was gone, the memory of it died as well, and one could not assess its usefulness without the most careful note taking. I considered the machine a failure and a danger yet the guards took use of it, as they did every machine of my invention, and made it into an instrument of punishment and war.

"Many were consigned to its well-recorded oblivion before I had found the guards out. The victims were completely robbed of their own existence, including their past. All their works disappeared as well. Their wives had different husbands; their children, different fathers. Only written words about them remained. I protested but not before I had returned to the old city, where my assistant and I constructed a cabinet like unto the first. But in this device, the patterns were reversed and the focus of their all-binding was inverted. Do you understand, 'weaver?"

"Aye," replied Jeppo. "And probably better than any of my brothers for I have experimented with such use of the forces. I have constructed a reckoning machine that can mimic the lines of force with lengths of yarn and in my reckonings such play would be possible. I have read the secret histories only recently as well. But I have not seen such things in fact." But then he thought of the heirophant's tower and his speedy ascent there, if it could be called an ascent at all.

"Then you know, Jeppo," said Atos. "You know I speak the truth. At least you know I speak what is possibly true. When I had protested and fought to stop the Lord Bezek of the guards, he had me put inside the cabinet as he had done to others. But I knew I would return through the door of the other cabinet, the one I had built in Koosh. These cabinets share a conduit of sorts, yet one that has no length. It is a paradoxical idea, I know, but brickweaving is full of such absurdities.

"I had instructed my trusted assistant, Oku-kuk, to travel to the old city and open the other cabinet if I were missing. I even wrote these instructions twice on paper and left them marked to be open at a later date. This was to assure that even should he not remember me due to the effects of the cabinet, he might nonetheless complete the task that would free me."

"I have read of this cabinet," said Jeppo. "It seems like you took a chance that the cabinet itself would no longer exist due to your oblivion."

"I had calculated that to be a remote possibility," Atos replied. "It was still a risk though. This phenomenon had never been tested. It was a bigger risk for the guards, considering that were my oblivion as complete as it was for the other victims it might erase the very cabinet itself. Perhaps the heirophant's tower as well, and every product of brickweaving along with it. Imagine the possibility of such a world without our brickweaving."

"Aye," said Jeppo. "Even at that you would have had a victory."

"I would think the guards took no risk," interjected Kulkulla, so entranced was he with the discussion that he forgot himself and how quiet he should be. "If they think as I do, they took no risk at all that the machine would disappear."

"And how is that, boy?" asked Atos.

"It is simple to me," replied Kulkulla. "If they had thought it through, they would have realized that the device could not disappear because its creator had when the device itself was responsible for making its creator disappear. I would expect that something would just need to happen to prevent that. And something did happen."

"Aye," said Atos. "I prevented the paradox."

"Aye," said Kulkulla, smiling that the stranger understood his argument.

Atos and Jeppo looked at each other as though Kulkulla's theory were an amusing opinion of a youth less knowledgeable than either of them. Yet both had been unexpectedly disturbed by it and each assured himself that he would think about it more at a later time.

"So it has taken all this time for you to be freed from your cabinet?" Jeppo asked Atos.

"Aye," said Atos. "I know not what happened to Oku-kuk but he did not complete the task. And without the special key, no other soul could do it in all this time. How did you do this? Did you have a key?"

"Aye," said Jeppo. "It was most strange. My assistant Kulkulla here had found the key in the dirt, among some shards of pottery."

"Well that was fortunate, then," said Atos. "But how did the key find its way there? It was among pottery you say? Perhaps circumstances had required that Oku-kuk secrete the key in a jar."

"Nay," said Kulkulla, excited. "Excuse me, sir, for being so contrary but I have kept the pottery shards and can show them to you. They are on the sledge." He turned to Jeppo, saying "May I fetch the pottery from the sledge and show it to this man Atos?"

"Aye," replied Jeppo.

Kulkulla found his way back to Vomcot's chamber and from there, to the door through which they entered. Once outside, he noted the three bags lying undisturbed on the rear of the sledge's deck. He hefted the larger one, embracing it with his fingers locked together and walking with a slightly bent posture due to the burden's awkwardness and weight. As he turned to carry the parcel back into Vomcot's infirmary, he looked farther up the road and saw a large crowd had gathered. It was thick with people, perhaps a few hundred or so, and they appeared to be walking slowly and in unison. He heard chants of "murderers!" and "justice!" They had seen the crowd when they first arrived but by now it had grown and was beginning to advance north.

Kulkulla walked gingerly back through Vomcot's chamber and into the ward room next door.

"May I set this on one of the empty beds, sir?" he asked Vomcot.

"Aye," said the healer. "Set it down here. It is not soiled, is it?"

"Nay, sir," Kulkulla assured him. "I cleaned the pieces myself. Any sand was left on the floor of my sleeping chamber at my tower."

"Master Jeppo," he continued, turning to his employer. "Outside a large crowd has gathered and they are marching north, shouting 'murderers'. Is this a normal event?"

"Nay, boy," said Vomcot. "There is some issue at hand. I have never seen this before. The Morso woman Lavena is leading a protest over the death of her cousin."

"Lavena?" said Jeppo, with a look of shock on his face. "My housekeep?" He ran out the door through Vomcot's chambers and the others followed. They met together on the road just outside and could see the crowd moving away.

"This is a larger crowd now," said Vomcot. "These are most of the workers and it is well past the time they would leave for their work in the city. There will be trouble, I fear."

"Master Jeppo," said Atos. "Look north past the crowd and off to the left. In the desert. Do you see that?"

"Aye," said Jeppo. "It is a bark and there is some structure atop it that reflects the sunlight like a jewel."

"Master," said Atos with deadly gravity. "You must believe this one thing from me. You can think me mad and do nothing and you will be proven wrong in that. So think me sane for just this one thing. That is a warring machine of the most horrific violence. If there is any way you can stop this, you must."

Jeppo could make out more of the machine is it approached. At this distance he could block out the view of it with his hands but he calculated it to be nearly as large as the concussing machine he had helped Mincon prepare for use. This was a different shape though. It had a curved square at its front, a wall of ceramic bricks, he reckoned.

"Master Jeppo," Atos continued. "This is a machine called 'the compressor'. I designed it myself and, as with the cabinet, it was invented for the disposal of rubbish. But the guards used it against the tribes. Have you seen it before?"

"Nay, sir," said Jeppo. "We eschewed warring machines centuries ago. This is a new thing. I have read the secret histories and I know this. I believe you, master Atos. I should not, but I do. This is the second warring machine I have seen in the past few days, and I had never seen one before in my lifetime."

Jeppo ordered Kulkulla to fetch the sledge and the boy did so quickly, sensing the urgency in his elders' words. Soon Jeppo and Kulkulla both stood aboard the deck.

"I will stop this," said Jeppo to Atos. "I have read what this machine will do. Have you any wisdom on a route to it?"

"Aye, sir," said Atos. "Stay well clear of the front of it. That you must do regardless of what transpires. There will be a chair near the center and before that a block of bricks. Inserted in that will be a key. Remove the key to stop its effect."

Lavena was angry but tears continued to run down her cheeks. Her speech had had its effect on the crowd but a greater effect on her. As she walked in the first line of marchers, she was coldly silent, allowing her following to shout accusations and profanities. A few lengths ahead of her walked the lone guard carrying a water bladder but no bludgeon or sword. The Tawani chief who held the long leather leash that ended in noose around the guard's neck carried no weaponry either. None of the marchers carried anything in his hands. It had been decided that this march would be a protest and not an assault on Thujwa itself. It was their number that would keep the guards at bay. There were hundreds. All the tribal peoples who worked in the Thujwa homes, the housekeeps and gardeners, and those that toiled in the industries were there, as were the sellers and porters, and the mill workers. Taking a day from work was part of the attraction for some, and a great many had come along from solidarity with their kin and mates. But the vanguard was comprised of their otherwise quiescent leaders, tribal chieftains whose office was normally unrecognized save for weddings or charities. And along with them as well were the house servants who practiced the whisper war.

They had only advanced a few great strides to the road when Lavena caught a glimmer of something off to the west. It was a moving thing that traveled smoothly, straight and fast in her direction. Up the road, she could see the distant row of guards on sledges and barks, but they were too far away for her to discern what weaponry they carried. There was no glint of morning sunlight from them though, as would be noticeable even at this distance if they had been carrying shields. She had not watched that thin line to the north for long when it appeared to halt its southward advance. Why, she wondered, would they stop? She squeezed her eyelids shut and opened them again. Even as the steady cadence of the marchers continued, that first line of guards and whatever number followed behind them had halted. Had they chosen that spot to be their stand? She realized at this moment that she need be prepared for bloodshed.

No sooner had her stomach clenched with that thought, then she turned her gaze again to the west. What she saw there made no sense. Approaching her directly at great speed and now almost towering before her was a great brick wall a few arm-lengths taller than even her recently departed cousin. It was slightly concave as though it were a small section of a large and hollow sphere. The bricks were heavily glazed, and they sparkled and glimmered as the wall approached. It seemed as if the machine might run her over when suddenly it stopped as abruptly as the guards had done.

At once, Lavena felt the hair stand up on the back of her neck. She turned to look at the Tawani chieftain next to her and saw that his faced was contorted in a mask of fear and shock. He was entirely paralyzed, she noticed, as were all the other marchers. Only she could move about freely. She turned to look at the machine again and it was gone, as was the desert. She spun around to see more but then she could not stop spinning. A voice called her name. A man stood before her. There was nothing else to see. No darkness, just nothing for the eye fix on, or make sense of. It was her father, who had died many years before. As he came closer to her, she then realized it was not him but rather someone who looked vaguely like him.

"Lavena," said the man. "You do not know me, but we are kin."

"But why?" her voice trailed off even in her own hearing of it.

The man was saying something to her and smiling, but she could not make out all of it. "It is a lie." she thought he said. "It is all a lie. There is no such thing."

Jeppo directed Kulkulla to pilot the sledge alongside the rows of marchers, some of who were shouting at them, mistaking them for guards.

"We will need to steer clear of them," Jeppo had told him. "A sledge is not a good thing to be in... here... at this time. These people are angry at men on sledges."

Kulkulla had managed to do so and they were soon sailing over clear desert ground with the advancing compressor machine approaching before them. From their vantage point, they could see the machine's pilot. Jeppo recognized him to be Galel. He also noticed farther to the west that two sledges were following the bark. One appeared to be carrying Mincon. He could see the glint of gold trim on the brickweaving lord's purple robe.

As they sailed toward it, and were only two or three sledge-lengths away, the bark gradually slowed and then stopped.

They were close to the vanguard of the marchers now, Galel

having sailed toward them at an angle to their western side. Equidistant between the front of the machine with its shiny curved wall and the marchers, and roughly at the height of the very center of that curved wall, a small grayish sphere appeared to float in the air and spin at great speed. Both Jeppo and Kulkulla saw it yet only Jeppo was moved to exclaim, "Good Thujwun!" He remembered from his rare chance to access part of the secret history of the brickweavers that this was one of the warring machines of old, or at least a machine like the one he had read about. It was named 'the compressor' in those histories, the same name as Atos had told him, and he realized that the vanguard of marchers was in grave danger.

    The sphere grew quickly until it was nearly the diameter of an ordinary man's height, at which point it stopped increasing in size but continued to spin, its surface roiling with streaks of light and darkness that the eye could not focus on for long. Its texture seemed improbable and alien to the sledge-riders and they kept well away from it.

    Kulkulla noticed that the hostage guard was freed and running north toward the army of guards that waited up the road. The leash that ended around the guard's neck now dragged behind him. The Tawani chieftain who had been holding it had let out a shriek that was followed by a strange popping noise as he appeared to be consumed by the spinning grey sphere. Jeppo shouted out Lavena's name as he watched her suffer the same fate, and all of the marchers closest to the ball as well. As marchers continued to be sucked into the sphere, its color changed from grey to more the colors of sand or flesh. Jeppo could make out faces with long hollow opened mouths and large wide eyes beaming from the edges of the thing. Limbs seemed to protrude out of the surface of the sphere at times only to be pulled back in, and sometimes a head would appear and always with a look of mindless shock on the wildly distorted face.

    Screams replaced the shouts of the protesters, and the sound of each was somehow repeated until it grew weak beyond perception. Kulkulla was unnerved by these events yet not so shaken as Jeppo because he was concentrating on piloting the sledge without harming himself or his master. As they came close upon Galel, who did not appear to notice their approach, Kulkulla realized he had little time to stop and he nervously adjusted the iron key to slow down the sledge.

He halted the vehicle abruptly and though he remained aboard due to his reflexive gripping of the sledge's hull, his master was flung forward like a missile aimed directly at the pilot chair on the machine's bark.

As Jeppo's body slammed into Galel, the brickweaver grabbed Mincon's assistant by the shoulders and turned him around to plead with him. What Jeppo saw surprised him for the usually able and confident apprentice was now wild-eyed with a wide toothy grin spread across his face, his lower lip thick with spittle.

"Turn this off!" Jeppo shouted to Galel, who made no response but fell to the deck of the bark, finally lying there on his back with the same crazed look on his face, his limbs slightly raised and shivering. Now seated in the chair himself, Jeppo reached for the key and pulled it from its receptacle.

A loud trumpeting emanated from the machine. Through the viewing slit before him, Jeppo could see the ball shrink to a point, surrounded by a crimson nebula of blood droplets. All around it limbs, and heads, and sections of bodies fell to the sand. The abrupt removal of the machine's effect had left some of its victims incompletely consumed. A few such persons were still alive as the ball seemed to disappear, though a roaring sound came up from the earth as the tiny but massive particle drilled into the desert crust with its terrific weight. These last victims did not live for long as so much blood was lost from them or their organs were so compromised of their normal function.

Jeppo quickly scanned the base of the control block and recognized a pattern to the lower bricks. He reached down to the base and carefully pulled out the brick penultimate to the end corner of the block. The bark shuddered as the large forward wall of the machine began to fall apart. The bricks had only lost a little distance in their previously impermeable embrace of each other when they clattered to the sand, raising a small cloud of dust near the gory collection of viscera that had once belonged to the humans they were woven to destroy. The base and chair collapsed as well, some of the bricks harmlessly hitting Galel's recumbent form before resting on the bark's deck.

Jeppo had destroyed the machine. Looking around, he realized that his housekeep was gone, either her limbs or torso or head were part of the gruesome scene on the road, or she had disappeared completely into that strange little ball that had suspended in the air just ahead of the machine. Whatever fate befell her body, Lavena was truly gone to the world and according to his faith, she would return as the child of a Thujwani couple some day forth. I would hope, he thought to himself, that she would have herself a brother who would himself be her cousin Olmak reborn. The thought made him feel slightly guilty, as though such a wish insulted the will of Thujwun, but he wished it just the same, his heart now in the grip of the powerful sentimentality that often arises in a witness to shocking events. He turned again to Galel and knelt down to get a better look at the apprentice, who was still conscious but unspeaking and shaking, still saucer-eyed and wide-grinned.

"Master," shouted Kulkulla. "Hurry back to the sledge." The youth beckoned him with a waving hand. Jeppo's sledge was nearly abutting the side of the bark but there was inadequate time for the brickweaver to rise and turn to it as two guards who had just jumped aboard the bark seized his arms. Ollon and, momentarily, Mincon himself accompanied them.

"Master Ollon," said Mincon. "I will need to have this man brought to the guild. I need to question him about this matter."

"We have better ways, your lordship," Ollon replied. "At the tower of guards."

"Nay," said Mincon with some exasperation. "I will need to ask him technical matters. This man is a brickweaver and I have first jurisdiction, brother. That is the law."

"Very well, lord," conceded Ollon. "Guards! We shall take the prisoner to Mincon's chambers."

As Jeppo was being taken, he raised his palms in Kulkulla's direction and shook his head to signal that the youth was not to follow. "Go away, boy," he shouted. "Go quickly. Notify my wife. You know how to find my tower."

"Aye, master," shouted Kulkulla, who managed to restart the sledge and turn it about. The marchers all were gone now. The last of them could be seen running back toward the farm town and dispersing to its many obscure corners. He turned to looked back and saw the two sledges carrying Mincon, Jeppo, Ollon and a pair of guards race away to the north across the desert. The line of guard sledges across the road that had earlier appeared on the horizon was gone as well. The dispersal of the marchers had rendered their presence unnecessary, and they were likely to be unwelcome at the farm town on any wise, and more than usually so. Kulkulla did not want to linger near where the event had occurred but he was curious and made the mistake of perusing the area ahead of the now dormant bark. Scores of twice-fired bricks that had formed the compressor machine lay in a great heap, still glistening in the desert sunlight. Below them, the ground rumbled occasionally as the compressed matter worked it's way into the heart of the earth. Just beyond the pile of bricks lay another pile of randomly tossed pieces of human flesh. Beyond that, the mutilated bodies of the marchers, who had not yet completely crossed what had been the widening horizon of the machine's action when Jeppo abruptly halted it, lay scattered around like the fallen of an ordinary battle, the tortured expressions of fear and shock still on the faces of those for whom any expression could still be discerned.

Kulkulla paused to vomit onto the sand and then turned to shakily adjust the key and sail his sledge forward. When he had finally reached the infirmary, a raucous crowd of people had gathered there, some of who eyed him and his vehicle suspiciously.

Someone shouted "Kulkulla!" and the apprentice turned his sledge toward the north entrance of the infirmary, where Vomcot and Atos were standing.

"Kulkulla," said Vomcot as the sledge came to a halt just before him. "The ward is full now with marchers. Some have terrible injuries. Is there any place you can take Atos for now?"

Kulkulla thought for a moment. "Jeppo told me to find his tower. I could bring him there."

"And what of Jeppo?" Vomcot did not breath after asking the question, as though that would hurry an answer.

"My master is well enough," said Kulkulla. "But he has been taken away by the guards. He ordered me to get word of this to his woman, whom I have met myself."

"He was not harmed, then?" said Atos.

"Nay," replied Kulkulla. "And he is with Lord Mincon, the brickweaver lord. That is a good thing, is it not?"

Neither man knew the answer to that question.

"We will hope that is good," said Vomcot. "But I need you to take this man away from here, as you must do the same. The towners are not friendly to our kind now, and for good reason. They trust me but I cannot protect the two of you."

"Aye," replied Kulkulla. "But first I must retrieve the bag of pottery I left in your hospital."

"Yea," said Vomcot. "But retrieve it quickly."

Kulkulla and the healer went into the ward and found the large bag set aside on the floor. Vomcot's towner assistants had removed it from the bed where it lay in favor of one of the marchers who had gone into shock. There was much shouting and moaning and crying in the wardroom, and patients were waiting for beds as the hospital filled. Vomcot had never seen such activity at any one time before. Most of the patients were in shock and while that required urgent attention, it would not be difficult to stabilize them, nor treat them either as Vomcot's usual remedy, the denatured essence of a poisonous flower, generally worked in one application.

With Kulkulla's parcel in place, he and Atos sailed up the south road and out of farm town. As they passed the site of the massacre, Atos looked on with astonishment and horror. "Master Jeppo destroyed the machine, sir," said Kulkulla, grateful to be at the helm with a passenger behind him who could hear his words but would lose his own to the wind. "He stopped it as you told him, but he also pulled out a brick from it, and the entire thing collapsed. Lord Mincon was there and he had the guards take Jeppo. Master Jeppo destroyed the machine, so Lord Mincon was not happy. He said he needed to question him at the guild, and that is all I know. That is all I know. Just one brick. The machine collapsed into a heap. It was a worthless heap of shiny bricks. Worthless."

Kulkulla continued, repeating the same facts, over and over. To anyone else standing behind the youth on the sledge, he would have appeared to be an overly talkative sort and not well educated. But Atos knew better. He knew what the boy had seen and wondered if Vomcot should have reserved a bed in his ward for the lad as well. He would need to watch him, recalling how he himself had first reacted to such sights so long ago. Save for the constant chatter, he seemed steady enough in his piloting of the craft but Atos could not see the boy's face, which was ashen and wide-eyed, and sported a mournful grin.

The guards had held their prisoner's arms on the short walk from the sledge to the double doors of the guild temple. Two of Mincon's assistants opened the doors and took custody of Jeppo, asking the guards to wait outside. From there they walked down a curving hallway that ended in the door to the library.

"Lord Mincon awaits you here," one of the assistants said to Jeppo. "He asked to see you alone. We will be waiting here, master."

With that, he was brought into the high-ceilinged room and told to sit in a brickwork chair near a long table, at the center of which sat Mincon. The assistants bid their leave and Mincon waved them away.

"Tell me now, master Jeppo," said Mincon. "Do you know why you are brought here?"

"I am not sure," replied Jeppo. "Whether it was halting the horrific machine or destroying it. Or both."

"That is part of it, sir," said Mincon with restrained exasperation. "It is both those things and two others as well. First, let me thank you for aiding my apprentice, Galel."

"How is Galel?" said Jeppo, reminded now of the man's strange behavior. To have seen such a thing, thought Jeppo, was onerous enough, but to have also been the instrument of such a horror must be unbearable to the mind.

"He is in a surgery," said Mincon, squinting his eyes and raising his brow high at the same time, pulling his eyelids tight. "The surgeons have determined he has too much blood and are treating him accordingly. He will be well anon. Thank you for your concern, sir.

"Now the fourth item at issue," Mincon continued. "The

fourth is your assistance in the construction of the concussor machine. That was invaluable to our efforts, sir, and for it you should be praised."

"I was not aware, milord," replied Jeppo. "That the machines would be used against our own people."

"Our own people?" said Mincon, shocked. "You mean the captured guard? He was in no danger. Galel made sure of that, praise Thujwun."

"The Morso who were killed by the machine, and the others. Tawani, and Howoo," said Jeppo.

"They are not our people, brother," replied Mincon. "They are our servants, our laborers, not our people. Most, after all, are unfaithful."

"One of the slain was my housekeep," said Jeppo, and then he noticed he could not rise from the chair. It was likely a device of torture.

Mincon's eyebrows rose again. How might he feel, he wondered, if his housekeep were to be killed? It would be a great inconvenience at the very least. This was no doubt the hardship that weighed on Jeppo, he thought. But there might be something else. The man is no doubt lust-mad for keeping that barren woman. Was he lust-mad for the housekeep, too?

"Now it was not the concussor that was used," argued Mincon. "You well know that that was to be a show of force to intimidate our trading partners. This machine that we used was another, a secret machine. But I had a writ to use it."

Jeppo had not thought about the legalities of what had occurred. The violence of it was so horrific and it seemed so pointless that he did not consider whether it was legal.

"A writ?" asked Jeppo.

"Aye," Mincon reached into his robe and produced a scroll. "This was signed by Lord Kulla himself."

"No writ can excuse such a horror. Your own assistant Galel was so unnerved by what her saw," said Jeppo.

"Galel will be fine as soon as he has lost sufficient blood," replied Mincon dismissively. "And no excuse is needed when the safety of Thujwani is at risk. Had I not stopped their advance, they would have attacked our towers."

"They bore no weapons," said Jeppo, sharply. "The were protesting for justice. I heard them. They were no threat."

"No threat?" said Mincon, turning his head about in different directions, as he spoke and as his resentment grew. "There was no factory work today, brother. There was no trading in the marketplace. It is possible the rebellion had spread so far that no workers farmed the land or herded goat and cattle today. Accounts are already down and this is another sharp blow to them. Yea, accounts are down but they will rise anon. The servants will return to work on the morrow and the laborers to the mills and fields, and the sellers to their markets. And we shall have greater trade with the foreign cities, which we will ensure with our armaments. And to complete this work, we will need clever brickweavers like yourself."

Jeppo realized he was being scouted to join in Mincon's ambitions.

"What you did, Jeppo, in ruining the machine, was a crime," Mincon continued. "Though I have waived the charge. But I am curious about how you knew to do that? How did you know how to ruin this machine without ever seeing its plan? Halting its action was obvious. Any brickweaver would know to pull the key. But you removed one brick, and it collapsed."

"I have made a great study of the patterns, milord," said Jeppo blandly. "I study them in all places without choosing to. I had seen the brick-binding pattern before and knew where it could be compromised."

"I cannot say, brother," replied Mincon. "That I have ever known a 'weaver to do that. We follow the patterns from the scrolls, and when they are constructed, they are designed to conceal their plan. But you make claim to discerning such hidden plans. That is very interesting to me."

Jeppo saw a chance to ensure his freedom, at least temporarily. "Would this skill of mine be of use to you, milord. And would it pay well?"

"Aye," said Mincon, hesitating, then with some relief. "I would welcome your allegiance, sir. There would be better licenses from this work than you have known, brother. And," he continued with a slight leer. "Once the servants have returned, we may find you a very young housekeep to aid your woman in her duties."

Jeppo had to restrain himself to conceal his disgust at Mincon's words. Had he ever had the tiniest portion of love for this man, it had just been cleaned away like a dollop of spilled soup. "Let me bid my leave, then, Milord," he said. "I must tell my wife that I am safe."

"Be on your way, master Jeppo," said Mincon. "Report to me on the morrow. At the guild temple." Then Mincon rose again and awkwardly moved forward, adjusting the key in the hovering platform upon which his knee rested. He approached Jeppo and grasped his wrist and looked at him sharply. "We will accomplish great things for our well-planned city of Thujwa, Jeppo. Great things."

Chapter 23

By midday, the cool breezes of the city made the plaza near Jeppo's small tower an idyllic place, well brightened by the desert sun's light but unburdened by its heat. As the sledge carrying Kulkulla and Atos pulled off the south road, the youth carefully slowed its advance and finally brought it to a hovering stop in the square's center.

"I have never been to Jeppo's tower, sir," Kulkulla said to his passenger. "But I know it is in this area." His eyes scanned about the perfectly identical towers. None had sledges parked outside or gardens. This was a neighborhood of merchant managers for the most part, and they were not showy with their properties, saving their treasures for the interior chambers. While the towers were of plain brick colors, their doors were painted to identify the resident's station. Most were blue or orange or brown, but one was a deep purple.

"It must be that one," said Kulkulla. "The brickweavers' color is that hue." He sailed the sledge slowly toward it, and left the vehicle hovering a few body-lengths from door. "Please wait here, master Atos," said Kulkulla and the paleness of his face now appeared almost white in the midday light. Atos was shaken by the sight of the youth's pallor but nodded his head. As Kulkulla approached the door, Atos continued to look about the plaza for any sign of guards but aside from the two travelers, the area was deserted.

Kulkulla knocked on the door and in a moment it opened narrowly.

"Aye?" said Matanya suspiciously. "Who... ? Oh, it is Kookulla. Should you not be with my husband at this hour?"

"I should be, madam," replied Kulkulla. "But I have bad news.

Master Jeppo has been taken away by the guards."

"What?" she said, tucking her head out of the door and looking around. "Please come in," and she motioned the youth to enter.

"I have a companion, madam," said Kulkulla. "He is a colleague of the master's. The guards may seek him as well."

"Bring him along as well, then," said Matanya, her face etched with worry.

Kulkulla returned to the sledge and lowered it to the brickwork edge of the plaza. "Please join us inside master Atos," said Kulkulla. "We will be safe there." The two walked in and Matanya closed the door behind them. She then motioned them to go into the dining chamber were they each found a pile of generous pillows to rest upon.

"Now tell me, young man," said Matanya. "What has become of my husband?"

Kulkulla related the events of the day to her. The march of the servants, the advance of the guards down the south road, and the horrific effects of the compressor machine on the marchers. And finally he spoke of Jeppo's crime, for which he was detained.

"I knew there would be trouble from what happened at the banquet," she said. "But this is beyond my ken. None of the servants have arrived at the towers but I had not imagined such a reason for it. My own housekeep, Lavena, must still be among the towners who dispersed. She must be fearful to come here."

"Lavena?" said Kulkulla. "There was a woman of that name in the march. Master Jeppo called out to her by that name. She was in the first row of the marchers. They were all executed by the machine."

"Lavena?" Matanya said, her voice cracking. "My Lavena is gone?" She began to cry. "Am I to lose both my husband and my friend in the same day? These are burdens I do not want... I do not want."

Kulkulla looked with a frown toward Atos, and held his hands out palms up to show he did not know how to console the woman.

"Please, madam," Kulkulla said at last. "Do not worry so much about Jeppo. He was taken to the guild temple, not the prison. He was taken by Lord Mincon. I think that may be a good sign."

"I must hope then," she replied through her tears. "Pardon my

220

weeping. I have known Lavena many years. She and Jeppo are the only people I have really known all this time. I cannot bear the loss of either. If they are both gone, I am done. Done."

And she tried to wipe the tears from her eyes with a white cloth. "What can we do?" she said.

"We must wait," Atos interjected. "Both Kulkulla and myself may be wanted by the guards. But I suspect Jeppo will return. The brickweavers have a code that adjures their common protection. Or at least they did in my time."

Matanya collected herself and noticed that Kulkulla was no longer the fresh-faced lad she had seen at the banquet. His description of what had happened at the march was hesitant and fragmented, and at times repetitive, and he was no doubt shaken by what he had seen. She realized he would need consoling as well.

"Then you shall wait," she said. "We will expect Jeppo's return and all this will be sorted out. I will make some tea."

She excused herself to the kitchen and at moments they could hear her sobbing there.

"Master Atos," said Kulkulla turning to his companion. "If we are to be here for long, I should retrieve the parcels from the sledge. They are Jeppo's belongings anyway and should be kept here for the time. Save for the fruit and sausages in my bag, which could spoil in the sun."

"I will aid you," replied Atos. "We should be swift."

"Madam Jeppo," Kulkulla shouted to the kitchen. "We must retrieve Jeppo's parcels from the sledge just outside. We will only be gone shortly."

"Aye, lad," Matanya shouted back. "But call me 'Matanya'. That is my name, dear."

The two moved quickly and managed to bring the three bags into the entranceway of the tower and close the front door securely.

"This is Jeppo's bag," said Kulkulla, holding up a cloth bag the size of an adult goat. "It has his tools and water bladder." He set it down on a bench. "And this is mine. It has the food I had thought we might enjoy at midday."

"And this large one?" asked Atos.

The thought struck Kulkulla that this third bag may indeed belong to Atos himself, as its contents were found in his old workshop. In the strange events of the morning, he had nearly forgotten the strangeness of Atos' history.

"Perhaps you should see this," said the youth as he widened the mouth of the bag. "These are the pottery shards I found in Koosh, not far from were you were found. In fact, the key to the cabinet was found among them. I have pasted them together as I reckoned they would fit, with potters pitch. I have imagined it to be a type of brickwoven clothing but you may be a better judge of that."

Kulkulla produced the green ceramic object traced with black lines of dried pitch. It looked like a crude sculpture of a child but was missing hands, feet and head. Only the torso, pelvis and limbs were depicted but crudely so. Kulkulla rested it on the floor and Atos was stone faced as he reached down to touch the statue's shoulder.

"And so it is true," said Atos, his voice breaking. The horrors of that morning seemed like a nightmare to him but now he knew there was no waking from it.

"Sir? What is true?"

"Do you know of the Gelgak?" asked Atos as he gently held the sculpture and turned it in different directions to examine the detail.

"The mud people? Aye, sir. I have heard of them before but I first saw one on the journey to the old city. Jeppo pointed them out. There were three, with different colors of mud covering them. My grandfather says they are nearly beasts and live wild in the forest."

"You grandfather is wrong on this. The Gelgak are a shy people but they are wise, far wiser than the brickweavers. And if you saw them on that journey, it is truly a sign. But of what, I do not know. One among them was my assistant, Oku-kuk, and I last saw him, in my time, only days ago. But his coat had lain in the sand for all these years." Atos seemed to choke at what he said next, "This was his mudcoat. Green is its color, green as the last day I saw him, but the heat of the desert has baked it into this shell of pottery."

"I found the key to the cabinet among these pieces," said Kulkulla, wide-eyed. "And the point of an arrow as well."

"Indeed," replied Atos, taking a deep breath. "He had followed the plan. He had come to rescue me but had fallen. The guards may have wounded him and yet he still tried."

"But what of his remains? The Gelgak have bodies do they

not?"

"Aye, they are men like you and I, lad. Wild animals would have taken his flesh and bones and left the hardened mud for which they would have no interest. So much time has passed, so much time."

"And how long ago was that, sir? I have heard your story and I believe you, because Jeppo does. But I am not sure how long ago you were taken by the guards."

"Do you know of the 'rescue'?"

"Aye," said Kulkulla proudly. "I learned of the 'rescue' in the scholastics. It was more than nine hundred years ago, soon after the founding of Thujwa."

"Then before you opened the cabinet in Koosh, I had not breathed air since the time of the 'rescue'," replied Atos. "Do you still believe my story then, lad?"

"Aye," said Kulkulla. "After what I have seen with my own eyes today, I am ready to believe all things, especially the strange occurrences that are not so horrific."

"Oh I would not say this is not horrific," said the old brickweaver. "I have lost all my kin and mates. All that is left of them is this crude pottery, this shell of my dear friend."

"Then I am sorry for, you, sir," said Kulkulla. "I had lost my father many years ago, when I was only a boy, and yet I still think of him."

Atos thought of the first time he had met Oku-kuk. He had been working on a brick home in Koosh when this child, or at least he assumed it was a child, appeared at the site and asked him questions about the masonry.

"Do you make these rocks?" Oku-kuk had said. "They are very good rocks."

"I did not," he had replied. "Other men make the rocks, 'bricks' we call them, and these men put them together. I draw the way they are put together."

"Do you know what they are made of?" Oku-kuk had asked earnestly, in perfect Thujwani speech.

"Yes," Atos had replied. "They are baked from clay and mud. The muds are not unlike your skin covering."

Atos recalled the look on Oku-kuk's face as the small Gelgak had turned his eyes to him in that long ago time. It was that moment, he though, when Oku-kuk's eyes widened, that the idea was born.

"Can you sir, please tell me, can you make the bricks of different mud?"

"Aye. We do that for different buildings."

And then Oku-kuk had said a very strange thing that Atos believed he would never forget: "It takes many different Gelgak with many different skin-mud to move the sands."

From the dining room, Matanya was calling. "Please come here, men, and rest," she shouted. "I have a tray of tea and some food. We will wait here for my husband."

Atos picked up the remains of Oku-kuk's mudskin and carefully returned them to the large bag, which he then placed on a bench in the entranceway. He joined Kulkulla and Matanya in the dining chamber and all three ate heartily of pomegranate, bread, goat cheese and sausage meat. Each was surprised at his own hunger but none spoke of it.

It was late afternoon before the front door opened and a haggard, innerved Jeppo entered his own tower. Matanya heard him and ran to the entranceway.

"Oh dear husband," she cried, embracing him at first sight. "Are you well?"

"Aye," he replied. "Well enough. Do you know what happened?"

"Aye, husband," she said leading him into the dining chamber. "I was told by your assistant and his companion."

Jeppo was grateful that Kulkulla had made his way to the tower but surprised to see Atos as well.

"Atos," he said. "You are surely welcome, but why are you

here?"

"I was adjured to leave the farm town by Vomcot," he said, smiling and grasping Jeppo's wrist. "There were many ill people after the event and Vomcot feared it was a dangerous place for Thujwani, and with good reason, I would reckon."

"It is probably a good thing that you are here," said Jeppo gravely. "I fear that Mincon has set upon a dangerous path and he must be stopped."

"The machines?" said Atos. "He is not restrained from using them again. Is this not true?"

"It is true," said Jeppo. "And I am confounded as to how I may stop him. I do not want to ever see the horrors I have seen today again. To ensure my release, I agreed to aid him. But he is suspicious of me in any wise. I cannot fool him for long."

"I may have an idea, then, brother," said Atos. "I will need paper and brush but I will show what I think can be done."

"Matanya," said Jeppo to his wife, now clutching his robe dearly. "Fetch paper, brush and ink and we will consider Atos' plan."

"Aye, husband," Matanya said, wiping her eyes.

"You know of Lavena?" he asked.

"Aye," she replied, and Jeppo embraced her mightily, triggering her sobbing that till now had been restrained.

"We will find her justice, Sparrow," he assured her.

As they gathered around the great dining chamber table, Matanya provided Atos with his writing instruments and a fresh bowl of tea for her husband.

"There is a door in the heirophant's tower around the back from the entrance. It will open from any door key but I will show you the secret way to turn it. I am not sure any man alive besides myself would know this."

"Will this key suffice," said Jeppo, producing a key to his tower's front door.

"Aye," Atos replied, turning it around several times. "This will do. Now the door leads to a staircase that continues downward many flights to a great room. In that room are three walls with different brick patterns." And Atos began to sketch the three walls to reveal their placement. "The walls are control blocks for three important city-wide effects. One controls the flow of water. It is the system that pulls the water deep from below farm town and distributes it to the farms and the city. This cannot be disturbed or many will die from thirst and hunger. The second controls the cooling breezes that keep the desert heat at bay. The third is the one I will sketch for you in detail. It is the control of the stabilizer."

"The stabilizer?" said Jeppo.

"It is the system of forces that pervades the brick streets of Thujwa," said Atos. "Have you ever wondered why the forces of the many towers and devices do not conflict? Do not exert too much influence on each other?"

"Aye!" said Jeppo. "I read the patterns of the city carefully and I have sometimes thought that there should be more influence among their effects, but I have not imagined this system."

"It is the strangest wall of the three because you will notice that the bricks are not all flush with one another." Atos continued. "They will move in and out of the wall, in response to any new brickweaving placed in the city. You must remove this brick completely," said Atos pointing to the sketch of a brick and its surrounding pattern that he had made on the paper. "Remove that brick, and the stabilizing will end."

"What will happen, then?" said Jeppo. He was fascinated by this new knowledge and a broad grin grew on his face as he digested it. Despite the events of the morning, the loss of Lavena and her comrades to the horrible machine, his own precarious status with Mincon and that lord's plans for more violence, Jeppo was delighted by the acquisition of such knowledge as only a brickweaver could be.

"It cannot be said with any certainty," replied Atos. "But there will be some cracking and wobbling of the towers and any later additions to them may fail. As will cooking and heating bins, in fact any device of brickweaving within a tower may fail."

"There could be harm to people, then?" asked Jeppo.

"There could be," said Atos. "But the effect will not be immediate and citizens will know that something is amiss before there is much danger. The will hear cracking and scraping noises, and notice subtle movements among the bricks. But, yea, there will be danger, there could be hurtful happenstance and even, I must warn you, some deaths should a tower fall. Mostly the effects will be small. A full bathing cabinet may collapse and water will cascade along floors and down steps. Steps themselves may be harder to climb or descend. Lamps may go out."

"And how will this stop Mincon?" Jeppo replied, his expression now more grave than before.

"There will be far too much effort consuming the work of the brickweavers to correct these problems," replied Atos. "There will not be any worth to pursuing the machines when the city itself is in such disrepair. Addressing this action will take many years away from Mincon's plans."

"I do not wish that my neighbors will die," said Jeppo.

"That is left to Thujwun, as it is always," said Atos. "There will be more deaths if Mincon has his way."

"Aye," said Jeppo with some resignation. "I would not have believed that some days ago but I believe it now."

"Then the choice is yours, brother," said Atos. "But I fear we have not much time from what you have said."

"We must do this anon," replied Jeppo. "I pray that Thujwun has shown us the best way and will protect his people."

"Am I to accompany you, master?" said Kulkulla.

"Nay," said Jeppo. "This is too dangerous for you. You shall remain here."

"But sir," replied Kulkulla. "I may be of more use at my home. I will not betray the plan but I worry for my mother, and my grandfather as well. I could be a help to them when that wall you spoke of is undone."

Jeppo looked at the boy's face and realized the day had taken its toll on him.

"That is probably a good thought, Kulkulla," he said at last. "I will take you home before I go to the hierophant's tower. Speak not of this plan. Do I have your assurance on that?"

"Aye, sir," said Kulkulla.

"Then this is how we will proceed," Jeppo described that he and Kulkulla would take to the sledge and the boy would be brought to his home. Then Jeppo was to sail to the tower, find the door and the underground chamber, and undo the stabilizer.

"You must remain here, in hiding, master Atos," Jeppo continued. "There is far too much danger in revealing you existence. And you shall aid my wife should any problems occur with this tower."

"I wish that I could be with you, sir," said Atos. "But like you, I fear I may be of too much use to your lord should he capture me."

"Then it is agreed," said Jeppo.

"It is agreed, husband," interjected Matanya. "But promise me you shall be careful and return to me anon."

"I will," said Jeppo hesitantly. "Worry not, Sparrow. I will return to you." And he forced a convincing smile.

Chapter 24

Taveef followed the sledge at some distance. Mincon had ordered him to keep his eye on Jeppo but not reveal himself. It was a mission well suited to the apprentice's furtive nature, and his blind loyalty to the lord. Jeppo and Kulkulla had no sense that they were being watched and their minds focused on their plans of the afternoon. When they reached Kulla's tower, Kulkulla bid his leave with a worried face.

"I wish to take this opportunity, master," said Kulkulla with gravity that would seem mocking in anyone else. "To thank you for your mentoring. I have great respect for you, sir, and I wish that all goes well. I will pray to Thujwun for your safety." And he grasped his master's wrist so hard that Jeppo was forced to remove it to relieve the pain.

"Worry not, boy," said Jeppo. "Thujwun will preserve us all if that is what is best for His people." He showed the youth a smile to allay his fears, and turned the sledge away, and sailed on toward the center of the city.

At the front door, Kulkulla was surprised to be greeted by his mother. The servant T'Mota was still in farm town that day, as were all the servants of the great towers, at least those that had survived the morning.

"Why have you returned from your duties, son?" said Antilla. "Is no one working today?"

"There has been much discord in the farm town, mother," he said, his eyes welling with tears.

"Son...," she replied and she embraced him reflexively at the sense of his troubled manner. The boy began sobbing at once.

"What is the matter here?" said Kulla walking into the atrium from his study. "Have you lost your position, boy?"

"Nay, grandfather," said Kulkulla, his cheeks wet with tears. "I have seen horrific things today, grandfather, horrific things."

Kulla's tone changed from admonishment to alarm. "What did you see?"

"It was a machine," said the boy. "It was a machine that killed many towners. It was so fast in its killing...."

The old judge felt a wave sweep over his body, like every capillary had been drained of blood, when he heard the words *"It was a machine"*.

"Come to my chamber, lad," said the judge. "We must not burden your mother with this. Antilla," he said, turning to the woman. "Fetch us some tea, please."

Kulla waved the boy to follow him to his study. He bid Kulkulla sit down and took for himself the chair of his writing desk.

"What exactly did you see, boy?" said Kulla, in his courtroom tone. "I must know all of it. I am aware of this machine."

Kulkulla related the events of that morning: the marching towners, and the appearance of the compressor and the massacre that it caused. Kulla's expression was at times puzzled, then horrified.

"How long was this machine in operation?" he quizzed Kulkulla. "Was it still in force after the marchers dispersed?"

"Aye, sir, well after. I think the man operating it may have been shocked by its effects and unable to turn it off. My master Jeppo... we took the sledge to it and my master Jeppo stopped it but not before many, I think maybe a hundred, were slaughtered by it."

"A hundred?" said Kulla aghast. "And so the marchers dispersed before it was finished? That is an important point boy, and you must be sure of it."

"Oh yea, I am, grandfather," said Kulkulla. "And they had no weapons either. The marchers. That is what seemed so cruel to me. They were in no danger."

"No weapons? Are you sure of that too?" said Kulla, his brow now deeply creased.

"They did not carry weapons, sir," said Kulkulla. "They were marching. They were shouting the word 'justice'."

Though he was careful to avoid any mention of Jeppo's plan,

or the existence of Atos, he answered the judge's questions as best he could.

"I fear there will be more trouble, sir," said Kulkulla. "There are still many who survived the event but are not well. There is a healer in the farm town that is treating them. He bid us leave because the crowds were angrier than they had been before but many were hiding. They are full of fear."

"That is not good, son," said Kulla. "A little fear is necessary for their labor. Too much will bring us down. I must think of what can be done."

"I have a suggestion, sir," said Kulkulla, an idea to protect his family from Jeppo's plan had entered his mind and found companionship with a possible course of action for his grandfather.

"And what is that, boy?" replied Kulla. "I am not sure what can be done to settle this."

"What if you were to go to farm town?" said Kulkulla, wincing. "The marchers were calling for justice. Are you not the figure of justice, grandfather? Would that not soothe their anger?"

"And what would I tell them?" said Kulla, entertaining the strange notion.

"That the guards would be tried for the giant's murder," said Kulkulla. "And the machine would not be allowed to come again. It is already destroyed."

"Let me give this some thought," replied the jurist, his chin resting on his hands. If what the boy says is true, he thought, there are certain actions he should be taking. The guards must be tried to show the towners Thujwani justice. That would be a salve to them. But Mincon is in violation of the writ as well and he must be dealt with. If he goes to farm town and breaks the strike, Mincon will have no allies. But he himself might also be killed by the mob. Yet Kulkulla does not seem so worried about that. He is worried about something else, the judge thought. These towners marched for justice, as he said. Can they be trusted to abide by the principles of justice as well?

"You are sure they had no weapons," Kulla said at last. "And that they only marched in protest."

"Aye, sir," said Kulkulla. "These are not bandits or thieves. These people are more fearful of us than we of them, and yet they sought to march without arms. And they sought to march for justice as well."

Kulla looked around his chamber at the many trappings of his office and prestige. Here were old writs of great import, framed in glass, and ornate stamps used to seal the laws of times past, and preserved brushes that were used to sign them. Here, in this room, were the souvenirs of a thousand years of Thujwani law and their presence weighed heavily on the old judge's mind.

"I will go to the farm town," said Kulla, at last. "We will go there, my grandson, and I will offer the towners their justice. Let us pray that Thujwun's hand guides us in this."

"And my mother should go with us, sir," Kulkulla said.

"Why is that?" said Kulla.

"She will be good company sir," said Kulkulla, weakly.

Now Kulla was sure that there was something his grandson was not saying. Perhaps he had a good reason for it and the judge did not question him on it. "Yes, she will be good company for us, son," he said with a questioning look. "Let us go at once, then."

As Jeppo sailed alone through the old streets of Thujwa, he took special notice of the bridges and platforms that threw the streets below into shadow. These may fail, he thought, and the lamps that hang under them as well. He saw few people in the streets as many were in their homes, doing the work normally performed by their servants, cooking, cleaning, gardening and caring for the small children. As Jeppo sensed his doubts about the plan, he reminded himself of the sight he had seen that morning. He conjured the images in his memory of human flesh dissolved and pulled into that spinning ball. He remembered their cries, how they were oddly repeated as the victims were consumed, and the screams and bloodletting of the compressor's incomplete victims, when the force was halted.

When he approached the front door of the hierophant's tower, a guard was standing there, surly and angry looking as before but he spoke first. "What business have you at this hour?" said the guard, raising his bludgeon slightly.

Jeppo had not contemplated how to deal with the guard. The hierophant's guards are not of the same barracks as those of the city and may not have yet been told of the day's events. He was worried he might be discovered but more worried that he could not fabricate a suitable story to gain entry to the tower.

"I am here to inspect the brickwork," he said with quickly gathered authority. "I was in this place a few days past and I am dogged by the memory of a faulty casement in the first story. I wish to examine it to be sure it does not become unstable."

"Unstable?" the guard lowered his bludgeon. "Are you a 'layers then?"

"Nay," said Jeppo with feigned distaste. "I am a 'weaver."

"And where is your warrant, then?" replied the guard.

"I have none, sir. It is my own worry that warrants this visit."

"You cannot enter without warrant. I have not been told to let any man pass today."

At that, Jeppo heard weak, scuffling footfalls behind him. He turned around and saw an old priest, who was smiling.

"Master Jeppo," said the old man. "How art thou on this fine day in devout Thujwa?"

"Yea, I am well, Amagh," Jeppo had just then remembered the priest's name. "On this glorious day in sturdy, *sturdy* Thujwa."

The priest guffawed and then straightened his posture as best he could, a little embarrassed by the outburst.

"What business have you at the tower, good master?" Amagh asked.

"I'm afraid I am without warrant, Amagh. But I have brickweaver business nonetheless. Do you recall that I was invited here some days past, by yourself in fact?"

"Aye. Of course, master. You were genial to me as I remember."

"I did keep my appointment, reverend, and I was careful to be prompt and quick to do the bidding of his holiness on my leave."

"Aye," said Amagh. "Go on."

"And now with all that business done, I have returned because of something I noticed that day, on the first floor of the tower."

"Aye?"

"A casement pattern I saw. In my trained eye it was broken though to the eyes of yourself or the guard it would appear normal."

The priest knitted his brow.

"It is a worry for me but I had not the time to address it till now," Jeppo continued. "I only wish to appraise the casement, to be sure in my heart it will not fail."

The priest thought for a moment. He turned to the guard and bid him stand off a ways, and then he whispered into the guard's ear, "This man I know is a charitable sort. I fear no danger from him. He worries about small things, such as the embarrassment of an old priest. I think he is of a sensitive manner and is easily plagued by false doubts. This tower has stood without need of repair for centuries so we can weather his inspection. It is only for him to cease a worry, I reckon."

The two returned to Jeppo's side. "Please, master Jeppo," said the old priest, weakly bidding him to the door. "Please examine the casement and leave your mind to rest."

"I am hopeful for a good result, reverend," said Jeppo, a little relieved. "But I will be as thorough as my oaths require."

"I trust all that you have just said as well," said the priest bidding his leave.

The guard opened the tower door and Jeppo walked into the large atrium with the base of the seemingly endless staircase before him. The door closed behind him and the brickweaver found himself alone. If only I might ascend to the hierophant's chamber and take his wisdom on this, he thought. But the plan was to be followed. He trusted Atos' judgment and turned his gaze from the center door he had noticed on his first visit only days before. He did not try that door or use the staircase. Instead he walked around to the back of the center tower. Here was a small, ceramic brick door without ornamented casement or signs or symbols of any kind. Even the gloss of its twice-fired glazing did not glow so brightly. He took out his house key and inserted it into a hole at waist height. He was careful to follow Atos' instructions for turning the key and the door opened without protest.

Beyond the door was a poorly lit staircase that seemed to circle down endlessly into the earth. As Jeppo closed the door behind him, his eyes adjusted to the dim blue light that was just beginning to grow, illuminating the way before him. The turn of the key had engaged these quartz lamps, he thought, as he listened to the cracking and hissing from the brick-binding pressure that was applied to them. It seemed dreamlike here, as the plazas of Thujwa appear at dark, when the quartz lamps begin to glow.

He followed the brick steps down and down. It seemed like an eternity as he made his way deeper into the earth like this and gave him ample time to consider the worst effects of what he was planning to do. "Dear Thujwun," he whispered to himself. "Grant me the courage to complete my task and protect my people from its consequences."

The steps ended in a great room, now well lit by the bluish light of a ring of quartz lamps. He easily identified the wall that controlled the water, and the stabilizer wall was exactly as Atos described, the bricks eerily moving in slow dance of small steps as the forces of the all-binding were mitigated throughout the city.

But the last wall he noticed struck him with surprise. It was as familiar to him as his own designs. Here in the bluish light, he could see the pattern of it clearly and it made him pause. This was the same pattern he had seen in countless dreams on countless nights, when he would awaken without knowing its nature or purpose. In a few moments of analysis, he realized that he could remove a single brick and ruin this wall's action. There must be a reason for my dream-filled nights, he thought. And that there must be a reason, I feel, now compels me. He decided to alter the plan and eschew the stabilizer wall. He would remove a brick from the pattern that keeps the great desert city from the encroachment of the desert heat. He did not know what would transpire but with an odd sense of confidence, he pulled out the brick, which came easily.

A sound like a great belch suddenly filled the chamber and the place felt clammy and much colder, then a rush of hot air surrounded him. He leapt to the staircase and made his way up as fast as his legs could climb it. He heard other belching sounds in the distance, somewhere beyond the walls, which cracked and heaved intermittently. Once in the atrium, he could feel the oppressive heat of the afternoon. He made his way quickly and opened the front door. In the plaza beyond the gardens, he saw his sledge but it was not alone. Surrounding it were city guards and he recognized one of Mincon's assistants. He looked around for a means of escape, but the guards were approaching the door and he would be trapped here if he sought refuge in the tower. The surly doorman who had let him pass now grasped his arms and handed him to the custody of the men standing with Taveef.

"What have you done?" asked Taveef, the sweat streaming from his face and those of the guards, unused as they were to the sudden rise in temperature.

"I have done what was needed," was all Jeppo said as they brought him to another sledge.

"Then you can explain that to my lord," said Taveef angrily. "He can judge what is needed."

The sledge carrying Kulla, Antilla and Kulkulla had left the city before Jeppo's action. They had brought full water bladders to deal with the heat of the open desert and the unmanaged climate of the farm town. Kulkulla was at the helm, happy to show his grandfather what a skillful pilot he had become. He was taking them straight to Vomcot's infirmary. From there, he had reckoned, the healer could direct them to the towners' leaders if any of them still lived. Kulla could give his assurances that the guards would be tried and the machines would no longer be used against the people of the tribes.

This was a dangerous task for Kulla, the youth realized. Even if he found no danger in the farm town itself, he could lose power for taking such an action. He sensed this was true when he and Kulla were discussing it but the judge seemed committed to the task. What could save them is the trust of the towners, he thought, and whether they would end their strike without discord. How do people find trust in others?

When Kulkulla was only a few years younger and set to apprentice in the law, his grandfather had given him a lecture that he recalled now as the desert wind rushed past them. He remembered that Kulla had compared the lawyers and their work to that of the brickweavers and the merchants. "It is the brickweavers that make our living possible in this desert city," the old judge had told him. "It is the merchants that make us wealthy and enrich our lives. But it is the law that holds all of this together. It is the law that must be abided. And we as lawyers must ever remind our brother guildsmen of this. That like the secret forces with which the brickweavers surround us and that which we may take for granted, so is the law a secret force that makes all our efforts possible. And we must never take the law for granted, or abandon it when conditions raise objection to it. For as soon as that is done, so are we done."

Kulkulla could not see the expression on Kulla's face as the old judge stood behind him on the deck of the sledge, but he imagined it did not belie any fear and that thought gave the youth great comfort.

"Are you a madman?" shouted Mincon.

Jeppo had been taken to the guild temple but not to Mincon's chambers. Instead, the guards had brought him down an ancient staircase not unlike the one he had just climbed in the hierophant's tower. The journey across the city had been unpleasant as the great towers seem to press the heat against the skin more cruelly than in the open air of the desert. They encountered swarms of insects and flocks of small birds, as the creatures of the desert returned to the streets of Thujwa for the first time in numberless years. The guards and Taveef and Jeppo himself all dripped with sweat, and the brickwoven chair into which he was seated was uncomfortable and moist.

"Do you realize what you have done?" the brickweaving lord continued, gulping air as he shouted while the oppressive heat worried his breathing. "It will take years to correct the cooling. I will have to clear my entire tower because of the great holdings of food I keep. They will rot from the heat."

Mincon's complaints produced no sense of fear or regret in Jeppo, but he was careful not to show his amusement at the man's raging discomfort.

"What have you to say in your defense, brickweaver?" said the angry lord, as perspiration wicked into his heavy robes.

"I did what was needed, milord," said Jeppo. "I did this to stop you."

"Oh you did?" said Mincon with mock amusement. "And what have I done that you would harm the people of Thujwa so?"

"You have ...," said Jeppo. "At the least, you have broken the law. You have used a machine of war on our soil without sanction." He wasn't sure that what he said was true but he wanted to see how the lord would react to it.

"I?" said Mincon. "I am a guild lord. I cannot break the law. The law is there to serve me and my brother lords. You need to learn more about the law, I think, for you have broken it twice today without regret."

"Yet I have taken no lives," replied Jeppo bitterly.

"Those were not Thujwani lives. It is Thujwani lives that you have risked now. Thujwani lives. Now tell me, if you prize your own life, master, how did you halt the cooling?"

"I will never tell you, milord," said Jeppo. "You may torture me with this chair, and I will not tell."

Mincon said a few things under his breath and then produced a scroll from his robes. He held it up with one hand, adjusting the floating platform beneath his knee with the other to straighten his posture.

"I will give you one more chance, sir," said Mincon. "How did you effect this? You were in the hierophant's tower when this happened. The old writings mention a deep chamber and controls that need never be touched. But that is all."

"I cannot say," said Jeppo, at which Mincon raised his index finger in the direction of one of the guards, who dutifully turned a key in the back of Jeppo's chair.

Jeppo felt the holding forces of the chair increase. No longer just bound there, he felt a tremendous squeezing on his muscles, even unto his bones. His heart started to beat faster. All the men in the stuffy chamber were perspiring yet Jeppo's sweat ran copiously down his face in waves, as the forces emanating from the chair stressed his body, and instead of running down his chest, the fluid pooled near the center of his back, in line with the those same forces.

"I will not tell you," said Jeppo, weakly now but with anger increasing in his voice. "But I will demand to know why you are keeping me here? What is your charge against me?"

At once Taveef and the guards turned their heads toward Mincon who tried to look amused.

"The charge is that you have...." Mincon paused to collect his thoughts. "That you have undone the cooling of the city."

"And how did I do such a thing?" said Jeppo hoarsely, his eyes squinting from the pain. "Where is the evidence?" Then he closed his eyes in a grimace and continued, "What law have I broken?"

Mincon started to think. It could not be the law against damage to brickworks, though Jeppo had certainly broken that law earlier that day. There was no law he could think of that specifically addressed damage to the cooling system of the city, probably because its operation was not entirely understood, even among the brickweavers. But there was a general law against "presenting as a hazard to the public" that had been used in the case of a man who drank too much Tawani beer at a festival and began to pilot his sledge into crowds. That was not as serious a charge as Mincon thought the act demanded.

Jeppo continued to grimace and sweat in the torture chair, the forces pulling him against the chair at just enough strength to cause pain. His heartbeats were sickly rapid now and he was starting to gasp for air. Mincon watched as Jeppo's eyes began to bulge, his mouth hanging open.

"Guard!" Mincon shouted at last. "Turn the key back! You should never have turned it that far! We do not torture a guildsman with this chair!"

The guard looked puzzled as he scrambled to turn the key back, which he did completely, diminishing the forces to the point of releasing its hold on the prisoner.

"Take hold of him lest he escape," said Mincon and the two guards held Jeppo by the arms. "I will give you one more chance, sir," said Mincon. "You and I both know you have done this. Tell me how to undo it, and you are free."

"I will not tell you," said Jeppo, still weak from his agony in the chair.

Mincon realized there was little that he could legally do to Jeppo under these circumstances but he also realized that there would be harsh consequences for him if Jeppo reported what had been already done. And the brickweaver witnessed this morning's events as well. The brickweaving lord could not imagine any resolution to the problem of Jeppo that was not fraught with peril for himself. Then he thought of the cabinet. It was written in the secret history that Atos was the last man placed in there and it had not been used since, precisely because the door could not be opened. And yet he had examined it only a few days ago, using the key turns he had found in the secret history, and the door had opened cleanly. If it truly worked the way the histories described, he could place Jeppo inside and close the door. Neither the guards nor Taveef would even remember he had been there.

Mincon briefly considered the other effects. With Jeppo gone, the concussor machine would not be finished but the compressor would not be destroyed either. And Jeppo's latest action, the halting of the cool breezes, would not occur. *This problem would disappear.*

"Taveef," he said after a moment. "Fetch me my scroll case, and ink and brush."

"Aye, master," said Taveef who loped up the staircase despite the heat.

Mincon turned again to Jeppo. "I give you one more chance, brickweaver," he said firmly, with the air of one who is suddenly freed of worry. "Tell me how to fix this problem with the heat."

"I know not what problem you speak of," said Jeppo.

"I can abide you no longer, master," said Mincon angrily. Taveef had just returned with the scroll case and held it out for his master to open. Mincon lifted the lid and produced a scroll from it. "This paper bears the names of worthless lives remitted to oblivion. The last name on it is that of Atos, the brickweaver who had gotten too smart and too prideful. Your name will be written below his and I will have written it there with my own hand."

Mincon took brush and ink and proceeded to inscribe the words "Jeppo, a brickweaver" on the ancient document. He then commanded two guards to take Jeppo out of the chair. A third was told to open the door of a brickwork cabinet in a shadowy spot of the deep chamber. The guards held him by his wrists, oddly reminding Jeppo of the common gesture of respect among the Thujwani, and the two men pushed him into the cabinet, let go their grasp of him, and saw the puzzled look on Jeppo's face as the door was shut firmly in front of him.

The sun was setting as the sledge approached the edge of the farm town. The controls were similar enough to those of Jeppo's sledge that Kulkulla wondered whether his master had designed it as well. He was careful to mind the instructions Jeppo had given him, repeating them in his head as he looked forward to navigate. The south road was empty of people but he could see a crowd gathering near the great fountain. He would have to race quickly past them, he thought, and make his way to Vomcot's infirmary without undue notice. But as the people at the edge of the crowd grew near, Kulkulla's plan was foiled.

"It is he!" shouted one of the towners. "The young man on the sledge!"

A group of the towners broke off from the crowd and came running to the conveyance.

"Please, slow down, sir," one of them shouted. "Please slow down!"

"I saw him myself, at the infirmary," another shouted. "It is truly he!"

Kulkulla slowed the sledge to avoid hitting any of the towners and brought it to a halt as the people surrounded him.

"Please, sir," said one of the towners. "We mean no harm. We wish to thank you."

At this Kulla's expression went from fearful to surprised. "Be it known," he bellowed. "That we have important business here with master Vomcot. Please do not delay us."

"Please, sir," said another towner to Kulkulla directly. He was an older man, thin and shaking, with watery eyes. "I was in the march," he said. "And you have probably saved my life. We saw you go to stop that machine."

Kulkulla realized he was being welcomed for his small part in Jeppo's destruction of the compressor.

"I am no hero, sir," he said. "It was my master who stopped the machine. But he is on other business now. I am here to meet with your leader Vomcot."

"Vomcot is a good man," came another voice, from a dark-skinned young man who had parted the crowd to reach the travelers. "But I am the leader of these people," he cleared his throat, which had tightened from the declaration. "I am Effel, of the Morso," he said. "My dear mother, Lavena, had led the march but now I take up her office. Now that she has passed."

Antilla and Kulla were silent. It seemed odd that they would be witnessing such an exchange between those much younger than they. The old jurist watched and listened.

"I am Kulkulla, apprentice to master Jeppo," said the youth, imitating the stentorian manner of Effel's speech. "I bring here my own mother, Antilla, and my grandfather, Kulla, who is the high judge of all Thujwa."

Effel smiled to Antilla, but the smile left his face as he looked up to Kulla's stern countenance.

"Are you followed by guards?" Effel said, craning his neck to look past them to the road far behind. Long shadows crossed the path of ruts and pounded dirt as the sun began its descent, but there was no sign of other sledges.

"Nay," Kulla spoke at last. "I have no use for guards on this mission. I am here because you have stopped working in the city and the factories. I will not sanction against that action if there is a good reason for it. My grandson tells me there is. There was a killing, he told me, and your people have demanded the guards they blame for it."

"Aye, sir," said Effel. "My cousin Olmak was killed by guards after his arrest. My mother wanted justice. She wanted the guards to be tried. That is when your guards brought the machine."

Kulla looked like he had eaten something sour, his face was so contorted. "Then that must be sorted out by the law," he said. "Do not think that we bring you justice as a gift, sir. It is not a thing that can be kept in a bag and opened with pleasure and grateful surprise. It is the strangest of things for it can only exist when all men crave it, as though water were found only where men are thirsty. Now we must talk. Tell me of this Olmak, and tell me of this machine and what it has wrought."

Kulla stepped down from the hovering sledge and Kulkulla and his mother followed after the youth had lowered the vehicle and taken custody of the iron key. Effel and the old jurist talked on and on as the sun disappeared and night descended on the farm town. Kulla listened intently to the story of Olmak, the return of his body, the anger of Lavena and her call to protest. Kulkulla had already told him of the massacre caused by the compressor machine but the people gathered around Effel provided more testimony. The darkness of evening demanded lamps and tapers be bought, and with them scrolls, and brushes and a jug of good Tawani ink.

Chapter 25

Morning came like a bludgeon to Thujwa, as the coolness of the desert nights, which their technics had permitted the Thujwani to enjoy throughout the day as well, now receded to the merciless heat of the desert sun. The streets grew hot to the foot as the sun rose. Blistering gusts of air blew around the city, a consequence of the many forces at play around and among the towers, which themselves concentrated heat within their interiors, little effort having been made in their design to reduce such an effect.

And so the streets became crowded with Thujwani trying to escape their domiciles, which had once beckoned them with comfort and repose, but now seemed to discharge them the way a man with an overheated belly might disgorge his most recent meal. They stood around in their layers of robes, which some were busy at shedding, and fought for shade, and complained of the heat, and fanned their sweaty faces with sheets of paper, and drank draughts of cool water from their bulging bladders. Some even ventured back into their towers, the way a thirsty man lost at sea might try a sip of salt water at intervals, but they always returned to the street, grateful to be away from those stuffy chambers.

With the coming of the heat, the creatures of the air returned as well. Birds flew about and their songs and chatter were heard throughout the usually quiet streets of the bricklined city. But also came the flying insects and there was no scarcity of beetles or flies, or even the long prodigal ants and other crawling creatures of the past, especially in the ill-protected kitchens and pantries of the complacent citizenry. The city was alive with life now as it had not been before in anyone's memory. But the portion of that life that walked on human legs was unanimously miserable.

Three travelers on this morning first noticed the change in the city air when they approached the first few brickwoven buildings well past the kilns along the south road. Here the cooling breezes had always come, shyly but noticeably, and the first hints of that refreshing city air would greet the laborers on their daily journey to work, but not on this morning. There was not the usual throng of servants and sellers, either, and Kulla, Antilla and the pilot Kulkulla sailed along the road unobstructed by pedestrian company. The old jurist carried a bundle of scrolls tied with a blue ribbon. He had been awake all that night before, negotiating with the tribal chiefs, and writing writs and treaties. He planned to call a special session of the council. He took notice that the sledge was now farther into the city yet there was no diminution in heat and the frequent sight of respectable Thujwani loitering outside their homes, and suspected the sledge had taken the wrong turn. He tapped Kulkulla on the shoulder and the youth carefully reduced their speed.

"What is it, grandfather?" Kulkulla spoke as the sledge puttered toward Jeppo's neighborhood.

"You are turning wrong, son," said Kulla, "We must get back to the tower anon."

"First, sir, I want to see how Jeppo is doing," replied Kulkulla. "His tower is very nearly on the way to ours and this will not take long."

"Very well," said Kulla, who reminded himself that the discourse of the night just past would not have gone so well had it not been for that brickweaver. "It is still early so I expect we will have time."

Kulkulla piloted the sledge through plazas normally quiet at this hour but now peopled by citizens escaping the oppressive heat of their homes yet finding little relief in the morning air. And there were no servants arriving as they would at this hour on days past. The travelers certainly understood about the servants but were puzzled by the appearance of so many Thujwani, as well as the absence of the cooling breezes. Kulkulla said nothing about it, but he expected to find damaged buildings here or there due to the plan that Jeppo and Atos had fashioned just the day before. He knew that Jeppo had been on his way to the hierophant's tower after taking him home. But he would not know what had happened till he saw the master. He wondered if the heat and the displacement of people were caused by Jeppo's action.

"Try again!" Mincon shouted to the apprentice. "I am not assured that you cannot open it."

"But milord," said the apprentice. "I cannot open a sealed door like this. I have placed a thin knife to it and I could find no space between the door and its jam."

"Then we shall have to call a guard or two," the brickweaving lord said, as drops of sweat highlighted the furrows of his face, which was now contorted with anger.

"I shall go for one, then," said the apprentice, anxious to leave the stuffy chamber and the company of his angry master. "There are crowds on the street, milord," he added. "Perhaps some men among them might help with this task."

"Nay," said Mincon, slumping into his chair as much because of the heat as the realization that he had discarded the only solution to the crisis currently plaguing the city, a crisis for which the blame will surely be laid at his foot. "Nay, you cannot allow the common people to see this chamber. They would ask too many questions. We are bound by our oaths but city guards can be trusted for their lack of curiosity. And the guards know of this place on any wise."

"Aye, milord," said the apprentice who bid his leave and ascended the steps at a quickened pace.

The brickweaving lord remained in the chamber and as he was alone now, with no one to do his bidding, he began to think of the events of the past few days. It had been a time of great promise, he thought. The building of the warring machines would lead to greater wealth for all Thujwani, and greater power for himself. His readings of the secret histories had inspired him with thoughts of empire. How great the technics of the brickweavers are, he thought, and how thoroughly those skills have been wasted on trifles like bridges and bathtubs and cooling bins.

How will matters fall out now? How can his plans be salvaged from the crimes of Jeppo? Surely that man was in the wrong. But he had been too clever to abide. He had let Jeppo go once, after all, and the city had become feverishly hot. He did a great favor for Thujwa, but what would be his reward? He would be ravaged by the council for allowing this to happen and -- and this was the worse part of it -- for lacking the expertise to correct the problem.

The cabinet stood across the room from him, still appearing like a box covered with quiescent beetles glistening in the cool light of the quartz lamps. He had two mysteries before him but he really only needed to solve one: the failure of the air cooling engines, those tunnels and chambers of brickwork sealed beneath the earth and operating for a millennium without the need for intervention. He knew there was a control wall for such a system, but where could it be? The secret histories were mute on this point, perhaps deliberately so. Now if he could solve the second mystery, the intractable door on the cabinet of forgetting, he could release Jeppo and torture him to reveal the truth. Or torture his woman. If Jeppo were still alive that is, which was increasingly unlikely, as the chamber did not appear to have any facility for ventilation. Why, he thought, could they not open that cabinet door in his many years as lord and yet just a few days ago it suddenly opened with ease, as it did again at the time that Jeppo was consigned there? Now it appears to be as firmly shut as if it were a solid wall! Perhaps, he thought bitterly, the secret histories were a sham, a fable like the stories told to children that purportedly explain the perplexities of life and set their minds at rest until they are old enough to understand the truth. The cabinet of forgetting, he thought, was so strange a concept that it might indeed be fabulous, but surely the two war engines are equally strange, and yet they truly behave as the writings had told.

The trio arrived at the plaza near Jeppo's tower at nearly midmorning. There were a few citizens standing outside their homes, clutching great bladders of water and bemoaning the heat. But no one stood outside Jeppo's tower. Kulkulla halted the sledge near the front door, disembarked and rapped his fist on it. Even after several moments, there was no response from inside. Kulkulla turned around to look at his mother and grandfather, both of them stood patiently on the still hovering sledge but were beginning to feel the heat, which was more intense in the city now than even the farm town had been the day before.

A few moments more of waiting and the door opened.

"Kukulla?" said Matanya in a raspy voice. "Come in, boy. Do you have news of Jeppo?"

"Nay, madam," replied Kulkulla. "I expected to find him here at this hour."

"He has not returned from the hierophant's tower," said Matanya with a note of alarm. "What is this heat?"

Another figure appeared behind Matanya, scratching his head and yawning. "Madam," said Atos. "I think I know what has happened." Then he turned to Kulkulla, "We fell asleep at the dining chamber table waiting for Jeppo to return. But he has not done so. I fear for him. But I think I know what has happened to the city."

Kulla was standing close enough to make out some of what was being said. At first he was disturbed by the sight of the strange man appearing with Matanya, with Jeppo nowhere in sight. It had all the appearance of miscreancy, he thought.

"Let me introduce my mother, Antilla," said Kulkulla, anxious that someone might reveal too much to his grandfather about what the four had planned. He reached out his hand to help his mother step off the sledge.

"Matanya," said Antilla, needing no introduction, for she had known Matanya from the women's temple. "What strange things have happened. I am still not sure why I needed to be brought along on this adventure, but I have seen many things I have not seen before. I was in the farm town today!" She emphasized the novelty of the event by opening her eyes wide.

"And my grandfather, Lord Kulla," Kulkulla interrupted, extending his hand in Kulla's direction, which the aged jurist took as his cue to disembark at last.

"Greetings to you, madam and sir," said Kulla in his well-studied, officious manner. "Please tell me all that you know. I have important business to conduct this day and I must know what has transpired. Where is the man Jeppo?"

"That is a mystery for us all, I reckon," said Atos, and Matanya waved them all inside. Though the atrium was stuffy it was not as severe as in other towers, especially the taller ones. Even the hierophant suffered the unexpected heat concentrating effect of his tower's brickwork yet he was singularly unable to escape to the street as his neighbors were doing in large numbers.

"My grandson said that Jeppo was returned from Mincon's custody," said Kulla. "Where is he now?"

"We do not know," said Matanya. "He was to return some time ago. We fell asleep waiting."

"Something has no doubt transpired," said the jurist. "I must know what has happened if I am to conduct my business this day. I have an important agreement with the farm town people that I will bring before the council. Jeppo's fate may be of significance to that effort, so what can you tell me?"

"We know little," said Atos. "The last we saw of Jeppo was when he left here to take Kulkulla back to your tower yesterday."

"Enough!" shouted Matanya, her face reddened with anger. "Enough of your secrets! My husband is missing! Tell the judge what you know!"

Kulkulla spoke up at once. "Grandfather," he said to Kulla. "You know I have my oath but I must break it if Jeppo's life is at risk. My master was released by Mincon yesterday and he told us that the lord had not wavered in his plans and that we must do something to stop him anon. Atos here," and he looked to the brickweaver. "He told Jeppo of a way to disturb all the brickweaving in the city so as to confound and preoccupy the lord... to ruin his plans for warring machines."

"Aye," said Atos. "What the lad says is true. But Jeppo did not act as we had planned. He disturbed another system instead, the system that brings cool air to the city. In this he may have made a wiser choice, I think." It still confounded Atos himself that Jeppo would decide in that way, or that he would know how to effect the disturbance.

"Ah," said Kulla. "That would explain the great heat and the discomfort of the citizens. Tell me, sir, do you know if Mincon can solve this problem?"

"I think not," said Atos. "Unless he can extract the answer from master Jeppo, he would have no knowledge of such technics."

"And you?" said Kulla, who eyed Atos as though he were accessing some miscreant at trial. "Do you know how to correct this?"

"Aye," replied Atos. "It is a simple action if Jeppo has not done too much damage. I could correct this with ease."

Kulla stared at the brickweaver with squinted eyes, taking his measure of the man and his words. "Are you sure of that?"

"Aye," replied Atos with some curiosity. "No matter the damage, this can be corrected. It is only a matter of time."

"Very well, then," said Kulla. "I may have the makings of a plan myself this day."

By late morning, Mincon's assistant had not yet returned but another came down the steps to the chamber in which the lord waited, pondering a solution to the problem of the great heat that plagued the city and hoping for the retrieval of the brickweaver who could solve that problem himself.

"Lord Mincon," said the assistant, breathlessly. "I have an

urgent message for you. Lord Kulla has called a meeting of the council. He requests your presence at the council temple anon."

"Good Thujwun!" replied the brickweaving lord. "What is the reason for this meeting?"

"I do not know, milord," said the assistant. "I was only told that it is an urgent matter."

Mincon looked again toward the cabinet and, resting his elbow on the arm of his chair, he cradled his head in his hand, as though deep in thought. "Very well then," he said at last. "Have you a sledge?"

"Aye, milord," replied the assistant. "We should probably leave soon. The other lords have been called as well."

"First," said Mincon with desperation. "First I want you to try opening that cabinet. Then we can go."

The assistant looked perplexed but went to the cabinet and fussed with the key still lodged in its receptacle on the door. But he had no luck with it.

All twelve seats of the council were filled that morning. Unlike the meeting some days before, which only the lords of brickweaving, guarding, merchanting, and surgery attended, the full council was present, including the lords of brickmaking and bricklaying, the scribes and scholastic lords, and the industrial and farming lords. The jurists had no councilor as the judge himself, who served as a presiding officer, represented them. He sat in a chair on a raised platform so that his head would be above the others, as the law should be above all men. On his lap rested a pile of scrolls and at his right side stood his nervous but resolute grandson.

"Greetings, milords," Kulla spoke strongly and loudly as the last lord, Mincon, finally arrived and took his seat. "On this sweltering day in the just city of Thujwa." At the mention of the heat, all eyes turned to Mincon, who tried to avoid some but glared at others.

"I have many urgent matters to discuss this day," said Kulla looking around randomly to the councilors. "And I will not delay in my presentation of them. I would ask that you show no delay in your actions as well, for we have much to decide in this meeting." The councilors were careful not to speak, but as their clothes slowly wicked up their sweat in the stuffy chamber, all hoped and expected some early resolution to whatever business Kulla had brought to them.

"First is the matter of a brickweaver named Jeppo," Kulla continued. "This guildsman has disappeared and he must be found, for he is a witness to other matters of urgency. What say you of this guildsman, Mincon?"

The brickweaving lord was flustered by the question and suddenly reckoned a distant chance to deflect the issue, if the secret histories could be believed. "I know of no brickweaver by that name," he said assuredly. "Have you a writing with such a name?"

"Nay," replied the judge. "I have known this man myself. He sat at my table only days ago at the banquet in your own tower."

Mincon was crestfallen. The cabinet had not really worked as was written. Why?

"Yea, of course," said Mincon. "I may have heard of this man now. The name is familiar."

"As well it should be," replied Kulla. "Had you not taken him into your custody only yesterday?"

"Aye," said Mincon. "I remember it. He was released though and I have not seen him since."

Kulla did not believe him but would not waste time forcing an admission from the lord for the moment. "Then there is the matter of the warring machine that was used against the towners," he continued.

Mincon reached into his robes and produced Kulla's writ permitting him to use the machine. "That was done to protect the city, milord," he said. "I have your writ approving its use in my hand."

"Aye," said Kulla. "There was a writ, which I signed with some urgency. But I have a witness to the use of that device beyond the permissions of the writ." He then turned to Kulkulla and told him to speak of what he saw the day before. "Grandson, tell these lords what you witnessed of the use of the warring machine near the south road."

"Please, milord," said Mincon with false geniality. "You are bringing a witness who we know as your grandson. You are accusing me of a crime and yet your own blood serves as witness. Surely his words must be suspect."

Kulla grew angry at the accusation but sought to reply without noticeable malice. "You are wise in the dicta of the law, milord," he replied. "And should you have a grandson that was also a witness to these events, say so now and we will send for him at once."

"I do not, of course," said Mincon, catching the sarcasm of Kulla's reply. Kulkulla looked up toward Kulla with woeful eyes. He had not thought such words from Mincon could still hurt him, so many years after his father's death, so many more after Mincon's disowning of the man, but he felt the blow just the same. Kulla returned a glance of assurance to the boy as Mincon continued, "But I have an apprentice who was there."

"Then we shall send for him," replied the judge. "What is his name?"

"It is Galel but he is not...." Mincon realized there was no means by which Galel could serve as a witness. The apprentice was being kept in a surgery chamber as they spoke, incapable of saying even his own name. "He is ill at present, and so I would seek to delay these proceedings until he is well."

"This apprentice," said Tovis. "He has gone quite mad with too much blood. My own apprentices attend him now."

"Then we shall not delay," said Kulla. "Please," he said, turning to Kulkulla, "tell us what you saw on yesterday morning near where the south road enters the farm town."

At that, Kulkulla took a deep breath and began to describe the events of the previous morning, the words running from his mouth in a steady stream, as though he were vomiting them. He described the marchers he saw and the arrival of the compressor machine. His face was flushed and his words shuddering as he described the machine's effect on the marchers, the wild look in Galel's eyes when they found him, and Jeppo's actions to halt and finally disassemble the machine.

"And how many of the marchers fell to this machine?" asked

Kulla.

"Many, milord," said Kulkulla, taking pains to speak formally to his grandfather. "Over a hundred as I saw."

"I have been told," said Kulla. "By the leader of the towners that some one hundred thirty-seven of the marchers were killed by this machine. They have taken a careful reckoning of the fallen and have given me a list of the names. Of this number, only nineteen bodies were found. All the remainder had been taken into oblivion."

"Yea, it was a tragic event, milord," said Mincon. "But I have done no wrong. These marchers had threatened the city, and I was dutiful in attending to the problem, as were you in issuing the writ."

"I contend," replied Kulla. "That there are two problems with the writ. The first being that it was issued in response to a fraud. There is proof that the marchers were no danger to the city, and you knew that they were not a threat. The second is that the writ constrained the use of the machine, a constraint that you exceeded. Now Orten," he continued turning to the guards lord. "When you gave the call to send guards to the farm town on yesterday morning, what arms did they carry?"

"They carried bludgeons and swords, milord," said Orten, a little worried that he may not give the correct answer to support his brother lord. "They were prepared to stop the march and protect the city."

"And yet they had so little regard for their own safety, then?" replied Kulla.

"I know not what you mean," said Orten. "The guards are brave men and they have risked their own skin to defend Thujwa."

"I am told by witnesses to these events," replied Kulla. "That they carried no shields. Is this a common practice?"

"Aye," said Orten. "When the guards are equipped for battle in the desert, they forego the shields because they are cumbersome...." Orten paused before saying the rest of his sentence, for which he could think of no alternate phrasing. "And if they face an unarmed challenge to them."

"So the marchers carried no arms, then?" asked Kulla.

"Aye," replied Orten. "We knew they had no arms. Yet they were in violation of the work laws, and they held one of our guards as hostage. They were miscreants. Surely that is sufficient danger to the city."

"Not sufficient by my reckoning, milord," said Kulla. "That is not the picture of the threat presented to my office when I issued the writ. On the second problem, I must ask my grandson for his witness. Tell me," he continued turning to the youth at his side. "How long was the machine in operation after the marchers had scattered?"

"Many moments," replied Kulkulla. "It is not likely it would have been halted had Jeppo not intervened."

"Surely that is a fine point," argued Mincon. "Galel had lost his mind somehow and was not able to act as I had ordered."

At this Kulla's face turned red and the councilors braced themselves at the sight of it.

"You are a guild lord, sir!" Kulla bellowed to Mincon, his voice growing louder still. "You can make no excuse for such incompetence! You had unleashed a power that you could not control. The law sees little difference between malevolent purposes and such profound negligence. I am told by those wise on these matters that had this machine not been halted, the entire city would have fallen to it. What have you to say to that, lord?"

Mincon was shocked. He had not contemplated that possibility before now but he realized that what Kulla said was true. The secret histories told of whole villages consumed by the same sort of machine. Had he really so threatened his beloved Thujwa? And how did Kulla even know of this danger?

"I say," said Mincon, weakly, almost imperceptibly, "I say that I am grateful that one of mine own guildsman acted so to stop the machine." And then in a stage-whispered monotone, "Let us remember that I am his superior."

"Remembered. But let us not decide this now," said Kulla, feeling at this point he had made his argument well. "But let us continue to the other matters. The towners are not working but I have spoken with them and we have reached an agreement." He produced a scroll from the collection on his lap and held it up for all to see. "The towners will return to work in the fields and mills and households if we agree today on these points: that Mincon is to be tried for the massacre near the south road, a crime for which the sentence will be banishment, or he may admit his guilt and remain in Thujwa but one-third of his wealth will be divided among the survivors of that massacre." In the oppressive heat of that chamber, Mincon suddenly felt a shock of cold across his body. "That the people of the farm town will not be ignored by our justice, " Kulla continued. "They can no longer be punished without cause and they cannot be held or put to death for harm of a Thujwani without a trial. The first trial of this new order of justice will be a trial of the guards who the towners believe murdered the giant Olmak."

"Let me interrupt, sire," said Orten. "I know of that incident and the guards did no wrong. We cannot maintain our guards if they are brought to trial each time they attend to a miscreant."

"Lord Orten," responded the judge. "I know you have as great a faith in Thujwani justice as I. I believe you when you say the guards are innocent and so sure am I that a trial causes me no worry. Nor should it cause you any."

Orten was not pleased with the response but could not conjure any rhetoric to argue otherwise that would not make him appear incompetent himself in his own office. "I look forward to their acquittal," was all he said.

"And lastly, the towners have requested that they be allowed to use the devices of brickweaving, for which they are now forbidden." Kulla paused here to read the reaction of the councilors, who appeared stunned by the suggestion.

"That is an old law," said Mincon. "It was designed to protect us from them. If they can use brickweaving, how can we control their unfaithfulness? They are sure to use this gift of Thujwun for ill."

"It is an old law," said Kulla. "And it has been with us too long. Mazrash," he said turning to the mercantile lord. "What effect would increasing thrice over the demand of our finer products have on accounts?"

"Thrice over?" replied Mazrash. "That would solve our accounts problem for many years to come, sire." He did not mention it but he had roughly calculated just the effect of the dispersal of Mincon's vast wealth to such a market and even without paper and brush he could determine that effect to be considerable. He took pains to avoid looking at the brickweaving lord.

"That, my lords, is the sum of the treaty," said Kulla. "What have any of you to say against it?"

All eyes turned to Mincon who in turn, looked to Orten, the

lord who would have shared in the power of the machines. But Orten was fearful of Kulla, and his influence on the others. Moreover, he feared his brothers' fealty to the law, a sentiment many of them had expressed on occasion. He turned his head away from Mincon.

"Brother lords," said Mincon at last, turning the key on his leg sledge so that he could stand. "Let me say in my defense that my actions were only to save Thujwa. It was an error in judgment, I now admit, to have put the machine in the hands of an apprentice. But the danger from these towners was real and it was my action that restrained them. Is it any better sign, brothers, of the intentions of the towners that in this treaty they would put aside justice for a share in my gold?" He smiled stiffly as he asked the question. Looking around at his brothers, he continued, "And how could the dispersal even be reckoned properly? These people breed like animals. I swear they could not recognize their own kin past the birthing chamber." He laughed at the slur but only briefly as no others joined him.

"I would not normally reveal the content of such negotiations," Kulla responded. "But I will reveal that the option to divide your fortune, yet allow you to live as citizen here, was not their suggestion. It was mine. And I had to argue for it at that. They are poor people yet they abide well enough. They want only justice. And some of the survivors, those of the M'butu tribe, will not be able to accept the bounty because their religion forbids it. So their share will be distributed equally among all the others. It is not so much justice from their point of view, but it is from ours. Brother Mincon, I argued for that option, myself, because of your many years of service to our Thujwa."

At this Mincon mumbled, "Then that is my defense, then, milord." And he adjusted the key again so that he could return to his chair.

"I am not sure," said the elderly Tovis. "This may be an urgent issue, but the heat of this city is what must be addressed before all other things."

"That is a good point," replied Kulla, ready with his answer. "If you all agree to sign this treaty, I know of a man who can restore the cooling breezes. But he is in favor of this treaty and is unlikely to act without its passage."

Who is this man? Mincon wondered. It could not be that

grandson of his, he thought. That fellow was not very bright, he had heard from others, as he had had no contact with his son's family for many years. But perhaps Jeppo had left detailed instructions for the boy. He stared at Kulkulla but the youth turned his face away from the gaze.

"Then let us agree," said Mazrash, who sought to restrain his enthusiasm about the new market infused with Mincon's gold. "I raise my hand to this." At that ten other lords stood to grasp his wrist. The last of them being the brickmaker and bricklayer lords, who hesitated out of fealty to Mincon but joined the others when it appeared the treaty would pass.

"My thanks to you, lords," said Kulla. "Let it be remembered that Lord Mincon chose not to vote in a matter relating to himself, as is the most honorable practice." Then he turned to Kulkulla and told him to report the news to Atos at once and assist him in restoring the cool breezes.

"Grandfather," the youth whispered excitedly to Kulla. "I may have the best news of all. Something Lord Mincon said may have revealed Jeppo's fate. I believe I now know where he is, and I believe, sir, that he is safe."

Chapter 26

The crystal lamps that lined the walls of the staircase glowed to life as Atos and Kulkulla made their way down the steps that seemed to form an endless path into the earth. The guard at the entrance to the hierophant's tower had waved them through. He had been alerted to their visit by the priests that attend to his holiness, the singular bridge between Thujwun and His children. They had not even needed to show him the writ that Kulla had signed and sealed with his own stamp.

"Is it not strange that the guard allowed us passage?" said Kulkulla, nervously questioning Atos as they continued descending, past coldly lit, circular brick walls.

"Nay," Atos replied. "The hierophant can see what will occur. That was true in even my time. I believe it to be a property of the disk of floating brick upon which he lives. It was an unexpected effect. I designed this tower myself. Did you know that?"

"Aye?" said Kulkulla. "You designed this tower, sire?" The thought of it made him a little dizzy. That and the sweltering heat that plagued even this deeply plumbed passage.

"Yea, I did, apprentice," replied the master. "And it is the work of which I am most proud. Every trick of brickweaving known to me was employed here to an extent unimagined before. This building plays with forces like no other and I had abandoned as futile a thorough understanding of its power. I had not even fully calculated the brick patterns as I constructed the model. Instead, I chose to *feel* my way through its design, creating patterns that intrigued my heart instead of my thinking organs."

"Sire, is it then safe to be here?"

"Aye, apprentice," said Atos. "I was guided in my work by a master much older and wiser than myself."

"What was his name?" the youth replied.

"I do not know," said Atos. "As a man who deals with solid bricks and dangerous forces, I can not apply a label to something so incompletely understood. All I know is that my hand was guided."

"Perhaps...," said Kulkulla in a whisper. "Perhaps it was Lord Thujwun himself that guided you."

Atos laughed at the youth's solemnity. "I am a faithful man," said Atos. "But I worship His Lordship through His creation rather than directly. It is full of wonders and many have yet to be discovered. It is that discovery that pleases Him, I would guess. And how are we to discover these wonders if we always claim His hand to be the immediate cause of them? Is it no wonder that He is so shy and fails to greet us on the street each day with a wave of that hand?"

"Then if not Thujwun, sire," said a puzzled Kulkulla. "Who guided you?"

"My guess," said Atos, with a sigh, the heat and the exertion of the descent tiring him. "Is there is more inside us than our wakeful minds can know."

Kulkulla reflexively bent his neck down to briefly look at his own belly, as if to see some sign of the unknown things within himself. But he knew that Atos spoke of matters less crude than that. Not religion so much as something close to it, something akin to the invisible principles about which his grandfather often spoke.

"I am thankful, sire, that you have included me on this task," Kulkulla said at last. "But I am wondering how much longer we must continue down these steps."

"Not much longer, apprentice," said Atos. "We have descended the equal measure of four stories and we have only a few more to go."

"I am anxious to go to the old city, too," said Kulkulla breathlessly.

"So am I," said Atos. "You are a good fellow, Kulkulla."

"Thank you, sire," replied the youth. "I have been very fortunate of late. It was not always so."

Atos was a student of many things aside from brickweaving and the culture of the Gelgak. He was keenly observant of the dynamics of human affairs as well, and he had recognized that Kulkulla's presence had usually meant the better of possible outcomes in recent events. He was not assured that that was a truth but rather believed it was only an emerging pattern, and like any such pattern, it deserved to bear further testing.

"You have lived through a great time, young man," Atos said. "I hope the days ahead are not too tame for your liking."

"I would welcome some quiet times," said Kulkulla.

"How long have you been a brickweaver's apprentice, then?" said Atos slowly, the temperature and exertion taking its toll on them both.

"This is my eighth day, sire," he answered.

Atos laughed and Kulkulla joined him anon. "Eight days," Atos said after a moment. "And you are about to see what no other brickweaver, save for your master Jeppo, has seen in many lifetimes."

Shortly thereafter the walls appeared to widen and the steps continued, freestanding, down into a large chamber whose lamps were just now beginning to crackle and glow. As the light from those lamps increased, Kulkulla's eyes widened at the sight of the wall with bricks that laboriously slid in and out in a seemingly random pattern that could easily mesmerize a hapless observer.

"The stablizer," Kulkulla said in a breathless hush of awe.

"You have listened well," said Atos. "That is the wall we had planned to subvert. But over here," and Atos pointed to another wall adjacent to the undulating one. "This is the wall we must correct." The wall was motionless but had a striking pattern of yellow, red and brown bricks. And one of the bricks was missing, or rather removed. It was lying on the floor nearby. Atos hefted it and turn it over, first vertically, then horizontally, and then he gingerly slid it back into its former niche.

At once they heard sounds of heaving and belching, and soon a roar like that of a lion, which shook them as it began. The roar did not relent but continued without pause, only slowly diminishing in volume. Kulkulla shivered as cool breezes suddenly buffeted his sweat-soaked robes. Atos instinctively hunched over and folded his arms at the chill.

"I think we are finished, apprentice," said Atos, motioning him to return to the steps.

"Aye," replied Kulkulla as he began the ascent, now somewhat refreshed.

As the sun passed its midday position in the sky, the streets and towers of Thujwa were suddenly and once again enveloped by the cool winds pulled from draughts of chilly underground pools. The complicated network had been built long ago and only minor repairs had been done on some of its older sections, those that still employed the less sophisticated plain brick-and-mortar method for constructing their ductwork. But they had been replaced by brickwoven ducts long ago and no one living had remembered any time when the system had even partially failed, and at no time in the written history, or even the secret texts of the brickweavers, had the system ever so completely failed.

But the Thujwani were grateful for the return of the breezes. Many of those sun-burnt and sweat-sodden citizens, who had crowded around outside the housing and commerce towers to complain and guzzle water from their bladders, cheered and shouted as they made their way back indoors. They had no clue as to what had occurred save for the rumors and speculations that swarmed along Thujwa's avenues, filled as they rarely were with crowds of bored and plaintive companions in misery. In many homes food had spoiled, and kitchens and pantries had been infested with insects. Birds flew about soiling whatever was below them.

The worst hit had been those towers that maintained great larders so that their owners could host extravagant banquets. Their cooling chambers were no match for the heat produced by the tower's brick-binding force that had only become noticeable when the cooling of the city air ceased. Returned to normal, they still contained many spoiled dairy foods, and meats, and wilted vegetables, or tainted grains. But the servants would arrive again on the morrow, and their efforts would be doubled by the task of clearing away the refuse. Their masters would probably know less of the details of the treaty that the council approved than their own servants, but the news eventually found its way into every household and workshop. There would be little discussion of it, though, between laborer and master. But there would be some.

At the brickweaving guild, Mincon had retreated to the stuffy library and was rereading the ancient texts, searching still for a clue to an end to the city's misery. As the first breezes came through, his body accepted them gratefully but his mind protested in frustration and the resignation that his rule had finally ended. He lifted his arms from the scroll anon, and it furled into two rolls and closed. Then he adjusted the key in his leg sledge and rose awkwardly out of his chair but managed even in his troubled walk to the library door to carry the air of a prince or a king. He wasn't plagued by the thought of that moment in the council meeting when he realized the machine could have continued operating indefinitely, or that he owed Jeppo more than he could ever pay. That moment was forgotten.

In the highest chamber of the city's tallest tower, a servant arrived with freshly laundered robes for the bathing holy man, who had sought refreshment in an ornamental pool that had, only eight days earlier, borne an image of towers crumbling, their bricks like sand swirling in a desert storm. He had worried when no other image appeared again for moments afterward as the pool's water had turned as black as kiln smoke. He had known from his own experience and from the secret histories of the hierophants that such visions were foretelling though not inevitable. But it had been a relief nonetheless when he had called that old priest to his chamber. Almost as soon as he had dispatched the messenger, the darkness in the pool had abated, revealing the image of a man in a purple robe surrounded by dark-skinned people, some reaching for a touch of the man's garment.

His holiness rose from the pool and dried himself with towels, then motioned to the servant to dress him in the fresh raiment. From his vantage point high above the city, he watched as the countless clots of humanity far below moved and separated and seemed to ooze back into the towers.

At the tower of the merchant Emblin, a young girl with a bandaged arm returned to the lonely chamber where she would normally have spent her day. She had enjoyed the sunshine and the crowd of people around her as she played with the homely, Tawani-made dolls, including the oft-renamed baker doll, now known as Stumble-Foot. The heat and sun did not bother her as it had the adults and the sudden coolness of the tower air made her shiver.

In a surgeon's infirmary in the northern section of the city, the brickweaving apprentice Galel lay alone, held fast to a brickwork bed in a locked cell. The heat had been enough to halt his shaking and calm the frenzy in his limbs. Now the breezes hit him like a chilly splash of water and dried the sweat off his robes. His muscles had finally gone limp, and his eyes had finally closed, and he fell into a restful sleep so deep that he had no dreams.

Chapter 27

No sooner had the door closed than it opened again.

Jeppo had to restrain himself lest he attack Mincon's person, as the guards would not be quick enough to stop him. But something was different. Something had happened in that short moment of darkness. The light that squeezed through the widening doorway was not the bluish sort of the quartz lamps but the golden, squint-inducing rays of the desert sun cascading through the open windows of Atos' old workshop in Koosh.

"Monkey!" a familiar voice shouted. "Come to me my husband."

There stood Matanya crouching over the cabinet, tears streamed down her cheeks but her smile had never been broader. As soon as Jeppo was free of the cabinet, he embraced her. Standing behind her were Atos and Kulkulla smiling broadly as well, the latter jumping up and down and shouting hurrahs.

"What has happened?" said Jeppo.

"Oh let me tell him," said Kulkulla excitedly. "It has been two days since your disappearance, sir. Two days!"

"Two days?" replied Jeppo. "It was only a moment to me."

"As I reckoned," said Atos. "It was the same for me but I had lost a great many more days than you, brother."

"Where are we?" asked Jeppo.

"We are in my old workshop at Koosh," replied Atos. "The same place from which you rescued me many days past. I am happy to repay the debt I owed you."

"Master Jeppo," Kulkulla interjected. "You must know this. Mincon has given much of his wealth in reparation to the towners who lost kin in the massacre. He was charged with using a warring machine beyond the restraint of grandfather's writ. It is a serious crime. He is no longer lord of the brickweavers, or even one among them."

"Then what about the machines?" asked Jeppo. "What of Mincon's plans?"

"They are undone," said Kulkulla. "The council has censured him."

"What did the other brickweavers make of you?" Jeppo asked, turning to Atos. "Did you reveal your strange history to them?"

"Nay, not as yet," replied Atos with a smile. "I was careful to go by the name 'Brumajin'. A few, I suspect, think me a demon of some sort, in disguise. But none could challenge my skills after I restored the cooling."

"And the towners?" said Jeppo.

"That is the best news," said Atos. "This good fellow here saw to that," and he grasped Kulkulla's shoulder. "He convinced his grandfather Kulla to go to farm town and break the strike. He is a good man, this Kulla."

"He told the towners he could offer them justice," said Kulkulla. "And they were like starving men offered a bowl of stew. Grandfather had not been there in ten years, he told me. You do not know, master, how fearful he was of the farm town. Had we not the use of a sledge, he might not have gone. But I think it was a brave thing for him to do on any wise, and the towners were much affected by it. He told me that a people so thirsty for justice could not truly be the miscreants he imagined them to be."

"Perhaps," said Jeppo in jest. "I should return to the cabinet so that more wondrous things will happen."

"You will not!" scolded Matanya. "You will stay with me till the day I die, Monkey."

"Here," said Atos, handing Jeppo a water bladder. "Drink. Then we must be off. We must return to the farm town. The Morso are holding a vigil for their dead this evening. It is called the 'densolem', and the Howoo will join them, as well as the Tawani and the M'Butu. And Kulla himself, I am told, will be there as well."

As Jeppo drank, Atos spoke again with some hesitancy, as though he debated whether to raise the issue or leave it unspoken.

"You will have many more questions, master," he said to Jeppo. "And they will be answered anon. But I have one for you. The pattern that you broke, the cooling pattern. That was not the plan though it worked well enough. Why did you change the plan?"

"I answer you truthfully," said Jeppo between draughts. "That the choice had come to me in a dream. Despite my rage, I did not wish to harm my own people and the choice of the dream was convenient to that wish."

Atos thought for a moment and spoke at last. "I feel like a man," he said. "Who might have studied sledges for many years and had just discovered that they could rise from the ground."

"Aye?" said Jeppo. "The meaning of your words escapes me."

"That can be discussed later," said Matanya, with impatience. "For now we must hurry to honor our Lavena. We must be there when her name is read, Jeppo."

"Aye," said Jeppo. "Let us go then."

The trip back to Thujwa as uneventful, save for the appearance of a line of black-robed bandits, Chief Bakau and his minions, who only stood and watched as the travelers passed the great rocks. Soon after that, Kulkulla piloted the sledge through the forest and the rush of wind past their ears muted the strange clicking noises emanating from the shadows beyond the trees that lined the road. At the south gate, guards bowed and waved them on. By dusk they had reached the great fountain square where a crowd had gathered, many holding small oil lamps that were just flickering to life as the sun began to set.

In the center of the square stood a group of young people, each in his distinct tribal dress. These were the remaining chieftains of the various tribes, the last inheritors of their lines. They surrounded a tall, robed figure, a man much older than they, who stood at a platform with the young Morso chief, Effel.

Kulkulla brought the sledge to a graceful halt and the passengers left it to take their places among the crowd. They stood among the tribal peoples, some of whom recognized Jeppo and reached to quickly touch his robe, or lifted up their small children to do the same. A few managed to pull flowers with prickly stems from its hem. Jeppo was embarrassed by the attention but Matanya held a prideful smile. The crowd quieted as Effel, a thin, nervous young man of eighteen years, made a few halting attempts to speak.

"People of The Surrel," he said, and with every word he uttered he feared his throat would close on the next one. "We now begin the den-solem. This is a remembering of our dead for we Morso. But we invite all the tribes here and we will remember all among them who have fallen as well. For this evening, we are proud to be Morso, and Tawani, and M'Butu, and Howoo. And we are proud to be the people of the Surrel, and we are proud of our fallen. The reading of the names will be made by Judge Kulla, for it is an honor appropriate to the keeper of the law." With that Kulla stood forward and unrolled a large scroll and, with the resounding and well-modulated voice of the practiced jurist, he began to read the names.

"Olmak al-Lora, a Morso prince," he read and many of the Morso prostrated themselves as was their custom.

"Lavena al-Lora, a Morso princess and defender of justice," even more of the tribe, and many of the other tribes, embraced the stony ground. Jeppo and Matanya saw this and laid themselves flat in homage to their fallen housekeep.

"Pandrix, an elder of the Tawani; Tabshir al-Denis, and Lallokin al-Denis, kitchen servants who bravely insisted on marching in the vanguard; Senta, a Howoo chieftain and teacher of animal husbandry..." Kulla continued reading the list well into the night, as over a hundred names were so honored. At the end, Effel once again took to the platform, and with a voice he had tried to make stronger, he began the final prayer of remembrance.

Kulla spotted Jeppo in the crowd and made his way to him.

"My grandson was right," he whispered to the brickweaver. "He reckoned you might be found in the old city."

Jeppo turned to Kulkulla and grasped his shoulder, looking at him with a smile and raised eyebrows, as though he were surprised by the youth's canniness.

"There is much work to be done, master," said Kulla. "Mincon has fallen and taken some of your brothers with him. We are short of brickweavers."

"Worry not," said Jeppo. "I am a master brickweaver myself. And standing with me is one as you know, as well as a second in some time." He briefly clenched his grasp on Kulkulla's shoulder and the embarrassed youth looked down at his own feet.

Kulla could not hold back his own prideful smile.

"There is something I may have for you, master," said the judge producing a smaller scroll from his robes. "It was in Mincon's hands. It has your name on it. I can make no sense of it but perhaps you can."

Jeppo opened the scroll. Across the top read the words "Manifest of the Cabinet of Forgetting" followed by a list of names and epithets.

"May I see that?" said Atos looking over Jeppo's shoulder. "You know what that is, do you not?"

"Aye," said Jeppo. "I will consign it to you, for your name is on it as well."

Atos took the scroll and perused the names. As Effel was finishing the prayer, Atos ran to the platform and stopped him. Jeppo could see that Atos was showing Effel the scroll and saying something to the young Morso. The fellow scratched his head, then looked at the scroll, and then he smiled.

"People of the Surrel," said Effel at last. "We cannot complete the prayers of the den-solem. We have found a list of more names, a very old list. These names have been long forgotten, but this man wishes to read them to you now."

At that, Atos began reading the list but first he spoke one name from memory: "Oku-kuk, loyal assistant and a member of the Gelgak tribe," he said. There were startled reactions and murmuring throughout the crowd. A savage Gelgak, they wondered?

"Al Tureengah, a Tawani spy," he continued. "Buta-lora, a Morso general; Andistee v'ens, a Dazglash freedom fighter; Keffe-ra, a Morso messenger; Boo-azizi, a Tawani merchant...."

And as Atos continued reading the list of names of those who had been placed in the cabinet, names never spoken before now, the crowd became quiet. By any rational measure the list was a fiction as the persons on it had truly never existed, but the crowd of towners were nonetheless moved to silence, perhaps by some vague familiarity with the sound of the names, or by some connection deep within their blood that like the written word had escaped the cabinet's influence. So still was the air save for the sound of Atos' voice that one could hear the rushing winds aloft and the distant crying of an infant, the calling of an unseen bird and the mooing of an unhappy cow far off in the farmlands to the east. Atos was nearly halfway through the list when Jeppo detected another sound, one he had noted in the past at times. It was a buzzing, like a thousand tongues clicking. The noise began as a muffled cacophony but slowly grew in volume, and as it did, it acquired a rhythm, and then Jeppo thought he could detect a pleasing pattern to it, a melody.

"What is that strange noise?" said Matanya, clutching her husband closer. "I was not sure at first but it sounds quite... pretty."

"I am not sure myself, Sparrow," said Jeppo, smiling. "But I suspect it may mean that I will no longer be plagued at night by strange dreams."

She gave him a puzzled look, and Jeppo laughed.

THE END

Afterword

In his writings, the Greek historian Herodotus mentions an ancient people he called the "Garamantes". They had developed the means to pull water from deep, prehistoric aquifers and their empire flourished where others failed as the Sahara Desert advanced across Northern Africa. The ruins of their cities remain in what is today southern Libya but little is known about them, except that they kept slaves, they lived comfortable lives and, despite their technological prowess, they had no weapons of war.

Acknowledgements

The author is eternally grateful to a number of people whose support and feedback helped to shape this book, including the first full manuscript readers Linda Craig and Larry Gonyea, early readers Jennifer Brown, Lisa Farnan, Lynne Marie Godfrey, Kevin Godfrey, Charles Meade, and Karen Northrup, and the extremely helpful crowd at Authonomy.com, especially fellow authors James David Audlin, Shalini Boland, Jim Heter, and Ashen Venema.

Made in the USA
Middletown, DE
25 May 2024

54696539R00165